X MARKS THE SPOT
DARKNESS FALLS
TIGER, TIGER
SQUEEZE
HUMBUG

Other *X-Files* titles in this series
available from Voyager

THE (X) FILES™

Based on the television series
created by Chris Carter

X MARKS THE SPOT

by Les Martin, based on
the teleplay written by Chris Carter

DARKNESS FALLS

by Les Martin, based on the
teleplay written by Chris Carter

TIGER, TIGER

by Les Martin, based on the
teleplay written by Steve de Jarnatt

SQUEEZE

by Ellen Steiber, based on the
teleplay written by Glen Morgan and James Wong

HUMBUG

by Les Martin, based on the teleplay
written by Darin Morgan

HarperCollins*Publishers*

Voyager
An imprint of HarperCollins*Publishers*
77–85 Fulham Palace Road,
Hammersmith, London W6 8JB

This omnibus edition 1997
1 2 3 4 5 6 7 8 9

*X Marks the Spot, Darkness Falls, Tiger, Tiger,
Squeeze* and *Humbug* first published in Great Britain by
HarperCollins*Publishers* 1996

A catalogue record for this book
is available from the British Library

ISBN 0 00 225646 0

Set in Aldus by Rowland Phototypesetting Ltd,
Bury St Edmunds, Suffolk

Printed and bound in Great Britain by
Caledonian International Book Manufacturing Ltd, Glasgow

X MARKS THE SPOT

To Stephanie,
Keeper of the X-Files

CHAPTER
ONE

The young woman ran through the dark woods. Her feet were bare. They stumbled on stones, slid on slick fallen leaves. Her nightgown left her arms exposed. Branches and thorns tore at her flesh. But still she ran. Her face told why. It had the look of a hunted animal.

Sweat beaded on her skin. Her breath came in gasps. Tears filled her eyes. Then her eyes opened wide as she felt herself falling.

She had tripped over a jutting root. She fell in a clearing on her hands and knees. She stayed there, panting. She was too tired to get to her feet.

She knew the chase was over. She could only wait.

A moment later, it was over.

A whirlwind of dust and leaves rose from the forest floor. Faster and faster the dust devil swirled around her. Flying grit stung her skin like a million bees. Her eyes blinked desperately. Then they blurred in an explosion of blinding white light.

The unearthly white light flooded the clearing. With it came a high-pitched humming. The girl put her hands to her ears. But the sound cut through like the whine of a high-speed saw. Then it grew even worse, with clanging like pounding heavy metal.

The girl's whole body tensed, bracing itself for what was to come.

A figure emerged from the white light. Only its outlines showed. The light grew even brighter. And everything – the figure, the girl, the clearing, the forest, the night – vanished in it.

Only the girl's voice remained. It screamed out a word. Perhaps a name. There was no way of telling. Pain had shredded the sound.

The echoes of her scream died. The light faded. The dark woods were silent as a grave. Then birds began chirping. Leaves rustled in the wind. Life resumed, leaving the girl behind for the living to find.

They found her the next day. A quail hunter spotted the body in the first light of dawn. He drove full speed to town with the news. By the time the morning sun turned the Oregon sky deep blue, the law was on the scene.

'I'd put the time of death eight to twelve hours ago,' the town coroner told the chief police detective. They stood looking down at the dead girl, who was lying facedown. Beside her knelt the coroner's two assistants.

'And the cause?' the detective asked. He was a big, powerful man. But right now, his broad shoulders slumped.

The coroner cleared his throat before answering. 'No visible cause. Just a few scrapes and bruises. But no sign of a beating or a physical assault. All we have is this.'

The coroner bent toward the girl. He lifted the hem of her nightgown. He exposed two red marks on her lower back. They were welts the size of dimes.

The detective looked at them, then traded looks with the coroner. There was no surprise in either man's eyes. Only grim recognition.

The detective's jaw clenched. He couldn't put off the next step any longer.

'Turn her over,' he said.

The assistants turned the stiffened body of the girl onto her back. Leaves and soil clung to her face. Dried blood ran like brown paint from her nose. But the detective had no trouble seeing who she was. It was just hard for him to get the words out.

'Karen Swenson,' he said.

'Is that a positive identification?' one assistant asked.

'She went to high school with my son,' the detective said.

Without another word, the detective straightened up. He turned and started walking toward his four-wheel-drive truck.

'The Class of '89, Detective?' the coroner called after him.

The detective made no reply. He only walked faster.

That didn't stop the coronor from shouting after him, 'It's happening again, isn't it?'

His words weren't a teasing question.

They were a terrifying answer.

CHAPTER
TWO

Dana Scully stood looking down at a corpse. It wasn't the corpse of a woman, though. It was the corpse of a pale young man.

Her face showed no emotion. She might have been looking at an eggplant. It was just part of a day's work.

Scully was a beautiful young woman. But that was not why she had her job. She had it because of her brains. She was smart as a whip and not afraid to show it. She was the kind of agent the FBI was looking for when she came looking for a job.

Her latest job in the FBI was teaching a class in its Training Academy. Today she was using a corpse to show how to spot death by electrocution. She spoke clearly. But she also moved along fast, with technical terms flying like sparks from a train wheel. If her students didn't follow her, tough luck. They wouldn't make good FBI agents, anyway.

'Electrocution disrupts the heartbeat and most of the autonomic systems. Death occurs from tissue damage, in the heart itself, and in the sinus and arterioventricular nodes. We all conduct electricity in different degrees. While I may survive a lightning strike, others might die from putting their finger in a light socket. In the same way, a cattle prod can kill. In an investigation, you would be looking for a round reddish bruise . . .'

Scully paused. Another agent had entered the classroom. Her smooth brow furrowed. She didn't like anyone interrupting her class. But she forgot her anger when she read the note the agent handed her.

'Your attendance is required in Washington at 1600 hours sharp. Contact Special Agent Jones.'

Scully might have a mind of her own. But she also obeyed orders. That was what made her the kind of agent the FBI liked best.

At four in the afternoon sharp, Scully was at FBI headquarters. She flashed the receptionist her badge. 'I have a meeting with –'

'Agent Scully,' a deep voice behind her said.

She turned to face a large, impressive man. He looked to be in his 50s. She had never seen him before. But she sensed who he was.

'Jones,' he said. 'Follow me. We're late.'

He led her down a long empty hallway. Their footsteps echoed on the cold marble floor. Scully had to half run to keep up with his long-legged stride.

'Am I in some kind of trouble?' she asked.

'You're being interviewed,' Jones said, 'at a very high level.'

Jones ushered her through a set of large double doors. Inside was a conference room. Six men sat around an oval table. They were in their 60s. Scully didn't have to know their titles to feel their power. It flowed out of them like the chill from an open freezer door.

Jones showed Scully to a chair. He remained standing behind her.

The man who spoke first looked to be the oldest one there. But age had not dimmed his gaze. Scully could feel it boring into her. And there was nothing feeble in his voice. It was as hard and cold as steel.

'Agent Scully, thank you for coming,' the man said. 'We see you've been with the Bureau for two years.'

'Yes, sir,' Scully said.

'You have an undergraduate degree in astronomy,' the man went on. 'You then graduated medical school. But you chose not to practice. Instead you got an advanced degree in physics. Please explain your different studies.'

'Well, sir, I come from a very bookish family,' Scully said. 'I guess science was my way of rebelling.'

Scully saw her little joke fall flat. Not a single smile appeared in the room.

Scully cleared her throat and went on. 'After med school, I considered doing research for the National Space Institute. I thought physics would help me there. But I decided to join the FBI instead. I finished my physics degree at the FBI Academy.'

The men at the table leafed through thick folders. Scully knew that her whole life was there in black and white. For long moments, the only sound was rustling paper.

Then a second man suddenly asked, 'Are you familiar with an agent named Fox Mulder?'

'Yes, I am,' Scully said. The name did ring a distant bell.

'In what way?' the second man asked.

'By reputation,' Scully replied. 'Other agents sometimes talk about him. At the Academy I heard him called by a nickname. "Spooky" Mulder.'

Jones cut in. 'I assure you, that reputation is not accurate. Mulder is a superbly capable agent. He graduated from Harvard and Oxford with honors in psychology. His paper on serial killers and the occult helped us crack one of our toughest cases. He may be the best analyst in the Criminal Division.'

That was as far as Jones got. The first man bluntly interrupted him. 'Unfortunately, on his own, Agent Mulder has developed a strong interest in a rather odd project. More than a strong interest, in fact. A total obsession. Are you familiar with the so-called X-files?'

'Vaguely, sir,' Scully said. 'I believe they have to do with strange happenings, unexplained phenomena.'

'They're a grab bag of outrageous ghost stories,' the second man growled.

The first man gave the speaker a sharp look. Then he turned back to Scully. 'Agent Mulder insists on spending his and the Bureau's time investigating cases in these files. He will not listen to suggestions that he take other assignments.'

The first man let Scully digest this information. Then he went on, 'Ms Scully, because of your excellent qualifications, you will assist Mulder in investigating the X-files. You will write field reports of these investigations. You will also give your frank opinion of their value. You will submit your reports to this group and this group only.'

Scully cased out her assignment instantly. It was a no-brainer.

'Am I to understand you want me to debunk the X-files project, sir?' she asked.

There was a moment of tense silence.

The first man said, 'Agent Scully, we trust you'll make a proper scientific analysis. If your reports cast doubt on the X-files, so be it. I'm sure we can use Agent Mulder's great talents elsewhere. And yours of course as well. Your career will flourish – when the X-files are behind you.'

His tone was clipped. It cut off further questions.

Scully knew the only thing to say and she said it. 'Yes, sir.'

'Agent Jones will give you a full briefing,' said the first man.

'We look forward to your reports,' said the second man.

'Your *candid* reports. Don't mince words. You can call a spade a spade – and a nut a nut.'

Scully waited until she was out in the corridor with Jones. Then she asked, 'So what is Mulder really like?'

Jones pursed his lips, clicked his tongue. 'Mulder? Bright. Very bright. Also highly independent. Often difficult. In short, weird by FBI standards.' He paused, and added, 'He'll know exactly what you're up to.'

Scully gave him her best innocent look. 'I'm not up to anything, sir. I'm just following orders.'

CHAPTER
THREE

Scully expected just one thing when she went to meet Fox Mulder. She expected the unexpected.

She was not disappointed.

Mulder's office was in the basement of FBI Headquarters. His door was unmarked. Without Jones to take her there, Scully never would have found it.

Jones knocked but did not wait for an answer to open the door. Scully followed him inside.

It was not like any other FBI office she had ever seen. Books lined the walls from floor to ceiling. Tables were piled high with old newspapers and stacks of papers and reports. They overflowed onto the floor, along with photos of blurred objects. Scully read a wall poster that said: I WANT TO BELIEVE.

Mulder was standing at a table when they entered. He was examining a photo slide under an intense light. He reluctantly looked up from it to greet his visitors.

Scully got her first good look at him. Even then it was hard to get a fix on him. It was like trying to put together two parts of a puzzle that didn't seem to fit.

His face was young, even boyish, for an FBI agent. His hair was a lot longer than the Bureau liked. He could have landed a job as a veejay on MTV.

Except for his eyes.

There was something old and haunted in his eyes. Something knowing. Something wise.

Mulder gave a crooked smile of welcome. 'Sorry,' he said, 'nobody down here but the FBI's most unwanted.'

Jones replied in a no-nonsense voice, 'Mulder, I want you to meet your new assistant. Special Agent Dana Scully, Fox Mulder.'

'An assistant? Nice to know I'm suddenly so highly regarded.' Mulder turned to Scully. 'Who did you tick off to get stuck with this detail, Scully?'

Scully kept her cool. She could already see that Mulder would take all the cool she had – and then some.

'Actually, I'm looking forward to working with you.'

'Really?' Mulder said. He looked into her eyes. 'I was under the impression you were sent to spy on me.'

Scully's polite smile stiffened. 'If you doubt my qualifications, I'll be glad to list them for you,' she said.

Mulder didn't bother answering. Instead he rummaged through a stack of papers. Finally he came up with a thick folder.

'"Einstein's Twin Paradox – A New Interpretation,"' he read. 'Dana Scully's master's thesis. Now there's a qualification, rewriting Einstein.'

'Did you bother reading it?' Scully asked. She could not keep a touch of ice out of her voice.

'Oh, yes,' Mulder said. 'I liked it. The trouble is, in most of my work, the laws of physics don't seem to work.'

'You should also know that Agent Scully is a doctor of medicine,' Jones told him. 'She is teaching at the Academy.'

'Yes, I know,' Mulder said. 'Maybe we can get her medical opinion on this.'

Mulder flipped off the lights in the room. He turned on

his slide projector. He inserted the photo slide he had been looking at. The picture appeared on a wall screen.

Scully saw a dead young woman lying facedown in a forest clearing.

'Oregon female. Age twenty-one. No explainable cause of death. Zip.'

He showed a second slide. 'Two distinct marks, however, found on her lower back. Can you ID them, Dr Scully?'

Scully moved closer to the screen. She studied the twin marks.

'Needle punctures, maybe,' she said. 'An animal bite, perhaps. Or possibly electrocution.'

'How's your chemistry?' asked Mulder. 'This is the substance found in the surrounding tissue.'

Talk about snap quizzes, Scully thought, as she studied the fresh slide. She hadn't had one like this since her first year in college.

She bit her lip, then said, 'It's inorganic. But it's not like anything I've seen. Is it some kind of synthetic protein?'

Mulder shrugged. 'Beats me. I've never seen it either. But look at this – from Sturgis, South Dakota.'

He flashed a new slide. This time the corpse was a big burly male biker. But the marks were the same.

Then yet another slide appeared. A man was lying facedown in the snow. Again the marks were in the same place. 'Shamrock, Texas,' Mulder said.

'Do you have a theory?' Scully asked.

'Me? I have plenty of theories,' Mulder said. 'But maybe you have a theory, too. A theory why the Bureau won't listen to me. Why the Bureau labels these cases unexplained phenomena. Why the Bureau thinks they should be filed away and forgotten.'

Abruptly Mulder stopped his tirade. He asked Scully

the hardest question of the day. 'Do you believe in extra-
terrestrials?'

Scully played for time to come up with a good answer.
'I've never exactly given it much thought,' she said.

'As a scientist,' Mulder pressed her.

'Logically, I'd have to say no.' Scully kept her tone hesi-
tant. She had to work with this guy. No sense starting off by
rubbing him the wrong way. 'The distances from the far
reaches of space are too vast. The energy needed alone would
exceed a spacecraft's –'

'Spare me your textbook wisdom,' Mulder snapped. 'That
girl in Oregon. She's the fourth member of her graduating
high school class to die mysteriously. Science as we know it
offers no answers. Don't we have to go beyond it? Don't we
have to consider what you'd call "the fantastic"?'

Scully had gone as far as she could to keep the peace.
Pussyfooting wasn't her style. Speaking her mind was.

'If we don't know why the girl died,' she said, 'it's because
something was missed in the autopsy. It must have been a
sloppy postmortem. There's only one thing that I accept as
fantastic. The notion that there are answers beyond the realm
of science. The answers are there. You just have to know
where to look.'

A smile of delight lit Mulder's face.

'I'm glad you think so, Agent Scully,' he said.

'I'm sure Agent Jones here agrees with you. As does
everyone else yanking the chain of command. Hey, that's
what the "I" in the FBI stands for. Investigation is our job.
And we'd better get started on it right away.'

Mulder turned off the slide machine and snapped the
lights back on.

'See you bright and early tomorrow morning, Scully,' he
said cheerfully. 'We leave for Oregon at eight A.M. sharp.'

CHAPTER
FOUR

The next morning, Scully was on a Boeing 747 flying to Oregon. She sat in a center aisle seat. Beside her, Mulder lay stretched over four seats fast asleep.

Scully had her Walkman on, playing folk-rock. She had a thick file folder on her lap. But she wasn't listening or reading. She knew the songs by heart. And she had already digested the files. They dealt with the strange deaths of four of the Bellefleur High School graduating class of '89. She'd think more about them later. Right now she was thinking about seeing her boyfriend, Ethan Minette, last night.

Ethan had not minded when she broke their weekend date. She knew he wouldn't. All she had to tell him was that she had a job to do. He'd do the same thing to her. In fact, he had many times. Work came first for both of them – and especially for Ethan.

He said he had heard of Mulder, though. A year ago 'Spooky' Mulder had convinced an Iowa congressman to fund UFO research. By now it was a Washington, DC, joke. Ethan knew all about that kind of thing. His job was bending congressmen's ears, and sometimes their arms, to vote the way his bosses wanted. The job paid well, and Ethan worked at it night and day. He went out with Scully when he happened to be free – if she could fit him into her own crowded schedule.

They were spare time sweethearts. The most that Scully could say was that it was better than nothing.

It was easy to stop thinking of Ethan. Out of sight, out of mind. But she couldn't stop remembering her last conversation with Jones.

After leaving Mulder's office, Scully had asked Jones, 'Why do they want Mulder so badly?'

'They have their reasons,' Jones said.

'And why did they choose me?' Scully asked.

'Actually, I chose you,' Jones said.

'So why did you choose me?' Scully asked.

'Because I knew you would be – fair,' Jones said.

Jones had said nothing more. But the look he gave Scully did. It said that he was counting on Scully to give the Bureau the straight scoop. It also said that he had different ideas about Mulder than did the old men upstairs.

Scully glanced sideways at Mulder. Sleeping, he looked innocent and defenseless as a baby. Was he a genius in trouble or a troublesome nut? She'd have to wait, watch, and see.

Suddenly the seatbelt lights flashed on.

The flight captain's voice came over the loud-speaker. 'I'd like to ask all passengers to fasten their seatbelts as we begin our descent into –'

That was as far as he got. His voice died as a jolt ran through the plane. It felt like it had been slammed by a gigantic fist. Baggage bins flew open overhead. The cabin lights blinked off. The sound of the jet engines stopped. Shouts and screams of passengers filled the darkened cabin as the plane began to dip.

Don't panic, Scully told herself. She looked down and saw that her hands were holding her armrests in a death grip.

Abruptly the lights came on again. The engines resumed

their roar. And Scully saw Mulder open his eyes and give a happy smile.

'This must be the place,' he said.

Mulder smiled again when he handed Scully their rental car keys.

'If you didn't like that plane ride,' he told her, 'you definitely won't like the way I drive.'

Scully didn't argue. She got behind the wheel and started the car. It moved along the airport access road and out onto the blacktop highway.

Beside her, Mulder put on a pair of wraparound sunglasses. He clicked on the car radio and fiddled with the dial. After he found a station he liked, he opened up a white paper bag and held it out to her.

'Sunflower seeds?' he offered.

'Nope,' Scully said. 'Never touch them when I'm driving.'

'They're to die for.' Mulder grinned. 'Pardon the expression.'

'I was reading those files,' said Scully, keeping her eyes on the road. 'You didn't mention that the FBI has already investigated this case.'

'The FBI looked into the first three deaths,' Mulder acknowledged. 'They suspended the investigation. Lack of evidence, they said.'

Scully couldn't see his eyes behind his shades. But she had a hunch they had narrowed.

'You obviously think there's a connection between the girl's death and the deaths of her three classmates,' Scully said.

'It's a reasonable assumption,' said Mulder. 'There's only one difference. The girl was the only one with both the strange marks and the unidentified tissue sample.'

Scully nodded. She thought of the files she had scanned on the plane. 'The girl was also the only one of the group autopsied by a different medical examiner.'

Mulder brightened. 'Pretty good, Scully. Better than I thought you'd be.'

'Or just better than you'd hoped?' Scully said.

'The limitations of science often make for limited scientists,' Mulder replied.

'I hope those words taste as good as your sunflower seeds,' Scully snapped back.

But Mulder wasn't listening. He was leaning toward the radio.

Elvis had stopped singing. A loud, low humming came out of the radio instead. It was ear-splitting. Overwhelming. Scully had never heard anything like it.

'Stop the car!' Mulder said. 'Stop the car!'

Scully slammed on the brakes. The car came to a halt so hard that the trunk popped open.

Instantly Mulder was out the door. He went to the trunk. He grabbed something out of it. Scully's mouth dropped open.

Mulder was holding a can of spray paint.

Bright orange spray paint.

Mulder walked back down the highway about ten yards. There he painted a big orange X on the asphalt.

'What the hell was that about?' Scully asked when Mulder got back in the car.

'Probably nothing,' Mulder replied with a shrug. Then he looked at Scully and added, 'On the other hand, you never know, do you?'

Scully had to agree with that.

She sure didn't know what was going on around her. She had no idea what was in Mulder's head. And she didn't have a clue to what was waiting for them down the road.

CHAPTER
FIVE

The roadside sign said in big letters: WELCOME TO
BELLEFLEUR – THE FRIENDLY CITY.

But the local folk had missed the message.

The crowd in front of the town civic center looked ready
to throw rocks.

'I was afraid of this,' Mulder said.

'What's going on?' asked Scully.

'I faxed the coroner's office,' Mulder said. 'I told him we
were coming.'

'That's all?' said Scully. 'They have something against
the Bureau around here?'

'I also said we'd be taking a look at the other dead class
members,' Mulder explained.

He didn't have to say more. The crowd said it all when
Scully and Mulder got out of the rental car.

'You the FBI?' shouted a middle-aged man. 'Stay out of
our personal business!'

'What gives you the right?' a woman demanded at the
top of her lungs. 'Those are our sons and daughters!'

'These people have suffered enough loss, enough grief,'
said a priest.

A well-dressed man with an air of authority called out,
'A man's been convicted of the crimes! He's been tried and

sentenced! There's nothing in those graves worth all the pain!'

None of this wiped the calm smile off Mulder's face. Scully was getting a little tired of that smile. It was the smile of someone who knew something that you didn't. In her opinion, it was a smile that asked for trouble.

Mulder kept smiling when a cop blocked their way.

'Agent Mulder,' he said. 'The papers are for you. The people of Bellefleur have gotten court orders against your action.'

Mulder took the papers. He scanned them and shrugged.

'Wait here while I go into the coroner's office,' he told Scully.

'Thanks a lot,' she said to his back as he went inside the building. Scully was left to listen to the crowd. She now knew what umpires felt like when they called the home team out.

Mulder's meeting with the coroner wasn't much better. More low-key, maybe. But no more friendly.

'Mr Truit?' Mulder said.

'Yes, sir. That's me,' the coroner said. His voice was cold, his eyes were icy. Beside him, his two assistants looked at Mulder just as coldly.

'I'm Special Agent Mulder, FBI,' Mulder said. 'We spoke on the phone. How soon can we get to work?'

'Well now, because of those court orders, there's not much we can rightly do,' Truit said. He looked like a cat who had swallowed several canaries.

'Gotcha,' Mulder said. 'But I'm going to need access to an autopsy room. And whoever does your lab work.'

'Maybe I should make myself clear,' Truit said. 'This may be just a little hick town. But we go by the law. I surely wish we could help you. But there you are.'

'Good news,' Mulder said. 'You can help me. There are three cases we're interested in. But there are only two court orders. We're missing someone, right?'

Truit stayed silent.

'I'm FBI,' Mulder reminded him. 'I represent the law.'

'That'd be Ray Soames,' the coroner said reluctantly.

'Why didn't his family go to court to stop us from digging up his body?' asked Mulder.

''Cause Ray Soames's family up and disappeared three years ago,' said Truit.

'Disappeared? Just like that?' demanded Mulder.

But Mulder had gotten all he was going to get out of Truit. The coroner's lips were pressed together tight. That was okay with Mulder. He had what he needed to start work. A name. Ray Soames. He said a cheerful good-bye. Truit and his assistants didn't answer.

'Crowd give you trouble?' Mulder asked Scully when he reached her outside.

'Trouble? Oh no. Just a little small town hospitality – at the top of their lungs,' Scully said. 'So, do you always blow into town like the Prince of Darkness?'

'My style bothers you?' Mulder asked mildly as he headed for the rental car.

'We came down here to investigate a possible murder,' Scully said sharply. 'How can we hope to get any cooperation from the locals?'

The irritating smile was back on Mulder's face. 'What did you expect, Scully?' he said. 'Marching bands and a parade? The FBI failed to turn up anything using your Academy approach. You don't like my methods, you can always cut out and file your report blasting me. Isn't that what you were sent to do?'

'I'm here to help you do a job,' Scully snapped back.

'Really?' Mulder said, raising his eyebrows. 'Really and truly?'

Scully was saved from having to come up with a good answer when a big, red-faced man stormed up to them.

'Who do you people think you're dealing with here?' he raged.

'All depends,' said Mulder. 'Who are you?'

'Dr Jay Nemman,' the man announced.

'The county medical examiner,' Mulder said. Scully had to admit, Mulder did do his homework.

'That's right,' the doctor huffed. 'Are you accusing me of missing something in those kids' autopsies?'

'No, sir,' Mulder assured him. 'We're running a separate investigation. Don't mean to step on any toes.'

'Yeah,' Nemman said suspiciously. 'Just remember, I'm doing any examinations you plan of those bodies. This is my county.'

'How come you didn't do the last one, Karen Swenson?' Mulder asked.

'I was on vacation and –' Nemman started.

'Sorry,' Mulder said flatly. 'This is a federal matter now. Dr Scully will be conducting any postmortem examinations.'

'Listen,' snarled the doctor. 'If you think you're going to make those parents relive their worst nightmares –'

With that he shoved Mulder hard against the rental car. He raised his big, hamlike fist.

Scully didn't know if Mulder was any good at karate. But she was. She tensed to make her move – then relaxed.

'Daddy, quit it!' a young woman's voice pleaded. 'Please! Let's just go home!'

The voice came from a car parked down the street from the rental car. The young woman in the front seat had a pale face and wild hair. Her eyes had a shadowed look. They seemed haunted by the same dark fear that was in her voice.

Dr Nemman kept glaring at Mulder. But he walked backward to his car. He climbed in. The car burned rubber as it roared away.

'Nice guy,' Mulder said. 'Nice tan. Lovely daughter.'

He opened the door of the rental car. 'Coming to the cemetery, Scully?'

'Yeah,' Scully said. 'I want to make sure we're not digging our own graves.'

CHAPTER
SIX

Truit wasn't exactly eager to dig up Ray Soames's grave. Mulder had to flex all his FBI muscle to make the coroner give the order.

Truit and his assistants huddled with a couple of local cops as a gravedigger went to work. Sweat rolled off the man as he dug. The Oregon sun was hot. The noontime air was humid. The Bellefleur Hillside Cemetery felt like a steambath.

Mulder, though, stayed cool as ever. He munched on sunflower seeds as he watched the black dirt fly. He looked like a cow munching cud, thought Scully. She felt her blouse dampen under the armpits.

'This is a waste of time – and sweat,' she griped. 'What about this Danny Doty we've heard about? He was convicted of one of the killings. He could have done them all.'

'Danny Doty turned himself in,' Mulder said. 'He said he killed all three. Trouble was, the cops could connect him to just one. Even then, they didn't have much on him. A tiny bit of evidence, and a lot of guesswork. Without his confession, he would have walked free. But everybody was so eager to find a killer, they took his word as gospel. The locals like to think Danny killed the others, too – just so they can put it all behind them.'

'So you say,' Scully protested. 'But why would he confess to murders he didn't do?'

'Happens all the time. Some folks just like to call themselves killers,' said Mulder. He munched on a sunflower seed and spit out the husk. 'Anyway, Danny's in a prison sixty miles north of here. We can go ask him.'

'And get what for an answer?' Scully grimaced. 'More stuff you won't believe? Maybe he'll confess to the latest murder, too. He'll say he slipped between the bars and did it.'

'Never underestimate what a man doing life will say,' said Mulder.

Scully watched the coffin being hoisted out of the open grave. 'It'll be more than we get from this guy here,' she commented grimly.

The grave didn't want to give the coffin up, though. Roots had wrapped around it underground. The strap from the hoist strained to break that stranglehold. Scully found herself holding her breath as the coffin lifted into the air. And she froze with everyone else when the strap snapped.

The coffin dropped and hit the ground. It started to slide downhill. A moss-covered headstone stopped it.

Mulder headed for it, with Scully close behind. The coroner and his assistants were at their heels.

The lid was knocked partly open. Mulder eagerly reached down to lift it all the way up.

Scully leaned forward to get a good look. She was a pro, and this was part of her job. As far as Scully was concerned, anyone with a weak stomach should be in a different line of work.

'Stop,' Truit commanded. 'This isn't official procedure.'

'Uh-huh. Right. I'll check it out in the rule book before I go to bed tonight,' said Mulder.

Slowly, carefully, he lifted the coffin lid.

Scully was looking over his shoulder as the lid came up.

'Uggh.' She couldn't stop the sound from coming out of her throat. She couldn't stop her skin from going clammy with cold sweat.

It didn't make her feel better to see Mulder's expression.

It was a look of absolute bliss, as if he had stumbled into heaven on earth.

'I guess Ray Soames didn't make the varsity basketball team,' he said.

The figure in the coffin lay on moldy white satin. It was the size of a small child. Its big head was shaped like a football. Its skin looked like shriveled brown leather.

'Is it – human?' gasped Scully. She was not sure she wanted to find out.

'I never –' the coroner managed to say, before he realized he had nothing to say.

'Seal it back up,' Mulder commanded. 'Nobody sees or touches this. Nobody.'

But Scully knew that wasn't what Mulder meant.

What Mulder meant was that nobody but himself was going to have the fun of examining this.

With Scully at his side, of course.

The coroner was more than happy to give them a lab room all their own.

He didn't object to Mulder ordering everyone but himself and Scully out of the room.

'It's your baby – and you're welcome to it,' Truit told Mulder just before Mulder closed the door in his face.

Mulder locked the door from the inside.

'Let's see what they taught you in medical school,' he said to Scully.

'Don't worry,' said Scully, 'I've examined cadavers before.'

'Really?' said Mulder. 'Any like this one?'

'A corpse is a corpse,' said Scully.

'That's for you to find out, isn't it?' asked Mulder.

'I'll do just that,' Scully said shortly. 'Just give me time to set up a tape recorder. I want to voice-record my findings.'

'For posterity?' asked Mulder. 'Or for your report to the big brass?'

'Let's say, for both,' said Scully. 'And maybe even for you, too, partner.'

'Okay,' said Mulder. 'You do the probing and talking. I'll take the pictures.'

He produced a small Polaroid camera. He walked around the corpse, clicking off shots from all angles, as Scully went to work.

'Subject is one hundred fifty-six centimeters long,' she said into the tape recorder mike. 'It weighs fifty-two pounds. It is in an advanced state of decay. It has large ocular cavities and an oblate cranium. They indicate the corpse is not human.'

'Why, Special Agent Scully, what else could it possibly be?' Mulder cut in sarcastically.

Scully kept her voice calm. 'It's some kind of mammal. My guess is it's from the ape family. Probably a chimpanzee.'

'Try telling that to the townspeople. Or to the Soames family,' said Mulder. His eyes danced with pleasure. His camera kept clicking away.

'I want tissue samples and X rays,' he added. 'Blood typing. Toxicology. And a full genetic workup.'

'You're serious?' said Scully, though she knew it was a foolish question.

'What we can't do here we'll order to go,' Mulder said.

Scully could take it no longer. 'You honestly believe this

is some kind of space alien? Look, I guarantee somebody is laughing his head off right now. The same person who switched Ray Soames's body with Bonzo here. We're wasting our time.'

She was wasting her breath.

'Can we do those X rays now?' said Mulder.

Scully's voice rose. She was going to make him listen to reason or go hoarse trying.

'Somebody's yanking your chain, Mulder,' she told him. 'Whoever killed that girl is still running around loose. They could kill again. Easily. At any moment.'

'Right you are,' said Mulder. 'And we'd better stop him right now.' Mulder looked at his watch. 'It's just after ten. We can strap on our six-guns. Then we can go out stalking a killer that the FBI gave up looking for years ago. That everybody else has, too. On the other hand, we can be wimps. We can do a proper scientific examination of the body here. We can remove any questions about who or what this thing might be.'

He paused. His look almost begged Scully to listen to him.

'Look, Scully, I'm not crazy,' he said. 'I have the same doubts you have. What say you help me settle them?'

CHAPTER
SEVEN

By dawn the next morning, Scully was back in her motel room. Her work wasn't over yet, though. X rays of the mysterious creature were taped to the lampshade. She gave them one more look. Then she opened up her laptop computer. She pushed the 'play' button on her tape recorder. Her voice came out loud and clear. She started typing out her report.

'X rays confirm that the creature is a mammal. But they do not explain a small implant in its nasal cavity. This object is gray and metallic. It is four millimeters long. I do not yet know what it is.'

Scully stopped typing. She turned the recorder off. She got up to take another look at the object found in the corpse.

The small metal cylinder was now in a glass vial. Scully stared hard at it. But she still had no idea what it was. Maybe Mulder did, but he wasn't talking. And she wasn't asking. She didn't want to hear any more of his ideas right now. Maybe because they were sounding more and more convincing. If she didn't watch out, she'd soon be as nutty as he was.

There was a knock at the door.

It was Mulder.

He was dressed in faded purple running shorts and a white T-shirt. The T-shirt had a small hole on one shoulder. He had a baseball cap marked 'Brooklyn Dodgers' on backward. His face wore a sunny smile.

'I'm too wired to go to sleep,' he said. 'I'm going for a jog. Want to join me?'

'I'll pass,' said Scully.

'Figure out what that thing in our friend's nose is yet?' Mulder asked, teasingly.

'No,' Scully snapped. 'But I'm not losing any sleep over it.'

Mulder shrugged and handed Scully a piece of paper. 'The motel desk had this for you.'

Scully watched him jog away. He moved smoothly, almost as if he were floating. The air was still cool, but she could feel the heat starting to seep in. Already the sky was changing from pale dawn to deep blue. It was going to be another scorcher.

Scully closed the door and looked at the piece of paper. It said that Ethan had called her and asked her to call back.

Scully punched in Ethan's home number in Washington, DC. He wouldn't be wild about a call this early. But Scully felt like talking to someone who wasn't connected with this case. Someone, anyone, who didn't believe in little invaders from outer space.

Ethan picked up his phone on the first ring.

'Hello?' His voice did not sound happy.

'It's me, Scully,' Scully said. 'Sorry to wake you.'

'I was awake,' Ethan grunted. 'Somebody called me a few minutes ago, then hung up.'

Scully smiled to herself. That had to be Mulder. He was checking her out. He still didn't trust her. Well, he wasn't so wrong about that. She still had a job to do. A job of checking *him* out. A fine pair of partners they were. Each spying on the other.

'Bad way to start the day,' she told Ethan.

'You're telling me,' Ethan agreed. 'What time is it, anyway?'

'Five here,' Scully said. 'That makes it eight where you are.'

'What're you doing getting up so early?' asked Ethan. 'The birds loud there or what?'

'I haven't been to bed yet,' Scully said. 'Up all night working. I got your message and thought it might be something important.'

'Nope, just felt like shooting the breeze,' Ethan said. Scully heard him yawn.

'Yeah ... well ...' Scully said, realizing how little she had to say to him. It was not the first time she had thought that. She had a hunch that Ethan and she did not have a long future together.

'Hey, that guy you're working with must be a slave driver,' Ethan said. 'What's his name, again? Spooky something?'

'Yeah, that's right, Spooky something,' Scully said. The phone was feeling heavy in her hand. She had a growing impulse to hang it up.

'So, you guys find any little green men running around yet?' Ethan asked.

'Well, to tell you the truth –' Scully said, looking at the X rays and the object in the glass vial. But she cut herself short. She could imagine Ethan's reaction. His raised eyebrows. His finger tapping his forehead. And she wouldn't be able to blame him either. She would have reacted the same way a couple of days ago. What a difference a couple of days with Mulder made, she thought. A couple of days seeing the world through his eyes. Would she ever see things in the same way again?

'Hey, well, just try not to get slimed, okay?' Ethan said, and yawned again. 'And don't let old Spooky work you so hard. Threaten him with the funny farm.'

'Well, I'm not so sure that –' Scully began.

'Look, I'd like to talk more, but I have a long day ahead,' Ethan said. 'Catch you later.'

'Yeah, later,' Scully said to the buzzing on the phone. Then she hung up herself.

Shaking her head, she went to the X rays again. Why would anything have a little metal implant in its nose? It didn't make sense. And if it did, then almost nothing else she believed made sense.

There was a tapping on the window.

She saw Mulder's happy, sweating face looking through the glass.

She opened the window.

'You should have come with me,' Mulder said. 'A jog really wakes you up. A cold shower and I'll be all set to really get moving.'

Scully groaned. 'I'll pass again. I want a *hot* shower – and a nice long nap.'

'Aw, come on,' Mulder said. 'You don't want to miss this. It's the chance of a lifetime. How often can you have a heart-to-heart with a real live mass murderer?'

CHAPTER
EIGHT

Danny Doty was a slight young man. But the prison was taking no chances with him. Handcuffs bound his wrists together. Metal shackles, connected by a short chain, bound his ankles. He could take only half steps when the guards brought him into the interview room.

'You can leave us alone with him,' Mulder told the guards.

'We warn you,' said one of them, 'this guy is dangerous.'

'He might not look it,' the second one said, 'but he's a killer.'

'Besides which, he ain't all there,' the first one said. 'You know, he's not playing with a full deck.'

'That's okay,' Mulder said. 'We can take care of him. We're FBI.'

The first guard looked doubtfully at Scully.

'Don't worry about her,' Mulder told them. 'Black belt in karate.'

The second guard shrugged. 'Okay. It's your funeral – pardon the expression.'

The guards left the interview room.

'Actually, it's just a brown belt,' Scully told Mulder.

'Who's to know?' Mulder said. 'Besides, Danny here won't give us any trouble. Will you, Danny?'

Danny didn't answer. But the gleam in his eyes made

Scully's muscles tense. The guards weren't kidding. This guy was definitely around the bend.

Mulder, though, was looking at him like a long lost brother. 'Hello, Danny,' he said, his voice friendly as could be.

'Hi, folks,' Danny chirped like a chipmunk. 'Come to see little old me? Not many people do. Danny here's not so popular. Like they locked me up and threw away the key. Like it was file and forget. But that's cool with me. One thing about the slammer. It's safe, man. Safe as the grave. And not near as cold.'

There were three chairs in the big white empty room. Mulder and Scully sat side by side. Danny sat down facing them.

'Danny, I'm FBI Agent Mulder and this is –' Mulder began.

'Hey, man, I know why you're here,' Danny said. 'They popped Karen Swenson.'

'You know Karen?' asked Mulder.

'Yeah, sure,' Danny said. 'She was a good chick. But, hey, it had to happen. Only a matter of time. Bet they did it real nice.' He laughed. 'One of their special custom jobs.'

'Who are "they"?' Mulder asked, leaning forward.

Danny rolled his eyes so that only the whites showed. Then he stared straight at Mulder.

'Did I say "they"?' Danny said. 'My mistake. Truth is, I did it. From in here. Telepathically. Like, it was no sweat. I just thought, "Karen, baby, you're dead." And wooosh, away she went. Don't worry, though. I'm willing to pay for my crime. Another life sentence, please.' Danny cackled crazily.

Mulder didn't blink. 'What can you tell us about these marks on Karen Swenson's back?' he asked, showing Danny a photo.

'Cleopatra's snakebite,' said Danny quickly. 'Yes sir, had to have one to be in the club.'

'Really?' Mulder said. 'What club was that?'

'What club you think, Mr FBI?' said Danny.

'Was Ray Soames in the club?' Mulder asked.

'Ray Soames?' Danny's brows wrinkled. Then he brightened. 'Oh yeah, good ol' Ray. Sure. Ray got a – what-ya-call-it? A family membership.'

Again he gave his nutty laugh.

Mulder turned to Scully. 'You have any questions for Danny?' he asked.

'No, you keep handling it,' Scully said. 'I can see Danny and you are soul mates.'

Mulder turned back to the prisoner.

'Look, Danny, we want to help you,' he said.

'Man, dig it. I don't want no help,' Danny said. There was nothing crazy in his voice now. 'I'm guilty, hear me? Guilty, guilty, guilty. I don't want out of here. I like those big high walls around me. I can't get out – but nothing can get in. I sure as hell wouldn't want to be in Billy Miles's spot. That's for sure.'

'Who's Billy Miles?' asked Mulder.

'Billy?' said Danny. 'I thought everybody knew Billy. He's the quarterback. Of course, he ain't calling no plays no more. Not since they put him in the nuthouse.'

The State Psychiatric Hospital was on the outskirts of Bellefleur. It was a handsome white building, surrounded by a well-tended green lawn. It looked like a first-rate institution.

The hospital head, Dr William Glass, seemed first-rate as well. His face was intelligent, his manner polite. His answers were clear. He was one person in Bellefleur who wasn't hostile to an investigation. He seemed eager to help.

'Yes, Billy Miles is a patient here,' he told Mulder and Scully. 'He's been one for over three years.'

'And you're his doctor?' Mulder said.

'I oversee his treatment, yes,' Dr Glass said.

'Billy was in the Class of '89,' Mulder said. 'You're familiar with what's happened to a lot of those kids?'

Dr Glass gave a grim nod. 'I've seen several of them over the years. Including Danny Doty.'

'What did you treat them for?' Mulder asked.

'I'm not free to discuss their cases,' Dr Glass said. 'Medical ethics.'

Mulder nodded. 'Of course. But can't you talk in a general way?'

'I suppose so,' the doctor said. 'I can tell you that they all suffered from a similiar problem. Post-traumatic stress. A backlash from a terrible shock.'

'What kind of shock?'

'I have no idea,' the doctor confessed. 'I don't think even the kids knew. But one thing is sure. Whatever it was, it shook them from head to toe. It scrambled their brains.'

Scully meant to stay out of this quiz. Her job was to watch how Mulder operated. But she couldn't resist asking one question.

'Do you think Danny Doty killed his classmates?' she asked.

'I leave those things to the police and the courts,' Dr Glass said carefully.

'But surely you have an opinion,' Scully said.

'My work is healing the mind,' Dr Glass said. 'It isn't putting a body behind bars.'

'To heal the mind, did you try hypnosis?' Mulder cut in.

Dr Glass gave a wry smile. 'People here are suspicious of psychiatry. They'd be up in arms if I tried anything fancy. I have to keep treatments simple. It might not be the best way. But Band-Aids are better than nothing.'

'Have you ever treated Dr Jay Nemman's daughter?' asked Mulder.

Dr Glass hesitated. 'Yes,' he said finally. He cleared his throat. 'Though not with her parents' knowledge. She came to me by herself. I did my best, but –' He stopped himself. 'I'm sorry. As I said, I can't discuss individual cases.'

'Not even Billy Miles?' said Mulder.

'Not even Billy Miles,' agreed the doctor.

'But you will allow us to ask him a few questions,' Mulder persisted.

Dr Glass raised his brows. 'I'm sorry, I thought you knew. Billy Miles is in a strange coma. A waking coma. He's conscious, we think. But he doesn't react to anything. And he hasn't spoken to anyone in years. I'm afraid you'd be wasting your time.'

Mulder winced. It was as if he had been slapped in the face. But he recovered fast. 'Then can we just take a look at him?' he asked.

The doctor shrugged. 'Of course. Though I can't see what good it will do. And I warn you, Billy is not a pleasant sight.'

That was an understatement.

Billy was sitting up in bed. He was a good-looking young man, clean-cut and well-built.

But he might have been in another world.

Breath came in and out through his slightly open mouth. Every now and then he'd blink. Those were his only signs of life.

'Look at him,' the orderly said, shaking his head. 'The

41

greatest football player Bellefleur High ever had. Figured to
be all-American in college. Then some bozo ran him down
out on State Road. A hit-and-run. They never caught the
guy. That was nearly four years ago.'

'He's been like that ever since?' Scully asked. She felt a
little sick. She could handle corpses fine. But a living corpse
was another thing.

'Never changes,' the orderly said. 'A vegetable. If it was
me, I'd rather be buried six feet under. His folks visit only
once a month now. Only one who cares about him is Peggy
O'Dell.'

Then the orderly spoke over Scully's shoulder. 'Isn't that
right, honey?'

Scully turned with Mulder to see a young woman in a
wheelchair. She was matchstick thin and pale as a ghost. She
didn't give Billy's visitors a glance. She had eyes only for the
figure in the bed.

She wheeled herself to Billy's bedside. She picked up a
book from her lap.

'She's Billy's girlfriend,' said the orderly. He gave Scully
a wink. 'Isn't that so, Peggy? Talk to the nice people. They've
come to visit Billy, just like you.'

The girl's eyes narrowed. Her mouth twitched – but she
said nothing.

Mulder asked gently, 'Did you go to school with Billy?'

Peggy ignored his question. 'Billy wants me to read to
him,' she said in a tense voice.

Mulder tried again, 'Did you know Billy before his
accident?'

Peggy's voice grew dreamy. 'Everyone knew Billy,' she
remembered. 'He was the most popular boy in school.'

'Does he like you to read to him?' Mulder asked her.

'I have to take care of Billy now,' Peggy said, still in the same trancelike tone. 'We're joined forever.' She paused. Then she said in a voice that seemed to bounce off the walls, *'Billy and I have seen the light!'*

CHAPTER
NINE

'Billy and I have seen the light!'

Peggy's words sent a shock wave through the room.

Mulder's and Scully's mouths dropped open.

But Billy Miles was hit even harder.

His eyes bulged. His face twitched. Veins stood out on his neck. His Adam's apple bobbed. His lips parted. An animal grunt came out of them, as if he were trying to speak.

Then it was over.

Billy was a vegetable again.

Scully heard Mulder say, 'Peggy, I don't want you to be afraid. We're just going to have Dr Scully take a look at you.'

Scully turned to see Peggy's pale face twisted in panic.

'No! Don't want . . . don't want . . .' Peggy cried. Panting with effort, she wheeled herself toward the door.

The orderly grabbed the wheelchair from behind.

'It's okay, honey,' he soothed. 'It's okay.'

Peggy wasn't buying it. She pushed herself out of the wheelchair. She started crawling away on the floor.

The orderly pushed an emergency button on the wall.

Meanwhile Scully tried to ease Peggy back up into her chair. Peggy wasn't grateful. Her arms flailed wildly as Scully tried to lift her. Mulder came to Scully's aid.

'Thanks. It's like holding an angry cat,' Scully said.

Mulder paid no attention to her. He was looking at something else. Scully followed his eyes. She saw what it was.

Peggy's hospital gown had lifted to show her lower back.

Two red welts stood out on her milky skin.

Mulder looked pleased. Very pleased.

As for Scully, she suddenly felt a little dizzy. A little sick. All this was getting harder and harder to digest.

Scully didn't want any more of this nuthouse scene. She wanted out – before she wound up in a straitjacket herself. She brushed past the two male nurses coming to take care of Peggy. She went down the corridor and out the front door. On the green lawn, under the blue sky, she felt better. More like herself again. Sane. In control. She decided to go to the rental car. She wanted to reread the files on this case. She had a hunger for facts. Nice clear cold facts.

She sat in the car and reread the newspaper story on Karen Swenson's death. The headline read: FOURTH TRAGIC DEATH IN CLASS OF '89. Then the details about discovering Karen Swenson in the forest clearing.

There had to be a sensible explanation for all this, thought Scully. She'd just have to find it.

There was a eerie tapping on the car window.

Scully almost jumped out of her skin.

Then she saw Mulder grinning at her through the glass.

'Very funny,' she said, after she rolled down the window.

'Billy said he was sorry he didn't get to say good-bye,' Mulder said.

'Ha-ha,' Scully said. 'Look, Mulder, how did you know that girl was going to have those marks?'

'Girl? What girl?' said Mulder. Then he said, 'Oh, you mean the one who looked like Carrie at the prom.'

Scully lost the little patience she had left. She was sick

of Mulder's games. Especially since he made the rules and rigged the odds.

'Mulder, cut it out,' she said. 'I want answers. What's going on here? What do you know about those marks? What are they?'

'You want the truth?' Mulder inquired.

'Yes,' Scully told him.

'But can you take it?' Mulder wanted to know.

'Try me,' said Scully.

'I think these kids have been abducted,' said Mulder.

'By who?' asked Scully.

'You mean, by *what*,' Mulder corrected.

Scully got out of the car. She stood face to face with Mulder. It was time to have this out with him.

'You really believe in *things* from outer space?' she demanded.

'Look, I'm open to a better explanation,' he said. 'If you've got one.'

'I think you're crazy,' Scully told him flatly. 'I think those young people were involved in some kind of cult. You know, one of those satanic cults. People, especially when they're young, fall for stuff like that.'

'That so?' said Mulder.

'Of course it is,' Scully said. 'And the forest is the perfect place for weird midnight rites. That's why they found Karen Swenson there in her nightgown. We should go to the forest. There have to be clues there. Candles. Crosses. Something. Anything. Lots of things.'

'Good thinking,' Mulder said, smiling. 'Lucky they put you on my case. I'd be lost without you.'

'Funny, funny,' Scully said. 'Anyway, I say we head for the forest.'

'I say so, too,' Mulder said. 'But after dark. No sense

stirring up the locals anymore. They're getting pretty edgy about our poking around. Any problem with that?'

'No problem,' Scully said. 'I'm a big girl now. I'm not afraid of the dark.'

That night, though, she did feel shivers running through her.

She was alone in the forest. She and Mulder had staked out different parts to investigate.

'Come on, girl, chill out,' she told herself as she played her flashlight through the trees.

She saw a clearing ahead. She made her way to it, branches brushing her face. She knelt where the grass in the clearing was scorched. She ran her hand over the spot. Her fingers came up covered with gray ash.

She remembered the newspaper story. This must have been where Karen Swenson's body was found.

She heard a low humming sound.

Wind in the trees, she told herself. But she didn't feel a breath of breeze.

The sound grew louder. Scully decided to go find Mulder. She stood up. She turned toward the way she had come.

Bright white light half blinded her.

She heard a clanking noise, like some kind of metal instrument. Or else strange footsteps.

She froze. She found it hard to breathe.

The sound grew louder. It was coming closer.

Then she saw it. The blurred shape of a dark figure in the center of the dazzling light.

'Mulder? That you?' she called.

But she already knew the answer.

It wasn't Mulder that was coming for her.

TEN

'Fight fire with fire,' Scully said to herself – and put her words to action.

She beamed her flashlight into the dazzling light.

'Hey . . . what . . .' a voice said.

She saw who the figure was now.

It was a police detective, holding a shotgun at the ready.

'You're trespassing on private property,' he told her.

'We're conducting an investigation,' Scully said, after swallowing the lump in her throat. 'We're FBI.'

'I don't care who you are,' the detective said. 'Get in your car and leave now. Or I'll book you for trespassing.'

Suddenly Mulder's voice came from the dark. 'This is a crime scene.'

Scully swung her flashlight toward the voice. Mulder was standing on the edge of the clearing.

'And I'm the police,' the detective said. 'Now get in your car and leave.'

Mulder looked at the cop's hard eyes. He looked at the shotgun. He said to Scully, 'You heard the man. We have to obey the law.'

Scully followed Mulder past the cop's four-wheel-drive truck. She saw the high-power light bar over the driver's cabin. That must have been what had blinded her. The truck's diesel motor must have made the rackety sound she heard. Sure. That was it. With one weird thing after another, her nerves were shot. She had started imagining things. Impossible things. Especially in these creepy woods.

Suddenly she almost jumped out of her skin.

A flash of lightning forked through the sky.

A crack of thunder split the air.

'Let's get out of here,' she said to Mulder.

'Sure,' said Mulder. They reached their car. Mulder started for the passenger's side.

'You drive,' Scully said. 'There's some stuff I want to check out.'

'If you say so,' Mulder said. He put the compass in his hand on the dashboard. He buckled his safety belt. 'You'd better buckle yourself in, too,' he advised.

Lightning flashed again. Raindrops splattered on the windshield. Mulder clicked on the wipers. They did little good. The rain was coming down in sheets. But that didn't stop Mulder from pressing the accelerator to the floor. The car roared out of the forest and onto the highway.

Meanwhile Scully was examining the scorched earth and ashes she had scooped up in the clearing.

'What do you think caused this?' she asked.

'Brush fire?' said Mulder, deadpan. 'Campers?' He grinned. 'Why ask me? You know you don't like my ideas.'

'It could be some kind of rite. Maybe a sacrifice,' said Scully. 'I think I was right about a satanic cult. I want to go back there.'

'Uh-huh. Sure,' Mulder said. He did not seem very interested. Scully might have been talking about the weather. Mulder was paying more attention to finding a good station on the car radio.

His hand froze on a radio push button.

A humming sound came and went on the set, as if they had passed under a power line.

'Look,' Mulder said.

Scully followed his gaze to the compass. Its needle was moving for no reason.

Mulder looked out the window.

'You okay, Mulder?' asked Scully. 'What are you looking for?'

Mulder didn't answer. He just kept driving through the rain. Pools were forming on the highway. But the car roared along.

'Hey, Mulder, maybe you should –' she started to say.

An awesome flash of lightning cut off her words. The flash filled the sky. It filled the car with light as well.

Then everything went dark.

The car lights had gone off.

The only sound was the beating rain.

The engine was still.

The car was coasting on the asphalt, slowing down. It came to a stop on the side of the road.

'Wow,' Scully said. 'What happened?'

'We lost power. Brakes. Steering. Everything,' Mulder told her. But he didn't seem bothered. If anything, he sounded pleased. Happy, even. Like a kid who had grabbed a gold ring on a merry-go-round.

He looked at his watch.

'We lost three minutes!' he almost shouted with delight.

'We lost what?' said Scully.

'Three minutes!' Mulder announced again.

Then he was out of the car walking down the highway in the pouring rain. Scully sighed and went out after him. She was as bad as a kid following the Pied Piper, she thought.

Thirty yards up the road, Mulder stopped. He waited for Scully to catch up.

'We lost three minutes of time,' he told her again. 'I looked at my watch just before the flash. It was three minutes after nine o'clock. Right afterward, it was seven after nine. And right here, look!'

He pointed down at the blacktop. A big orange X shimmered in the rain. Scully tried to remember when Mulder had spray-painted it there. It took her a moment. Only yesterday. It seemed a year ago. So much had happened since. Around them. And inside of her.

This case was getting to be too much, thought Scully. She knew how a computer must feel overloaded with data. And with a power surge to boot.

She wished things would stop happening, for a little while at least.

But they refused to.

'Abductees report strange time loss,' said Mulder. 'So do people who have made sightings.'

Abductees, thought Scully with a grimace. Mulder wouldn't give up on his ideas about space aliens. He really and truly believed that such things existed. That they were out there in the night. Ready to jump.

'Look, you can't tell me that –' Scully began.

'Look!' Mulder said.

He pointed back up the road. The car headlights had flashed back on by themselves.

'What the –' Scully gasped.

'I warned you about my driving,' Mulder said. 'No telling what'll happen when I'm at the wheel. You have to be ready to get shaken up.'

'I'll tell you what I want to happen right now,' Scully said. 'I want you to drive us straight back to the hotel. No stops. No detours. No passing go.'

'Sure thing,' Mulder said. 'We've seen enough tonight.'

'More than enough,' Scully assured him.

She sighed with relief when she was at last back alone in her room. A good hot shower, a good night's sleep, and this would seem like a bad dream.

First, though, she had a job to do. She put her laptop computer on a table, opened it, sat down, and started typing:

'Agent Mulder's report of time loss, due to "unknown forces," cannot be supported by this agent. This agent believes it highly unlikely and instead believes . . .'

At that moment, the motel room lights flickered and went off.

Scully's computer screen stayed lit. It was operated by a battery.

Scully looked at her last sentence. 'This agent believes it highly unlikely and instead believes . . .' She looked into the darkness around her and bit her lip. She highlighted the sentence and pressed the 'delete' key.

She tried to think what she should write. She gave up. All this was too much. She was more than bone-weary. She was brain-dead. It would be easier to make sense of everything in daylight.

By the light of the computer she found candles in the room. She lit one. Then she yawned and stretched. Mulder would have to go for his morning jog alone again. She was going to sleep as long as she could.

She went into the bathroom with the candle and set it down on the shelf above the sink. Its flickering lit the room, reflecting off the mirror and the white tile walls.

Scully turned on the shower. She checked the water. It

was coming out nice and hot. She could hardly wait to get under it.

She stepped out of her clothes, leaving them in a heap. Then she screamed.

CHAPTER
ELEVEN

Scully held her candle in one hand. Her other hand pounded on Mulder's door.

Mulder's eyes widened when he saw the look on her face.

'What happened, Scully?' he said. 'See a ghost?'

Scully tried to keep her voice calm. 'Can I come in? I want you to look at something.'

Mulder stepped aside. Scully entered his room. It, too, was lit by candlelight.

Scully took a deep breath and took off the bathrobe she had thrown on. Another time she might have been embarrassed. Not now, though. She was too worried to be shy.

Besides, she knew that Mulder didn't have eyes for her. He had eyes for other things.

Scully was wearing just her underwear. She turned her back toward Mulder. With a trembling finger she pointed at her lower back. She wanted Mulder to see what she had seen in the bathroom mirror, when she was about to take her shower.

'What are they?' she asked him.

Mulder knelt down for a closer look.

When he stayed silent, she raised her voice.

'Mulder, *what are they*?'

Mulder stood up. 'You mean, those two raised red welts?' he asked.

Scully fought to keep from screaming. Her voice quavered. 'Yes, I mean those two raised red welts.'

'That's easy,' Mulder told her. 'Mosquito bites.'

'Mosquito bites,' said Scully with a gulp.

'I got about twenty of them myself out there in the woods. Look,' said Mulder. He started to take off his shirt.

'Don't bother. I believe you,' Scully told him. She hastily put her bathrobe back on. She started for the door. But she didn't make it.

A wave of trembling washed over her. She stood there, shaking. Outside the window the rain lashed and the thunder rumbled. Inside the candles flickered madly. She told herself not to be scared. There was nothing to be scared of.

It didn't work.

'You okay?' Mulder asked.

'Yes. Perfectly fine,' Scully lied.

'Yeah,' said Mulder. 'I can see that.'

'I tell you, I'm okay,' Scully insisted. Then she added, 'One thing, though. I'm not sleeping in my room tonight.'

'Oh?' said Mulder. 'Got something better to do?'

'It's time we talk, Mulder,' Scully said. 'It's time you tell me the truth.'

'The truth?' said Mulder. 'What truth do you mean?'

'The truth about what you know,' Scully said. 'And the truth about how you know it.'

'On one condition,' said Mulder.

'Which is?' said Scully.

'You're willing to listen to it,' Mulder said.

'After today, after tonight, I'm willing to listen to anything,' Scully assured him.

'Sit down, then,' Mulder said. 'Better yet, lie down on

the bed. I'll take the chair. You've got a lot to listen to. A lot to learn.' He held out a hand to her. 'Some sunflower seeds?'

'Don't mind if I do.' She munched on the seeds as she listened to Mulder's voice. They tasted good. She should have tried them sooner.

'I was twelve when it happened,' Mulder said. 'My sister was eight. We slept in the same bedroom. We had since we were babies. The next month, we were supposed to get separate rooms. But we never did. Because she just disappeared from her bed one night. Vanished into thin air.'

'How can a little girl just vanish?' asked Scully.

'Nobody knew,' Mulder said. His voice sounded as if he were far away. As if he had gone back in time. Back to when he was a kid – a scared, confused kid. 'My family had money. They had connections. We launched a big search. The police. Private detectives. The newspapers. The works.'

'And – ?' said Scully.

'Nothing,' Mulder said. 'Then we waited for a ransom note. We would have paid anything. It never came.'

'You never found her?' said Scully.

'It tore the family apart,' said Mulder. 'It took years to put it in the back of our minds. But it never really went away. It was like a wound that wouldn't heal – no matter how many bandages you put on it.'

'It's still there, inside of you, isn't it?' said Scully.

'It's still there,' Mulder agreed. 'I tried to put it behind me. I left home to go to school in England. I thought that might help. It didn't. I couldn't forget my sister. Her disappearance gave me a passion for looking into mysteries. First mysteries of the mind. Then mysteries of crime. I joined the FBI. I became their star agent. I was slated for big things. I was going all the way to the top.'

'So what happened?' asked Scully.

'One day I stumbled onto the X-files,' Mulder said. 'Cases so weird that everyone called them ridiculous.'

'Everyone but you,' said Scully.

'I knew I was supposed to,' said Mulder. 'But I couldn't. I couldn't stop myself from believing them. I read every case. Hundreds and hundreds of them. Then I read everything I could find about strange happenings. The occult. Paranormal phenomena. And finally I learned about deep regression hypnosis.'

'What exactly is that?' asked Scully. She wanted to make sure she was following him.

'Deep regression hypnosis is hypnosis that opens up closed parts of your mind,' Mulder explained. 'It lets you remember things you have completely blocked out. Things that are too scary to want to remember.'

'And you remembered – what?' asked Scully, half guessing the answer.

'Scully, look at me,' Mulder said.

Scully sat up in bed and looked him in the eyes.

'I've never told this to anyone else in the Bureau,' said Mulder. 'It sounds too crazy. I didn't want to believe it at first myself. I'm trusting you because I think you're like me. You want answers – right?'

'Right,' Scully said.

'I was hypnotized by an expert,' Mulder said slowly as if he were going into a trance. 'I went back in time. I went back to the night my sister disappeared. I saw myself lying in bed, suddenly waking. I saw the bright light outside the room. I saw the dark figure entering.'

Mulder's hands had clenched into fists. His voice was filled with pain. 'I saw me as a kid frozen with fear. I heard my sister's cries for help. They took her and I didn't make a move to stop them. Listen to me, Scully. This thing exists. I don't know what it is or why it is. But I'm going to figure it out. And I'm going to stop it. Nothing else matters to me. And this is as close as I've ever come to it. You can believe me or not, it doesn't matter.'

'I believe you,' Scully said.

'But I warn you,' Mulder said, 'it's dangerous. And the closer we get, the more dangerous it gets.'

'I believe that, too,' said Scully.

'So maybe you should back off,' Mulder suggested.

'So maybe I shouldn't,' Scully said. 'You forget, I have a report to write. You're not the only one who wants to finish a job.'

The phone rang.

Mulder ignored it. 'If you say so,' he said.

'I say so,' Scully said.

The phone rang again.

Mulder picked it up.

Scully saw his mouth tighten as he listened.

'Right,' he said into the receiver. 'We'll be right there.'

He hung up and said to Scully, 'It's happened again.'

CHAPTER
TWELVE

'Who was on the phone?' Scully asked.

'I don't know. They didn't say. Someone was disguising his or her voice,' said Mulder. He was already putting on his jacket.

'What happened?' Scully wanted to know.

'Peggy O'Dell, Billy Miles's girlfriend in the asylum,' Mulder said. 'She's dead. In the forest at a railroad crossing. That's all the voice would say. I want to find out the rest fast.'

'Give me a minute to dress,' Scully said.

She raced to her room and put on clothes. She splashed water on her face and ran a brush through her hair. There was no time for makeup. Mulder was waiting for her in the hall.

'Let's get the show on the road,' he said impatiently.

'Wait a second, let me lock my door,' said Scully.

He stood tapping his foot as she locked and double locked it.

'Locks won't do much,' he told her. 'Nothing will, not if it wants to get in.' Then he said, 'Come on. Let's go. I'll flip you to see who drives.'

'No way,' said Scully. 'I'm driving. I feel a lot safer that way.'

'You might be right,' Mulder agreed. He tossed her the car keys.

They left the motel. It had stopped raining. A brisk breeze was blowing. A full moon in the night sky lit racing white clouds. It shone on rippling puddles in the motel parking lot. Drops of water sparkled on the roof of their rental car.

They climbed in and buckled their seatbelts. Scully turned the ignition key and the engine roared to life.

As they pulled out of the lot, Scully told Mulder, 'You know, I have a funny feeling. Like someone is watching us. Someone – or something.'

Swarms of cops were on the scene when they arrived. Lights from squad cars lit up the forest crossing like a movie set. Scully saw splintered branches and uprooted saplings from the storm. She spied a locomotive and a string of freight cars halted on the tracks.

Mulder headed straight for a pair of cops standing by the tracks.

'What happened?' he demanded. 'The details. I want all of them.'

One cop squinted at Mulder. 'Don't worry, mister. Everything's under control.'

'I asked, what happened?' Mulder repeated. 'Come on. I don't have all night.'

'A young woman was struck by a train,' the cop said reluctantly.

'How did she get down here?' Mulder demanded.

The cop started to open his mouth. But before he could speak, his partner said, 'Hey, buddy, what's with all the questions? Like who are you to give us the first degree?'

Mulder ignored him. 'Was the girl in a wheelchair?'

The first cop scratched his head. 'Wheelchair? There was no –'

Mulder felt a hand on his shoulder from behind. He whirled around and stiffened.

It was the police detective who had found them in the forest. The one who had told them to clear out.

The big, beefy man kept his hold on Mulder's shoulder. He squeezed harder.

'I thought I told you to get out of these parts,' he snarled.

He let go of Mulder's shoulder. With the butt of his hand, he gave Mulder's chest a hard push.

'And I told you, I want to know what's going on around here,' Mulder answered, shoving back just as hard.

'This is the last time I warn you,' the detective said. 'One more move like that, and I book you for probable cause. You can find out what's happening in the jailhouse.'

He gave Mulder another shove. Mulder's jacket opened.

The first cop's eyes lit up. 'Hey, he's carrying heat,' the cop exclaimed. He yanked Mulder's pistol from its shoulder holster. He moved fast for someone who looked like an ox in blue.

'I'm FBI, you moron,' Mulder said, holding out his hand for the gun.

'Yeah, sure,' the cop said. He kept the gun.

'I've no time to argue,' Mulder said. He turned to the detective. 'Look, maybe you'll listen to sense. I saw that girl in a wheelchair just this afternoon. You tell me how she got here without it.'

'I'll tell you what I told you before,' the detective said. 'Butt out, buster.'

Scully watched Mulder and the detective facing each other. They looked like stags with their horns locked. Mulder was getting nowhere fast acting macho. It was up to her to do some digging.

She saw a blanket lying by the tracks and gently lifted it.

She looked down at the broken body of Peggy O'Dell. Peggy's eyelids were wide open. Her eyes were rolled back so that only the whites showed.

Scully tried not to think about Peggy alive. She tried not to remember Peggy looking with love at Billy Miles.

Peggy was just another corpse now. Peggy was another job to do.

Scully knelt down for a closer look. A lock of brown hair was clutched in the dead girl's hand. She thought about taking it as evidence. She decided not to. The cops wouldn't like her stealing evidence. That's all they'd need to lock her up with Mulder and throw away the key. She'd just make a mental note of it and type it up in her report later.

Then she saw something else. Peggy was wearing a watch. Maybe it had broken when she was hit. That would tell the time of death.

Scully took hold of Peggy's wrist. It was cold. She turned it over to see the watch face.

A shiver ran through her.

The watch read 9:03.

9:03.

The moment that time had stopped. And vanished.

She'd have to tell Mulder. She'd have to –

'Get to your feet, sister,' a voice barked at her. 'And come with me.'

She looked up. A cop was standing looking down at her. His gun was drawn.

Scully stood up. 'Look, officer, you're making a mistake. I was just –'

'You were tampering with evidence,' the cop said.

'But I tell you –' Scully protested.

'You can tell it to the judge,' the cop said. 'And you can also tell him what you're doing with *this.*'

The cop flipped open Scully's jacket. He plucked her pistol from her shoulder holster.

'Come on, let's go see your pal,' the cop said.

Mulder was standing spread-eagled against a squad car. He turned his head when Scully was spread-eagled beside him. He looked angry at the cops' actions, and disgusted with their stupidity.

'We'll run an ID,' the detective told them. 'You check out, you can come pick up your weapons.'

'I've got my ID right here,' Scully told him.

'Forget it. He's not listening,' Mulder said. 'He's been watching too much Smokey and the Bandit.'

Just then a voice said, 'You can let them go. I'll vouch for them.'

It was the coroner.

'Truit,' Mulder said with relief. 'Thank God you got here. Now we can start putting things together.'

'Ain't nothing left to put together,' Truit told him. 'Brace yourself, Mr FBI. 'Fraid you're back to square one.'

CHAPTER
THIRTEEN

Mulder grimaced. 'Okay, Truit, give me the bad news. I can guess what it is. But you might as well make it official.'

'Somebody just trashed our offices down in the civic center,' Truit said, shaking his head. 'I was afraid something like this was going to happen. Folks around here are law-abiding – but you got them so worked up.'

'They trashed your offices,' Mulder said. His voice sounded tired, resigned. 'But that's not all they did, is it?'

'Ain't that enough?' Truit said. Then he added, 'Oh yeah. Almost forgot. Hope you weren't too attached to that dog carcass you dug up. Or whatever that critter was.'

'They took it, right?' Mulder said. 'Funny how that doesn't surprise me.'

'Don't ask me why they wanted it,' the coroner said, scratching his head. 'Not the kind of thing you'd hang over your fireplace.'

'I wouldn't dream of asking you why,' said Mulder. 'I won't even ask you why you didn't have security.'

'Never needed security, before you people started stirring things up,' Truit answered. 'Outside agitators always cause trouble around here.'

Mulder opened his mouth to say something. Then he closed it. A thought had hit him – hit him hard.

'Scully!' he barked. 'The car keys! Quick!'

She handed them to him. Before she could ask him why, he was running toward the car. She dashed after him. By the time she slid into the passenger seat, he was already gunning the motor.

'What's the hurry?' she asked, as the car roared down the highway.

'I'm afraid you'll find out soon enough,' said Mulder, not taking his eyes off the road.

He was right.

Scully got her first hint of what was coming when she saw a glow in the sky just above the horizon.

'Is that what I think it is?' she asked Mulder.

Mulder didn't answer. His lips were pressed together grimly.

The car went around a bend in the road. She could see straight down the highway. She had a clear view of their motel.

She saw a mass of flames.

Mulder stopped the car by one of the fire engines parked on the road. He and Scully made their way through the firemen in their gear and motel guests in their pajamas and nightgowns. The two of them stood side by side looking at the blaze. Helplessly they watched the fire licking at their rooms. Streams of water from fire hoses had no more effect than spit.

'There goes my report. Not to mention my laptop. The latest model. I had to pull strings to get it,' said Scully. She felt as if she had lost a close friend.

'There go the X rays,' Mulder said. 'My Polaroids. The whole works. Every trace of what we dug up yesterday. I wonder who wanted it gone. Any ideas, Scully?'

Scully started to say something. Then she stopped herself. 'Not really,' she said.

'Or maybe you have some – and don't want to admit them,' Mulder suggested.

Scully was saved from having to give him an answer.

'Look who's coming,' she said, glad for the distraction.

'Dr Nemman's sweet little daughter,' said Mulder, as the figure emerged from the bushes into the light. 'She looks like she's had a rough night, too.'

Scully agreed. The girl had looked unkempt when they first had seen her in her dad's parked car. But now she looked like the bride of Frankenstein. Her hair was a wild tangle. Her long nightgown was streaked with dirt and ripped at the hem. Her feet were bare. Her face was streaked with tears. And her voice broke as she begged, 'Please, help me. You've got to protect me.'

Mulder took off his jacket and put it around the girl's heaving shoulders. 'It's cold out tonight,' he said. 'We don't want you to catch a chill.'

Then he said, 'Let's go somewhere we can get something warm into you. Then we can talk. Nice and slowly and calmly. Sort everything out. Get everything straight. Make everything normal again. You'd like that, wouldn't you?'

The girl nodded. 'Everything normal again. Oh yes, please.'

'We passed an all-night diner down the road,' Scully suggested. 'We can go there.'

'I was thinking the same thing,' Mulder agreed. 'Guess it's true what they say about great minds.'

The diner was empty when they entered it. A bored-looking waitress took their order for coffees. She didn't act curious about a girl who looked like a beat-up Raggedy Ann doll. She'd probably worked the graveyard shift so long that nothing could surprise her.

Scully waited until the girl finished her cup of coffee.

'Want some more?' she asked her.

The girl shook her head. 'No,' she said. 'It won't do any good. It won't take this taste out of my mouth.'

'What taste?' Mulder asked.

'Like metal,' the girl said, grimacing. 'Or something. Something worse. Uggh.'

Mulder nodded sympathetically. 'It must be terrible. You'll have to brush your teeth really well tonight.'

He was talking to her slowly, the way you talked to a child. The girl might be in her early twenties, but she had the look of a scared five-year-old.

'Now tell us, what's your name?' he asked.

'Theresa. Theresa Nemman,' the girl said.

'What were you doing outside in your nightgown tonight? You don't usually wander in the woods that way, do you?'

'I don't know,' Theresa said, shaking her head. 'I just found myself out there. That's the way it happens. Always. I'm out there and I don't know how or why.'

'So it's happened before?' Scully asked. She spoke softly, soothingly. The girl looked as fragile as crystal. And as skittish as a frightened rabbit.

Theresa's voice seemed to come from far away – from someplace deep inside her. 'It's happened ever since the summer I graduated,' she said. 'It's happened to my friends, too. That's why I want you to protect me. I don't want it to happen to me. I don't want to die like the rest of them. Like Peggy tonight.'

Her shoulders started heaving again. Tears ran down her cheeks.

Scully reached across the table to comfort her. She took the girl's hand in hers. The girl's hand felt as cold as Peggy's had been by the railroad tracks.

'You will protect me, won't you?' the girl pleaded between sobs. 'Promise me you'll protect me.'

'Of course we will,' Scully soothed her. 'You can be sure of that.'

Scully had a bitter taste in her mouth now. A metallic taste.

She knew what it was.

The taste of a lie.

CHAPTER
FOURTEEN

Scully couldn't lie to herself anymore.

She could no longer pretend that this was an ordinary case. She could no longer tell herself that science would give her all the answers. Or that her FBI training would lead her to the killer.

Even worse, she could no longer dismiss Mulder as a loose cannon, a screwball, off the wall, or cuckoo.

She was almost glad that her laptop was trashed. For the time being, she didn't have to worry about writing her report.

It would be tough to convince her FBI bosses that Mulder was onto something. Maybe impossible. She couldn't see them believing it. She wouldn't have believed it – until now. She'd have to watch her step when she wrote up this case. It wouldn't be just Mulder's job on the line. It was her future, too. Not to mention what would happen to the X-files. The Bureau brass would lock those files up and throw away the key.

Scully didn't want that to happen. She wanted those files to stay open. She wanted Mulder to keep on with his work. And she wanted to help him. She had seen enough to want to see more. Mulder was right about her. She was like him. She was the kind of person who wanted answers. She was the kind of person who *needed* answers – no matter what they turned out to be.

'It's time to tell the truth,' Mulder said.

Scully stiffened. Then she realized he wasn't talking to her. He was talking to Theresa.

'You were the one who called me tonight, weren't you, Theresa?' Mulder said. 'You were the one who told me Peggy O'Dell had been killed.'

His voice was no longer gentle. It was harsh, demanding. He had decided it was time to take off the gloves, Scully thought. He was like an animal smelling blood. Ruthless. Relentless. It was a side of him Scully hadn't seen before. But she wasn't surprised it was there.

Theresa bit her lip, stayed silent. She tried to turn her eyes away from Mulder's. But Mulder's piercing gaze held her like a vise.

'Yes,' she said in a weak voice. 'It was me.'

'How did you know where to call me?' Mulder wanted to know.

'I heard my father say where you were staying,' Theresa said.

Scully caught Mulder's eye. She raised her eyebrows. Was Dr Jay Nemman the firebug? He had acted mad as the devil the day before. But was he that mad?

Mulder gave a slight shrug. He didn't know. Then he turned back to the doctor's daughter. He was going to find out the truth, even if he had to yank it out of Theresa with pliers.

'Who was your father talking to?' Mulder asked. 'Who did he tell about the motel?'

'He was talking to Billy's dad,' Theresa said.

'Billy? You mean Billy Miles?' said Mulder.

'Yes. Billy is –' Theresa said. She paused. It was hard for

her to say the words. Finally she managed to. 'Billy's one of us.'

'I know that, Theresa,' Mulder said. 'You're all in this together. The Class of '89. But let's get back to the present. How did you know Peggy was dead?'

'My dad got a phone call,' Theresa said. 'I heard him asking over the phone, "Peggy's dead? You sure?"'

'What time was that?' Scully cut in. She wanted to get the time right – to the minute. Tonight minutes meant a lot. Maybe everything.

'Nine o'clock. A couple of minutes after,' Theresa said. 'I remember my favorite TV show had just come on when the phone rang.'

'And what happened then?' Mulder asked. 'After you heard your father talking?'

Theresa shook her head helplessly. 'I don't know. I can't remember. Next thing I remember, I was in the woods. Someone was chasing me.'

'Who?' Mulder said.

'I don't know,' the girl said. She seemed near tears again.

But Mulder did not let up. 'Was it your father?' he said.

'No,' Theresa said. Her voice was barely above a whisper. 'But Daddy said never to tell anyone. About any of it.'

'You're not supposed to tell anybody about any of *what*?' Mulder demanded sharply.

Scully couldn't blame him. By now she felt the same way he did. They were too close to the truth to let it get away.

'I'm not supposed to tell anyone about Peggy,' Theresa said. 'Or Billy Miles. Or how Daddy helped.'

'Your father helped? Who did he help?' Mulder wanted to know.

'Peggy,' Theresa told him.

'How did he help her?' Mulder asked.

71

'He was Peggy's doctor. She was ... she was going to have a baby,' Theresa said. 'But it died.'

'Did Billy know about the baby?' Scully asked, beating Mulder to the punch.

'No,' Theresa said. 'He wasn't around then – he hadn't been for months. He disappeared right before graduation. He didn't come back until almost the end of summer. Peggy said he was the father of her baby. But nobody believed her because he wasn't even here.'

'Did your dad know who the father of the baby was?' Mulder asked.

Theresa hesitated again. Then she said, 'He helped Peggy. But ... but there was no baby. There was something else. Daddy said it was because Peggy had the marks.'

Scully swallowed hard. She didn't like to think of what Peggy had instead of a baby. But there was no escaping it.

She saw in her mind the remains of the creature they found in the grave.

Her stomach turned over.

She looked at Mulder. He didn't seem bothered. He was leaning forward.

'The marks?' he asked. 'You mean the marks on her back?'

'Yes,' said Theresa. 'We all got them. In the forest. *And we're all going to die.*'

FIFTEEN

That was as far as Theresa could go.

Now she put her hands over her ears, lay her forehead on the table, and broke into violent sobs.

Scully reached out to touch her hand. It was still icy cold.

Then Theresa raised her head.

'Oh, God,' Scully said.

Blood was pouring out of Theresa's nose.

Scully grabbed a handful of paper napkins from a dispenser. She handed them to Theresa.

As she did so, a picture flashed into her mind. The creature in the coffin. The implant in its nostrils.

Was the same implant in Theresa's – ?

That was as far as Scully's thinking got.

Out of the corner of her eye, she saw the diner door swing open.

Dr Jay Nemman stormed into the diner. Close behind him was the police detective from the clearing in the woods. He looked meaner than ever.

The waitress pointed to the table where Scully and Mulder sat with Theresa.

'There's your little girl, Doc,' the waitress said. 'Goodness only knows what they've been doing to her, poor thing.'

Scully realized the waitress must have made a phone call.

Folks around here stuck together – especially when outsiders were concerned.

Outsiders from earth, anyway.

Dr Nemman ignored Scully and Mulder. He had eyes only for his daughter.

He put his hand on her shoulder. 'Let's go home, honey,' he said. 'You'll be best off there. Away from these prying people and their painful questions.'

But Theresa shrank from his touch. Her eyes were wide with terror.

'I don't think the girl wants to leave,' Mulder said in a flat voice.

'Now you just stay out of this,' the doctor snapped. 'She's a sick girl. A very sick girl. She imagines things. All kinds of things. She's on the verge of a mental breakdown. She should not become excited.'

By now Theresa had retreated to the corner of the diner booth. She formed her body into a half ball. Like a baby in the womb.

The police detective reached out his arm toward her.

'Your daddy wants to take you home, Theresa, honey,' he said soothingly. 'He'll get you all cleaned up. Put you to bed. Give you some nice hot chocolate. Now wouldn't that taste good?'

'We're going to take you where you'll be safe, sweetheart,' Dr Nemman chimed in. 'You know that Detective Miles and I won't let anything happen to you.'

Mulder suddenly sat ramrod straight in his seat.

'You're Billy Miles's father?' he asked the detective.

The big detective turned toward Mulder. 'That's right.' He looked down at Mulder menacingly. 'And you stay away from my boy, hear? Bad enough he's like he is. I don't want outsiders gawking at him like he's something in a zoo.'

'Come on, Joe, help me,' Dr Nemman said to Detective Miles.

Nemman took one of Theresa's arms, and Miles took the other. Together they hauled her and half dragged her out of the diner.

Neither Mulder nor Scully made a move to stop them. No way they could argue with the rights of a parent and power of the law. Theresa give them one last terrified look as she went out the door.

'You have to love this place,' said Mulder, finishing his coffee. 'Every day's like Halloween.'

'Can we believe a word she said?' Scully said. 'Maybe her father was telling the truth. Maybe she is crazy. This town seems to breed them. Maybe it's something in the diet.'

'Do you think anybody, crazy or not, could make all that up?' said Mulder.

'You know the answer to that,' Scully said. 'But it's still hard to make sense of it. For instance, Peggy O'Dell's watch stopped at three minutes past nine o'clock. That's when she was supposed to have been hit by the train. But Theresa said that Miles told her father about the death just after nine. He couldn't have.'

'Who knows?' said Mulder. 'She could have been wrong about the time. People make mistakes about things like that. Or she could have been lying. Lying to us – or even to herself. There are things that are hard to admit. Like her having a telepathic connection with Peggy. Those kids in the Class of '89 were linked together by something. Something they couldn't break free of.'

Mulder raised his coffee cup to his lips. He realized it was empty.

'Anyway, whatever the truth is, it wouldn't stand up in

court,' he went on. 'Nothing Theresa said would. A girl as upset as she. A girl whose own father says she's unbalanced. No court would take her word against a doctor's. Or a cop's.'

Scully nodded. 'Imagine you describing what happened on the highway where X marked the spot. At three minutes after nine o'clock, when you said time took a three-minute holiday. I won't say it did or it didn't. But for sure don't try telling it to a judge.'

Mulder smiled bitterly. 'I've long since stopped trying to tell things to judges. What you need is hard evidence.'

'You're not the only one who knows that,' Scully said. 'Whoever wrecked the coroner's office and torched our motel rooms knew it, too. All we have to show for our work is ashes.'

'Who do you think the firebug is?' said Mulder. 'The good Doctor Nemman?'

'Could be,' said Scully, thinking hard. 'He's not exactly our pal. Maybe Billy's father was working with him. I can see both of them against us. Both of them covering somebody's tracks.'

Suddenly Mulder stood up from his seat.

By now Scully recognized the signs.

She got up, too.

'Where to now?' she asked.

'It just hit me,' Mulder said. 'There still may be some evidence they haven't destroyed.'

'Where?' Scully said.

But Mulder was heading for the door.

Scully raced after him to the car. He beat her to the driver's seat.

'Careful,' she told Mulder as they raced down the road. It had clouded over again. A fine rain was falling. The asphalt was slick. 'We won't solve this case if we're corpses.'

'At least we'd wind up in the right place,' said Mulder. He kept the accelerator down to the floorboard.

Finally the car braked to a sharp stop. Scully peered out. They were at the edge of Bellefleur Hillside Cemetery.

Mulder got out, and so did Scully. Mulder turned on his flashlight. Then he led the way over the wet grass and muddy soil.

He stopped.

'Too late,' he said.

His flashlight played over two opened graves. Beside them were two coffins with their lids off.

Mulder shone his flashlight into them.

Scully looked over his shoulder.

'Both empty,' Mulder said. 'I should have known.'

'What's going on here?' asked Scully. 'Is everything in this case crazy? Or are we the crazy ones?'

Mulder wasn't listening.

He stood there, his face vacant, off in a world of his own.

All Scully could do was wait.

Slowly life came back to his face.

He took Scully by the shoulders. His eyes were shining brightly. It was the light of pure joy.

His voice was lit with the same joy.

'It just came to me,' he told her. 'I know who it is.'

'Who *who* is?' said Scully.

'Who did it,' said Mulder.

'Did it?' Scully said. 'You mean, killed Peggy?'

Mulder nodded happily.

'And the rest?' said Scully. 'Stole our evidence? Scared Theresa out of her wits? The same person?'

Mulder kept nodding.

'One and the same,' he said. 'I know who it is.'

CHAPTER
SIXTEEN

'I hate to spoil your fun – but I think I already know the answer,' said Scully. She had been putting a lot of pieces together in her mind. She thought she had the puzzle solved.

'Do you?' said Mulder. 'Do you really?'

'Is it the big cop – Detective Miles?'

'Good try,' said Mulder. 'You're a credit to the Academy. But – no.'

'No?' said Scully.

'No – but you're close,' said Mulder.

'Close?' said Scully.

'It's his son – Billy Miles,' Mulder declared.

Scully could see that Mulder might be a nice guy. Well-meaning. Talented. With his heart in the right place.

But his head was definitely screwed on wrong.

She smiled at him as she shook her head.

'Billy Miles?' she said. 'You mean the kid who's been a vegetable for the last four years? He got out here and dug up these graves all by himself?'

Mulder nodded.

'I don't know if I completely understand it,' he told Scully. 'All the details. But it fits a profile of alien abduction. Believe me, I know what I'm talking about. I've run hundreds of cases through a computer and –'

'*This* fits a *profile?*' said Scully. She thought of the total insanity of the past couple of days. Some profile that must be.

'Listen,' Mulder said. 'Peggy O'Dell's watch stopped at three minutes after nine o'clock. You saw it. That's exactly when we lost three minutes out on the highway. Meanwhile, at the same time, Theresa Nemman somehow left her house and wound up running for her life in the woods. I think something happened in those three minutes. When time as we know it stopped.'

'Sure, Mulder, sure,' Scully said. 'Now why don't we go back to the motel. You can have a nice glass of hot milk. Get a good night's sleep. You'll feel better in the morning.'

Mulder raised his eyebrows.

'You don't believe me?' he said.

'Agent Mulder, I'm standing out in the mud and drizzle,' said Scully. 'I'm looking at two empty coffins. I'm in a cemetery where we dug up someone or something I can't explain. Meanwhile, a whacked-out kid just told me she's going to die because she has "the marks." Sure, I believe you, Mulder. But that doesn't mean you're right. It means I'm going around the bend myself. At this point, I'd believe anyone or anything. It wouldn't surprise me if we both started howling at the moon.'

'Calm down, Scully, and listen,' Mulder told her.

'Calm down?' said Scully. 'I'd need a couple of good strong pills for that.'

But strangely enough, she did feel herself calming down. Maybe it was something in Mulder's voice. His passion for the truth. His complete conviction. Whatever it was, she shut up and listened.

'I think there's a force at work here in Bellefleur,' Mulder told her. 'We felt it on the plane just before we landed. We experienced it out on the highway. There was a strange force at work there. Our watches played tricks. My compass went haywire. What I'm saying is – I think this force can bend time. So that Billy Miles could go dig up these graves. And loot. And burn. And kill. With no one around to see that he was gone from his bed.'

Scully told herself not to listen to Mulder. But it was like being in the water and fighting an undertow. She felt the pull of his thinking – its power and its purpose. She was losing her footing, being pulled farther and farther out to sea.

'This "force" – it expands time?' she heard herself asking.

'Yes,' he answered. 'And it's what caused the marks on those kids' backs. The kids with the marks have been abducted and used in tests. They're taken to that clearing in the woods. The substance we can't identify is put into their bodies. It causes a genetic mutation.'

'So this "force" was chasing Theresa through the woods tonight?'

'No,' said Mulder. 'It was Billy Miles. He was acting from an impulse implanted in his DNA. Danny Doty feels the same kind of impulses in his genes. That's why he wants to stay in prison. He knows he can't obey them if he's behind bars.'

Scully nodded. Of course. It made sense. Complete sense. No question about it. Mulder was perfectly sane in telling her all this. And she was perfectly sane in listening to it and nodding and urging him to tell her more. It was the rest of the world that was –

She doubled over as a wave of laughter hit her.

Mulder looked at her and started laughing, too.

They stood there in the cemetery in the darkness and the drizzle, laughing their heads off.

'You know, we're crazy,' Scully finally said.

'Of course we are,' Mulder gasped out.

At last he caught his breath.

'Come on,' he told Scully. 'Let's go.'

'Where are we going?' asked Scully, still feeling weak with laughter.

'Where we belong,' said Mulder. 'To the funny farm. To see Billy Miles.'

CHAPTER

SEVENTEEN

Scully stood with Mulder at Billy Miles's bedside. The orderly who took care of Billy was there as well.

'We can wait 'til the second coming for Billy to get out of this bed,' the orderly told them. 'It ain't gonna happen.'

Billy lay there, quiet as a corpse. Only the smallest rise and fall of his chest showed he was breathing. His face looked like a death mask. His eyes were blank as glass.

'Three years he's been lying here like this,' the orderly said. 'And a year before that at home.'

'You're sure?' Scully asked. 'He never makes a move?'

'I keep a close eye on him,' the orderly assured her. 'His old man, he pays me extra to do that. He made me swear that if there's any sign of life, I tell him first. Believe me, Billy even blinks, and I know it.'

Mulder had been listening. Now he stepped forward and took over. 'Did you change his bedpan last night?'

'Nobody else here gonna do it,' the orderly said.

'You notice anything unusual?' Mulder asked.

'Unusual?' said the orderly, puzzled. 'What you mean? What kind of unusual thing could happen here with Billy? Like I already told you, he hasn't moved in –'

'What were you doing last night at nine o'clock?' Mulder cut in.

'Probably watching TV,' said the orderly. 'Yeah. Sure. That's right. I was watching the tube.'

'What were you watching?' Mulder asked sharply.

'Sure. It was ... it was ...' The orderly paused. He was suddenly confused. 'Funny about that, I can't exactly remember what –'

He stopped abruptly. Scully was leaning over Billy's bed.

She had spotted something. A black smudge on Billy's clean white sheets. She moved to the foot of the bed. She started pulling at the blanket.

'Hey, what are you doing?' the orderly wanted to know.

Scully paid no attention to him. She pulled the blanket free and looked down at Billy's bare feet.

'What you looking for?' the orderly demanded.

Scully found what she was looking for under a toenail. Dirt. Black dirt.

The orderly was angry. He didn't like this stranger meddling with Billy. Billy was his job. More than his job. His meal ticket.

The orderly opened his mouth to shoo Scully off. Before he could, Mulder shot him another question. 'Who was taking care of Peggy O'Dell last night?'

'Not me,' the orderly defended himself. 'That's not my ward. Not my part of the vegetable garden. It's a shame about that girl, though. She sure enough liked Billy here. I think she did him more good than all them doctors. I sometimes even thought Billy actually kind of knew she was there.'

'How could she have gotten out of here?' Mulder asked. 'Without her wheelchair?'

'I don't know,' the orderly insisted. 'Like I said, that's not my thing.'

Then he noticed Scully again. She had taken a metal instrument out of her purse. She used it to scrape dirt from under Billy's toenails. She put it in a small glass vial. She finished the job before the orderly could tell her to stop.

All the orderly could do was ask, 'What the devil you want to do that for?'

Mulder answered for Scully. 'Thank you for your time,' he said.

The orderly was left openmouthed as Mulder and Scully made their exit.

The orderly was back to having only Billy to talk to. He didn't mind, though. He was used to it. He talked to Billy every working day. It didn't bother him that the conversation was so one-sided. The orderly liked the sound of his own voice.

'Now look what that girl did,' the orderly said. 'Messed up the nice hospital corners of these sheets. Gotta fix them again. 'Course, she did give your nails a nice cleaning, though how they got so dirty I don't know. Guess you must sweat or something. I mean, you are alive, Billy boy. Else your old man wouldn't give me that little bonus every week. Still, I earn my pay. No fun being cooped up with you all the time. I mean, you ain't my dream companion. Besides which, I think it's affecting my mind. I could have sworn you actually gave that girl a look when she scraped your nails. Which means I'd better take some time off this job. Else soon some-body's gonna be looking after *me*.'

Meanwhile, outside, Scully was saying to Mulder, 'Guess where I want to go now?'

'It'll just take twenty minutes to drive back to the motel – or what's left of it,' Mulder said.

'Then I guess I don't have to tell you what we're looking for,' Scully said.

'Let's hope we can find it,' Mulder said.

Scully wrinkled up her nose as they went through the

charred remains of her motel room. Fire left an awful stink. But a second later she forgot the smell.

'We're in luck,' she told Mulder, picking up a half melted baggy. Its contents were intact. 'I knew I was right taking a sample from the forest clearing.'

'Score one for your Academy training,' Mulder agreed.

'Here's something else that survived, too,' she said. She picked up a glass vial. It had cracked, but the tiny metal implant – the implant from the creature in the coffin – was still inside.

'Our firebug friend might be good – but he's not *that* good,' Scully said.

'Time to see how good we are,' said Mulder. 'Let's get to the lab. There's work to do.'

'No sweat,' Scully assured him. 'It'll be child's play.'

She was right. The job was a snap. She put the dirt from under Billy's toenail on a glass slide. Beside it she put the sample from the forest clearing. Once the slide was under a microscope, she needed only a quick look.

'We've hit pay dirt,' she announced. 'They're a perfect match.'

'Put 'er there, partner,' Mulder exulted. His palm went up to slap Scully's in a stinging high-five. 'Goal to go!'

CHAPTER
EIGHTEEN

'Looks like we're not alone,' Mulder said.

Their car headlights lit up a four-wheel-drive truck. It was parked at the forest edge.

Scully recognized it right away. 'Our old pal, Detective Miles,' she said. 'He sure does like these woods at night.'

'Must be a boy scout who never grew up,' Mulder said. 'Wonder what good deed he's planning tonight.'

'I'm sure we'll find out,' Scully said. 'But let's not worry about it now. There's more to find out first.'

She parked the car beside the truck. They got out and lit their flashlights. They followed the bright beams through the dark trees.

'You'd think we'd know our way by now,' Scully said. 'But in these woods, I always feel a little lost. Or maybe it's not these woods. Maybe it's this whole case. I keep losing my bearings. Every time we find one answer, a new question pops up.'

'Welcome to the club,' Mulder said, brushing aside a branch. 'I've felt that way for years now. It's like being in a maze. A maze with endless twists and turns. A maze built to confound you no matter how smart you think you are.'

He fell silent. There were only the night sounds of the forest. The wind in the trees. An owl hooting. The scurrying of unknown animals. And the soft crunching of their footsteps on fallen leaves.

Then Mulder said, 'What about you, Scully? What do you think about this maze? Does it spook you? Does it make you want to turn tail and get out while the getting's good? Or are you like me? Have you gotten in too deep to turn back?'

'Do I have to answer that question right now?' she asked, half joking. 'Or am I allowed to consult my notes?'

'Take all the time you want,' Mulder said. 'But you'll have to give the answer sometime, you know. Not to me. To yourself. And of course to the folks who sent you into this with me. Our dear bosses.'

'I'll worry about that later,' Scully said. She found the spot where she had scooped the gray ashes and black earth. 'Look,' she said. Her light shone on imprints in the ashes.

'Footprints,' said Mulder.

'Bare footprints,' Scully said. 'It figures.'

'Listen,' Mulder said. 'Someone's running.'

Scully heard it, too. The sound of a body crashing through the underbrush.

Mulder swung his flashlight toward the sound. He was fast enough to spot a figure moving into the trees. But he wasn't fast enough to see who it was.

Scully watched Mulder take off. She hesitated for one violent heartbeat. Then she broke into a run. Maybe she couldn't catch up with him. But she wanted to keep him in sight.

Scully was a Redskin fan. Now she knew what it was like to follow a zigzagging blocker on a broken field run. Mulder darted in and out of the trees ahead of her. Scully tried not to lose him. For a second she was sure she had. Then she saw him through a break in the trees. He was drawing away from her. She had to speed up. Her legs felt like lead weights. Her breath ripped at her lungs. But she made herself breathe deeper, move faster –

Blatt.

Something hit the back of her legs very hard.

Suddenly her legs were no longer under her.

She was falling.

She felt the impact to her elbows as she hit the ground palms first.

Her chin was resting on the ground. She slowly lifted her head. She stared at a pair of scuffed and dirt-covered boots.

Her eyes traveled upward over massive legs in dark blue pants. Next she saw a big stomach straining shirt buttons as it hung over a taut belt. Then her gaze fastened on a gleaming shotgun pointed at her head.

She didn't have to bother checking out the man's face. 'Detective Miles,' she said. 'Fancy running into you here.'

'Touch my kid and I'll kill you,' he promised.

Then he was off and running.

Scully knew where Miles was going. But maybe she could catch up with Mulder before the kill-crazy cop did. She didn't know what she could do to help him. But there had to be something. Anything. How she wished she had her gun. Or that Mulder had his. Karate was fine. But even a black belt couldn't beat a bullet.

She picked herself up and raced through the woods. But now she was running blind. She had lost sight of both Mulder and Miles. All she could do was run and hope and pray she got to Mulder in time.

Then she was at the edge of another clearing. Her heart skipped a beat. She saw Mulder.

He was standing on the far side of the clearing, shining his flashlight at the center of the open space.

There, frozen in the beam of light, was Billy Miles standing in his pajama bottoms.

Scully gripped a tree trunk to steady herself. She could see two red marks on Billy's back.

Seeing them shook her up enough. But the limp figure cradled in Billy's arms shook her up even more.

It was Theresa Nemman. The doctor's daughter was in her nightgown and bathrobe. She was dead to the world.

'Billy!' Mulder shouted. 'Put her down, Billy!'

Billy looked at Mulder blankly. He might have been on a different planet.

Then it was Scully's turn to shout.

She saw Detective Miles coming out from the trees behind Mulder. He had his shotgun at the ready. And he had murder in his eyes.

'Mulder!' Scully screamed out at the top of her aching lungs. 'Look out! Behind you! He's got a gun! He's going to –!'

But even as the words left her mouth, she knew they were too late.

CHAPTER
NINETEEN

Mulder heard Scully's shout. He had time to turn around. He had time to see Miles charging out of the forest. But there was no time to stop Miles from gunning him down.

But the big detective didn't even seem to see Mulder.

He had eyes only for his boy.

'Billy! I love you! But this is the only way!' Miles roared like a wounded grizzly – and raised his gun.

It went off – up into the air.

Miles had gone down – hit by Mulder's tackle.

The Redskins could use this guy, thought Scully.

She saw Mulder bending to grab the shotgun. She started forward to help him. Meanwhile, Billy stayed frozen, with Theresa in his arms. He looked like an incredibly lifelike statue.

Then Scully froze, as the clearing came to life.

A twister of dust and leaves swirled up from the ground. It formed a whirling wall around Billy and his burden. Wind howled through the trees. Above the wind a humming rose. Behind the humming, a clanging began. And with the clanging, dazzling white light flooded the clearing. Mulder and Miles vanished in the blinding blaze.

It ended as suddenly as it began.

Scully blinked, trying to focus. She saw Billy and the girl

side by side on the ground. They were covered by fallen dust and leaves.

Mulder and Miles saw them, too. The two men got to their feet and ran to the fallen pair. Scully arrived at the same time they did.

Miles knelt beside his son.

'Billy,' he said in a choked voice.

Billy raised his head. 'Dad . . . ?' he managed to say. He rose to his feet, his father helping him. Beside him, Theresa stirred. Scully helped her get up.

'Who are you?' the girl said. 'What am I doing here?'

Scully looked into the girl's dazed eyes. Then she felt a hand on her arm. It was Mulder. She followed his silent gaze. He was looking at Billy's back. Scully had to stifle a cry.

The red marks were gone.

'Detective Miles,' Mulder said, 'you don't mind if we ask Billy a few questions.'

'Mind? No. Not at all,' the detective said. He held Billy in a gentle bear hug. He was looking at his son with wonder and joy. 'You kept me from doing the craziest thing a father could ever do. You saved my boy's life. You helped bring him back from the dead. Anything you want is okay by me.'

The detective insisted on driving Billy back to the mental hospital himself. Mulder and Scully dropped Theresa off at her home. Then they headed for the hospital.

'Hey, slow down,' Mulder cautioned Scully. 'We both can't be reckless drivers.'

'How true,' said Scully. She reluctantly slowed the car to the legal speed limit. Mulder was right. She didn't want to crash – not before they got their answers from Billy.

Billy was back in his bed when they arrived. Dr Glass was with him. The psychiatrist looked puzzled.

'A most unusual case,' he said. 'In all my years, I've never seen anything like it.'

'You're right,' Mulder said. 'It is a most unusual case. That's why it's important we question Billy.'

'Of course,' Dr Glass agreed. 'But keep the session short. He's still weak. Recovery will take a while.'

Billy did look weak, lying in the bed he had lain in for three years. But his eyes were alive now. And though his voice was faint, it was clear.

Mulder kept his own voice low-pitched. He did not want to disturb Billy's mental balance. It was still as fragile as a house of cards.

'Tell me about that light, Billy,' Mulder said. 'When did you first see it?'

'In the forest,' Billy said. 'We were all in the forest. We were having a party. All my friends. We were celebrating.'

'What were you celebrating?' Mulder asked.

'Graduation,' Billy said.

'But you never graduated,' Mulder said.

'No,' said Billy. 'The light took me away.'

'Where did it take you?' Mulder asked.

'To the testing place,' Billy explained.

'Did they do tests on you?' Mulder asked.

'Yes,' Billy said.

'Did you help them test the others?' Mulder asked.

'Yes,' Billy said. 'I would wait for their orders. To gather the others.'

'How did they give the orders?' Mulder asked.

'Through the implant,' Billy said. 'But the tests didn't work. I –'

Billy's voice was wavering now. It was like a candle flame flickering in a breeze.

'You what?' Mulder urged him to try to answer. Mulder

leaned forward to catch his words. Behind Mulder, Scully did the same.

They saw tears rolling down Billy's cheeks. They heard Billy say between sobs, 'They said it would be okay. They didn't want anyone to know. They wanted everything destroyed. I'm afraid. Afraid they're coming back.'

'Nothing to be afraid of,' Mulder tried to assure him. 'Now if you can just tell me –'

But Billy had said everything he was going to that night. He was weeping uncontrollably.

'I'm afraid that has to be all,' Dr Glass told Mulder. 'I hope you've heard enough.'

'Don't ask me,' Mulder told him. 'Ask Agent Scully here.'

But Mulder did it himself. 'What about it, Scully,' he asked her. 'You heard enough? Enough for your report?'

CHAPTER
TWENTY

'They're waiting for you,' Special Agent Jones told Scully.

Scully almost turned to exchange looks with Mulder. But she didn't. Because Mulder wasn't there.

Funny, she thought, how she had gotten used to Mulder being around. Funny how fast they had turned into a team.

She was alone now, though. Back at FBI Headquarters in Washington. The big brass had read the report she turned in. Now they wanted to see her.

Jones led her into the conference room. She saw the same men around the table as before.

Did she look the same to them? The same sound and sane agent they had put on a crackpot's case?

She tried to look like her old cool, composed self as she sat down. Then, she waited for the questions to begin.

The elderly man who was top gun was the first to speak.

'We've been going over your report, Ms Scully,' he said. 'Frankly, we don't know what to make of it.'

The man next to him demanded, 'Did Agent Mulder try to trick you in some way? Throw dust in your eyes? Brainwash you?'

Scully answered firmly. 'No, sir. Agent Mulder allowed

me to make up my own mind. No smoke. No mirrors. Fair and square.'

A third man joined in. His voice had a nasty edge. 'So you think we have space aliens flying around America? Zapping people with ray guns?'

Scully forced a polite smile. She acted as if he were making a little joke. 'No, sir,' she answered. 'I don't think we have enough evidence to say that. Not for sure.'

'I've read about the evidence you do have,' the second speaker growled. 'Time warps. Grotesque corpses. And what about that other thing? What you call an implant?'

Scully pulled a glass vial from her pocket. Maybe it would do what her report clearly had not. Maybe these men would believe their own eyes.

The men passed the vial from hand to hand. Each in turn squinted at the metal object inside.

'Our lab tests could not identify the metal,' Scully told them. 'This came from the corpse's nasal cavity. Billy Miles described the same object. He said it was in his nose, too. It told him to kill. You could call it a kind of fax – used to deliver a message of murder.'

The vial rested in the top man's hand. He stared at it, trying to think what he could say about it.

In the end, he could only look at Scully hard and say, 'Let's get back to earth. What's happened to the boy? Billy? Are they putting him on trial?'

'They've decided that Billy's father and the county medical examiner obstructed justice,' said Scully. 'Billy, of course, has confessed his part in the deaths.'

'His *part*?' exclaimed the second speaker. 'Who else could be involved?'

Before Scully could answer, the top man demanded, 'Are you saying the boy will be put on trial for murder?'

'No, sir,' Scully said. 'We persuaded the local law to drop the case. We said it would be best for all concerned.'

'Darn right,' the second speaker declared. 'That's all we need. A slick lawyer putting Mulder on the stand. Using an FBI agent to beat a murder rap with an "alien abduction" defense.'

The third speaker asked Scully sharply, 'Did anyone stop to think that the boy might just be an insanely clever killer?'

Scully fumbled for an answer she didn't have. But the top man saved her from having to pull a rabbit out of a hat.

'Let's get back to the point of this meeting,' he said. 'What does Agent Mulder believe?'

Now Scully faced another problem. There was too much she could say. Too much that Mulder had revealed to her. Too much that almost nobody else in the world would believe.

Certainly not the men waiting for her answer.

She did the best she could. She said the least she could.

'Agent Mulder thinks we are not alone.'

The top man gave her a long hard look. Then he made a tiny movement of his shoulders. It just might have been a shrug.

'Thank you, Ms Scully,' he said. 'You may go.'

'I just want to say that –' Scully began.

'Thank you, Ms Scully,' the man repeated.

'Yes, sir. Thank you, sir,' Scully said.

Her stomach was sinking as she got to her feet.

Only one thing stopped it from sinking still more. The small smile that Agent Jones gave her as he let her out the door. That smile seemed to say that she had done just fine.

Jones's smile faded as he closed the door from the inside. His face was deadpan as he went back to join his bosses.

The men at the table were busy comparing notes.

'Her report is a match with those classified Pentagon papers,' the third speaker said. He shook his head.

The second speaker shared his concern. 'It would be murder if this got to the press. Or if Congress got hold of it. We'd have to spend all our time chasing ghosts and spacemen.'

A previously silent man said sourly, 'FBI would stand for Federal Boogeymen Investigators.'

'It would cause mass hysteria,' the third speaker declared.

The top man listened quietly until they were finished. All eyes turned to him, waiting for his decision.

He cleared his throat.

'Gentlemen,' he said. 'This report offers no hard evidence. We will have to let Agent Scully keep her eye on Mulder. She must give us enough facts to close the X-files for good. Until then, the information in Agent Scully's report will not leave this room. Special Agent Jones, file the evidence in the usual manner.'

'Yes, sir,' Jones said.

He collected all copies of the report from the table. They made a thick stack. Scully had done a thorough job.

Then the head man handed him the glass vial with the metal implant.

'Take special care of this,' he told Jones.

'Yes, sir,' Jones said.

Jones's first stop was in the basement of Bureau Headquarters. He let himself into a room that few agents knew about. And to which even fewer had a key.

Inside was a a stainless steel furnace. He opened its door and tossed in the reports. He pressed a button. He watched orange flames leap up hungrily.

He waited until the fire did its job. Then he left, walking quickly.

He went to the Headquarters parking lot.

'I need a Bureau car,' he told the attendant.

'Another special assignment, Jones?' the man said. 'Nice day for a drive. Some guys get all the luck. Me, I have to stay on post 'til six.'

'Yeah, lucky me,' Jones said.

He left the city. He crossed the Potomac and drove through the green Virginia countryside. He turned off the highway down a narrow unmarked blacktop.

He stopped before iron gates in a high stone wall. It looked like the entrance to a private estate. But private estates did not have two soldiers with semiautomatics on guard.

'Hi, Jones,' said the sergeant in charge as Jones flashed his ID. 'Another job?'

'Another job,' agreed Jones.

The gates swung open, and Jones followed the blacktop to a huge, square, windowless concrete building.

Jones showed his ID to the soldier at the door and entered.

The inside was a maze of floor-to-ceiling shelves. They were crammed with steel boxes, all locked.

Jones did not pause. He knew exactly where he was going.

At the far end of the warehouse he stopped. He took out a key and opened a steel box marked with a code number.

He carefully placed the glass vial inside.

Right next to four other identical glass vials.

As he closed and locked the box, he wondered how many more trips he would have to make.

He thought of Scully. He thought of Mulder. He thought of the X-files overflowing with cases.

As he left the building, he said to the guard, 'Be seeing you.'

DARKNESS FALLS

To Janet,
with love and kisses

CHAPTER
ONE

Dense morning fog filled the forest.

It curled like gray smoke around the thick trunks of evergreens hundreds of feet tall.

It swirled around the bushes and brambles of the undergrowth.

It blanketed the carpet of pine needles on the forest floor.

The shrouded forest was as still as death. The only sound was the croaking of a lone tree frog.

It could have been a scene hundreds and hundreds of years ago. When the trees were slender saplings. When only Native Americans lived here on the Pacific coast.

That was before pale-skinned strangers arrived. And made this territory one of the United States. And named it after their first president. The state of Washington.

Now, in the 1990s, new strangers had come to the forest. Men who made their livings from it. Loggers. They stood in a clearing that they had made themselves. Around them were stumps of trees they had felled.

There were thirty of them. All of them were as hard and tough as the iron and steel in their axes and power saws. All of them were used to dealing with every challenge and danger of the wilderness.

And all of them now were shaking in their boots.

Jack Dyer was the man they looked to as leader. His voice boomed through the mist. 'This thing could kill us all!'

A big, burly logger named Bob Perkins answered, 'I told you we should have cleared out two days ago! But no! You wouldn't listen! Dyer, remember what you called me? Chicken. So tell me, who's squawking now?'

Dyer strode over to Perkins. They stood glaring face-to-face. Their callused hands were clenched in white-knuckled fists.

Then Dyer dropped his hands. 'No sense in slugging each other,' he said. 'We got bigger fish to fry. If I could only get my hands on it, I'd –' His hands opened and closed on empty air.

Perkins would not let go of his anger before taking another shot. 'Still Mr Macho Man, huh? Just like two days ago.'

'Nobody knew what it was two days ago, Perkins,' Dyer snapped. Then he shook his head. 'Nobody knows now.'

'Somebody's got to go for help,' Perkins said.

His idea stirred bitter muttering and sour laughter from the other loggers.

Dyer spoke for them. 'And what about the rest of us?' he demanded. 'What are we supposed to do? Wait here until help arrives?'

'We have to take a chance,' Perkins insisted. 'One of us has to hike out.'

'That person might not make it in time. He might not get to the road before nightfall. Then what?' Dyer asked.

Perkins did not answer. He did not have to. They all knew what to expect if you were still in the forest when darkness fell.

Dyer turned to the others. 'I say we make a run for it. Split up and take our chances.'

Perkins opened his mouth to argue.

Before he could, one man shouted, 'It's our last chance!'

'No more nights here!' shouted another.

'Each man for himself! Sink or swim!' a third joined in.

Perkins made a last try. 'It's suicide! You know that as well as me, Dyer!'

'Fine,' Dyer said. 'You stay here tonight and let us know how things come out.'

Dyer was already unbuckling the heavy belt he used for climbing trees.

Around him the others did the same.

Nobody wanted anything to slow him down. They were all in a race. A race through the forest against the sun moving above the tall trees. A race against nightfall.

Late that afternoon, Dyer was still running. Or trying to. He had a stitch in his side. It felt like a spike driving into him. His legs felt like stone. His mouth tasted like pennies. Every breath hurt. But the sight of the daylight dimming through the branches above was enough to keep him lurching forward.

Dyer wondered how the others were doing. He didn't figure they were much better off than he. He wished now that they had stayed together. Maybe you traveled faster when you traveled alone. But you also got more scared. He had never felt so alone and scared in his life.

'Owww,' he screamed. His cry echoed through the silent forest.

He had tripped over a fallen branch. His body fell forward, but his foot stayed wedged under the branch. He could almost hear his ankle crack.

He tried to keep tears of pain from his eyes. He got his foot free of the branch. He eased himself into a sitting position. He unlaced his boot. He gingerly eased it off.

'Is it bad?' asked a voice.

Perkins was looking down at him. His chest was heaving.
'I think it's broken,' Dyer said.

'Come on,' Perkins told him. 'You gotta get up.'

Dyer put his hand on his ankle. He winced. 'I don't think
I can make it,' he said.

'I told you, come on,' Perkins said.

He put his arms under Dyer's shoulders. With a grunting
heave, he lifted Dyer to his feet.

'Put your arm around my shoulder,' Perkins said. 'We'll
make it out of here together.'

'Thanks,' Dyer said. 'But why are you doing this? You
know you hate my guts.'

'Forget about that,' Perkins said. 'Maybe we have our
differences. But at least we're humans. And right now humans
have to stick together.'

'Yeah,' said Dyer. 'I remember what old Ben Franklin
said. I learned it in history when I was a kid. "We gotta hang
together – or else we'll hang separately." Except it won't be
hanging for us. It won't be so nice.'

'Come on. Enough jawing,' said Perkins. 'It's getting dark
already.'

They started moving again. But they couldn't go fast.
Three legs weren't enough for two men. They staggered like
a mechanical toy with a part missing.

'How many more miles, you think?' Dyer panted.

'No idea,' Perkins gasped back. 'Wish there were some
landmarks here.'

'You hear that?' Dyer said. He stopped moving. He
listened to a distant humming.

'Insects, just insects,' Perkins said. 'They come out in the
dark.'

'And it is dark now, isn't it?' said Dyer. He stayed frozen.
'We can't make it.'

The humming got closer, louder.

'Guess old Ben was wrong,' Dyer said. 'Hang together – and die together.'

'No!' said Perkins. 'We ain't giving up!'

He yanked Dyer forward, half dragging him along.

But the humming was all around them now. And the forest around them was growing bright.

Perkins looked up. Through the treetops the darkness was gone, replaced by a dazzling cloud of whirling green light. Perkins's shoulders slumped. He let Dyer go.

Dyer fell to his knees. Perkins stood over him, trying to shield him, as the blinding light descended.

The humming was deafening.

It drowned out the last human sounds in the forest.

Perkins's screams of pain.

CHAPTER
TWO

'It's show and tell time, Scully,' FBI Agent Fox Mulder said. 'Come into my office.'

'Said the spider to the fly,' replied FBI Agent Dana Scully. She finished the last bite of her doughnut. She took the last sip of her coffee. Then she left the FBI Headquarters basement cafeteria with Mulder. They headed down the long corridor toward his office.

Scully braced herself for what was coming. She recognized the gleam in Mulder's eyes. Mulder had spotted a case that interested him. A case that belonged in the X-files. A case that nobody in the Bureau wanted to touch. Nobody except Mulder . . .

The X-files contained cases that the FBI brass called strange, weird, bizarre – in short, nutty. They would have liked to lock the X-files up and throw away the key. Mulder, however, kept opening them up.

For the FBI brass, that was bad enough. Even worse, Mulder had too brilliant a record to be dismissed as a loose cannon. His bosses had to find another way to protect their peace of mind. They did. They made Scully his partner.

Scully had what it took to do the job. She was not only a doctor, she was a scientist as well. She had the knowledge and skills to check out Mulder's theories about unknown aliens spreading havoc on earth. And she had plenty of down-to-earth common sense. Enough of it to keep Mulder from going completely out of orbit. As a last resort, Scully was there for damage control. Her bosses told her to blow the whistle the moment Mulder started acting as freaky as the cases he loved. Except by now Scully was no longer following that set of orders. By now, Scully had worked on Mulder's side long enough and hard enough to start seeing through Mulder's eyes.

Right now Scully could barely keep up with Mulder's eager stride. Out of the corner of her eye she saw heads turn as they hurried past. She knew tongues would start wagging as fellow agents wondered what they were up to. She wondered the same thing herself. With Mulder you never knew what the next case would bring. You could only wait and see.

'You've gotta see this,' Mulder said as they entered his office. 'It'll impress even you, Scully.'

Scully had been in Mulder's office many times. But it still made her shudder.

Shelves lined the walls from floor to ceiling. Crammed on them were folders bulging with reports, stacks of yellowing newspapers and magazines, floppy disks with curling labels, and every kind of book from science textbooks to science-fiction paperbacks. Piled on the floor were more records and writings.

Scully liked neatness and order. This office was her notion of a nightmare. She had no idea how Mulder ever found anything he wanted. But he always seemed to.

Right now he had his slide projector loaded and his projection screen pulled down.

'Take a good look at this,' he said, as a slide came onto the screen. It was a candid photo, a little blurred, showing a group of about thirty men. They had on well-worn outdoor gear. Most were bearded. Many held axes. In front of them was a huge fallen tree. Behind them stood a towering forest.

'Loggers, right?' Scully said.

'You've won the set of Tupperware,' Mulder said. 'Want to try for the microwave?'

'Come on, who are they?' Scully asked.

'A logging gang working in Washington,' Mulder said.

'Washington?' Scully said. 'I didn't know they had trees like that around here.'

'Not Washington, DC,' Mulder said. 'The state of Washington. Now tell me, what else do you see?'

'They look tough,' Scully said. 'Men's men, I believe is the term.'

'Very good,' Mulder said. 'And what else besides that. Anything strange? Out of the ordinary? Hard to explain?'

Scully took a hard look. She shook her head. 'I give up,' she said.

'You give up,' Mulder said, nodding. 'Funny. That's exactly what the Federal Forest Service has done.'

'What do you mean?' Scully asked. 'What happened to them?'

Mulder pressed a button. The photo vanished. 'They vanished,' he said.

He flashed on another photo. This one was of just two men. They wore bright flowered shirts, ragged blue jeans, scruffy high-tops. They had unkempt beards and long dirty-looking hair. One had his hair in a ponytail. The other had a bandanna tied around his forehead.

'They look like they're going to a 1960s costume party,' Scully remarked. 'All they need is bell-bottoms.'

'Meet Douglas Spinney and Steven Teague,' said Mulder. 'They call themselves "monkeywrenchers." And they're very good at what they do.'

'What do they do?' Scully asked.

'Everything they can think of to foul up lumberjacks and lumber mills. One of their favorite things is driving spikes into trees to make saws break,' Mulder said.

'Ecoterrorists,' Scully said grimly. As an FBI agent, she knew the type. People who claimed that they loved nature. That they were fighting for the environment. That it was okay to trash anyone and anything in the name of ecology. 'Do-gooders who do bad things. They can be the worst.'

'Teague and Spinney *are* the worst,' said Mulder. 'Two weeks ago, we got the latest word on them. The loggers I showed you in the first slide radioed from the middle of Olympic National Forest. Seems that Teague and Spinney went on a spree: spiking trees, wrecking equipment, the works. A week later, all radio communication was cut off.'

'Anyone know why?' asked Scully.

'No,' Mulder said. 'The lumber company that hired the men asked the Federal Forest Service to check it out. Two officials went into the forest a week ago. Nobody has heard from them since.'

'Looks like the monkeywrenchers aren't just playing games,' Scully said. 'They're playing for keeps.'

'That's what the lumber company and the forest service say,' Mulder said. 'They've asked the Bureau to investigate. I had to pull strings to make sure we got the case.'

'Pull strings? To get an ecoterrorism case?' Scully said, puzzled.

Then she saw Mulder grin, and braced herself.

'Dare I ask why you want this case so badly?' she asked.

'Take a look at this picture,' he answered.

A new slide came up on the screen. It showed more loggers. Tough men, too. But their outdoor gear was old-fashioned.

'This was taken in 1934,' Mulder said. 'Long before eco-terrorism was even in the dictionary. This crew was working for a government agency, the WPA. They vanished in the same forest without a trace. Not one of them was ever found or heard from again.'

'And you suspect what?' Scully asked. 'Bigfoot, maybe?'

'Not likely,' Mulder answered deadpan. 'That's a lot of flannel to choke down. Even for Bigfoot.'

Scully sighed. She should have known better than to joke about Bigfoot to Mulder. Bigfoot wasn't a joke to him.

'Come on, Scully,' he responded cheerfully. 'What could be nicer than a trip to the forest? I bet you were a Girl Scout when you were a kid.'

Mulder was right as usual. Scully *had* been a Girl Scout. And she had earned every merit badge.

But those wouldn't be of much use to her now. Mulder's favorite territory – the uncharted regions of the X-files – wasn't covered by the Official Girl Scout Handbook . . .

CHAPTER
THREE

'I feel like an ad for L. L. Bean,' Scully told Mulder. She was dressed in jeans, a flannel shirt, and hiking boots. All were brand-new.

'When in Rome,' said Mulder. He was dressed the same way. But his clothes were broken in.

'Some Rome. More like nowhere,' Scully said. She looked out the window of their rental car. Thick forest ran to both edges of the road. 'I hope we're going in the right direction. They're not big on signs around here.'

Scully was doing the driving, which she preferred. Mulder knew only two speeds: fast and faster.

Right now Scully would have liked to go faster herself. Crawling ahead of them on the narrow blacktop was a big flatbed, loaded high with huge logs.

'We're fine,' Mulder said. 'That truck is going to the same place we are. There's just one lumber mill around here. I hope the guy from the forest service is there. He said he'd be waiting for us.'

'He's pals with the lumber company?' asked Scully.

'I don't know about being pals,' Mulder said with a shrug. 'But they know each other. This is government forest. The forest service tells the lumber company where they can cut and how much.'

They followed the flatbed as it turned off onto an even narrower road. Soon they saw the mill. And smelled it.

'Whew – what an odor,' Scully said, closing her window. 'I always thought sawdust smelled nice.'

'They use a lot of chemicals to process the wood,' Mulder said. 'They say if you work here long enough, you stop noticing it.'

'I guess you can get used to anything,' Scully said. 'Like in morgues. I've seen attendants playing cards on corpses. Probably folks around here have forgotten what clean air smells like.'

'There aren't many folks around here,' Mulder said. 'That's why they put the mill out in the wilds. Otherwise they'd have protesters in front of the gates. And pressure to pass laws.'

'I can understand that kind of environmental action,' Scully said, as she found a spot in the mill parking lot. 'Eco-protest – not ecoterror.'

She parked next to a four-wheel-drive truck. The truck was a wilderness special. It had mud tires, winches, bumper guards, a windshield screen, and the emblem of the Federal Forest Service on its front door.

A tall, lean man in outdoor gear stood by the truck. He had a map spread out on the hood.

'Looks like our boy,' Scully said.

'Hi,' Mulder said to the man by the truck. 'Agent Mulder here. This is Agent Scully. We're with the FBI.'

The man took his time looking Mulder and Scully up and down.

'Got identification?' he asked.

Mulder produced a photo ID from his wallet. Scully did the same.

The man glanced at the pictures, gave the two agents

another slow look, and handed the IDs back. Then he stuck out his hand to shake Mulder's, then Scully's. He had a grip like iron.

'Larry Moore, Federal Forest Service,' he said. 'You can put your gear in the back of the truck.'

'What's that on the windshield there?' Mulder asked. 'A bullet hole?'

'Twenty-two calibre,' Moore said shortly. He started folding up the map.

'Somebody shoot at you?' Mulder asked.

'That's what it would appear,' Moore said. 'Sure wasn't a hunter's stray shot. Not much to hunt around here with that kind of ammo. 'Cept Freddies.'

'Freddies?' asked Scully.

'Employees of the Federal Forest Service,' Moore said. 'That's what the ecoterrorists call us.'

'That who you think shot at you?' Mulder asked. 'You have a problem with them?'

Moore fixed Mulder with a level gaze.

'Let's get this straight right now,' he said. 'I've got no beef with what those people claim they want. I want to save the forest, too. It's their methods I can't condone. There's never any reason to cause unlawful damage – not to mention taking human lives.'

'Point taken,' said Scully. 'But you really think they'd go as far as killing?'

'There are over thirty men missing in the forest,' Moore said. 'All of them with survival experience. *Something* happened to them.'

A station wagon pulled up on the other side of the truck. A big, muscular man got out.

He easily lifted two heavily loaded packs out of his car and tossed them into the back of the truck. Then he grabbed a couple of large containers from his front seat. Scully glimpsed what they were. Cases of shotgun shells.

'At last,' Moore said. 'Now we can get this show on the road.'

'Sorry I'm late, Larry,' said the man. 'I was just down talking to Bob Perkins's wife.' He turned to Mulder and Scully. 'Perkins is one of our missing loggers,' he explained.

Then he introduced himself. 'Steve Humphreys. Head of security, Schiff-Immergut Lumber. You must be FBI.'

'I'm Mulder,' Mulder said. 'She's Scully.'

Humphreys gave them a nod. Then he handed the cases of shotgun shells to Moore. 'Take good care of these,' he said. 'I have a hunch we could need them.'

'Maybe,' Moore said. He stowed the shells in the cab of the truck.

'Let's get rolling,' said Humphreys. 'Got about four hours' driving ahead of us.' He climbed into the truck, followed by Moore.

Scully turned to Mulder. 'I have a feeling we're riding into a war,' she told him. 'A war that's already started.'

CHAPTER
FOUR

Scully knew that in a war, the first casualty was always the truth. Which made it all the harder to get the facts in this case. She couldn't take what Moore and Humphreys said as gospel. She'd have to decide for herself who were the bad guys and who the good. And so would Mulder.

Soon they left all signs of civilization behind. They turned off the highway onto a rutted dirt road. A loggers' road. It was just wide enough for a truck to squeeze through, and it led higher and higher up through the tree-covered mountains.

Scully and Mulder were squeezed in the front seat between Moore and Humphreys. The two FBI agents used the long drive to start probing. They had worked together enough to be a good team.

'Why do the loggers work so far up in the wilderness?' began Scully.

'That's where the trees are,' said Humphreys.

Scully looked out the window. All she saw were trees. All she had seen since they began were trees. 'You're kidding, right?' she said.

'It's those environmentalists.' Humphreys snorted. 'They worry more about trees than about people. They've managed to keep us from touching a single branch around here. They make us go to the most remote spots to do our cutting.

Even there, we have to replant saplings for every tree we take.'

'So why do you think that the ecoterrorists are targeting you?' asked Mulder. 'Seems they've gotten all they're after.'

'Nothing is enough for them,' said Humphreys. 'Those tree huggers won't be happy until we can't touch a tree on the planet. Until we go out of business and our loggers go on welfare.' He shook his head. 'What gets me is they won't come out and fight like men. They're the kind who dodged the draft in the Vietnam war. They're cowardly and so are their tactics. I'd like to get my hands on them and –'

Bang! Bang! Two sharp explosions.

Instinctively Scully ducked her head, hands shielding her face. But there were no bullets, no flying glass. Instead, the truck bucked like a bronco. A moment later, it was lurching from side to side.

'What was that?' Scully asked Moore, as the forest service agent put on the brakes.

'Tires,' Moore said. He did not look surprised. Just angry.

As soon as the truck stopped, he was out of the driver's cab. The others followed.

'I'll check the left side,' Moore told Humphreys. 'You take the right.'

Scully and Mulder stood behind Moore as he kneeled by the left front wheel. The tire was flat as a pancake.

Moore pulled out a long sharp piece of metal. 'Homemade tire spike,' he said.

'Serious damage?' asked Scully.

'Right through the sidewall,' Moore said. 'Unfixable.'

'You've got a spare, don't you?' Mulder asked.

Before Moore could answer, Humphreys came around to their side. 'The right tire's history, too,' he said.

He handed Mulder a bent piece of metal with four spikes

sticking out of it. 'Maybe you'd like to put this in the FBI files,' he said.

Mulder passed it to Scully. 'Nasty-looking piece of work,' she said.

'Monkeywrenchers call it a caltrop,' Humphreys told her. 'They litter these roads with them. Doesn't matter what comes over them. Blind terrorism pure and simple.'

Scully handed the device back to him. Humphreys flung it into the trees.

'Imagine someone putting these down on the Washington, DC, beltway,' he said. 'I'd like to see what lawmakers would do then. And how much sympathy these environmentalists would get.'

Before Humphreys could say anything else, Scully changed the subject. 'How do we get to the loggers' camp now?' she asked.

'We do it the old-fashioned, low-tech way,' Moore said. 'We hike.'

'Well, these boots were made for walking,' Scully said. She looked ahead at the dirt road. It snaked upward through the forest, climbing out of sight. 'I just hope the salesman was right.'

Hours later, it was a toss-up whether Scully's feet were breaking in the boots – or vice versa. She wished she'd stuffed less in her backpack. A lot less. And she wondered how Mulder's step could still be springy. In the future, she decided, she'd up her daily jog to match his seven miles. Her usual three didn't cut it.

She breathed easier when she spotted a vehicle parked up the road.

'Signs of life at last,' she said.

'Signs of something at least,' said Moore.

'What kind of vehicle is it?' Mulder asked.

'A skiploader,' Humphreys told him. 'For lifting felled trees onto transport.'

'But useless now,' Moore said. He pointed to a giant flat tire. The blunt end of a spike stuck out of its sidewall. 'Come on. The camp can't be far away.'

The camp was ten minutes up the road. Two big logging trucks and a small crane came into sight first. Then a small wooden cabin. Beyond the cabin was a cluster of medium-size olive-green tents.

The open truck doors swung back and forth in the forest breeze, creaking eerily.

'Anybody here?' Moore shouted.

There was no answer.

'Brrr,' Scully said to Mulder. 'Looks like a ghost town.'

Mulder headed for the cabin. Scully followed him inside.

'Somebody forgot to clean his plate,' Mulder said. Moldy, half-eaten portions of food covered the crude wooden dining table.

'Maybe they got tired of franks and beans and went after bear,' said Scully. She looked around the cabin. Chairs lay upended on the rough plank floor. The bunks in the other room were unmade. 'Looks like they left in a hurry.'

'And they forgot to pack,' Mulder said, standing by the refrigerator. Its door was open. He reached in and pulled out a Ziploc bag. It was stuffed with tiny buds.

Scully took a quick look. 'A controlled substance?' she asked.

Mulder sniffed one of the buds and nodded. 'I guess loggers have to find a way to pass the long nights without TV.'

He ran his finger over the top of the bag.

'Something interesting?' asked Scully.

'Some kind of grease,' Mulder said.

He was still studying it when Humphreys came into the cabin.

'Find anything?' Humphreys asked.

'Party favors,' Mulder said. 'And you?'

'Vehicles have all been monkeywrenched,' Humphreys said. 'Power generator's busted.'

'Somebody really did a number here,' said Scully.

'And that somebody didn't want the news broadcast either,' Humphreys said. He picked up what was left of a shortwave radio transmitter. It had been smashed to bits.

'Let's see what Moore's up to,' Mulder suggested.

They found him at one of the trucks. He had lifted the hood and unscrewed the radiator cap.

'The radiator's full of rice,' he said. 'So are the others. Plus sugar and sand in the crankcases. Our pals didn't miss a trick.'

'Wonder what else they pulled off,' said Mulder.

'Not much more time to find out today,' Humphreys said. He looked at his watch. 'Sun's going down in an hour and a half.'

'I'm taking another look around here before it gets dark,' Moore said.

'You do that,' Humphreys said. 'I'll see if I can get the generator working.'

As the two moved off, Scully peered into the radiator. Moore was right. Plump grains of rice filled the radiator. She fished out a few grains.

'Well, you were right about one thing,' she told Mulder.

'What's that?' Mulder asked.

'It definitely wasn't Bigfoot.'

CHAPTER
FIVE

Mulder looked around at the camp. 'Of course, we're not even sure *what* was done,' he said. 'Much less who did it.'

'Yeah. It's like being in a cemetery with no corpses,' said Scully. Then she said, 'Here comes Moore. Maybe he's found something.'

'Nothing here,' the forest service agent reported. 'Nothing that works. Or breathes. Those monkeywrenchers made a clean sweep.'

'We still don't have proof of that,' Mulder said.

'Hard evidence is what we need,' Scully agreed.

'We still have an hour of daylight,' Moore said. 'Enough time to check out the forest around here. Might turn up something.'

'Good idea,' said Scully. 'The sooner we clean this case up and get out of here, the better. I have to admit, this place gives me the creeps.'

'The creeps?' said Mulder with a smile. 'Just because a bunch of big, strong men cleared out so fast they didn't finish their food? And then vanished into thin air? Don't be silly. I'm sure there's a nice scientific explanation. Oh, sorry, Scully. You're the one who's supposed to be telling me that, right?'

Scully winced. Mulder loved to remind her of what she had once told him. Everything had a scientific explanation.

That was when she had first met him, before their first case together. That seemed a long time ago. She still clung to her faith in science. But her grip was loosening bit by bit, shock by shock.

All she could say now was, 'We'll see, Mulder. We'll see.' She changed the subject. 'Think Humphreys wants to join us?'

'He wants to play around with the equipment,' Moore said. 'See if he can patch it up.' He turned toward the trees. 'Let's go.'

Scully and Mulder followed Moore into the forest. It was slow going. Then they hit an open space. Suddenly the late afternoon sky spread wide above them.

Tree stumps filled the clearing. The stumps were fresh. A few tall pines still lay where they had been felled.

'The men were hard at work – right to the end,' Moore commented.

'Busy as bees,' agreed Mulder. Then he paused. He was staring up at a towering pine on the edge of the clearing. 'Speaking of bees, are there many in this neck of the woods?'

'Not many,' Moore said. 'Why?'

Mulder pointed to a branch of the pine. Something that looked like a big gunnysack was hanging from it. But its dirty gray strands weren't made of cloth.

'Could be a hive,' said Moore, scratching his head. 'Or maybe some kind of cocoon.'

'A hive?' said Mulder. 'A cocoon? What kind?'

Moore shook his head. 'I can't say for sure. I've never seen anything exactly like it.'

'I think I can make out something inside it,' Scully said. 'See that dark shape?'

'Hard to tell from here,' said Moore, squinting.

'We'll have to investigate,' Mulder said. 'How about it, Scully? Want to give it a spin? You're the scientist.'

For Scully, there was only one way to respond to a challenge. 'Love to,' she said. 'Let's figure out how I do it.'

'Shouldn't be hard,' said Moore. He took a long rope out of his pack. 'We can rig up a harness for you. Throw the rope over that branch. And haul you up there. Then you cut that thing down. Mulder's right. You're the best one to do it. You're the lightest. The branch can support your weight.'

'As usual, women and children first,' said Scully. 'Well, I've been wanting to test out this hunting knife.' She patted the brand-new knife in its brand-new sheath on her brand-new belt.

The rope harness that Moore rigged up was crude but effective. It went around Scully's waist and under her armpits. Moore got the loose end of the rope over the branch on the third heave. He and Mulder pulled at it and Scully rose into the air.

This is fun, Scully thought. Then her smile faded. The sack was coming closer and closer. And the closer it came, the nastier it looked. Its grimy gray strands glistened with some kind of grease or slime. It certainly seemed to be a cocoon. But Scully didn't like to imagine what kind of creature had made it.

'Can you reach it?' Mulder called from below.

'Just a little bit more!' she called.

Another pull, and it was in range of her knife blade. She reached out her arm as far as she could. She started to saw away at where the cocoon was joined to the branch.

Then her knife hand froze.

Her stomach did a slow somersault.

Something was sticking out of the gap she had carved.

A bony human finger.

'You see something?' shouted Mulder.

'Yeah, I do!' she managed to shout back.

'What is it?' Mulder asked.

'Let me take a better look,' she forced herself to answer. Scully felt the rope yank.

She moved closer to the opening.

She squinted past the finger into the cocoon.

Staring back at her were two empty eye sockets. She was face-to-face with a skull.

'So what do you see?' Mulder shouted.

'You take a look!' Scully shouted back. She finished cutting the cocoon loose. It fell to the ground by the two men's feet.

Mulder and Moore wasted no time in hauling Scully down. Then they turned toward the cocoon. By the time Scully was free of her harness, Moore had cut the cocoon wide open.

'Oh my God,' said Scully, looking down.

Inside the cocoon, was a body. It was the size of a baby, curled up inside its mother. But it was definitely not a baby. It was shriveled and shrunken, almost mummified. Or like an orange that had been sucked dry.

But what had it been when it was alive? And how long ago had that been?

'Time to go to work, Scully,' Mulder said. 'This one looks right up your alley.'

Scully gritted her teeth. She reminded herself that she was a trained scientist. She had a medical degree as well. This was just another job. She reached down and touched it.

'It's hard and dry,' she announced. She wished she felt as calm and cool as her voice. 'Almost as if it's been preserved.'

'Or embalmed,' suggested Moore.

'More like all the fluids were bled from the body,' Scully

observed. 'Like it's been – cured.' She gave the corpse another close look. 'It's a male, I think.'

Meanwhile Moore was examining the cocoon. 'I'd say it's some kind of spider's nest,' he said. 'Some kind of insect cocoon, anyway.'

'And what kind of insect could have gotten a man all the way up that tree?' Scully wanted to know.

All three looked up at the branch high above.

All three shook their heads.

CHAPTER
SIX

Back in the deserted camp, Humphreys was whistling while he worked. He was finishing his repair job on the broken electric generator. It gave him a good feeling to do his best for the Schiff-Immergut Lumber Company.

Schiff-Immergut had been good to Humphreys. It had given him his first job after high school. It had promoted him year after year. It had paid for his station wagon, his ranch house, his two kids' college tuition. It covered his medical bills and would take care of his retirement when he got old. He owed everything to the lumber company. In return, he gave it his all.

He was screwing in a new spark plug when he heard a noise outside. It wasn't loud, but Humphreys wasn't a top security man for nothing. He had ears like a cat's.

He moved fast as a cat as well. He grabbed his shotgun. Then he was out of the generator shed to see who the intruder was.

Humphreys didn't know whether it was a man or a grizzly invading the camp. It didn't matter. He stroked his shotgun. Both chambers were loaded.

He was just in time to see the cabin door closing behind someone or something. He pumped his shotgun. He leveled it and kicked the door open.

The tall, rangy man stood by the table, with his back to the door. He paid no attention to the sound of Humphreys's kick. He was too busy grabbing moldy food with his bare hands and wolfing it down.

'Freeze!' shouted Humphreys. 'Turn around slowly – with your hands in the air.'

The man stuffed one more handful of food into his mouth. Then, without hurrying, he obeyed.

His bearded face was framed by long, matted, dirty brown hair.

'Doug Spinney,' Humphreys snarled. 'I ought to shoot you where you stand.'

Spinney, unfazed, looked wearily at Humphreys and his gun.

'Might as well shoot yourself, too, Humphreys, old pal,' he said. His voice was as empty of fear as his eyes.

'You're in no position to be testing me,' Humphreys warned him. 'Now talk fast, Spinney. What the devil happened to my men?'

'What men?' Spinney asked.

'The men working in this camp,' said Humphreys, fighting to keep his trigger finger still.

Spinney shrugged. 'I don't know what happened to them. Not for sure. But I can make a good guess.'

'And what's that?' demanded Humphreys. He raised his shotgun so it was pointed right between Spinney's eyes.

Spinney looked into the barrels without blinking. 'The same thing that'll happen to us when the sun goes down,' he said.

Suddenly a voice demanded, 'What's going on here?'

It was Mulder. He stood at the open cabin door. Behind him were Scully and Moore.

Reluctantly Humphreys lowered his gun. 'This animal is Doug Spinney,' he said. 'The man who did all this monkey-wrenching. And a murderer. I'd like to make him pay right now.'

Scully just had to take one look at Spinney to recognize him. He was one of the monkeywrenchers in Mulder's slide show. She wondered where Spinney's sidekick Teague was hiding.

'I'm no murderer,' Spinney protested.

'You're a liar,' snarled Humphreys, raising his gun.

Mulder put his hand on the barrel and gently pushed it down.

'We're investigators – not executioners,' he told Humphreys. 'Let's hear what Mr Spinney has to say.'

'We stand here taking much longer and there won't be anything left to say,' Spinney said. 'We've got to get that generator started. The darkness is our enemy.'

'What are you talking about?' Humphreys barked. 'Stop the horse manure.'

Spinney ignored him.

'Any of you want to give me a hand?' he asked. Without waiting for an answer, he calmly shoved Humphreys's gun aside and walked out the door.

Openmouthed, Humphreys watched him go. It took him a moment to get back his balance. His hands tightened on his gun. He started for the door.

Mulder raised his palm to stop him. 'Not so fast, Humphreys,' he said. 'I have a hunch he knows what he's doing.'

'Him run the generator?' sneered Humphreys. 'He just knows how to smash things, not make them work. I'm the one who had to pick up the pieces and try to put them back together.'

'But he seems to be the only one who can put the

pieces of this puzzle together,' said Mulder. 'I say we help him.'

He went out the door after Spinney.

'Agent Mulder has a funny habit of being right about things like this,' Scully said, and followed him.

Humphreys exchanged looks with Moore.

'We'd better go along,' he told the forest service agent. 'We don't want to leave Spinney alone with those two. He's too good at selling his line of phony goods. Especially to folks from the beltway who don't know any better.'

When the four of them caught up with Spinney, he was holding a five-gallon gas can.

'Putting sugar in it?' asked Humphreys. 'Or have you decided to burn the camp down?'

'Piece of advice, Humphreys. Keep your mouth shut – and your eyes and ears open,' said Spinney.

He hauled the gas over to the generator. The others followed, watching his every move.

'What did you mean about the darkness being our enemy?' Mulder asked him.

Spinney started pouring the gas into the generator fuel tank. 'That's when they come,' he said, not looking up.

'When *who* comes?' asked Mulder.

Spinney finished pouring, set the can down, and screwed the fuel tank cap back on. 'They come from the sky,' he said. 'Can take a man right off his feet. Devour him alive. I saw it happen.'

'Happen to whom?' Mulder asked.

Spinney ignored the question. 'God, I hope this works,' he said, gripping the starter rope of the generator. He gave the rope a sharp, powerful yank.

Scully, watching him, found she was desperately hoping the generator would start, too.

She didn't know why, but she sensed she would soon. She would find out why light in this forest suddenly seemed the most precious thing on earth.

CHAPTER
SEVEN

The generator turned over once. Twice. And roared to life.

Scully ran her fingers over her forehead. She realized she had been sweating.

'I need to eat,' Spinney announced. 'I haven't eaten in three days.'

Without another word, he headed for the cabin.

Humphreys turned to the others. 'What a line of bull that guy puts out. As if any of us would believe a word of it,' he said.

The other three were silent.

'Hey, what's with you?' Humphreys asked. 'I tell you, Spinney wouldn't tell the truth if his life depended on it.'

'We found something in the forest,' Scully told him.

'What?' said Humphreys.

'A man caught in some kind of insect cocoon,' Moore said.

'A cocoon?' said Humphreys.

'Or something,' Mulder said.

'I never saw anything like it,' Moore admitted.

'We have to find out exactly what it was,' said Scully.

'We have to get some more answers from Mr Spinney,' Mulder declared.

Scully looked at the cabin. The windows were glowing in the dusk.

'Well, at least we know the lights are working,' she said.

'And we know he turned them on the second he got into the cabin,' Mulder said. 'He was more eager to get light than food.'

The four of them went into the cabin. They found Spinney opening up cans of franks and beans. He had already finished off the moldy food on the plates.

Spinney looked up and gave the security man a crooked grin. 'Got a beef, Humphreys?' he asked. 'Worried about me eating company property? Believe me, that's the least of Schiff-Immergut's worries in this neck of the woods. Not to mention ours.'

'Speak for yourself, Spinney,' Humphreys said. 'You're the one who's going to have worries.'

'You mean, when we get back to civilization?' Spinney said. 'I don't see that as a pressing problem right now.' He went back to spooning cold beans into his mouth.

Mulder sat down across from him. 'I have some questions for you, Mr Spinney,' he said.

'I'll make some tea,' Scully offered. 'It's going to be a long night.'

'Yeah,' said Spinney between mouthfuls. 'Nights are long around here. Real long.'

Moore sat down at the table, too. Humphreys kept his shotgun on his knees, and his eyes on Spinney's every move.

'What happened to you out here?' Mulder asked.

Spinney took his time answering. He finished his can of beans and opened another. He wiped his mouth with the back of his hand and belched loudly. Then he said, 'We're camped two valleys over. Four of us. Three now – after last night.'

Humphreys spat. The blob of spittle hit the plank floor near Spinney's feet. 'No wonder things smell funny around here,' Humphreys said. 'These woods are filled with skunks.'

'Filled with worse things than skunks, believe me,' Spinney told him. Then he turned back to Mulder. 'Our Jeep has a dead battery. We drew straws to see who'd hike over here and swipe one that works from the loggers.'

Humphreys started to say something. But Mulder silenced him with a sharp look.

'Why didn't all of you just hike out of the forest?' Mulder asked Spinney.

'It's more than a day's hike,' Spinney said. 'No way we wanted to be out in the forest at night. Not after what happened to Teague.'

'Teague is the man who was – devoured alive?' asked Scully, as she poured them all tea.

Spinney nodded, remembering. He pushed his can of beans away. He had lost his appetite.

'So what are you guys doing up here?' Mulder continued.

Spinney raised his eyebrows in phony innocence. 'Camping,' he said.

'Yeah, sure,' Humphreys said. 'The kind of camping you do is a federal offense.'

'Hold off for a second,' Mulder told him.

But Moore took Humphreys's side. 'He's right,' he told Mulder. 'This man is a criminal. He could be placed under arrest.'

'He could be – and should be,' said Humphreys.

Spinney and his pals were on too many wanted posters for him to waste his breath defending his innocence. Instead he went on the attack.

'And what about you, Humphreys?' he demanded. 'What about the crime against nature you commit?'

'We operate completely under the law,' Humphreys said. 'We pay for the right to take those trees and after we do, we –'

Spinney cut him off. 'I got news for you, Mr Law and Order. Your loggers were taking trees nobody has a right to. Trees here for hundreds, even thousands of years. Trees that are marked. Trees that are supposed to be protected. Except that out here nobody is looking. Or maybe they're looking the other way. So don't talk to me about breaking the law, *sir*.'

Moore leaned forward. 'Schiff-Immergut loggers were taking marked trees?'

'You bet they were,' Spinney assured him. 'Marked in bright orange by your own people. The big no-no for cutting. Or am I wrong about that, Mr Forest Service Man? Are you maybe more interested in greenbacks than green space?'

Moore's face flushed. He turned to Humphreys. 'Old growth trees. You know anything about that, Steve?'

'No. Of course not,' Humphreys declared.

But Moore kept looking at him. Looking at him hard.

'You're going to take *his* word over *mine*?' Humphreys said indignantly.

Moore said nothing. But his silence said a lot.

Humphreys got to his feet. 'I'm not going to sit here and take this bull,' he snarled. Angrily he stomped toward the door.

Spinney leaned back in his chair and watched him. A strange smile was on his face.

'You don't want to go out into the night, Humphreys,' he warned ever so mildly. 'Take my word. It's out there.'

Humphreys paused with his hand on the doorknob. He chuckled.

'What?' he said. 'If I walk out this door I'm going to be

attacked? By something that will eat me alive? And then spin me in its web?'

Spinney's smile grew broader. 'Yes,' he said.

Humphreys chuckled harder. He had to pause for breath before he said, 'And this *thing*, I suppose it's too polite to come inside to get me.'

'For some reason it's afraid of the light,' Spinney told him quietly.

'It's *afraid* of the light?' Humphreys was gasping with laughter now.

Moore interrupted his fun. 'There might be something to what he's saying, Steve.'

Humphreys stopped laughing. His voice was grim. 'You know what I think? I think this man is a liar and a murderer. I think he's just clever enough to make up a story like this. Even to whip up that phony cocoon thing. Just to monkeywrench anybody who wants to take any trees. And I'm going to prove I'm right.'

He swung open the door.

He stepped out into the night.

He was holding his shotgun at the ready.

Spinney leaned back in his chair. 'You can't say I didn't warn him,' he said.

Mulder went to the open doorway to look out into the night. Scully followed, and the others came after her.

Scully heard a series of strange buzzes. Sharp little sounds, quick as the blink of an eye.

'What's that?' she wondered aloud.

'An insect zapper,' Mulder said. He pointed at a brightly lit device hanging outside the cabin. 'It attracts bugs at night. Then it fries them. A swarm must have hit it at once.'

'Lots of bugs in the woods,' Scully said.

'Lots and lots of bugs,' Spinney agreed. 'They're part of

nature's great plan. When we kill them, we upset the balance. Just like with almost everything we do out here.'

The sound stopped as suddenly as it had begun.

The night was filled with silence.

Then they heard Humphreys's mocking voice.

'Come out, come out, wherever you are!'

CHAPTER
EIGHT

The next morning, Humphreys was still crowing. The whole group was sitting at the breakfast table. They were finishing flapjacks and coffee that Moore had made.

'Hey, Spinney,' Humphreys taunted, 'the boogeyman didn't get me, did he? And the cookie monster didn't eat me up. I didn't even run into the big bad wolf. I wonder why.'

'You know, Humphreys,' Spinney said with disgust, 'I saw macho men like you in Vietnam. They'd go out on night patrol in the jungle. They'd come back laughing. "A piece of cake," they said. Then one night, they wouldn't come back. We'd have to go out to find them. And ship them home in body bags.'

'You were in Nam?' Moore asked. The forest service agent looked surprised. 'I didn't figure that.'

'Yeah, I was there,' Spinney said. 'Jerk that I was. I was one of the guys who dumped poison on the jungle. You remember, Agent Orange. Then I saw what it did to the trees. And to the people. I swore I'd make up for it. I'd stop the destruction of Mother Earth. Even if I had to fight another kind of war to do it.'

'I was in Vietnam, too,' Moore said. 'And I'm proud of it. I was there to do my duty. Serve my country. Protect its way of life. Preserve its laws. Just like I'm doing now.'

'You serve your country,' said Spinney. 'And I'll serve mine.'

'There's just one country,' Moore said.

'So you say,' Spinney sneered.

'So I know,' Moore replied.

Scully listened to the two men argue. The Vietnam war had ended a long time ago, when she had been a little girl. But for these two, it was still going on. She had a hunch it was never going to end for them.

Mulder spoke her thoughts when he said, 'Let's forget Vietnam. We're in a different war now. Against a different enemy. And we're all in it together. I suggest we head out into the forest. See if we can pick up traces of the missing men. Figure out what happened to them. We don't want to waste any daylight.'

'And I say we don't waste any more time,' Humphreys said. 'There's nothing out there but a bunch of trees. Trees that this sicko values more than human life. I'm going to see him tried on murder charges.'

Humphreys turned to Moore. 'Come on, Larry. What say we march this monkeywrencher back to civilization. Put him behind bars where he belongs.'

Moore gave Humphreys a level look. 'I need more evidence. And a few answers, too. I want to take a closer look at those trees that were cut down.'

'Do you really?' Spinney said. 'I'll show you one of them. I warn you, though. You'd better have a strong stomach.'

'I tell you, you can't trust a word this guy says,' protested Humphreys. 'He lies like he breathes.'

'I'm not asking you to believe my words,' Spinney said. 'Just your eyes.'

'It's like following a crooked Pied Piper,' grumbled Humphreys. But he joined the others following Spinney out of the cabin.

Spinney knew exactly where he was taking them. He did not hesitate as he led the way through the forest.

'Here we are,' he announced. 'Take a look at this. A good look.'

'My God,' Scully said, wide-eyed. 'What a tree!'

'You mean, what a hunk of dead wood,' Spinney corrected her.

The tree lay on the forest floor. It was at least a hundred and fifty feet long. Its trunk was more than ten feet in diameter.

'This redwood was standing here since time began,' Spinney said. 'Until a bunch of greedhead men came and cut it down.'

While Spinney stood smiling bitterly, Scully and Mulder walked along the tree's length. They had never seen a giant like it before.

Moore squatted by its base. He carefully inspected the bright orange *X* spray-painted on its side.

'Who marks these trees?' Scully asked him.

'Federal Forest Service,' Moore answered. 'You're only allowed to cut trees marked with a blue *X*.'

'You must get a lot of lumber from a big tree like this,' Scully remarked.

'Thousands of board feet,' Spinney said. 'It's a lot easier than taking smaller, young trees. A lot cheaper, too. They make tons more money with these giants.'

'Stop, or I'll start crying,' said Humphreys sarcastically. He turned to Scully. 'Let me remind you, these monkey-wrenchers often mark trees with their own paint.'

Moore looked up from the orange *X*. His eyes were hard.

So was his voice. 'This tree's five hundred years old if it's a day, Steve.'

Mulder was more interested in the tree stump. 'Hey, take a look at this,' he said.

The excitement in his voice drew them all to the stump. Their eyes followed Mulder's finger. It went across the rings in the wood from the outside inward. Then it stopped. It rested on a ring that was thicker than the others. And a different color as well. Not brown, but sulphur yellow.

'What would this ring be?' Mulder asked Moore.

'I don't know. I've never seen one like it before,' the forest service agent said.

'These center rings. These are the oldest ones, right?' Scully asked.

'Yeah,' Moore said. 'Every ring represents a season of growth. You can count them to see how old the tree is. And measure them to get an idea of the temperature and rainfall. But I don't know about this yellow one. I should take a sample.'

'Are we finished with our nature walk?' asked Humphreys. 'Because I just want to know one thing. What happened to my loggers?'

'That's what we're trying to find out,' said Scully.

'By looking at a tree stump?' Humphreys demanded. 'It's this monkeywrencher you should be looking at. Look inside him – and you'll see he's guilty as sin. He's the one who offed my people.'

'I don't think he did it,' Mulder said calmly.

'Well, I think he did,' Humphreys said. His hands tightened on his shotgun. His voice was loaded with menace. 'I want him arrested. And I mean right now.'

'There's no rush,' Mulder said. 'He's not going anywhere.'

'Not with a gun on him,' said Humphreys, pointing his

weapon at Spinney. 'But what if his two buddies show up while you're poking around? Remember your forest service buddies who vanished?' he asked Moore. 'You can imagine what the monkeywrenchers did to them.'

'I have to take a core sample of this tree, Steve,' Moore answered.

'I got families down there who want answers about their loved ones,' Humphreys insisted. 'So do you, Larry. Answers you're not going to find in that tree. We've got a crime to solve, and the faster the better.'

'The death of that tree's the only crime to investigate,' Spinney said.

Humphreys looked at Moore. Then at Mulder. Then at Scully.

He made one last try at winning them over. 'Come on, you guys. Don't let this killer pull the wool over your eyes.'

No one said a word. Or made a move.

'If you wimps feel like that,' Humphreys said angrily. He turned and started striding away.

'Where are you going, Steve?' asked Moore.

'I'm going to hike back down to your truck,' Humphreys said over his shoulder. 'And get on the horn. Get some people up here. People who'll take action.'

'Steve!' Moore called after him.

But he had already vanished in the trees.

'Let him go,' Spinney said. 'Let him find out for himself.' He smiled. 'And he will. Just as soon as the sun goes down.'

CHAPTER
NINE

The sounds of Humphreys stomping through the forest faded. He was gone.

Moore returned to the tree stump.

'Let's see what we can find out – before sunset,' he said. 'I'll bore out a sample from the core. We can take a good look at it back at camp.'

'Sounds good to me,' Mulder said. 'The yellow ring might give us some answers.'

'I hope so,' Scully said. 'All we've found so far is questions.'

Spinney shook his head. 'You people won't listen to me, will you? You won't believe what I've seen. As for myself, I just have one question. Do we have enough gas for the generator? Can we get through the night?'

When they got back to camp, Spinney said, 'I'm going to the generator shed. Check out the fuel supply.'

The others followed Moore into the cabin. He set his tree sample, a cylinder of wood the size of a long pencil, down on the table. Then he squinted at it through a magnifying glass. 'This is odd,' he said.

'Something odd in this case?' said Scully. 'Surely you jest.'

'What is it?' asked Mulder.

'This yellow ring,' Moore said. 'It's got something living in it. Some kind of tiny bug. It doesn't make sense.'

'Why not?' asked Scully. 'Lots of insects live in trees.'

'Right,' said Mulder. 'What makes this bug so strange?'

'Insects attack a tree in different ways,' Moore explained. 'But they always invade the living parts. The leaves. The roots. The new growth rings.'

'Maybe they're borers of some kind,' Mulder suggested.

'They still wouldn't be working so deep in the tree,' Moore said. 'Here, take a look for yourself.' He handed Mulder the magnifying glass.

Mulder looked through it. He saw what Moore was talking about. Crawling over the yellow wood were countless mites. Mites too small for the naked eye to see. Mites unlike any Mulder had ever seen. They looked like miniature spiders.

'Maybe the wood in this ring is different,' Mulder said. 'They seem to be feeding on it. Take a look, Scully. You might know what they are.'

He passed her the magnifying glass.

She peered through it and shook her head.

'Never saw these in any textbook,' she said. 'Can you identify them?' she asked Moore.

'They seem to be wood mites of some sort,' Moore said. 'But nothing I've run into before. I can't really explain them.'

I can't really explain them. The sentence made Mulder's eyes gleam. Scully knew why. Mulder was on home turf now. His favorite hunting ground. X-files territory.

'Could they have been living in that tree for hundreds of years?' he asked. 'Maybe even longer?'

'I don't see how,' Moore said. 'The yellow ring was too close to the core. A tree provides water for its outer rings only. Insects need water to survive.'

'Insects that we know about,' Mulder said.

142

Meanwhile, Scully was taking another look through the magnifying glass.

'It appears they might be hatching out of the wood,' she said. 'Maybe when you took this sample, you disturbed their nest.'

'Can they build a cocoon?' a voice cackled from the doorway. It was Spinney.

'Now listen up, lawpeople,' he told them. 'I've been in this forest awhile. I know these trees like I know my friends. And I know what's going on here.'

'And what do you say is going on?' Moore asked.

'I'll tell you – if you're willing to listen to a monkey-wrencher,' Spinney said.

'Come on, Spinney,' Moore said. 'It's too late in the day to start playing games.'

'You're right about that – it is too late in the day,' said Spinney. He had stopped joking. Nightfall was something he didn't joke about. 'My pal Teague died just after that tree was cut down,' he told them. 'Right about then the loggers disappeared, too.'

'You think these mites are what killed them?' Scully asked.

'Maybe they've been lying asleep for hundreds of years,' Spinney said. 'Maybe thousands. Maybe they woke up hungry.'

Spinney paused. No one said anything. They were all busy thinking about what he had said.

Spinney grinned. 'You know, I almost miss old Humphreys. It feels funny not hearing him laugh like a donkey. I wonder if he's still laughing now.'

Many miles away, Steve Humphreys wasn't laughing. He was cursing.

It was still daylight when he reached the road. But day-light was fading fast.

The truck was where they had left it. He glanced at the two blown tires. Driving on the tire rims would ruin them. But it would get him out of the forest.

He swung open the driver's door. He tossed his shotgun onto the front seat. He climbed behind the wheel and reached out to turn the ignition key.

His fingers closed on empty air.

'Rats,' he muttered. 'Where is it?'

He looked on the sun visor. Nothing. In the glove compartment. No luck there either.

He looked out the window. The last of the daylight was going.

'Here's something at least,' he said to himself. He pulled a flashlight from the glove compartment.

He turned it on just as darkness descended.

He shone it out the window. The night was huge. The flashlight beam looked pitiful.

But it would do. It would give him enough light to see what he was doing. He'd hot-wire the engine. Then he'd be out of this cursed place.

He went to work under the dashboard. Good thing he knew how to take care of Number One, he thought. Maybe he wasn't any Vietnam hero. Though it wasn't his fault he wasn't drafted. Not with his wife expecting a baby. But he'd like to see any of those vets beat his survival skills. He was a guy who knew the way the world worked. It was the law of the jungle. Dog eat dog. Only the fittest survived. The weak ones got eaten.

He got hold of the ignition wires. Here we go, easy as pie. He smiled, and touched the wires together. His smile grew as they sparked. He heard the engine turn over. Once, twice –

Then it died.

Rats, he thought. Must be damp or something. He tried again. Again the wires sparked. Again the engine turned over. Once, twice, three times –

Then silence again.

He climbed out of the truck. He opened the engine hood. He played the flashlight beam over the engine. He'd find what was wrong. Fix it. And –

Hmmmmmmmmmmmm.

The humming came from the forest. It rose, then fell away.

He straightened up. He turned his flashlight toward the sound.

He saw nothing. Just trees. Endless trees.

He grabbed his shotgun from the cab of the truck. Pointed it at the trees.

The humming rose again. But from a different direction.

He whirled around, shotgun in one hand, flashlight in the other.

'You monkeywrenchers come out now,' he shouted. 'You ain't scaring me. I know what you're up to.'

The only answer was more humming. Louder and louder.

Then Humphreys's mouth dropped open. The flashlight dropped from his hands.

He didn't bother picking it up. He had all the light he needed. The forest edge was flooded with light. Green light. Dazzling. Hovering above the treetops.

As he watched openmouthed, the cloud broke up into glowing pinpricks. And they came swarming down toward him.

Humphreys blasted away with both barrels of his shotgun.

The humming drowned out the echoes of his shots.

He threw away his gun and dashed into the truck,

slamming the door. He rolled the windows shut. Then he tried the ignition wires again.

The engine turned over once, twice – and roared to life.

'Go, baby, go,' he urged between clenched teeth. The truck started to move, staggering like a drunk on its flat tires.

Looking out the window, Humphreys saw the points of light close up. They were bouncing against the glass.

Some kind of bug, he thought. Bugs that glowed green in the dark.

But he'd soon be rid of them. He'd soon be out of this – *Aghhhh!*

He screamed as he felt the first bite on his hand.

Only then did he see the bugs streaming in through the air vent.

Even as he watched, the whole cab filled with them. They covered him. Every inch of exposed skin. His hands. His face. His neck. He flailed away but they ignored him. Their bites burned and stung like hot needles.

'Gotta get out of here!' his mind screamed. He turned the door handle. It was jammed.

There was no way out.

No way.

No –

'Nooooooo!'

His last living sound merged with the humming that ruled the dark.

CHAPTER
TEN

In the cabin, the lights stayed on.

Scully kept studying the tree sample. She was a scientist who never gave up on a problem.

Mulder went to make himself more tea. He believed in relaxing his mind, and letting answers come to him.

Moore stood looking out the window. He was anxious for Humphreys to get back. Whatever their differences, Humphreys and he had been friends for years.

Spinney was the only one in the cabin smiling. He enjoyed seeing Moore's worry grow.

'Humphreys should have been back by now,' Moore said. 'I know Steve. He gets hot under the collar. But then he cools down. He wouldn't cut out on us. He's a team player.'

'Why don't you go out and look for him?' Spinney asked.

Moore didn't answer.

'On the other hand,' Spinney said, 'why bother? What could happen to a good old boy like your good old pal? A tough guy like him who isn't afraid of the dark?'

From the table, Scully announced, 'These bugs aren't moving anymore. They're either dead or asleep.'

'Don't count on them being dead,' Spinney told her. 'Or asleep. It's the light. They don't like the light.'

'That's weird,' Scully said. 'Bugs are usually attracted to the light.'

'These are not your usual bugs,' Spinney said. 'Or haven't you noticed?'

Meanwhile, Mulder noticed something else unusual.

He ran his finger over a kind of grease that covered the wood countertop in the cooking area.

He had seen the same layer of grease on the refrigerator.

He checked out the rest of the kitchen space. The grease was everywhere. Either the loggers had been the sloppiest cooks in the world, or – ?

Or what?

He didn't know. He filed the question in the back of his mind. It was like putting aside a piece of a jigsaw puzzle. It might not fit in now. But it would later, when a few more pieces fell into place.

'Scully,' he said, 'you know much about insects?'

'Got straight *A*'s in biology,' she said. 'But that was a while ago.'

'What do you remember about them?' Mulder asked.

'Let's see,' Scully said. 'They're a key link of the chain of life. You could even call them the foundation of all life on earth. And there are a lot of them.'

'They outnumber humans, right?' Mulder asked.

'To put it mildly,' Scully said. 'Something like two hundred million bugs for every human on the planet.'

'And they've been around a long time,' said Mulder.

'Much longer than us,' Scully told him. 'Even long before the dinosaurs. Six hundred million years is the latest guess. Why?'

Mulder moved to the table. He looked at the sample from the tree. He touched it gently, with respect.

'This tree's how old?' he said. 'Five, six, seven hundred years?'

'Yeah. That old at least,' said Moore.

'And these rings show changes of climate?' Mulder said.

'Right,' said Moore.

'That means something strange happened in the year that this yellow ring was formed,' Mulder said.

'Looks like it,' agreed Moore.

'What kind of strange thing?' wondered Scully.

'I'll make a guess,' said Mulder. 'A volcanic eruption. Volcanoes still hit this mountain chain. All the way from Washington to Oregon. Remember Mount Saint Helens? The whole mountain just blew its lid one day.'

'How would that explain the bugs?' asked Scully.

'Look at Mount Saint Helens,' Mulder said. 'When it erupted, radiation was released. It came from deep inside the earth. Suddenly strange things started to grow.'

'What kind of strange things?'

'One was an amoeba they found in a lake,' Mulder said. 'No one had ever seen anything like it. It could suck a man's brains out.'

'Don't bother telling me how they found it,' Scully said. 'I can imagine.' Then she shook her head. 'A brain-sucking amoeba. That's too weird. I know you, Mulder. Sometimes your stories are just too much.'

But Mulder got back-up.

'It's true,' said Spinney. 'In Spirit Lake. There are documented accounts of what happened to swimmers. You're right, Scully. You don't want to hear the nasty details.'

'Okay, I'll buy that,' Scully said. 'But an amoeba is a one-celled life-form. It can mutate fast. Bugs are different. They're complex living things. Thousands of cells. A mutation would take years, decades, even centuries. Try again, Mulder.'

Mulder's eyes went remote. Scully could almost hear his brain working, whirring like a computer.

'Then maybe what we have here isn't a mutation,' he said finally. 'What if they're some kind of insect eggs? Thousands, maybe millions of years old? Eggs from deep inside the earth. Eggs that volcanic eruptions brought to the surface? Eggs sucked up into the tree through its root system? Eggs lying quietly in the tree for hundreds and hundreds of years –'

'Until those loggers cut down the tree – and those eggs hatched.' Spinney finished Mulder's line of thought. 'Yeah, hey, good thinking, Mr FBI Man.'

Spinney turned to Moore. 'That would be a good joke, wouldn't it?' he said to the forest service agent. 'Or maybe joke isn't the right word. Maybe justice is. Yeah. Poetic justice. Those loggers break the law. And let loose the things that kill them.'

Spinney paused. 'And maybe take out your friend Humphreys.'

Moore didn't answer.

'And maybe us,' Spinney finished. 'Maybe us, too.'

CHAPTER
ELEVEN

Doug Spinney woke up at dawn the next day. He woke with a start. He had been having a nightmare. A nightmare of bugs tearing at his old buddy Teague's flesh. Teague's screams filling the forest. While Spinney and his other pals watched and could do nothing.

Spinney's eyes were still glazed with horror when they opened. Then they blinked and focused. He saw the first pale light of day through the dirty cabin window. He had made it through another night.

He looked up at the ceiling. The light in the cabin was still on. The generator had made it through the night as well.

He looked around the room. The others were still asleep. They hadn't had nightmares to wake them. Not yet.

He climbed to his feet quietly, careful not to wake them. He stole out of the cabin, closing the door softly behind him.

As soon as he was outside, he started moving fast. He half trotted across the camp to the generator shed. The generator was still going. He didn't bother to shut it down. He didn't want the lights going off in the cabin. It might disturb the others inside. They'd turn off the lights fast when they awoke. They had enough sense to do that at least. That way, the generator would have enough gas to last another night.

Spinney picked up the five-gallon can of gas and shook it. He felt its weight and heard the gas inside sloshing around. There wasn't much left. But it would do. It had to.

He carried the can out of the shed to one of the monkey-wrenched trucks. He raised the truck hood. From the utility belt around his tattered Levi's he took a crescent wrench. Quietly and carefully he loosened a bracket. It was the bracket that held the truck battery in place.

He put the wrench back in his belt. Eagerly he reached for the battery.

There was a sharp click behind the back of his head. Spinney froze. He knew what it was. A pistol being cocked.

He turned and looked into the barrel of a pistol. A .45 calibre FBI issue.

'Going somewhere?' Mulder asked, his gun pointed between Spinney's eyes.

'Hey, man, you're quiet,' said Spinney. 'You would have done good in Vietnam. 'Course, I'm not as sharp as I once was. Used to have eyes in the back of my head.'

'I'm sure your war stories are quite interesting,' Mulder said. 'But they're not what I'd like to hear now. I'll ask my question again. Going somewhere?'

'Me? Why you ask that?' Spinney said. His eyes were darting, looking for a way out. He couldn't see one. All he could see was Mulder's pistol pointed dead at him. And Mulder's gaze, just as pitiless.

'Seems a funny time to do an auto repair job,' Mulder said. 'Tell me if I'm wrong – but were you planning to cut out of here?'

Spinney thought of lying. He didn't think about it long. Mulder wasn't the kind of guy you wanted to lie to. He might seem nice and gentle on the outside, but below the surface of this FBI agent, Spinney sensed something else. Something as hard and unyielding as a rock. Spinney didn't know what it was. But he didn't want to test it to find out.

'Okay, okay,' Spinney said. 'I'll level with you. I gotta go save my friends. They're still trapped in the middle of the forest. They only have enough gas to keep their generator going four hours tonight. Six hours max. They're dead if I don't get back there with this gas.'

'And what about us?' Mulder asked. 'Our generator. You didn't seem worried about it.'

'It's got enough to run as long as you need it,' Spinney said. 'I checked. It'll keep going until I can get you all out of here.'

'Get us all out?' said Mulder. 'That's real good of you. One detail, though. Mind telling me how you're planning to do it?'

'With this truck battery,' Spinney said. 'It still works, see. The only one in camp that does. We blew up all the others, but by the time I hit this truck, it was getting late. The sun was almost down.'

'Shame on you,' Mulder said. 'They should strip you of your monkeywrench.'

'Hey, look, let bygones be bygones,' Spinney said. 'I want to square things now.'

'How?' asked Mulder, still keeping his pistol level.

'Me and my pals, we've got a Jeep,' Spinney said. 'It's parked just two valleys over. All it needs is a battery. I could get to it. And be back here tomorrow morning. We could all drive out, easy as pie.'

'Sounds good,' said Mulder.

'Sounds good because it is good,' Spinney affirmed.

'One little question,' Mulder said. 'If it's the way you say it is, why the sneaking around? Why didn't you just tell us your plan?'

'It's Moore. The Freddie – the forest service guy,' said Spinney, shaking his head.

'What about him?' said Mulder.

'He wouldn't go for it,' Spinney said. 'He'd never trust me. I'm not one of his lumber company friends. Far as he's concerned, I'm an outlaw. Doesn't matter if it's the lumber company breaking the law. I'm the one who isn't making people money.'

'You think he's taking bribes,' said Mulder. 'You have evidence?'

'Nahh,' Spinney said. 'I don't. And he's probably not. It's just the way straight arrows like him think. If you got a corporate logo, you're one of the good guys. If you make waves, you're bad.'

'And me?' said Mulder. 'Why do you think I'd believe you? Remember, I'm FBI.'

'You may be a G-man,' said Spinney, 'but you're not like any I've ever seen. You don't have tunnel vision like most of them. You're weird, man. Weird enough to see things the way they are in this weird world. You should come over to our side. Or maybe you already are.'

'Not exactly,' Mulder said. He had to keep back a smile. But that didn't stop him from keeping his gun steady.

'Look, man, trust me,' Spinney pleaded. 'Maybe I've done some stuff you don't agree with. Maybe I've bent a few rules. Maybe I've even broken the law once or twice or three times. But there's a reason behind it. It's about the preservation of life. I ain't never killed anybody. Not since Vietnam, anyway. That place cured me for good. And now I'm asking for a chance to save you and your friends. You gotta let me. You gotta believe me.'

'And if I don't?' Mulder said.

'You know what'll happen,' said Spinney. 'You've seen it. Come on, what do you have to lose?'

'With you going off with the last of our gas?' said Mulder. 'That cuts our odds of surviving. They go from bad to worse. They go to zero.'

'It's a gamble you have to take,' Spinney urged.

Mulder bit his lower lip.

Gambling with his own life was one thing.

Gambling with the lives of others was something else.

Spinney gave him a big yellow-toothed grin.

'Hey, man, scout's honor I come back,' he said. 'What do you say?'

CHAPTER
TWELVE

Mulder didn't like to think what would happen if he was wrong about Spinney. Or if Spinney was wrong about being able to get back to them in his Jeep.

But he couldn't stop thinking of it.

He couldn't stop remembering the human remains in the cocoon.

He couldn't stop wondering how many other cocoons there were.

He couldn't stop counting off the number of people who had vanished here: the loggers a few weeks ago, the forest service men sent to look for them, the loggers fifty years ago, before there were laws protecting ancient trees. How many more cocoons were there? How many more victims, down through the years, as men felled the giant trees, woke the wrath of nature, and brought it down on their heads?

Mulder couldn't just sit and wait for Spinney to get back. He had to do something. Try to, anyway.

He found a tool kit in one of the trucks and took it into the cabin. The others were starting to stir. He ignored them. He went straight to the smashed radio, and started to take it apart.

'Didn't know you were a techie, Mulder,' said Scully, getting up and rubbing her eyes.

'I used to fool around with ham radios when I was a kid,' Mulder said, not looking up from his work.

'Let me guess why,' said Scully. 'Ever succeed in making contact with a spaceship?'

It was a private joke between them. Only Scully knew Mulder's story of how his younger sister had been kidnapped when he was a child. Kidnapped by alien beings. How he had seen it happen. How no one would believe him. How it had set him on the trail of all kinds of strange sightings and stranger disappearances. A trail that had finally led him to the X-files.

'No,' said Mulder. 'But it wasn't from lack of trying.'

'I can bet,' said Scully, as she watched Mulder at work. Mulder wasn't one to give up on anything. No matter what the odds, or how long it took.

'Want some tea for breakfast?' she asked.

'Sure, thanks,' he said, not pausing. By now the radio was in pieces. He started putting it together again.

'Make some for me, too, please,' said Moore.

The forest service agent got to his feet and stretched. He went to the sink and splashed cold water on his face. Scully gave him a mug of tea, and he took a sip.

'Thanks,' he said. 'What's your partner doing?'

'Tinkering with the radio,' Scully said.

'Wasting his time,' Moore announced. 'He'll be at it all day.'

'Tell him that,' Scully said.

Moore shrugged. 'He might as well do that as nothing. Myself, I'll check out the camp. I want to make sure old Spinney isn't up to mischief. One thing's for sure, though. He's not running away. Not him. Funny thing. A guy who says he loves trees – scared to death of the forest.'

Moore had just left the cabin when Mulder announced, 'Radio's back up.'

He touched two wires together. With a buzz of static, the radio came back to life.

Scully hurried to the table. 'It's working?'

'Sort of,' said Mulder. 'It's not getting any reception. The receiver was beyond repair.'

'But is there transmission?' she asked. 'Can you send out a message?'

'I'll give it a whirl,' said Mulder. He picked up the microphone, then flipped a switch on the radio a couple of times until the static held steady. He moved the dial to an emergency frequency. Then he spoke loudly and clearly into the mike. 'This is a call for help. Is there anyone on this frequency?'

There was only more static.

'As I said, no reception, I can only keep broadcasting and hope someone picks us up.'

Scully smiled wryly. 'You know that riddle?' she said. 'If a tree falls in the forest with no one to hear, does it make a sound? I guess we're going to find out the answer.'

Mulder spoke into the mike. 'This is Special Agent Mulder of the FBI with Special Agent Scully. We have an emergency. We have a suspected outbreak of life-threatening insect infestation. We have a possible quarantine situation. Our position is –'

Mulder paused. Scully thrust a map of the region in front of him.

But before he could read off their bearings, the static died. The radio face went dark.

'The generator's quit,' was Scully's guess.

'Come on. Let's check it out.' Mulder put down the mike and stood up. He clicked off the safety on his gun as he and Scully left the cabin.

They arrived at the generator to find Moore there.

'What happened to the generator?' Mulder demanded.

'I turned it off,' Moore said.

'Well, turn it back on,' Mulder said impatiently. 'I've got the radio working.'

'What happened to the gas can?' asked Moore.

Mulder hesitated. He swallowed. Then he said, *Spinney* took it.'

'Spinney took it?' said Moore in a stunned voice. He shook his head as if someone had slapped him in the face.

'Early this morning,' said Mulder. 'He took a truck battery, too.'

'He's gone?' said Moore, still trying to digest the news. 'When did you find him and the stuff he stole missing?'

Mulder hesitated a moment before he admitted, 'I let Spinney go. He's going to come back for us tomorrow morning.'

'Really,' said Moore. 'Did he give you his personal guarantee of that?'

'He gave me his word,' Mulder said.

'His *word*,' Moore snapped. 'And what do you think his word is worth? The word of a man who has made an art of sabotage? The word of a man who defies authority? The word of a man who laughs at the law? The word of a man who probably put a bullet through my windshield?'

'It was a judgment call,' Mulder said.

'I question that judgment,' Moore said. 'I call it crazy.'

'What would you have done?' asked Mulder.

'I would have stopped him in his tracks,' Moore said. 'Dead or alive.'

'At least this way there's a chance we can get out of here alive,' Mulder argued. 'That's one more chance than we had before.'

'Or one less,' Moore said.

'What do you mean?' Scully wanted to know. She wished she could back Mulder up. But when he went this far out on a limb, it was hard to do.

'Your good-hearted partner let Spinney leave with the last of the gas,' said Moore. 'This generator's got about a quarter of a tank left. Maybe less. We'll be lucky if we make it through the night.'

'What about the gas in the trucks?' asked Scully.

'Since Spinney isn't here to tell you, maybe Mulder here will,' Moore said with disgust.

'Mulder, what's the score?' asked Scully.

'There is no gas,' Mulder told her. 'The tanks have all been ruptured. Or filled with sugar.'

'By the same man we're supposed to trust to come back and save us,' said Moore.

'Then we've got to keep trying on the radio,' Scully decided. 'We've got to get a Mayday message out. There has to be someone on the emergency frequency. Someone to hear us.'

'Want to bet your life on it?' said Moore. 'Every drop of fuel we use to run the radio is fuel we'll need tonight. I don't want to be praying somebody got our message when the tank hits empty at two A.M. And the generator quits. And the lights go out. Do you?'

'So what do we do?' Scully said.

'Ask your partner,' Moore said. 'He's the one with all the brilliant answers.'

Their eyes turned to Mulder.

'Whatever we can,' he said. 'Before darkness falls.'

THIRTEEN

'We have to circle the wagons,' Mulder declared. 'We have to turn the cabin into a fortress.'

'Against what?' asked Scully.

'Against the night,' Mulder said. 'Against whatever's out there in the night.'

'Wish we knew exactly what it was,' Moore said. 'It's like fighting blindfolded.'

'Nobody ever said it would be easy,' said Mulder. 'Come on. Let's find out what we have to work with. We can rummage through the camp. One thing you have to say about Western civilization. It produces a lot of useful junk. Maybe we can recycle some of it.'

It was Scully who spotted what they needed. A pile of dirty plastic sheets in the camp garbage dump. Logging equipment must have come wrapped in it.

'Beautiful,' said Mulder. 'We can make ourselves snug as a bug in a rug. Except that "bug" isn't the word to use.'

They carried the tarps into the cabin. There they found hammers and nails. They got to work nailing the tarps over the floor, the walls, the ceiling.

'Be sure not to leave any cracks exposed,' Mulder cautioned them.

'Looks like we're doing our friends' work for them,' Scully

said, as she nailed down a tarp over the window. 'We're building a cocoon of our own. With us in the middle of it.'

'That's the problem with building defenses,' Mulder agreed. 'You want to protect yourself. But you can wind up trapping yourself.'

'One more thing to check out,' Scully said. The lone lightbulb in the cabin hung down from the ceiling on a long cord. It was in easy arm's reach. She started to unscrew it.

'Be careful,' said Moore. 'It's the only bulb we've got. The lumber company seems to have cut corners in this camp.'

Scully nodded. She held the lightbulb as if it were a very thin-shelled egg.

'You know that new kind of bulb? The kind that only needs changing every seven years?' she asked.

'Yeah,' said Moore.

'Well, this isn't one of them,' Scully said. 'It isn't even a name brand. I think the filament is starting to go. I hope I'm wrong.'

'We'll find out soon enough,' said Mulder, as Scully screwed the bulb back in. 'The sun's going down.'

'I'll go start up the generator,' Moore said.

'Better move fast,' said Mulder. 'You don't want to be outside when it gets dark.'

'Agreed,' said Moore, already halfway out the door.

He was back in three minutes flat. He must have run all the way. Breathing hard, he nailed the last tarp over the door.

'Truth time,' said Mulder. He snapped on the light switch.

No one breathed until the light came on.

Mulder looked at his watch. 'Sunrise is about ten hours away.'

'With the tarp and the light together, we should make it,' Moore said.

'No problem,' Mulder agreed. 'Unless –'

'Unless?' said Scully.

'There are some surprises,' said Mulder.

He lay down on a bunk. Moore lay down on another, and Scully on a third.

'Funny, I used to think I hated TV,' Scully said. 'I wouldn't mind the tube now.'

'It would sure beat staring at that bulb,' agreed Moore.

'And listening to the generator,' said Mulder. They could hear the generator humming in the distance. 'My imagination, or is its sound going up and down?'

'I did the best I could to fix it,' said Moore. 'But it's still not working smoothly. We can just pray it doesn't conk out.'

'We don't have to hear it to know how it's working,' said Scully. 'We just have to look at the lightbulb. It keeps flickering. Watching it makes me feel like I'm on a roller coaster.'

'Try getting some shut-eye,' Mulder suggested.

'Easier said than done.' Scully felt her stomach tighten as the bulb dimmed. It brightened and her stomach unknotted.

She decided to take Mulder's advice. She shut her eyes. But she opened them quickly. Darkness wasn't what she wanted to see.

She turned over onto her stomach. She looked away from the bulb. She fixed her gaze on a tarp covering a wall. Suddenly she sat up, almost banging her head on the bunk above.

She tried to keep the panic out of her voice. 'I can see them – through the tarp. Come look.'

She led the way to the tarp. Dots of green light glowed through the dirty plastic. Hundreds of dots.

'They're coming through the walls,' Scully said. 'Down near the floor. Where the light doesn't reach. I want to get a better look at them.'

She pressed both hands against the tarp and started smoothing away the wrinkles.

'Aaaaah!' she screamed.

The glowing green dots were on her arm, crawling up it.

'They're on me!' she shrieked. 'Get them off!'

She leaped back, arms flailing.

'Watch it!' shouted Moore, as one of her hands hit the lightbulb.

It flung through the air, swinging out of control.

Moore almost knocked Scully down as he dashed for it. He caught it gently, then brought it to a safe stop.

Meanwhile Mulder had his arms around Scully. He could feel her shaking wildly. She was as out of control as the lightbulb had been.

'Scully,' he said. 'It's okay. It's okay.'

'Get them off!' she pleaded.

'Stop it!' Mulder commanded. 'Calm down. Stand still.'

Scully forced herself to obey. She stood with her fists clenched, her arms stiff at her sides. Her heart was beating like a hammer. Her eyes were shut. She couldn't bring herself to open them.

'Where are they, Mulder?' she asked. 'Do you see them?'

'They're not just on you, Scully,' Mulder said. 'They're everywhere. They've been leaving the slimy grease that's all over the cabin. I think they lit up on your arms because you were in shadow.'

'I thought we were safe here,' said Scully. She shook her arms to make sure they were free of bugs. They were. Or seemed to be. At least nothing was biting.

'There's a good chance we're okay,' Mulder said. 'Just a few of them don't seem to do damage. And it looks as if light keeps them from swarming.'

He glanced at the window. 'I don't want to think how many of them it would take to devour a human being. How many of them might be out there. Filling the sky. Covering the trees. Getting hungrier and hungrier.'

'Let's just hope they make these things well in Taiwan,' said Moore, still holding on to the lightbulb. 'Dawn is still a long way away.'

CHAPTER
FOURTEEN

Scully did not even try to go to sleep. She was trembling too hard. There was only one way she knew to calm down.

She had to get back to work. She lay on her bunk and thought about the case.

Suddenly a thought struck her.

She got up and went to her backpack. She took a glass jar from it and set it on the table.

'I thought so,' she said to herself.

She turned and said to the others, 'Come here. Take a look at this.'

Mulder and Moore joined her. They looked at the glowing dots of green light inside the jar. There were about a dozen. They flew furiously fast, as if struggling to escape.

'I collected these in the forest, from the cocoon we found,' Scully said. 'They appear to be like fireflies. If that's the case, the light they give off comes from waste from their bodies. When the waste hits the air, it produces a glow. In this case, a green glow.'

'Right,' Moore said, nodding. 'A chemical reaction from instant oxidation.'

'Except these aren't fireflies,' said Mulder, squinting

166

into the jar. 'Fireflies don't look like tiny spiders. Fireflies don't make cocoons. Fireflies don't suck the life out of you.'

'That must be how they make their cocoons,' Scully said. 'After they feed, they have to get rid of waste. It mixes with their own juices. They squirt it out. It hits the air with a glow. And it turns to strands of greasy gray fiber.'

'Judging from the cocoon we found, they're hungry little devils,' said Moore. 'They must suck every last bit of nourishment from their prey.'

'You'd be hungry, too,' Mulder said, 'if you hadn't eaten for centuries.'

'They're making up for lost time now,' said Moore.

'I wonder how many there are,' said Scully.

'No telling,' said Mulder. 'But I'd guess in the millions. There had to be that many to take care of thirty loggers. Trouble is, that may not be the worst news.'

'What is?' said Scully.

'I have an idea they're multiplying by the minute,' said Mulder. 'The more they eat, the faster they breed. When they found those thirty loggers, they hit the jackpot. It was a feast for them, and it must have set off a population explosion. Insects are like that. That's why they outnumber us by so much.'

'But they've never eaten humans before,' said Scully.

'There's always a first time,' said Mulder.

'And this one could mean the end of human life,' Scully said grimly. 'Other species have disappeared in the past: the dinosaurs, the mastodons. We're still not sure why. But we do know there were volcanic eruptions that disturbed the earth. They could have set off a plague like this one. It could be our turn now to be the victims.'

'We also know meteors from outer space have hit the

earth,' Mulder said. 'They could have brought deadly life-forms with them.'

'Whatever their origin,' said Scully, 'these insects are a threat to human life.'

'They're a threat to our lives for sure,' said Moore.

At that moment, the electric light flickered. In the distance, the hum of the generator faltered.

'Oh God,' said Scully, her fists clenching. Cold sweat beaded her skin. In her mind was a picture of the bugs swarming, closing in on them. Feasting on them.

Then the light steadied. So did the hum of the generator. Scully wiped the sweat off her forehead.

'Maybe we'll make it through the night,' said Mulder.

'Maybe,' said Moore.

'But then what?' Scully wondered. 'It's over a day's hike out of the forest. We could never make it before night-fall. By now the bugs must be ranging all over the woods, looking for food. If they find us outside after dark, we're dead.'

'Maybe somebody heard our radio call,' said Mulder. 'Help could be on the way.'

'You sent that call hours ago,' Scully said. 'Help would be here by now.'

'Stands to reason,' agreed Moore. 'The forest service has choppers. So does the lumber company.'

'Well, I'm not giving up on Spinney,' Mulder insisted. 'He gave me his word he'd come back to get us.'

'Spinney talks a good game,' said Moore. 'What he does is something else. I've been playing hide-and-seek with him for years. I've read all the pretty words in all the pamphlets he puts out. I've seen all the ugly damage he causes. I'm not buying anything he says. And I'm sure not staking my life on it.'

'Moore is right,' said Scully. 'Spinney isn't exactly a Boy Scout. We can't count on him. We have to figure out what to do if he doesn't show.'

'And we can't wait around too long hoping he will,' said Moore. 'Every minute of daylight will be precious.'

'Any ideas?' Scully asked Mulder.

'Don't worry,' he said. 'We'll think of something.'

'When?' asked Scully.

'When the time comes,' said Mulder.

Moore looked at his watch. 'The time is coming closer every second.'

'And those bugs are getting hungrier,' said Scully.

'Still hours until dawn,' said Mulder. He yawned. 'I don't know about you, but I'm getting some shut-eye.'

'Good idea,' said Moore. 'We'll have to be clear-headed when dawn comes. Tough choices to make.'

'If we're still alive when dawn comes,' said Scully.

'Well, pleasant dreams,' said Mulder, going to his bunk.

'I could use some,' said Moore, sacking out, too.

Scully lay down on her bunk as well. But she didn't shut her eyes. Mulder might act like Mr Cool. As for her, she was chilled with fear. She didn't feel like she would ever sleep again.

She stared up at the electric light. She told herself that as long as it stayed on, she was safe. It was like a life raft in a sea as dark as night.

She let her mind drift. She tried not to think of the bugs, the cocoon, the hideous shrunken corpse.

Then everything went dark.

She opened her mouth to scream.

Then she realized her eyes were closed. She had fallen asleep.

She opened her eyes and saw the bulb was still working. But it was dim.

Brighter light edged the dirty plastic covering the windows.

Dawn had come.

CHAPTER
FIFTEEN

An hour later, the day was not much brighter.

Morning mist filled the forest. It would take another hour or more for the sun to burn through.

Moore wasn't waiting. He looked at his watch and said, 'That's it. Spinney's not showing. We're on our own.'

He turned to Mulder. 'You got us into this, Mr FBI. Got any bright ideas about how we get out?'

'I've been thinking,' Mulder said.

'Don't tell me,' Moore said sarcastically.

'I want to check that truck,' Mulder calmly went on. 'The one that Spinney lifted the battery from.'

'Why bother?' said Moore. 'It's a wreck. Sugar in the fuel line. Battery gone. Tires slashed.'

'Let's just take a look,' Mulder repeated.

He headed for the truck, with Moore and Scully following. He circled around it, kneeling at each wheel in turn. He was examining the tires.

'This is the best of them,' he said, pointing at the front right one. 'It's practically new. The tread's barely worn. And the slash isn't bad. The tube is just nicked.'

'Yeah,' said Moore. 'The monkeywrencher must have been lazy. Or else arm-weary by the time he got to it.'

'Is there a patch kit back in your truck?' Mulder said.

'Yeah,' Moore said. 'It's still there. Untouched. There was no use trying it. The tires were beyond repair. The caltrops totaled them.'

'But we could use it to patch *this* tire,' said Mulder. 'Then we could replace one of your ruined tires with this one, and the other with your spare. It might not last long. But maybe long enough for the truck to limp out of the forest. Get us in the clear before nightfall.'

'Hey, it might work,' said Scully.

'And if it doesn't,' Mulder said with a grim smile, 'at least we can use the truck radio. Warn the people outside what's up here. Save them from what happened to us.'

'Right,' Scully agreed somberly. 'Stop them from being the bugs' next meal.'

'It beats waiting here,' said Moore. 'No way the generator will last another night.'

'Let's get rolling,' said Mulder. 'Rolling the tire, I mean. We can cut straight through the forest. It's a lot more direct than following the winding road to the truck.'

'We'd better hurry,' said Moore. 'We have no time to waste.'

Mulder went to the driver's cabin. He came out with a tire iron and a jack.

In minutes the tire was off the truck. Mulder rolled it in front of him as he jogged into the mist.

'Brrrr,' said Scully as they jogged. 'It looks like ghostland.'

Around them the trees loomed like dark giants. The fog swirled around the trail ahead. But as they ran, it began to lift.

By the time Moore took his turn rolling the tire, the sun had broken through. By then they had slowed from a run to a quickstep.

'Wish we didn't have to go so fast,' Scully remarked. 'This

forest is beautiful. It makes you feel good to be alive. Be nice to walk through it. Well, maybe some other time.' She paused. 'When our little insect friends are gone. If they're ever gone.'

She glanced admiringly at the huge old trees. Through the deep green of the pine needles the sky was a brilliant blue.

'It's God's country,' Moore agreed. 'I've loved it since I was a kid. I can't think of anything better than making sure my kids can grow up loving it, too. For me the forest service was the only way to go. I could never see working for just a paycheck. You have to work for something more than money.'

'Funny hearing that from you,' said Scully. 'You sound like you're on Spinney's side. You know, saving the trees and all. Yet Humphreys is your pal. Not Spinney.'

Then she said, 'Hey, my turn with the tire.'

Moore passed it to her without breaking stride.

'Humphreys and I are on the same side of the law,' he said after a moment. 'Spinney wants to take the law into his own hands. That's not the way we do things in this country.'

'Let's try jogging again for a while,' Scully suggested. 'The path is wide here. We can run three abreast.'

'I'm with you,' said Moore. 'Still lots of ground to cover. We'll be cutting it close.'

'It's looking good, though,' said Mulder, glancing at his watch. 'We should get to the truck by late afternoon. Then, if there are no hitches –' He paused, then said, 'Well, we'll cross that bridge when we come to it.'

As they started to jog again, Scully asked Moore, 'But you still think Spinney is the only one who plays fast and loose with the law? Seems to me that Humphreys is no angel either.'

'I don't like to think that,' Moore said. 'I've known Steve

for years. We golf together, play tennis together, our families have barbecues together. I always figured I could trust him like a brother.'

'That's the problem with enforcing the law,' Mulder said, jogging alongside Moore. 'You can't afford to get too friendly. Not with anybody you may have to collar.'

'Sad but true,' agreed Scully. 'Our jobs set us apart. With no one to trust but the people we work with. It can get kind of lonely. You have to believe in what you're doing.'

'You have to really believe,' agreed Mulder.

'Like Mulder does,' said Scully. 'Right, partner?'

They exchanged quick grins. It was a private joke.

Moore's face stayed grim. He wiped away sweat from his eyes. The day was getting hot as the sun moved across the sky. Its dazzling glare exploded like flashbulbs through the treetops.

'I suppose friendship could have clouded my judgment,' he admitted. 'Maybe I didn't notice as much as I should have. Maybe I didn't look as hard as I should have. When I see him again, I'll make sure he levels with me, pal or no pal.'

Scully stopped in her tracks.

'Tired?' asked Moore.

'We can take a break,' said Mulder.

'It's not that,' said Scully. 'A thought just hit me. Humphreys headed for the truck when he cut out. What if he managed to drive it out of here on its rims? What if there's nothing waiting for us? Nothing but the bugs?'

'The possibility already crossed my mind,' Mulder confessed, 'but I decided there was no sense worrying about it. Staying in the camp, our odds of survival were zip. This way, at least we have a chance.'

Scully didn't bother asking what kind of chance. Mulder had made it crystal clear. It was better than nothing. Barely.

'Come on,' she said, rolling the tire again. 'Last one to the truck is a rotten egg.'

They continued moving through the forest in silence. Silently they shifted from jogging to quickstep when the trail narrowed again. Silently they passed the wheel from one to another. They had run out of talk. They were all too busy thinking the same thing.

It was late afternoon when they reached the highway.

Scully gave voice to the relief they all felt.

'Thank God,' she said. 'There's the truck. It's still here.'

CHAPTER
SIXTEEN

Funny how fast things turned around, thought Scully. As fast as a rug pulled out from under your feet. One second, she was overjoyed to see the truck. The next, the truth hit her. It felt like a punch to the jaw.

'The truck,' she said. 'It's plowed into a tree.'

Moore had already seen it. He led their dash toward it. He reached it steps ahead of the others. He looked into the driver's cabin.

He turned around and said to Scully, 'Better not look, lady.'

'Don't worry. I'm used to –' she started to say.

That was as far as she got before she took a look.

Her mouth dropped open.

She saw Humphreys's face pressed against the inside of the glass. Part of his face, anyway. Part of a face twisted in horrible pain.

The rest of his face, his head, his whole body, was wrapped in a dirty gray cocoon. The cocoon filled the driver's cabin.

Scully turned away. She did not want the others to see her face turn a pale shade of green. She took pride in being an agent who always kept her cool.

She need not have worried. Moore and Mulder looked pale and queasy themselves.

Mulder recovered first.

'Humphreys made a good try – but no cigar,' he said.

'Poor devil,' said Moore. 'He was a good guy at heart. Maybe just a little too loyal to his company. Whatever he did, he didn't deserve a punishment like this.'

'Nobody does,' said Mulder. 'But when you mess with nature, justice turns blind. And everybody gets punished.'

'Right. Everybody,' echoed Scully. Her stomach had stopped turning over. But she still did not feel very good. Especially when she looked westward.

'The sun sure sets early around here,' she remarked.

Off in the distance, the sun hovered, glowing above the rim of the mountains.

'I guess that's it for us,' she said.

Moore nodded. 'Nowhere to run.'

'And nowhere to hide,' Mulder said.

Scully brightened. 'Maybe we can take refuge in the truck,' she said.

But before anyone could answer, she shook her head. 'Dumb idea. The truck is full of bugs. They'll swarm to life looking for dinner as soon as it's dark.'

'I've got a flashlight,' said Moore. 'Maybe we can use it against them.'

This time Mulder shook his head.

'You don't want to try it,' he said. 'There'd be too much shadow for them to swarm in. And you'd be trapped in a small space when they do. You'd wind up like Humphreys, with your face squashed against the glass. Better to take your chances with nothing caging you in.'

'Doesn't really matter,' said Scully. 'The end result will be the same. It'll take a miracle to save us.'

Nobody argued.

They stood there in silence, staring at the setting sun.

Then they all heard a distant sound.

A miraculous sound.

It came from up the highway, from the direction of the mountains.

The sound grew more distinct.

'It's a car,' said Moore. 'But who – ?'

'I think I know who,' Mulder said, grinning. 'And I think it's a Jeep.'

Minutes later, they saw the Jeep, coming toward them. Spinney was at the wheel.

He was driving full-out. He braked to a screeching, skidding stop when he reached them.

He didn't waste words.

'We've got to get moving,' he said. 'I wasted enough time, looking for you in that camp. Hop in.'

'But look, we've got a body,' Moore protested. 'Humphreys's body.' He motioned toward the truck. 'We can't leave him here. He's got a wife and kids. They'll want to give him a decent burial.'

'We're the ones who'll need burying if we don't move,' Spinney said, his voice harsh with impatience.

Then he saw the pain in Moore's eyes. Humphreys and Moore had been friends. He looked at the truck. It was easy to imagine what had happened to Humphreys. Spinney had seen the same thing happen to his friend.

'Don't worry about Humphreys,' Spinney said, his voice turning gentle. 'I had a radio back in my camp. I sent out a call for help. There'll be people coming in. They'll take Humphreys. I just hope for his family's sake that the coffin stays closed.'

Moore nodded. He gave one last look at the truck, and went to get his gear. He and the others tossed their stuff into the Jeep. Then Moore climbed in beside Spinney, and Scully and Mulder got in the back.

They had barely closed the doors when Spinney roared off. He pressed the accelerator to the floor.

The Jeep tore over the rough road, bouncing like a bronco. Mulder shouted a question to Spinney over the noise of the engine. 'Your friends? You found them?'

Spinney kept his eyes on the road, his foot to the floor. 'Yeah, I found them!' he shouted back. 'They didn't make it! But we will, by God!'

Scully looked at the forest whizzing by. It already lay in darkness. The long shadows of the trees edged the road. The lower rim of a bloodred sun dipped below mountains black as ink.

She saw that Spinney had turned on the headlights, and she opened her mouth to shout a question to him. Would they make it?

She closed her mouth without a word. There was no sense asking. They would find out soon enough.

Suddenly there was a loud sound. An explosion even louder than the motor.

A jolt ran through the Jeep.

It started bouncing crazily.

'No, no, it can't be,' moaned Spinney.

Desperately he struggled with the steering wheel, fighting to keep the Jeep from careening off the road.

It steadied, then slowed, as he braked it to a stop.

He got out, taking a flashlight with him. By now he needed it. There was a faint reddish glow in the west. But everywhere else night had fallen.

Spinney shone his flashlight on the right front tire. Slowly he shook his head.

Mulder turned to Scully in the backseat.

'Five'll get you ten that the tire is ripped to shreds,' he said.

'Same odds on what did it,' Scully said.

'The monkeywrencher's best friend,' said Mulder. 'A caltrop.'

They could read Spinney's lips muttering, 'Clean forgot about it.'

'Talk about shooting yourself in the foot,' said Moore.

Then he said, 'This I have to see. If it's the last thing I ever do, I want to make sure Spinney eats crow.'

He opened the Jeep door and stepped out into the night.

'No!' Mulder shouted at the top of his lungs. 'Get back inside! Close the door!'

Moore froze, bewildered.

'Get back in!' Mulder shouted again.

'Please!' Scully shouted in chorus.

'Wha – ?' Moore started to ask. Then his mouth gaped open like a fish.

He heard Spinney screaming. He turned and saw what Mulder and Scully had seen.

Spinney was bathed in blinding green light.

The bugs had scented their food.

They had swarmed.

And arrived.

Moore stayed frozen in shock.

Mulder moved fast.

He flung open the door. He leaped out of the Jeep. He shoved Moore back into the front seat and slammed the door on that side. He tore around the rear of the Jeep and slammed the driver's door. Then he jumped back inside beside Scully, slamming the door behind him.

'But Spinney –' Scully said.

'Too late,' Mulder said, panting, as they all looked out the window.

Spinney's flashlight lay on the ground, still glowing. Spinney's arms flailed uselessly. He ran blindly away from the Jeep, taking the glowing green swarm with him.

Down the highway, beyond the headlights, Scully could see the green light. It hovered motionless a few minutes. Then she saw it growing larger, coming closer.

'The bugs finished off their appetizer,' said Mulder. 'Now they're coming back for the main course.'

CHAPTER

SEVENTEEN

The light almost blinded Mulder.

He blinked, trying to focus, trying to think.

His first thought was: The light, it's not green.

His next thought: It's daylight.

Then he saw the eyes looking down at him. They were shielded by clear plastic. The man bending over him wore a hooded white cleansuit. He looked ready to go on a moon walk. Every inch of him was covered, protected from all contamination.

Gloved hands lifted Mulder out of the Jeep. He saw other men in cleansuits standing by. A short distance away were the three large white vans that had brought them here.

'Thank God you're alive,' the man said. 'When I got that stuff off your face, I held my breath until your eyes opened. What the devil happened?'

'It's a long story,' said Mulder.

'We got a few pieces of it on a radio call,' said the man. 'From some guy named Spinney. Said something about bugs. Deadly bugs. Is he around here? Maybe he can fill in the details.'

'I'm afraid not,' said Mulder. He remembered his last sight of Spinney, running screaming into the dark. 'You might find what's left of him up the road.'

Mulder shut his eyes. He tried to piece together what had happened.

He saw again the three of them in the Jeep. Moore in the front seat. He and Scully in the back.

For a few minutes they'd thought they were safe.

Then glowing green bugs had come pouring through the air vents in the dashboard.

They'd reached Moore first. Helplessly Scully and Mulder had watched them feasting.

Then some of them had broken off from the others. They'd swarmed toward the back. Mulder remembered the first stabs of pain when they reached his skin. He remembered Scully's shrieks of agony in his ear.

Then why was he still alive? Mulder wondered. Why hadn't they sucked the last drops of life out of him?

He couldn't remember. He had blacked out as the wave of pain crested.

Could the insects in the Jeep have been spread too thin with three victims to attack?

Had the edge been taken off their appetites after Spinney and Moore and –

Mulder's eyes flew open.

'There's someone else in the backseat. My partner, Scully,' he croaked. He was too weak to move. He could barely turn his head. He could only ask, 'Tell me, is she alive?'

'I didn't see her,' the man said. 'But I may have missed her. I barely spotted you. And then I was in a hurry to get you out. The whole inside of the Jeep is draped in some kind of strange fiber. Almost like a cocoon. Not to mention the slimy grease over everything.'

Mulder heard a voice shout, 'I've found two more. I'm looking for life signs.'

A second voice said, 'I think I see some movement in this

one. Around the face. Maybe a mouth breathing. Or trying to speak.'

The first voice said, 'Let's get this stuff off of it.'

A moment later, the second voice said, 'It's a female.'

'Alive?' the man with Mulder shouted to them.

'Affirmative,' said the second voice. 'But I don't know for how long.'

Then Mulder heard another voice. It must have been talking into a radio.

'We have an emergency evacuation situation,' it said. 'Urgently requesting a helicopter. Also prepare a quarantine facility. We have at least two victims of an unidentified infection. Or else exposure to unknown biological agents. They are to be handled with extreme care. Also a total news blackout. Definite potential for a deadly epidemic. And extreme danger of a public panic.'

Let's see how good medical science really is, was Mulder's last thought before he passed out again.

'Who are you?' Mulder asked the man in the white cleansuit bending over his bed.

'Dr Simmons, from the Center for Infectious Diseases in Atlanta,' the man said. 'I was flown in to take over your case three days ago.'

'And where am I?' Mulder asked.

'Hyman Rickover Naval Hospital, Seattle, Washington,' Simmons said. Then he added, 'You can keep talking. You seem to be strong enough. But keep on breathing though that oxygen tube in your nose.'

Mulder took a long drag of oxygen, then looked around him. 'This is a special ward, I take it,' he said.

'A very special ward,' Simmons said. 'You're a very special case.'

Mulder's bed was in a large white plastic dome. Attendants in cleansuits stood guard at the entrance. Others monitored high-tech medical equipment. Mulder turned his head and saw two other beds beside his. It figured. The medicos had three very special cases on their hands.

'How are you feeling?' Simmons asked.

'I think I'll live,' Mulder said. 'But you probably know better than I. Any test results yet?'

'Your respiratory charts are good,' Simmons said. 'That was our big worry. We thought that you might have breathed in a harmful material. But what we found wasn't that dangerous.'

'What did you find?' asked Mulder.

'A sizable amount of a chemical called luciferin,' Simmons said.

'Which is what?' Mulder wanted to know.

'The same enzyme found in fireflies and similar insects,' Simmons said. 'Our experts are still trying to determine exactly what species you encountered. So far, no success.'

'And what about the others?' Mulder asked. 'Moore. And Scully.'

'Moore's life is hanging by a thread. A very thin thread,' Simmons said. 'Medical science can do only so much when dealing with the unknown.'

'And Scully?' Mulder said.

'As I said, it's difficult to give you a definite –' Simmons began.

'Can I take a look at her?' Mulder requested.

The doctor hesitated. Then he said, 'I don't see why not. Just keep breathing in that oxygen.'

Mulder carefully got out of bed, the tube still in his nose. It was hooked up to an oxygen tank in a cart. He wheeled it with him as he followed Simmons to Scully's bed.

He looked down at her.

She lay still as death. Only a faint rise and fall of her chest showed she was breathing. Her face was blotched red with countless bites. Her features were gaunt, wasted away.

'Scully?' Mulder said softly.

'She's still not out of the woods – if you'll pardon the expression,' said the doctor. 'She's lost a lot of fluids. If there had been a few more insects, or if they'd had a few more hours, no way could she have made it. As it is –' Simmons paused, then went on, 'We're doing the best we can. But there are no guarantees in a case like this.'

'And I told her it'd be a nice trip to the forest,' said Mulder.

The pain he felt now wasn't from insect bites. But it was just as piercing. It was a bad case of serious guilt.

'No way you could have known,' the doctor assured him. 'No way anyone could have known. A totally bizarre phenomenon.'

'Yeah, a natural for the X-files,' said Mulder, half to himself, and half to the body in the bed.

Then he asked the doctor, 'How are you going to seal off the forest? What if the swarm migrates?'

'The government is giving it the highest priority,' Simmons said. 'They're using every available means of insect control – their whole arsenal of pesticides, plus carefully controlled tree burning. They're quite certain they'll be successful.'

Mulder couldn't keep from smiling a crooked smile. Spinney must be turning over in his grave.

And he couldn't resist asking the doctor, 'What if the government's best efforts fail?'

'Don't even think about it, Agent Mulder. They won't

fail,' the doctor said crisply. 'It's out of the question. Completely unthinkable.'

The doctor turned sharply and strode away.

Mulder sighed.

The people in charge were always the same.

They did not like questions that had troubling answers.

They did not want to think the unthinkable.

Mulder looked down at his partner.

'Please get better,' he said. 'I'm going to need all the help I can get.'

He might have been crazy, but he thought he saw her head give a tiny nod.

He'd have to wait and see.

TIGER, TIGER

To Nicole,
my greatest fan and severest critic

ONE

'Nobody is paying you to dance, Roberto,' Francisco García told his nephew. He spoke in Spanish, above the Latin music from Roberto's boom box. 'Remember, God is watching.'

Francisco pointed to the TV camera trained on them from the ceiling of the building where they were working. The building housed the Idaho Mutual Insurance Trust. The bank was the biggest in Fairfield, Idaho, with high ceilings and gleaming marble floors. Francisco and Roberto mopped those floors each night.

Francisco had to admit that he enjoyed the sight of Roberto dancing to the radio, using his mop as a partner. The young were entitled to a little fun. But as Roberto's uncle, he had to keep the young man in line.

'You lose your job, and it's back to the jungle in El Salvador,' he told Roberto sternly.

Roberto responded with a grin. He did one more fast step. Then he turned off the music and went back to work.

Satisfied, Francisco attacked a nasty stain on the floor with his squeegee.

Then a strange rumbling filled the air.

The marble floor trembled.

Back in El Salvador Francisco had felt earthquakes. And he had heard the sounds of war as well.

But this was Idaho. There were no earthquakes here. No wars either. This was a land of peace and plenty. But Francisco knew the sound of trouble when he heard it.

There was more rumbling, louder and closer.

Francisco's gaze darted around the bank, looking for a safe spot. The perfect place would have been the vaults. But of course the huge metal doors were locked. Perhaps behind the counter –

Before he could move, the plate glass front of the bank exploded. Instinctively Francisco shut his eyes against the splinters showering inward. He felt a stinging on his cheek. Then there was silence.

Slowly he let out his breath. He opened his eyes and touched his cheek. His fingertip gleamed with blood. But other than that scratch, he was untouched. He looked at his nephew. Roberto was safe, though shaking like a leaf. Francisco realized he was shaking too. He crossed himself.

He heard the rumbling again. It was more distant now. It was going away.

Cautiously Francisco led the way over the shards of glass glittering on the marble floor. He and Roberto reached the gaping hole that had been the window. They looked out.

'Mother of God. This cannot be happening,' Francisco said.

But it was. They saw a car down the street crumpling as if hit by a gigantic sledgehammer. They saw a wooden newsstand splintering into matchsticks.

But they could not see what did it.

The force that smashed into the bank, the car, the newsstand, was invisible.

Francisco and Roberto looked at each other. Each knew what the other was thinking.

Maybe they had not been so smart to come to Idaho after all. Back at home at least they knew where danger came from. Here they were suddenly strangers – and afraid.

Ray Hines was no stranger to Idaho. He had been born and raised there. He had helped build highways across the state's vast highland plains and through its rugged mountains. Tonight he was enjoying his job. The construction company was in a hurry to finish a new four-lane highway to Fairfield. That meant overtime pay.

Hines was taking a coffee break with his fellow workers when he heard the rumbling.

He peered down the unfinished highway.

'What the devil?' he said, his mouth dropping open.

One lane of the road was lined with barricades to keep off traffic. The barricades were heavy wood, but now they were being flipped aside as if they were cardboard. One by one they tumbled over.

Something big and strong was coming down the pike.

Hines would have said a twister, but he couldn't feel a breath of wind.

He couldn't see a thing either.

Not even when it hit him – and sent him flying through the air.

Out of the corner of his eye, Hines saw his Thermos in the air as well, spraying coffee.

That was the last thing he saw.

His body hit the last stretch of highway he had laid down. The last he ever would lay down.

Ray Hines's coffee break was going to last forever.

Thirty miles down the highway, Wesley Brewer was enjoying the newly paved surface. If all roads were like this, driving his big tractor-trailer would be a cinch. Especially when he didn't have a load. He could really let her go all out. As far as Brewer was concerned, it beat flying.

It had been a long night's ride, though. Brewer yawned as he turned on his CB radio.

'This is Wesley Brewer out on Route Seven,' he said. 'Looking like an eight o'clock estimated arrival time on that cargo pickup.'

He rubbed sleep out of his eyes as he waited for an answer.

Suddenly his eyes bulged.

Suddenly sleep was a million miles away.

Dead ahead, only a few hundred feet away, was a sight Brewer had seen before only on a circus poster.

A huge elephant.

This elephant wasn't on a poster.

It was charging up the highway straight at him.

Brewer slammed on the brakes. He prayed they would hold.

The tractor-trailer skidded. Started to spin out of control. Then came to a stop.

The elephant stopped too.

The huge machine and the huge animal faced each other, inches apart.

Brewer looked into the elephant's glinting eyes. He saw the menacing points of its long ivory tusks. He watched its gray trunk slap against his windshield.

Dimly he heard a voice on his CB. 'Give me that ETA again. Brewer? Brewer, you copy?'

Brewer didn't think of answering. His hands were white-knuckled on the steering wheel. They relaxed when he saw the elephant turn. It lumbered away, tail swishing, toward the blazing rim of the rising sun. Then, as if hit by an electric prod, it broke into a run. Huge as it was, it moved startlingly fast.

Brewer watched it disappear around a bend in the road. He waited for the pounding of his heart to slow. Then he said over his CB, 'I know you're not going to believe this, but –'

The sun was clear of the horizon when the police caught up with the elephant. It was easy. There was no chase.

A motorist had spotted it and reported it.

It was still lying on the highway in the same spot when the two squad cars arrived, lights blinking, sirens wailing. Other cars were already there. Men, women, and children stared at the fallen beast.

'Keep back!' a cop told the crowd. 'It's still alive and dangerous.'

The elephant *was* still alive. Barely.

Its flanks heaved painfully. Its trunk slapped the road feebly. It strained to rise to its feet.

Its effort seemed to exhaust it. It slumped back. It lay quivering a moment. Then it was still.

'Mommy, Mommy, it gone to sleep?' a little boy asked.

The mother bit her lip as the boy looked up at her. 'Yes, dear, it's gone to sleep,' she assured him.

The little boy's sister was old enough to take a step closer to the fallen elephant.

She was old enough to take a long look at it.

She was old enough to burst into tears at what she saw.

CHAPTER
TWO

The media had fun with the story.

A radio newsman joked, 'This elephant had his trunk packed but nowhere to go.'

A TV anchor wisecracked, 'Home, home on the range, where the deer and the elephants play.'

A paper sold in supermarkets ran this headline, MOVE OVER, DUMBO! REAL LIFE FLYING ELEPHANT MAKES A CRASH LANDING!

After a quick look, the local police tried to forget it too. The trail of destruction, the elephant on the loose – none of it made any sense. The cops had plenty of cases that did. They had no time to waste on a headache like this. They buried it in their files. Out of sight, out of mind.

But the case went into another set of files as well.

The X-files.

They were files kept in a top-secret room at FBI Headquarters in Washington, DC. They held reports of strange cases received from all over the country. Cases that no one could explain. Cases that even the FBI would have been happy to forget.

Except for a couple of agents who would not let those cases rest.

'When's the next flight to Idaho?' Fox Mulder asked Dana Scully.

'There's a red-eye flight to Boise at three A.M.,' she told him. 'We can rent a car there to drive to Fairfield.'

'Let's get packed, then,' he said.

'I already am,' Scully answered. 'I knew wild elephants couldn't keep you away.'

Mulder gave Scully a grin. She gave him back a half smile. She had come a long way since she'd started working with him.

At first she'd thought he was a little crazy, just as his bosses at the Bureau did.

But no longer.

She had moved a lot closer to Mulder's point of view. She had learned that crazy things could happen in the world.

And that it was really crazy to pretend that they didn't.

'Now I know where my taxes go,' Stan Weitz, the Camus County sheriff, told Mulder and Scully the next day as they sat with him in his office. 'Flying all this way from Washington on a wild-goose chase. Wild-elephant chase, anyway.'

Mulder waited patiently for the sheriff to stop chuckling at his own joke. He wondered how many elephant jokes he would hear before this case was over. Too many, for sure.

He looked at his watch. 'Well, no sense wasting government time,' he said. 'Let's get to work.'

'Sure,' the sheriff said. 'I expect you want to read our official report. I'll fish it out of the files.'

'We've already read it,' Mulder said. 'On the plane.'

'We got it out of our files,' Scully explained. 'It was forwarded to Bureau Headquarters. Part of a computerized system we've set up in police departments all over the country. It lets us react immediately to – emergencies.'

'Oh yeah, I forgot,' the sheriff said. 'I heard something about that from my staff techies. I gotta say, I don't hold much with all these new gadgets. Give me old-fashioned police work. Shoe leather beats computer chips every time.'

'I agree,' Mulder said. 'Can you take us to where the trouble started?'

'Can do,' the sheriff said. 'But you won't find out anything more than we did. Which was nothing.'

They left the Fairfield police station and got into the sheriff's squad car. The bank was a five-minute drive away. Its plate glass front still had not been repaired. Local citizens stood gawking at the gaping hole. Fairfield wasn't a town where strange things happened. A broken streetlight would have been big news here.

Two Latinos in janitors' clothes stood in front of the building. One was middle-aged, the other in his early twenties. Both looked scared.

'I told these two to show up here when you faxed me,' the sheriff said. 'I figured you'd want to see them. They were eyewitnesses to the . . .' the sheriff said. He paused, looking for the right word. 'To the whatever-it-was' was the best he could come up with.

'I think you should question them,' Mulder told Scully. 'I'll check out the inside of the bank.'

'Right,' said Scully.

But before she began, she said to the sheriff, 'Thanks a lot. We can take over from here. I'm sure you have other things to do.'

'Sure do,' the sheriff agreed. 'Well, I wish you folks luck. You'll need it.'

He got into his squad car and drove off.

Scully turned toward the two janitors. As she had hoped, they looked more relaxed now that the sheriff was gone. Police garb definitely put them on edge.

'What are your names?' she asked them.

'Francisco García, and this is my nephew Roberto,' the older man answered. 'Believe me, miss, we had nothing to do with the broken glass. We are good, careful workers. We never do anything wrong. We obey all the laws. We try always to be good Americans. We want to be citizens someday.'

'Please, don't worry. You have nothing to fear from us,' Scully assured him. 'We simply want to know what you saw the night the glass window exploded.'

'We saw nothing,' Francisco said.

'Nothing,' Roberto agreed.

'No one outside?' asked Scully.

'No,' Roberto insisted. 'I went to look. But I saw nothing.'

'Did you hear anything?' asked Scully.

'A noise. Yes,' Francisco said.

'Like thunder it was,' Roberto added. 'First it was loud, then it was fainter.'

'Anything else?' Scully said, jotting down their remarks. Both men shook their heads.

Scully waited to see if they'd remember anything more. They didn't.

'Thank you,' she told them. 'Your help is appreciated.'

'You are police too?' Francisco asked.

'Yes,' Scully had to admit. 'From the federal government. FBI.'

'Nothing will happen to us, please?' Francisco said.

'Nothing will happen to you,' Scully told him.

'Thank you, miss, thank you,' Francisco said.

The two men had learned back in El Salvador that the less you had to do with the law, the better. Now they moved away as fast as they could without seeming to run.

Meanwhile, Mulder had returned. 'Nothing inside except heaps of broken glass,' he said. 'What did the janitors say?'

'They claim they saw nothing,' Scully said. 'They just heard a loud noise that they couldn't identify. I have a sense that they're telling the truth.'

'They probably are,' Mulder said. 'The TV security cameras in the bank don't show anything either. Just a giant explosion of glass flying inward. As if from some kind of shock wave outside.'

'Which leaves us with nothing to go on,' Scully said, shaking her head.

'So what else is new, partner?' Mulder said. 'We're in X-files land. Starting with a blank slate comes with the territory. The fun is filling the blanks in.'

'Sure,' said Scully. 'Like working out a crossword puzzle in a language you don't understand.'

'A language you have to learn to understand,' Mulder told her, 'if you want to get a message you can't afford to miss.'

CHAPTER
THREE

Scully glanced at her notes. 'The police report said the trail of damage goes up this street,' she said.

'Let's follow it,' replied Mulder.

Before they started walking, Scully took one more look at the gaping hole in the glass.

'The noise the janitors described – it could have been a sonic boom,' she suggested.

'Yeah, well, no sonic boom did that,' said Mulder, pointing down the street to a car parked at a weird angle. Its trunk was bashed in. So was part of its side. Beyond the car, a metal street sign was twisted as if it were made of Silly Putty. 'Or that either,' he added.

'Or this.' As they walked past it, Mulder indicated a newsstand that had been smashed to splinters.

'Right. Cross off the sonic boom theory,' Scully agreed.

'Then there's this photo,' he said. He handed Scully a copy of a photo that had been faxed to FBI Headquarters along with the police report.

Scully glanced at it to refresh her memory. It was not a pretty picture. A corpse never was.

'This man had his spine broken like a toothpick,' Mulder reminded her. 'And there was a bruise on his body that was roughly the size and shape of an elephant's foot. The other men working on the road said they felt the ground shake. Then they caught the faint whiff of an animal odor on the wind.'

'I know what you're thinking, Mulder,' Scully said. 'That elephant they found dead did it all.' She shook her head. 'I don't buy it. It defies logic. Someone would have seen it.'

'If someone saw it, we wouldn't be here, Scully,' said Mulder.

He gave her a smile. Scully didn't smile back. She had her own ideas. And she used her own eyes.

She moved to check out the bashed car again. The twisted street sign. The totaled newsstand.

Mulder followed her as she made the rounds. 'A vehicle would have left evidence of a collision,' he told her. 'There would be bits of paint. Or metallic scratches. I see no sign of either. Do you?'

Scully examined the twisted sign. She shook her head.

'I'd allow there's the outside chance of a tornado,' Mulder went on. 'Even though it's not tornado season. I'd even allow there's a chance that a black hole in space might have passed over the area. But . . .'

He paused and waited until Scully asked, 'But what, Mulder?'

'But if I was a betting man, I'd say it was –' Mulder began.

'An invisible elephant?'

'You said it – I didn't,' said Mulder.

'You didn't have to,' said Scully. 'I know the way your mind works.'

'Do you know I once saw the magician David Copperfield make the Statue of Liberty disappear?' said Mulder. 'An elephant would be child's play for someone with the right tools.'

'Sure, Mulder,' said Scully. 'Some mad magician came to Fairfield with smoke and mirrors.'

'Maybe not a magician,' said Mulder. 'And maybe not smoke and mirrors. But someone, something, with some kind of –'

He got no further.

A large truck pulled up to the curb near them.

Painted on the side of the truck were the silhouette of a leaping tiger and the words FAIRFIELD ZOO.

The driver's door opened and a man in a green zoo attendant's uniform got out. His hair was graying and thinning, and his stomach hung over his belt. But there were strength and swagger in his stride as he came over to the two agents.

'Agent Mulder?' he asked.

'Yes,' Mulder said.

'I'm Ed Meecham, Fairfield Zoo. I got your fax to meet you. I checked with the sheriff and he told me you'd be here. Sorry if I'm a little late, but we had some trouble transporting Ganesha's body this morning.'

'This is Agent Scully,' Mulder said. Meecham nodded, as if he was noticing her for the first time. Funny how some people simply couldn't see a woman as an FBI agent, Mulder thought. Even one as sharp-looking as Scully. They had to keep being told.

'Hi,' Meecham said, and started to turn back to Mulder.

Before he could, Scully asked, 'Has it been determined what he died of?'

'She,' Meecham told Scully brusquely. 'Ganesha was a twelve-year-old Indian female. Far as I can see, she ran herself into the ground. Died of total exhaustion.'

'How did she escape?' Scully asked.

Meecham wrinkled his brows. 'Well, I gotta say it's a mystery. When I got the call that she was on the highway,

I thought I'd find her cage open or something. But it was locked tight. Just like I left it the day before at closing time.'

'Any idea how an elephant could have escaped a locked zoo cage?' Mulder asked.

'No sir,' Meecham said. 'No sign of tampering either.'

Mulder and Scully traded looks.

Meanwhile, Meecham scratched his head at the damage in the street.

'What a mess,' he said. 'You'd think they'd clean it up.'

'We asked the police to let us see it before any cleanup,' Mulder explained.

'Well, I guess you know your job,' Meecham said. 'Me, animals are mine. Been at the zoo for thirty years.'

'You know elephants, then?' said Mulder.

'I know all the critters in the zoo,' said Meecham. 'Like I said, that's my job.'

'Then maybe you can give me some information,' said Mulder.

'If it has to do with the zoo,' Meecham said.

'I've read about something called the elephant rebellion,' said Mulder. 'There have been reports from zoos across the country. A growing number of cases of elephants behaving violently. Turning on their keepers. Wrecking their pens. Was Ganesha ever a problem?'

Meecham's face stiffened. 'Elephants are very big, very willful animals,' he said.

Mulder waited for him to go on, but Meecham stayed silent.

'So there *were* problems?' Mulder probed.

Meecham's mouth tightened. 'I'm not the one to ask,' he said edgily. 'The person you want to talk to about that is Willa Ambrose.'

'Ambrose?' said Scully, making a note in her book. 'Who is she? Someone at the zoo?'

'Yeah,' Meecham said. He looked as if he had a bad taste in his mouth. 'She's what you call a naturalist. The Zoo Board of Supervisors hired her last year.'

'And her job?' asked Scully.

'She's supposed to make the zoo up-to-date,' said Meecham. 'You know, all the new stuff they're coming up with nowadays. She's supposed to be in charge now. Not that she ever worked in a zoo before. Not that she knows much about animals outside of books and maybe videos.'

'But you do,' said Mulder.

'I sure do,' Meecham agreed.

'Elephants included?' Mulder said.

'Elephants included,' Meecham affirmed.

'Then let me ask you this,' Mulder said. 'The damage here on the street. Is it something you think could have been done by an escaped elephant?'

'My honest opinion?' said Meecham. 'Yes.'

'You are sure of that?' Mulder said.

'Yes,' Meecham repeated.

'Thank you,' Mulder said, giving Scully a triumphant glance.

Meecham looked at his watch. 'If you don't want me for anything else, I got to be heading back to the job,' he said. 'Feeding time.'

'Thanks a lot for your cooperation,' Mulder said. 'We may have more questions later. You know, questions that Ms Ambrose may not be able to help us with.'

'Feel free,' Meecham said. 'Any time.'

Mulder waited until Meecham had gotten into his truck and driven off. Then he got down on his hands and knees and started rummaging through the papers littering the ground near the shattered newsstand.

'What are you looking for, Mulder?' asked Scully, bracing herself for the answer.

'A local paper,' said Mulder, not looking up. 'I want to see if David Copperfield's appearing in town.'

CHAPTER
FOUR

'Not much of a crowd here today,' Scully remarked, looking around her. She and Mulder had decided it was time to pay the zoo a visit.

'It's a weekday,' Mulder said. 'There's probably a better turnout on weekends.'

'There should be,' Scully said. 'It looks like a nice place. Better than a lot of zoos I've seen. Some of them, ugh. You really feel sorry for the animals.'

'Yeah,' said Mulder. 'You want to put the keepers in the cages.'

The Fairfield Zoo did look like a pleasant place. The animals' cages were big and clean. The outside enclosures had trees, rock formations, and streams of running water that imitated natural surroundings. The animals seemed healthy and well fed. As Mulder and Scully went along winding pathways and in and out of buildings, hunting an attendant, they saw lions and panthers, pythons and jackals, rhino and llamas, flamingos and seals.

Scully paused by an outdoor enclosure. She looked through the bars at a huge Bengal tiger. It was pacing back and forth, its muscles rippling. When it saw Scully, it opened its jaws and roared. Then, growling, it resumed its pacing.

'It's beautiful,' Scully said. 'It reminds me of that poem by William Blake.

> *Tiger! Tiger! burning bright*
> *In the forests of the night.'*

'It is beautiful,' agreed Mulder. He looked at the tiger's cage. 'And a little sad.'

'Maybe that's why I always feel funny at a zoo,' said Scully. 'Like something's wrong. The balance seems off. Take the way that tiger moves, back and forth, back and forth. And the way it seems to be looking off into the distance when it stops. It's like that with all the animals. They're made to have space around them, and it isn't here.'

'A lot of people feel that way,' said Mulder. 'There's quite a protest movement against the whole idea of zoos.'

The tiger turned toward them and roared again. Its wicked-looking teeth gleamed.

'Still, there's something to be said for iron bars,' said Scully, stepping back from the fence.

At that moment Mulder spotted an attendant, an elderly man in a green uniform.

'Hi,' said Mulder. 'We've been looking for someone to tell us where to find Willa Ambrose. Not too many attendants working today.'

The man shook his head. 'Not too many working any day. Been a lot of cutbacks here. Money troubles. Don't know how long my job is safe, and I been here thirty years.'

Then he remembered what the visitors wanted to know. 'Willa Ambrose. I saw her a while ago near the bird houses, down past the polar bears. You might try looking there.'

'Thanks,' Mulder said.

'Seems the human animals here have their own troubles,' he remarked as he and Scully headed off.

'Right,' said Scully. 'They're feeling squeezed too.'

They passed an enclosure where polar bears splashed in a shallow pool to escape the heat of the sun, and came to a building marked AVIARY.

The bird house was spacious and high-ceilinged, filled with tropical plants and rock ponds. Bright-plumaged birds of every color filled the air with their cries.

There was only one person inside – a woman in her thirties, tall and slender, dressed in a crisp white shirt and faded jeans. She carried an armload of books and notebooks. But they seemed forgotten as she stood gazing fondly at the feathered creatures.

'Ms Ambrose?' Scully asked.

'Yes, I'm Willa Ambrose,' she answered, smiling politely.

'I'm Agent Dana Scully,' Scully said. 'This is Agent Mulder. We're with the FBI.'

Willa's smile vanished. So did the warmth in her voice. 'Yes?' she said.

'May we ask you a few questions?' Scully said.

'Is this about Ganesha?' Willa wanted to know.

'Yes,' Mulder said. 'We spoke to a Mr Meecham. He works here, I believe.'

'My chief of operations,' Willa said.

'In any case, he seemed reluctant to answer some of our questions,' Mulder said. 'He told us to see you.'

'He did?' Willa raised her eyebrows slightly. But she seemed pleased by the news. Her face and her voice thawed. 'I'm sorry if I was abrupt. You took me by surprise. How can I be of help?'

'An employee of the Federal Highway Department was fatally injured recently,' Scully said. 'It seems possible that an escaped elephant from your zoo was involved in his death.'

Willa's smile vanished again. 'It was my understanding that eyewitnesses could not say how the man was killed,' she said coldly.

Scully glanced at Mulder. Her look told him that he could carry the ball from here on in. The killer elephant idea was his idea, not hers. She couldn't blame Willa Ambrose for rejecting a notion that seemed not only off the track but off the wall.

Mulder picked up the questioning without missing a beat. 'Actually, what we're trying to find out is how Ganesha escaped.'

'What did Ed Meecham say?' Willa asked.

'He said the cage was locked, the same way he left it,' Mulder said.

Willa shrugged. 'What more can I tell you?'

'A man was trampled to death,' Mulder said. 'Trampled to death by a very large animal. An elephant from your zoo was found forty-three miles from here. No one's blaming anybody. We're just trying to find out the facts leading up to the incident.'

'Okay,' said Willa. 'I guess you guys are just doing your job. Why don't I show you Ganesha's pen? It'll tell you more than anything I can say.'

The elephant pen was a short walk away. It was surrounded by a high fence of iron bars on three sides, and at the rear by a concrete wall. The gate in the fence was secured by a heavy lock.

'This is where Ganesha stayed when she wasn't in her habitat,' Willa said.

'And where is her habitat?' asked Mulder.

'Through those big steel doors in the back of the pen,' Willa said. 'She'd be there during the day for the public to see. Then at night she'd be taken back to this side. The habitat is quite nice, actually. Care to take a look at it?'

'No, thanks,' Mulder said. 'The holding pen is what interests me at the moment. This is where she escaped from, right?'

'Seems so,' Willa said.

'Who has the key to the lock?' asked Mulder.

'Only me and Ed Meecham,' said Willa.

Then she noticed that Scully was looking up at the high iron fence.

'Elephants aren't very good jumpers, if that's what you're thinking,' Willa told her.

'Actually, I was wondering why you had such a small pen for such a large animal,' Scully said.

Willa did not look happy as she answered the question. 'This zoo was built in the 1940s. Many pens and habitats are much too confining. I was hired to help redesign the facility. I plan to expand the animals' living spaces, make them more humane. But these things take time.'

Mulder pointed to two heavy chains coming out of the ground. 'What are they for?' he asked.

Willa looked even more uncomfortable. 'Those are tie-downs,' she said. 'They're used to restrict an animal's movements.'

'They were used on Ganesha?' asked Scully.

'No,' said Willa firmly. 'I stopped their use when I came to work here.'

'Stopped their use by whom?' asked Mulder.

Willa's face hardened. 'By Ed Meecham,' she said, an edge in her voice. 'He belongs to a different generation of zookeepers. Many of his practices are . . . not enlightened.'

'How is your relationship with Mr Meecham?' asked Mulder.

Willa gave a tight smile. 'I'm his boss and I'm a woman,'

she said. 'Ed doesn't like that combination much. He also doesn't like the way I run the zoo. But that's his problem.'

'Would he be angry enough to commit an act of sabotage?' asked Scully. 'Would he be angry enough to let an elephant out of its cage?'

There was a silence as Willa pondered the question.

From a distance came the sound of the tiger roaring again.

CHAPTER
FIVE

Finally Willa shook her head. 'I can't see Ed Meecham doing something like that,' she said. 'Not that he likes me much. Or that he likes the idea of the kind of zoo I want. But he does like his job. And this zoo is in trouble – money trouble. The city is cutting back funding, and we need private contributions to keep going. Any kind of scandal, and the contributions would stop. This place would go down the drain.'

'Have you and Meecham talked about the elephant's escape?' asked Mulder. 'How it could have happened? What the elephant might have done outside before she died?'

'No,' Willa said. 'Ed and I aren't exactly buddies. We're barely on speaking terms. Besides, Ed's pretty busy now. He has his hands full just dealing with the WAO.'

'The WAO?' said Scully.

'The Wild Again Organization,' Mulder said.

Scully smiled to herself. She could count on Mulder for information like that. There wasn't a far-out group in the country, in the world, maybe in the universe, that Mulder didn't know about.

'Who are they?' she asked him.

'They're a group that believes any captive animal is a crime against nature,' Mulder told her. 'They also believe that they can break any human laws to stop this crime.'

'They're going to have a field day with Ganesha,' said Willa grimly. 'In fact, they've already started. One of their leaders has set up shop out where that highway worker died. He's handing out leaflets to every driver who slows down to rubberneck.'

'Who is he?' asked Mulder.

'A guy named Kyle Lang,' said Willa.

Scully heard an odd note in Willa's voice when she said the name – a kind of wavering.

'You know him?' Scully asked.

Willa's mouth tightened. 'We . . .' She paused, then went on, 'We've had a few run-ins.'

'What sort of a person is he?' Scully asked.

'He's very committed,' Willa said. 'He sees things in terms of black and white. No shades of gray. You're either on his side or you're his enemy. He . . .' She paused again. 'But you'll find out for yourself when you interview him – as I'm sure you will.'

In the distance the tiger roared again.

'I'd better see if there's any trouble,' Willa said. 'Sometimes people get their kicks teasing the big cats. I'm trying to educate visitors not to be cruel, but it's tough.' She sighed, then shrugged. 'Gotta keep trying. You have to do the best you can. This world may not be perfect, but it's the only one we've got.'

Mulder and Scully watched her walk off in the direction of the tiger enclosure.

'She seems dedicated to her job,' Scully remarked. 'She's facing tough odds, though. Budget cuts. An outdated facility. Angry old-timers. And this fellow Kyle Lang. I got the feeling he bothered her more than all the rest. Wonder why.'

'Let's take Ms Ambrose's advice,' Mulder said. 'Go meet

Mr Lang. If nothing else, his flyers should be interesting.'

'Let's contact Washington first. See if there's a file on him,' Scully said. 'I have an idea there's something about him Willa wasn't telling us.'

'Sure,' said Mulder. 'Though facts in the files and facts in the flesh can be very different things.'

Kyle Lang stood with leaflets in his hand near the unfinished highway lane where Ray Hines had died.

Tall and lean, flannel-shirted and blue-jeaned, Kyle walked with the stride of a man at ease in his body and at home on the earth. He smiled at Scully and Mulder as they got out of their car, and extended a leaflet.

'Thanks. We'll read it later,' Mulder said, putting it in his jacket pocket. 'Right now we'd like to talk to you. And perhaps your friend over there.'

Mulder indicated a young redheaded man leaning against the door of a beat-up truck parked up the highway. He looked barely out of his teens. He also looked permanently angry. There was a scowl on his face and a hostile look in his eyes.

'And you are?' asked Kyle.

'FBI Agent Fox Mulder and my partner, Agent Dana Scully,' Mulder said.

Mulder half expected Kyle to react to the information. Most people froze at least a second when they heard 'FBI.' But Kyle was unfazed. If anything, he looked slightly amused.

'Come to investigate the crime scene?' he asked. 'You're in the wrong place. I suggest you try the zoo.'

'We've already been there,' said Mulder.

'Then you've seen the cage where Ganesha was kept,' said Kyle. 'Fifty feet by fifty feet. For an elephant.'

'You consider that inhumane?' Scully asked.

'I consider it criminal,' Kyle answered, all trace of

amusement gone. 'It would be like forcing you or me to live in a pickle barrel.'

'Speaking of criminal actions,' Scully said, 'according to FBI files, you've been arrested over a dozen times. For activities involving the kidnapping of zoo and circus animals.'

'The WAO sees it as liberation,' Kyle said calmly.

'Were you involved in the liberation of Ganesha?' Scully asked.

'That would make me an accessory to murder, wouldn't it?' Kyle said.

There was a moment of silence.

Then Kyle said, 'Sorry, G-people. I'm not confessing anything. Endangering an animal in any way is against everything the WAO believes in. And elephants are especially precious forms of life.'

'Really?' said Mulder, in a deliberately harsh tone. 'I wouldn't have thought it. They've got such thick hides.'

Scully knew what Mulder was doing. He was needling Kyle, trying to get under his skin. It was an excellent way to get a suspect to talk.

Scully joined in. 'I always thought they were just big dumb brutes with a yen for peanuts,' she said.

But Kyle didn't seem to get angry. He seemed interested only in setting them straight. 'You couldn't be more wrong,' he told them. 'Elephants are incredibly gentle, spiritual, intelligent creatures. Their behavior and their rituals are a link to a past that no humans have ever witnessed. Do you know that they actually bury their dead? That they have graveyards hundreds and hundreds of years old? That they instinctively know where the bones of their ancient ancestors lie? And that we humans have no idea how?'

'You know a lot about elephants,' said Mulder, smiling.

'I wish I knew more about them,' Kyle said. 'About them

and all animals. The more you know, the more you treasure them.'

'But you must have some idea of the facts about Ganesha's escape,' Mulder asked. 'Where was she going? What was she running from?'

'You really want to know?' said Kyle.

'That's what we've come all this way for,' Mulder said.

'Then come along with me,' said Kyle. 'I'll do better than tell you. I'll show you.'

CHAPTER
SIX

'**F**ollow our truck,' said Kyle. 'It's a half hour's drive.'

'Where are you taking us?' asked Scully.

'To a video show,' Kyle told them. 'Educational TV.'

He went to his truck and spoke briefly to the redheaded young man. The two climbed into the truck's cab and drove off toward Fairfield.

Scully and Mulder followed, Scully driving. Halfway to town, she switched on the headlights. The sun was setting.

It was dark when they reached town and the run-down neighborhood where the truck parked. Scully parked behind it and she and Mulder got out.

Kyle and his friend were waiting for them in front of a ramshackle two-story building. On the front of the building hung a WAO shingle. Kyle unlocked the front door and they all went inside.

'Welcome to our office,' said Kyle. 'As you can see, our organization isn't exactly well funded.'

The second-floor office was filled with beat-up furniture, several aging computers, an old printer, a very old copying machine, and stacks of books, papers, posters, and leaflets. In the corner was a battered TV, topped with an equally battered VCR.

'Sit down and enjoy the show,' Kyle said, pushing a video

into the VCR. 'I'll supply the commentary. Maybe Red here will add a few remarks. Probably not, though. Red believes in action, not words.'

As Mulder and Scully sat down, Kyle started the video.

An elephant appeared on the screen. One of its tusks was chained close to the ground, forcing it to its knees. Its great head and trunk lay twisted sideways against the ground. Two trainers were prodding it from behind with long poles.

'The tie-down chain is called a martingale,' said Kyle. 'It's one of Ed Meecham's favorite devices. This is how he treats these majestic animals. Some animal lover. All he loves is his power over them.'

Kyle froze the frame. Then he said, 'You wanted to know what Ganesha was running from? Take a good long look. You wanted to know what she was looking for? Look in the dictionary. The word you want is *freedom*.'

'This treatment is still going on?' Mulder asked.

'Meecham is a barbarian,' Kyle said. 'He's been torturing animals at the Fairfield Zoo for years. We're sure he's still at it.'

'So you have proof?' Scully asked, turning to look at him.

Instead she met Red's eyes. They were filled with ice-cold hate. She shivered. She didn't have to hear Red say a word to know that he would do anything for his cause. His were the eyes of a true believer. A fanatic.

'We'll get our proof, don't worry,' Kyle said.

'Maybe not,' Mulder told him. 'We've spoken to Willa Ambrose. She says she's put a stop to a lot of Meecham's old practices.'

'Willa Ambrose?' Kyle sneered. 'She's too busy with other things to keep tabs on Meecham.'

'With what other things?' Scully asked.

'With a lawsuit she's fighting,' Kyle said.

'Against whom?' asked Mulder.

'Against the government of Malawi in Africa,' said Kyle.

'What are they fighting over?' asked Scully.

'Sophie,' said Kyle.

'Sophie?' asked Scully.

'Sophie is a lowland gorilla,' Kyle explained. 'Willa rescued her from a North African customs house ten years ago. Smugglers were shipping her to a zoo in Europe. She was nearly dead from bad handling. Willa nursed her back to health and raised her like a child. But now the people in Malawi have tracked her down and want her back. They claim they're starting a nature preserve and want to give Sophie a home. What they really mean is they want a tourist attraction. Tough luck for Willa. She loves that animal.' But there was no sympathy in Kyle's voice. Quite the opposite.

'Then you think Malawi will win the case?' Mulder asked.

Kyle shrugged. 'What does it matter? Either way, it's a perfect example of what humans do to animals. We turn them into objects for our own selfish pleasure.'

'I thought you said Willa rescued this gorilla,' said Scully.

Kyle snorted. 'Rescued her so that Sophie could spend a life behind bars. Willa's duty was to return the gorilla to the wild. Because all animals should run free.'

Scully was getting a little tired of Kyle Lang. Supporting a good cause was one thing. But being holier than thou was another. She said with an edge in her voice, 'They should run free even if it means trampling a man to death?'

She made sure not to look at Mulder when she suggested Ganesha was the killer. She did not want to see the flicker of amusement in his eyes. She knew it too well. Sometimes she wished she didn't wind up agreeing with his theories so often.

'Maybe the guy should have gotten out of the way,' said Kyle, still with his irritating assurance.

'I'm sure he would have if he'd seen it coming,' said Mulder quietly, almost to himself. Then he got to his feet. 'Thank you for your time, Mr Lang. We'll be getting back to you.'

Outside the building, Mulder said to his partner, 'We're getting warm. Whatever's going on, it's all happening at the zoo, Scully.'

'And now we know who's behind it,' Scully said.

'Mr Lang and his WAO?' said Mulder. 'You think they busted the elephant out?'

Scully heard the amusement in Mulder's voice. She answered with a flush of annoyance, 'You heard what Kyle Lang said. All animals should run free. I'm talking facts that you can't deny.'

'Then how do you explain some other facts?' Mulder inquired. 'The eyewitness accounts? And the videotapes from the bank security camera? How do you explain why nobody actually saw the elephant until it was miles from the zoo?'

Scully did a fast mental run-through of the police report she had read. Then she said, 'The lights at the road construction site were mercury vapor, ten thousand candlepower. In other words, half blinding. Certainly strong enough to limit a man's ability to adjust his vision to the dark. And the bank security cameras were poor quality. A gray elephant may not have registered as an image on the tape. Especially in the dim light in front of the building.'

Mulder looked unconvinced.

'I don't know, Scully,' he said. 'Those guys may talk a good game. But that's what I think their game is. A lot of talk.'

'Those guys are dedicated to just this kind of trouble making,' Scully insisted. 'You can't tell me that Kyle Lang isn't into the movement heart and soul. And did you take a good look at that kid Red? He looked like he'd run over his own mother to save a chipmunk. Not to mention the fact that they have some pretty high-tech gear, despite the crying about poverty. Did you spot that night-vision camera lying on a shelf?'

'Speaking of spying at night,' said Mulder, glancing upward.

Scully followed his gaze. Looking down at them from the lighted second-floor window were Kyle and Red. Their mouths were hard and their eyes were narrowed. Their belief in gentleness and kindness clearly did not extend to the FBI.

Scully and Mulder walked down the street and around a corner.

As soon as they were safely out of sight, Scully stopped and said, 'I wouldn't be surprised if they tried to keep the ball rolling.'

'By doing what?' Mulder asked.

'Liberating another animal,' Scully said. 'Willa Ambrose said the zoo was having money troubles. The loss of another big exhibit might close it down for good. The WAO would dance in the streets.'

Mulder thought a moment, then nodded. 'You might be right,' he said. 'Why don't you keep an eye on the WAO? If there's any action, give me a ring on the cellular phone. I'll get mine out of the car.'

'But where are you going?' Scully asked.

'To talk to the animals,' Mulder told her.

CHAPTER
SEVEN

Their names were Frohike, Byers, and Langley. But they went by a different name. They called themselves the Lone Gunmen. They aimed to shoot down official lies and blow the lids off coverups. They refused to believe even their own government. They kept hunting for dark forces beneath whitewashes.

The media called them conspiracy freaks – paranoid oddballs who imagined evil everywhere.

Fox Mulder called them whenever he wanted information he couldn't get anywhere else.

Today he called them from a state-of-the-art telecommunication conference room in Fairfield. It was part of a big, gleaming new photocopying-and-faxing service center there. Even in Idaho, everything was getting up-to-date.

Outside the glass walls of the room, Mulder could see students and others feeding paper into copying machines. They showed no interest in him as he sat before a large video screen and punched out the number the Lone Gunmen had given him.

'Bingo,' Mulder said to himself as the images of two men blinked to life on the screen.

There was Frohike, with his buzz-cut hair, his surplus olive-drab fatigues, and his Marine Corps-issue watch. With him was Byers, looking as if he should be selling insurance, a clean-cut straight arrow with a white shirt and striped tie.

'Beam me up, Scotty,' Frohike wisecracked.

It was a typical beginning of a typical conversation with the Gunmen – weird, wired, and off the wall.

Mulder got into it without missing a beat. 'Did anyone ever tell you the camera loves you, Frohike?'

'Yeah,' Frohike said. 'The arresting officers at the last protest rally I was at.'

'So what's this costing the taxpayers, Mulder?' Byers cut in.

'A hundred and fifty dollars an hour,' Mulder told him.

'Ouch,' said Frohike. 'Almost as much as one of the president's haircuts. Not nearly as much as a NASA toilet seat, though. Still, I'll remember next time I do my tax return.'

'And when was the last time?' Mulder couldn't resist asking.

'Sorry, classified information,' Frohike said. 'Working for the Feds, I'm sure you know the term.'

'By the way, where's Langley?' Mulder asked. Langley was the third Gunman.

'Sitting here off camera,' Byers said. 'Seems he has an objection to having his image bounced off a satellite. Who knows who might be watching? Nothing personal, you understand.'

'Getting back to you, Mulder – what are you doing in Idaho?' asked Frohike.

'I'm on the job,' said Mulder. 'What do you guys know about the town of Fairfield?'

'Fairfield, Fairfield,' mused Byers. 'Let's see. No nerve gas plants. No missile silos. No underground nuclear waste dumps. But they do have a nice little zoo there. Lots of strange stuff going down. Animals escaping. Disappearing without a trace.'

'Any idea how or why?' Mulder asked.

'You're not far from the Mountain Home Air Base,' Frohike suggested, his eyes lighting up.

'Which means?' said Mulder.

'It's a major UFO hot spot,' Frohike said.

'Here's a weird fact, Mulder,' Byers put in. 'No animal at Fairfield Zoo has ever had any offspring.'

'Not a cub or a chick,' said Frohike.

'A real mystery,' Byers said. 'I know of someone who might give you answers.'

'Who?' asked Mulder.

'The woman who runs the zoo has a gorilla named Sophie,' said Byers. 'Sophie knows sign language. She has a vocabulary of over a thousand words. One thing about gorillas: Unlike humans, they always tell the truth.'

At that moment Mulder's cellular phone rang.

'Wait a sec, guys. Got a call,' he said to the two on the screen.

'If that's the lovely Agent Scully,' Frohike said, 'tell her I've been working out. I'm buff.'

'Right,' Mulder said. 'I'm sure she'll be happy to hear it. Now if you can just convince her you're not crazy.'

'That's your job, Mulder,' Frohike said.

'I'll put it on my list of things to do – but right now duty calls,' said Mulder. 'If you'll excuse me.' And he picked up the phone.

'Mulder, it's me,' Scully whispered into the phone. She was standing in the shadows on the street next to the zoo.

'What's up?' Mulder asked.

'I was right,' Scully told him. 'I've followed the kid from the WAO to the zoo.'

'Red?' said Mulder.

'Nobody else but,' Scully said. 'He's going over the fence right now.'

'I'm on my way, Scully,' Mulder said. 'Don't move.'

'No way,' Scully said. 'I'm going after him. I want to find out what he's doing.'

'But . . .' Mulder began. Then he realized it was useless to argue with Scully when it came to her doing her job. 'Be careful' was all he could say.

'See you,' said Scully, and hung up.

Moving fast, she headed for the fence that Red had gone over. Swiftly she scaled it. Working out in a gym might be a pain. But it paid off at times like this.

Inside the zoo grounds, she caught sight of the kid again. Wearing a backpack, he was going up the rock wall of an animal enclosure. Scully had to give him credit. He knew how to rock climb.

So did she. She let him get over, then went to the base of the rock wall. She tensed her muscles for the climb.

Then she froze as a hand brutally grabbed her shoulder from behind. It swung her around.

'What the devil do you think you're doing?' Ed Meecham demanded. He kept hold of her with one hand. In his other hand was a wicked-looking cattle prod. From the angry flush on his beefy face, she knew he'd be happy to use it on her.

'You've got a member of the WAO on the premises,' she told him.

Meecham's eyes narrowed. He tightened his grip on the cattle prod. He looked like a beast of prey scenting a kill.

'Come on,' he said to Scully. 'Let's get Willa Ambrose. I want her to see me nab this guy. Maybe then she'll learn

that they haven't repealed the law of the jungle yet. Sometimes you have to play rough.'

'Is she near here?' Scully asked.

'Just a few steps away,' said Meecham. 'She's in her play-
house, with her best friend, as usual.'

Meecham led Scully down a path to a windowless concrete
building. On the door, a large sign said in big letters, SICK
ANIMAL. AUTHORIZED PERSONNEL ONLY.

'"Sick animal,"' Meecham sneered. 'The only thing that's
sick is *her*.'

He opened the door without knocking and they went in.

The room inside was dimly lit by a single bulb. At one
end was a large barred cage with its door open. Near the cage
was a camp bed. Willa Ambrose was sitting on the bed. Beside
her was a large gorilla.

Ambrose was exchanging gestures in sign language with
the animal. Both of them stopped when they saw Meecham
and Scully.

'It's okay, Sophie,' Willa said soothingly to the animal.
She turned to the intruders. 'Meecham, I've told you never
to come in here unless there's an emergency.'

'Yeah,' Meecham said with a note of triumph. 'Well, there
is an –'

That was as far as he got.

A tiger's roar filled the night.

And as Sophie leaped off the bed and ran for her cage,
the whole zoo woke up.

Panthers and lions joined the roaring. Birds squawked and
screeched. Monkeys chattered, wolves howled, and hyenas
cackled hideously. The zoo sounded like an animal madhouse.

'We have to find out what's happening,' Willa said.
Swiftly she went out the door. Scully had to hand it to her.
Willa did not show a trace of fear.

Holding his cattle prod ready, Meecham followed.

Scully was at his heels.

She didn't know what they would run into. But she was sure of two things.

It had something to do with Red.

And it wouldn't be good.

CHAPTER
EIGHT

Red had loved animals as long as he could remember. As a child he had taken in stray cats and dogs and had fought with his mom to keep them. He had nursed injured birds back to health and joyfully watched them fly away. And he had been sick to his stomach when his dad had taken him on a deer hunt for the first and last time.

Anyone who hurt an animal filled him with rage. An animal in a cage was torture to him.

He and the WAO were made for each other. Maybe he hadn't been able to make his mom take in strays. Maybe he hadn't been able to stop his dad from gunning down deer. But he would help show the world that animals should be safe and free.

He was looking forward to his job tonight. Dropping down on the far side of the rock wall, he reached into his backpack. He pulled out a night-vision video camera. It was a lovely piece of equipment. It was worth more than the WAO could afford, but Red had a real talent for heisting. Not that he liked being a thief. But animal rights ranked way ahead of human laws in Red's book.

Inside the enclosure, he moved swiftly toward a cage near the far wall. He looked into it. The yellow eyes of the Bengal tiger stared, unblinking, back at him. The big animal stood tensely, watching the stranger's every move.

'Hi, tiger – snarl for the camera,' Red said softly. He pointed the camera and pressed the Start button. His video shoot tonight would capture the cruel sight of the magnificent cat in captivity. It would open the eyes of the world to the horror.

But suddenly the tiger and the cage started to swim before his eyes.

Waves of heat like those that rise from desert sands made his eyes water. The tiger and the cage were melting away.

Red blinked. He rubbed his eyes. He tried to focus them – and was blinded by white light exploding.

The light faded, and his vision returned.

His mouth dropped open.

The cage was empty.

'Where is the – ?' he started to ask himself.

A huge roar came from behind him.

A tiger's roar.

Red whirled around and saw – nothing.

It's gotten out somehow, he thought. *It's in the dark somewhere. It doesn't know I'm a friend. I gotta get out of here before –*

That was the last thing he thought before a smashing force knocked him off his feet.

It was like being hit by a car.

But he still could see nothing. Nothing except the red light of the video camera on the ground. The camera had flown from his hands, but it was still taping.

Stunned, he managed to sit up. Pain seared his chest. He looked down. His shirt had been slashed open. He put his hand into the opening. It came out covered with blood.

Then came another roar, even louder than the first.

Red staggered shakily to his feet. He started to stumble away.

Again he was batted down.

This time he didn't get up. Not on his own, at least.

He was picked up like a limp rag doll and tossed through the air.

His body landed and was picked up and tossed again.

And again.

And again.

Until playtime was over.

And Red lay still for good.

That was the way he was lying when Willa, Meecham, and Scully found him. The blood on his chest and face glistened in Meecham's flashlight beam.

'My God,' Willa said. 'Poor kid.'

'Guess he found out a tiger isn't a tabby cat,' muttered Meecham.

Scully shook her head. She had seen a lot of corpses in her career. This was one of the worst.

Out of the dark, Mulder's voice asked, 'What's happened?'

He reached them and looked down at Red.

'Sorry I'm late. I got here as fast as I could,' he said to Scully.

'Doubt you could have done anything,' said Scully. 'It all happened so fast. I thought I would give the kid enough rope to hang himself. But this wasn't what I had in mind.'

'Nothing to do now but call the police,' Willa said. 'And try to fend off the reporters.'

'Plus hunt down that cat on the loose,' said Meecham.

'There's one other thing to do as well,' said Scully. 'And I'm sure the police will agree.'

'What's that?' asked Mulder.

'Pay Mr Kyle Lang a visit.'

*   *   *

Scully had disliked Kyle Lang at first sight.

She liked him even less when she went to see him again.

She had told Mulder that she would take personal pleasure in grilling the WAO leader. Mulder told her to have fun. He would check out other leads.

Kyle kept a poker face when Scully and two sheriff's deputies showed up at his office. He sat at his desk, leaning back in his chair, as Scully questioned him. He looked a little bored.

'Why was Red at the zoo?' Scully demanded.

'Don't know what you're talking about,' Kyle said.

'You have no idea what he was doing,' Scully pressed him.

'Not the faintest,' Kyle said.

Scully showed him the video camera found at the scene of the slaying.

'What if I told you I saw this camera up there on your shelf yesterday?' she said.

'Guess I never noticed,' Kyle answered blandly.

Scully fought to keep the rising anger out of her voice. 'A tiger is missing. And a member of your organization is dead. For a man who claims to be so tenderhearted, you show a surprising lack of emotion.'

Kyle shrugged. 'If the tiger killed this person, it was a natural act.'

Scully glared at him. 'If I find evidence that Red was releasing animals under your orders,' she said, 'I'll make sure you go to prison and spend your life in a cage.'

Kyle met her gaze without flinching. Scully had seen cool customers before. But this guy was an iceberg.

She was trying to think of some way to melt his icy resistance when Mulder came into the office.

He was holding an evidence bag. He tapped it and motioned for Scully to follow him.

'Okay, guys, it's your turn,' she said to the deputies. 'See if you can make him squirm.'

She left the room with Mulder as one of the deputies took her place. 'That guy really gets my goat,' she told Mulder, her hands clenched into fists.

Mulder glanced at her fists. 'You okay, Scully?'

Scully took a deep breath and exhaled slowly. She let her hands go limp. 'Yeah,' she said.

'All calmed down?' Mulder asked.

'Yeah, yeah, I get your message,' said Scully impatiently. 'I'll be a good levelheaded agent. Now fill me in. They find the tiger?'

'No,' Mulder said. 'But I viewed the cassette from Red's camera. It was going when he got killed. And it shows he wasn't killed by a tiger.'

'*What?*' Scully exclaimed.

'Unless it's trick photography, the kid was killed by some kind of invisible phantom,' Mulder said calmly.

'But you saw the body, Mulder,' Scully protested. 'That kid was mauled to death. He had deep claw marks on his chest and back. It had to be the tiger.'

'I can't explain it, Scully,' Mulder said. 'But I think I know someone who can.'

'Who?' asked Scully.

'Can't you guess?' asked Mulder.

'No,' said Scully. 'Tell me.'

Mulder smiled. 'I don't want to spoil the surprise.'

CHAPTER
NINE

'I think we'll find her here,' Mulder said.

He and Scully stood before the zoo door marked SICK ANIMAL. AUTHORIZED PERSONNEL ONLY.

'So you figure Willa Ambrose has been keeping stuff to herself,' said Scully.

Mulder's only answer was a smile. He raised his hand to knock on the door.

Before he could knock, Scully said, 'Mind giving me your reasons, Mulder? Call me insecure, but when I go to see a suspect, I like to know why.'

'You'll find out soon enough,' Mulder assured her. Again he raised his hand to knock.

Before he could knock, the door swung open. Willa Ambrose faced them. She was just going out. When she saw them, her mouth tightened and her body stiffened.

'Ms Ambrose, may we have a word with you?' said Mulder.

'I don't know anything more than I've already told the police,' Willa said. 'I have nothing else to say.'

'I understand this is where you keep Sophie – your gorilla,' Mulder said.

'Sophie is ill,' Willa said curtly. She clearly wanted to cut the conversation short.

'Can we meet her?' Mulder asked.

Willa said nothing. But her hostile stare said a lot.

'We're not here to take her away from you,' Mulder assured her.

Willa looked hard at Mulder. She bit her lip, hesitating.

'All right. Come in,' she said, leading Mulder and Scully inside to the gorilla's cage.

Sophie was crouched in the rear of the cage. She stared suspiciously at the visitors. This was the first time Scully had had a chance to take a good long look at her. Scully wondered why so big and powerful a creature should seem so fearful. Especially since Sophie had to be used to human beings by now.

'Six weeks ago, I had to take her out of her public habitat,' Willa said, as if she were reading Scully's mind. 'She had become withdrawn and depressed. She would ball herself up in the back corner of her cage and just shiver.'

'Have you asked her why?' Mulder said.

Scully shot Mulder a look. Mulder's questions often took bizarre turns. But this one was really around the bend.

Willa seemed to find nothing strange about it. She answered matter-of-factly, 'I ask her all the time.'

'What does Sophie say?' Mulder asked.

Willa's hands made a few quick signs. Then she translated them. '"Light afraid." Which means she's afraid of the light.'

'She *speaks* to you!' Scully said.

'Over six hundred words, using American Sign Language,' Willa said. 'She understands over a thousand.'

Willa found a piece of paper on her desk and handed it to Scully. 'You might find this interesting,' she said. 'It's a recent article on the subject.'

Scully read it quickly. The article described studies

conducted around the world of gorillas who had indeed mastered sign language.

She looked up from the article and saw Mulder smiling again. Now she understood why.

'Is this who you wanted to talk to? A gorilla?' she demanded.

'I suggest you read your FBI training manual again, Scully,' he told her. 'It's a basic rule. "Question all possible witnesses."'

'But a gorilla!' Scully exclaimed. 'What could a gorilla know?'

'Perhaps Ms Ambrose can answer that,' Mulder said.

'Gorillas are extremely sensitive creatures,' Willa said. 'Sophie's language skills make her even more so.'

'But why would she be afraid of the light?' Scully said.

Willa gave Scully a sharp look. 'You've talked to Kyle Lang?' she asked.

'Yes. A couple of times,' Scully said.

'Then there's no sense in beating around the bush,' Willa said. 'I'm sure he's told you about my trouble with the Malawi government. There's a chance Sophie could be taken away from me. I think she knows it. And she's scared. In her mind, Africa may conjure up a picture of light. It never ceases to amaze me how Sophie can put things together.'

Scully looked at the gorilla again. Sophie was still crouched in the back of the cage. Scully saw for the first time how alert the animal's eyes were. How they seemed to take in everything that was happening. Scully still couldn't fully believe that animals could actually think. On the other hand, she no longer was absolutely sure that they couldn't.

'It is a possibility,' Scully conceded.

She turned to see if Mulder agreed. But his attention had

shifted elsewhere. He was examining crayon drawings taped to a wall. They looked as if they had been made by a pre-schooler.

'Are these drawings Sophie's?' he asked.

'Yes,' Willa said. 'She's always liked to draw. Though she hasn't done any new ones for a while. Not since she became ill.'

'Interesting drawings,' said Mulder. 'They seem to repeat the same pattern over and over again. A small brown blob in a circle. Any idea what it might mean?'

'I can't be sure, but I have a strong hunch,' Willa said. 'Up until recently, Sophie desperately wanted a baby. The brown object in the circle was her way of showing it.'

'Have you ever attempted to mate her?' Mulder asked.

'I was looking for a suitable partner,' said Willa. 'But then the Malawi government got into the act. With all the stress on Sophie, I didn't think it wise to go ahead. I decided to put the project on hold until everything was settled.'

Mulder nodded. He was looking at her intently, following her words closely.

'Let me make sure I understand you,' he said. 'Sophie showed strong signs of wanting a baby. Then she seemed to stop wanting one. And at the same time, she started being spooked by some kind of light.'

'That's right,' Willa said. 'Her desire to become pregnant was clearly diminished by some kind of stress.'

'Uh-huh,' Mulder said. 'That's one explanation at least. One among several.' He paused a moment, thinking. Then he said, 'I was told there never has been a successful pregnancy at the Fairfield Zoo.'

'I knew I could count on Kyle Lang to keep you fully informed,' said Willa with a grimace.

'Is it true?' Mulder asked.

'Yes,' she said. 'But I don't think it's for the reasons that Kyle claims. Not because of anything Ed Meecham has done to these animals.'

'Why, then?' Mulder persisted.

'For an animal to bear young is always difficult in captivity,' she said.

'But a perfect failure rate?' pressed Mulder.

'I know,' Willa said. 'It looks bad. It's one of the things I was determined to change when I came here.'

Mulder nodded and Scully saw a familiar gleam in his eyes. She started to pay even closer attention as he continued his questioning.

'Was there ever an attempt made to mate Ganesha?' he asked.

'No,' Willa said. 'Mating elephants out of the wild is rarely successful. There have been only six elephant births in captivity in the last ten years.'

Scully saw Mulder's face light up. She braced herself. She did not know what Mulder's latest brainstorm was. But she knew from experience that she should be ready for anything.

Anything except the expected, at least.

'Do you have a veterinary facility here?' Mulder asked.

'Yes,' she said. 'We have an excellent animal hospital. Bringing it up to date was one of the first things I did.'

'Ms Ambrose,' Mulder said, 'I have a rather unusual request for you. But it might help to explain what's been going on here.'

Then he turned to Scully.

'I'm going to need your help too,' he said. 'I can promise you it will be a most interesting challenge for your skills.'

Scully thought she had never seen Mulder look quite so eager.

'I bet it will,' she said.

CHAPTER
TEN

'Mulder, this isn't exactly in my job description,' Scully said.

She was wearing protective plastic gear, complete with hood. A surgical mask dangled around her neck. In her hand was a scalpel. It shined brightly in the glaring lights of the operating room.

'An oversight,' said Mulder. 'You have everything you need for the job. A degree in medicine. A degree in science. What more could you want?'

'A degree of sanity,' said Scully. Mulder had told her in private what her assignment was, but she still couldn't believe it. 'This is the craziest thing you've ever asked me to do.'

Mulder started to answer. But his voice was drowned out by an ear-splitting whine. It came from an electric saw.

He and Scully looked down from the scaffolding on which they stood.

Below them was a gaping hole.

The hole opened into the huge body of an elephant.

A dead elephant.

Ganesha.

The whining came from inside that hole. After a minute it stopped. A figure in protective gear and mask, wearing a miner's helmet, emerged.

'How did it go?' Mulder asked.

'I've carved the ribs away,' Willa Ambrose answered, laying aside her saw. 'There's room for both of us now, Agent Scully.'

Scully turned to Mulder. 'I hope you know what you're doing.' Then she added, 'I should say, what *I'm* doing.'

'I'm pretty sure of what we're going to find,' Mulder said.

'Pretty sure isn't enough for this job,' said Scully. She sighed. 'But I guess it'll have to do.'

Scalpel in hand, Scully climbed down to join Willa.

Working side by side, the two used their scalpels on the inside of the elephant. Slice by slice they carved their way toward the rear of the corpse.

'I'm glad you know your way around animals,' Scully grunted to Willa as they tunneled away. 'I'd hate to get lost down here.'

'Well, I'm lost myself in a way,' Willa said. 'I mean, you told me what you're looking for. But I don't have a clue what you expect to find.' She reached into the opening they had made. From it she pulled a large, dripping body organ.

She handed it to Scully. 'Now maybe you'll let me in on the secret,' she said. 'What exactly do you hope to learn from Ganesha's uterus?'

'Can't you guess?' Scully said.

'Considering the functions of the uterus, one possibility does come to mind,' Willa said. 'But I won't even mention it. It's too weird to take seriously.'

An hour later, in the laboratory, Scully looked up from a high-power medical microscope.

'You were right, Mulder,' she said.

Willa was watching. 'What did you find?' she asked.

'You want to tell her, Mulder?' said Scully. 'Or should I?'

'You're the doctor,' Mulder said.

'Ganesha had been pregnant,' Scully said.

'What do you mean,' said Willa, 'when you say she *had* been pregnant?'

'She was no longer pregnant at the time of her death,' Scully said.

'Then you're saying that not only was she pregnant – but she also gave birth.' Willa struggled visibly to make sense of it all.

'Exactly,' Scully said.

'I don't believe you,' Willa declared.

'See for yourself,' Scully said, making room for her at the microscope. 'See the traces of the offspring on the uterus wall? And the place where it exited?'

Willa looked into the microscope. 'I don't care what it looks like,' she said. 'It's impossible.'

'Of course it is,' Mulder said. 'But so is an invisible elephant. Unless you're prepared to look at things from a different angle.'

'What is going on here?' Willa demanded, shaking her head in disbelief.

'Whatever it is, it's been going on for some time,' Mulder said. 'And I think you're going to see evidence of the same thing when we find your missing tiger.'

'So you've come up with a theory about the case,' Scully said.

'I want more proof before I make it official,' Mulder said. 'You know the brass. They still find cases like this hard to swallow.'

Willa had been totally left behind. 'Is this some kind of joke?' she asked.

'I'm afraid there's nothing funny about this case,' said Mulder.

As if to emphasize his words, sirens sounded in the distance.

'A fire somewhere,' Willa guessed.

'Those are police sirens,' said Scully.

'I'm sure you know better than I,' Willa said. 'It's quite unusual to hear them around here. Except that recently everything has become so unusual.'

'Which is why we'd better follow them,' said Mulder, heading for the door.

Scully and Willa had to half run to keep up with his long-legged stride as he made tracks for the rental car outside.

'I'll drive,' he told Scully.

As she got in beside him, she told Willa, 'Better use your safety belt, even in the back. For somebody in law enforcement, my partner is not exactly into speed limits.'

The seatbelts had barely clicked shut when Mulder started the car with a screech. It tore out of the parking lot toward the sound of the sirens.

'Any idea what's in this direction?' Mulder asked Willa. 'What the trouble spot might be?'

'The only place I can think of is the new shopping plaza,' she said.

The wailing sirens were closer now – much closer.

They turned a corner.

'Watch out!' Scully warned Mulder.

Mulder was already stopping the car.

A crowd of people ran down the street toward them – men, women, and children with terror on their faces.

'Let's see what's up,' said Mulder.

He was out of the car fast, with Scully and Willa close behind.

By this time most of the crowd had passed.

A woman carrying a small child in her arms paused to warn them, 'Not in that direction! The other way, fast!'

Before they could ask any questions, she was running again. At the far end of the street, where she'd come from, were two squad cars, sirens blaring, red lights flashing.

'It's the shopping plaza,' Willa said, 'just beyond the squad cars.'

Mulder and Scully broke into a run, with Willa on their heels. At the squad cars they found six officers with drawn weapons.

Scully looked past them at the shopping plaza. She felt a chill run through her.

The plaza was gleaming new. It had a six-screen movie house, expensive stores whose windows were packed with goods, sit-down restaurants and fast-food places offering everything from Tex-Mex to Chinese. But now it was empty. The only traces of life were a few discarded paper plates and other litter on the rust-colored brick pavement. The only movement came from the bright dancing images on a row of TV sets playing in a store window. The scene was spooky, silent as a graveyard.

'Get back, mister,' a cop commanded. 'This area is off-limits.'

'FBI,' Mulder said, and both he and Scully flashed their ID.

'What's the trouble, officer?' Scully asked.

'Nothing for the FBI to worry about,' the cop said.

'Unless the Feds are into hunting tigers,' added his partner.

ELEVEN

'The tiger's been sighted!' Willa exclaimed.

'You know about it?' said the first cop, surprised. 'I gotta hand it to you. You Feds are on the ball.'

'I'm not connected with them,' Willa said, indicating Mulder and Scully. 'I'm Willa Ambrose, director of the zoo. I'm the one who phoned the police to report that the tiger had escaped.'

'Yeah,' the cop said. 'We went looking for you to get details. But we couldn't find you. Where were you?'

'I was taking care of an animal in our hospital. An emergency,' Willa said, and swiftly changed the subject. 'Who spotted the escaped animal?'

'Some guy chowing down on a Big Mac in the plaza,' the cop said. 'He said he saw the tiger appear out of nowhere, walking right through the shoppers. He gave our emergency number an instant call. We got here in minutes. But by that time the panic was on.'

'Yeah,' Scully said. 'We were almost knocked over in the stampede.'

'That must have been the last wave of people running for their lives,' the cop said. 'It took a few minutes for word to get around.'

'And the tiger – where is it now?' asked Mulder.

'I wish I knew,' said the cop. 'We've blocked off all streets leading out of the plaza. But it might already have gotten out. I understand those things move fast.'

'When they have to,' Willa said. 'When they're hunting – or fleeing.'

'We'll catch up with it,' the second cop promised. 'And when we do, we're ready to handle it.' He patted his rifle.

'That won't be necessary,' Willa said. She opened her large handbag. Scully had wondered why she needed it. Now she had her answer. Willa pulled out an impressive pistol.

'Thanks for your offer, Ms Ambrose.' The first cop smiled. 'But we have all the firepower we need.'

'You don't understand,' Willa said. 'We shouldn't kill the animal for simply obeying her instincts. It's not her fault that she's out of her natural environment. It's ours. There's no need to use bullets on her. This pistol shoots a tranquilizer dart. It will put her out of action without injuring her.'

'You really think that'll stop it?' he said dubiously. 'I saw that thing when I took my kids to the zoo. It's a monster.'

'I know it'll work, officer,' Willa said firmly. 'I've used this gun before.'

'Well, if you say so, ma'am.' He sounded unconvinced.

'Funny thing,' said his partner. 'The guy at the zoo didn't say anything about tranquilizer guns. In fact, he asked if he could join the hunt with his shotgun. Let's see, what was his name?'

'Meecham,' Willa said shortly. 'Ed Meecham. He works at the zoo. But I outrank him. I'm in charge there.'

'Yes, ma'am,' the first cop said.

'But we'll still keep our guns out, just in case,' his partner said.

Willa opened her mouth to argue further – but the squad car's radio blared.

'All-car alert! All-car alert!' a female voice said loud and clear. 'Tiger sighted at Dumont and Spencer! Tiger sighted at Dumont and Spencer! Proceed there immediately! Proceed there immediately!'

'Come on!' the first cop said to his partner.

'Right,' his partner said. 'That's twenty blocks downtown. That tiger moves like the wind.'

The two cops hurried to get into the squad car.

'Mind if we tag along?' Mulder asked.

'Sure, plenty of room,' the first cop said.

Mulder, Scully, and Willa crammed themselves into the backseat. Willa kept her pistol on her lap.

Siren wailing, the squad car joined the others racing across the city.

'Here we are,' the cop in the driver's seat said. 'Dumont and Spencer.'

But no street signs were needed. At least half a dozen squad cars were already there, their lights flashing.

'Not a good idea,' Willa said as they got out. 'The animal will be scared to death. It'll just make her harder to approach.'

'There's another possibility,' Scully said. 'I don't know that tigers are any different from humans when they're threatened. It's flight or fight. You can never be sure which.'

'One thing is sure,' said Mulder, looking around him. 'The animal has a great hiding place – or hunting ground.'

The corner of Dumont and Spencer was the site of a high-rise construction project. A huge hole had been dug. Nearby a thicket of steel beams rose toward the sky, linked here and there by newly built floors and ceilings. Workers in hard hats milled around in confusion. The authorities in Fairfield, thought Scully, were not highly trained in handling major emergencies.

'Right,' she said to Mulder. 'It's a perfect place for a tiger to roam. A man-made jungle.'

Willa said nothing. But she kept her tranquilizer gun ready as she looked around the site.

Suddenly her face hardened.

She strode over to a group of sheriff's deputies. They all carried shotguns. With them was Ed Meecham. He had a shotgun too.

Willa faced Meecham head-on.

'Put that gun away, Ed,' she said. 'And you can tell the local Wyatt Earps to do the same.'

Meecham kept a firm hold on his shotgun. 'You want another death on your hands, Ms Ambrose?' he demanded.

'That cat can be captured without harm to anyone,' she told him.

'This is no time for wishful thinking,' Meecham replied.

'*As your superior, I'm ordering you, Ed,*' Willa said, her voice like a hammer pounding in a nail.

Meecham stiffened, then shrugged. With a sneer in his voice he answered, 'Yes, ma'am. You're the boss. Anything you say.'

She gave him one last hard look. Then she headed into the maze of construction.

A cop tried to stop her.

'The cat may be anywhere in there, ma'am,' he warned.

'Don't worry,' Willa told him. 'I have the equipment to handle her.'

The cop started after her, but Mulder stopped him.

'Don't worry, officer,' he said, flashing his ID. 'Agent Scully and I will provide her with backup.'

Mulder pulled out his pistol. Scully did the same. They hurried after Willa.

'How many darts does your gun hold?' Scully asked when they caught up with her.

'One,' she said.

'Will that be enough?' asked Scully.

'Yes,' Willa said. 'It has to be.'

Scully dropped back to fall into step with Mulder.

'I'm all for saving the animals, Mulder,' Scully said to him in a half whisper. 'But just one dart? You know what I mean?'

Mulder nodded. Without a word both of them released the safety catches on their weapons.

Suddenly a burly worker came racing out of the unfinished building.

'It's there,' he said, white-faced.

Willa peered into the site and raised her dart gun.

'I think I see her tail!' she exclaimed. She dashed into the unfinished building, dodging a huge girder.

Her sudden movement caught Mulder and Scully by surprise. By the time they moved to follow her, she was out of sight.

Then they heard her voice. 'Over here!'

They walked through a forest of girders in the direction of her voice. But they still couldn't see her.

Then they heard her again – much closer.

This time the sound of her voice was a scream.

They raced toward it.

Then they heard another sound.

A shattering shotgun blast.

They ran around a girder and finally saw Willa.

She stood white-faced and trembling, her gun at her side.

Beside her stood Ed Meecham, his shotgun smoking.

Less than five feet away lay the tiger. Blood streamed from a bullet hole between its eyes.

'She was hiding up there,' Willa gasped, indicating an unfinished ceiling. 'She leaped at me from behind.'

She was shaking too hard to go on.

'Thought I'd keep an eye on you,' Meecham said. 'There are things I know about animals that you don't.' He shook his head. 'They don't all talk and draw pictures.'

CHAPTER
TWELVE

Mulder read the sign on the zoo entrance.

ZOO CLOSED TO THE PUBLIC UNTIL FURTHER NOTICE.

Mulder gave the sign a crooked smile as he passed it. Ed Meecham had saved Willa Ambrose's life. But Meecham hadn't been able to save Willa's job. Or his own.

Mulder walked through the zoo, hunting Willa. He wanted to tell her what Scully had found when she cut open the dead tiger.

Scully had asked Mulder to give Willa the news by himself. She had had enough of zoos for a while. She was going to clean things up at the animal hospital lab, then get some sleep. She just hoped she didn't see the tiger in her dreams. Such a beautiful animal, and so dead. She feared it might haunt her.

Mulder found Willa with a group of men and women in suits. They were standing near a whale tank, watching a pair of orcas swimming to and fro. Now and then the whales' mouths opened, revealing rows of evil-looking teeth.

The people with Willa didn't look much kinder. Their eyes glittered coldly as they shook hands with her and left.

Only then did she notice Mulder.

'Well, that's that,' she said. 'The tiger was the last straw. They've cut off all funding to the zoo. They've arranged to ship the animals to other zoos. My last job here will be to get them crated up.'

'I'm sorry,' Mulder said.

'Not as sorry as I am,' said Willa. 'The timing couldn't be worse.'

Mulder saw the pain in her eyes. 'You mean for Sophie,' he said.

Willa nodded. 'What I had in my favor was my job here,' she said. 'I was able to guarantee her a good home.'

Her face started to melt. Then, with effort, she pulled herself together. 'But that's my problem, not yours,' she told Mulder. 'You have your own problems. Tell me, did the results come back on the tiger?'

'Scully says the animal definitely had been pregnant.'

Willa shook her head firmly. 'Impossible. There's no chance these animals could have gotten pregnant. No way.'

'What if they were made pregnant by injection? By artificial insemination?' Mulder suggested.

'It's a very complicated procedure,' Willla said. 'I would have known.'

'Unless it was done somewhere else,' Mulder said.

Willa looked lost.

Mulder made himself clearer. 'What do you know about alien abduction?'

'You're kidding me, right?' Her eyes widened.

Mulder said nothing.

'You actually think these animals are being taken aboard spaceships?' she asked.

But Mulder couldn't be stopped by a look that said he was crazy. There came a point in a case when he had to state the facts as he saw them. They had reached that point.

'I don't know where the animals are being taken,' he said. 'But there seems to be trouble getting them back. Perhaps there's a technical foul-up, some hitch in a space-time-energy hookup. In any event, according to a computer analysis of available data, the animals are being returned roughly two miles west-southwest of the zoo.'

'Aliens making animals pregnant?' said Willa, trying to get a handle on the idea.

'And stealing the results,' replied Mulder.

'But why?'

'Who knows?' said Mulder. 'Maybe they've been observing us. Maybe they see what we're doing to the planet. Poisoning the sea. Cutting down the forests. Plowing up the grasslands. Spraying insecticides on food sources. Slaughtering animals for food, furs, hides, ivory, or simple pleasure. Destroying whole species and locking up the ones still alive.'

'So say – for the sake of argument – that they know what we're doing – and I won't argue about that,' Willa said. 'So what?'

'Maybe they're making a kind of Noah's Ark,' Mulder said. 'Maybe they want to save the animals left in the world from extinction.'

'What an idea!' said Willa, blinking.

'I'm just guessing at their motive,' Mulder said. 'But I'm almost positive that they're the reason why there's never been a successful birth at this zoo. They've gotten here first.'

It took less than a moment for Willa to make up her mind about Mulder's brilliant idea. 'I think that's the most ridiculous thing I've ever heard,' she declared.

Mulder didn't back off. 'If you don't believe me, then ask Sophie.'

'You think this is what she's so afraid of?' said Willa.

'I think Sophie is pregnant,' Mulder said. 'And she's afraid of them taking the baby.'

'Ridiculous,' said Willa again. But now her voice wavered.

'Then prove it,' Mulder said. 'If you dare.'

That last word decided it. 'Follow me, Agent Mulder,' said Willa.

She unlocked the door marked SICK ANIMAL, and Mulder followed her inside.

Sophie was in the rear of her cage. She stared at the visitors suspiciously.

She relaxed only when she heard Willa's voice. 'Sophie, come here. There's something I want to ask you.'

Cautiously Sophie moved toward the human being she loved most in the world. But in the middle of the cage she stopped and looked past Willa at Mulder. She started to make quick, nervous signs.

'What's she saying?' Mulder asked.

'"Man woman hurt,"' Willa said. 'She thinks you and your partner are here to hurt her. Or me.'

Willa made signs back to Sophie, saying as her hands moved, 'Man woman are here to help you. They want to know about Sophie's baby.'

Sophie stiffened, then retreated. She crouched in the back of the cage, making anguished grunts, her eyes big with fright, her long arms curled protectively around her stomach.

'Seems she got the message,' said Mulder.

'And it seems you're right – about her being pregnant, anyway,' said Willa.

'Can I ask her something?' Mulder asked. 'Can she understand simple words?'

'Probably,' Willa said. 'Try it and see.'

Mulder spoke slowly and clearly. 'Sophie – do you want to leave here?'

Sophie became still.

She looked at Mulder and he looked straight back at her.

Then she signaled her reply.

'She says, "light afraid,"' Willa translated. Then she asked Sophie, 'What are you afraid of ?'

Sophie made more signs and started to tremble again.

'"Baby go flying light,"' said Willa in a stunned voice. 'That could mean ... that is, if you're actually right about aliens trying to –'

Mulder started to say something, but Willa's raised hand stopped him. Then she rubbed her hand across her forehead.

'Let me try to put this all together,' she said. 'It seems so incredible. It's so hard to –'

Just then the door swung open.

It was Scully.

'Ms Ambrose,' she said. 'I thought I'd find you here. I'm afraid I have bad news.'

'God, what now?' Willa said.

'I've just come from the lab,' Scully said, closing the door behind her. 'There was a sheriff's deputy who came looking to serve you with papers. I think it's about Sophie.'

'Oh, no,' Willa said, going pale.

'He's waiting outside,' Scully told her.

'What am I going to do?' Willa said.

'Whatever you do, Ms Ambrose, you can't leave Sophie here,' Mulder said. 'Not if you want her to be safe.'

'But I've nowhere else to take her,' Willa said.

There was a knocking at the door. Willa took a long look at Sophie huddled in the cage. Sophie looked back at her. There were no signs or words exchanged. Just love.

Then Willa slowly went to open the door.

The man waiting said, 'Willa Ambrose?'

'Yes,' she said.

The man thrust of a piece of paper into her hand. 'I'm serving you with a court order,' he said. 'You are to release a gorilla named Sophie into protective custody.'

He left her standing there with the paper in her hand and her face bleak with despair.

But as she turned to look at Sophie again, her jaw firmed.

Mulder recognized the look on her face.

It was the look of a gambler with one card left to play.

Mulder knew better than to ask what her ace in the hole was.

The stakes she was playing for were too high.

Mulder was able to decipher the sign she made to Sophie.

'I love you.'

THIRTEEN

Kyle Lang heard an urgent knocking on the door. He got up from his desk and opened it.

'Willa,' he said. 'What brings you here this time of night? In fact, what brings you here at all?'

Willa stepped into the WAO office quickly, closing the door behind her.

'I had to wait until no one would see me,' she said. 'But I had to talk to you.'

'Willa, I'm touched, really touched. After all this time, you still care,' Kyle said mockingly. Then he stopped joking. 'What do you want? That I lay off the zoo? That I shouldn't kick it when it's down? Sorry, but I want to make sure it stays down – and out.'

'Kyle, forget the zoo,' Willa said. 'I'm asking you to help me. You're my last hope.'

'Hope for what?' asked Kyle.

'They're coming to take Sophie away from me,' Willa said frantically.

'If you're looking for sympathy, look somewhere else.' Kyle's voice was cold.

Then he saw the pain in her eyes. 'Let her go, Willa,' he said more softly.

'They're putting her in an iron cage as we speak,' Willa said. 'Without bars or windows. They're taking her to the warehouse. It'll kill her.'

'Sophie has spent her whole life behind bars,' Kyle said. 'Let her go home, Willa. She'll have the freedom she deserves.'

'Freedom to do what?' Willa asked angrily. 'To be killed by poachers? Who'll cut off her hands to sell to tourists?'

'Malawi promises to put her in a nature preserve,' Kyle said.

'You know what that promise is worth,' Willa said. 'Malawi can't even police the streets of its capital, much less its forests.'

'Freedom is worth a little danger,' Kyle said.

'Easy for you to say,' said Willa. 'But Sophie's mine. I can't bear to think of her being hurt. I won't give her up.'

'What choice do you have?' Kyle said.

'Please, you can help find a place for her in America,' Willa said. 'A secret place. A private preserve. You know people.'

'It's against everything I believe in,' Kyle said. But he found it hard to meet Willa's eyes.

'Just this once – for old times' sake,' Willa pleaded.

'Those days are over,' Kyle said. 'You know that. You made your decision when you went to work at a zoo.'

'But I work for animals too, Kyle,' Willa said.

'We've already had this argument,' said Kyle. 'As far as I'm concerned, it's finished.'

Willa bit her lip, then blurted out, 'She's pregnant, Kyle.'

'*What?*' Kyle said.

'Sophie's pregnant,' Willa repeated.

Kyle stared at her, then shook his head. 'You are

desperate, aren't you, Willa? But sorry, no sale. I'm not buying it.'

'But it's true,' she said.

'Say I believe you, which I don't,' Kyle said. 'What if Sophie was pregnant? The baby would live out its life in a cage too.'

Willa opened her mouth to answer, but Kyle cut her off. 'She doesn't belong to you, Willa. She's not your child. She should be with other gorillas, not selling tickets for a zoo.'

'You won't help me?' Willa asked in a voice that showed she already knew the answer.

'No,' Kyle said. 'Now, why don't you go looking for another job? And let me get on with mine.'

He saw Willa's head drop, her shoulders slump. He watched in silence as she went out the door. Then he went back to his desk and the pamphlet he was writing. He sat down in front of his word processor and punched the first key his eye fell on.

An hour later Kyle was still at his desk. The computer screen still had only one meaningless letter on it. And Kyle still was seeing Willa's beaten look in his mind's eye.

It was as cruel a sight as any tormented animal he had ever seen. And he had seen many.

He tried to call them to mind. He wanted to be reminded of his life's work. But all he could see was Willa.

Willa as she was now, so hurt.

And Willa as he had known her years ago, when they had been so happy together.

He clicked off his machine and stood up.

He knew what he was going to do.

There was one thing he never had been able to endure, no matter what the reasons were.

A living creature in pain.

He picked up a bag of tools. He left the office. He got into his truck. And he drove to the zoo.

They were already saving money at the place. The lights were off. That was fine with Kyle. He had a flashlight to see by as he picked the lock on the gate.

If Willa ever smiled again, she'd smile at this joke, he thought. He had learned to break into places like this to fight people like her. Now she had to be thankful that he was so good at it.

He didn't need his flashlight as he moved through the zoo grounds. He knew the layout like the back of his hand. He went to the building marked SICK ANIMAL. Willa might be there, staying close to Sophie till the end.

But Willa's camp bed was empty. So was Sophie's cage.

Kyle scribbled a short note to Willa. Just enough to tell her whom to contact tomorrow. He tucked it under her pillow. Then he headed for the warehouse.

He used his flashlight as he picked the lock, then snapped it off when the lock clicked open. The zoo still might have the money to pay for a watchman. But there was no sign of one as he entered the big darkened room, only the low murmur of animal noises.

Kyle gritted his teeth. He wanted to free every single creature boxed up in here – so badly that it hurt. But there was only so much he could do tonight.

His flashlight had an adjustable beam. He set it on low as he moved through the maze of stacked crates, examining their labels.

Suddenly he stopped and stared. Down a shadowy aisle was an open metal door.

Swiftly he moved to it.

It was the door of a large metal box. By the open door was a label:

GORILLA. NAME: SOPHIE. NO LONGER ZOO PROPERTY.

He shined his light inside.

It was empty except for the straw on the floor.

Kyle turned and whispered loudly, 'Willa? Where are you? Don't worry. It's me, Kyle. I'm here to help.'

Suddenly he sensed something behind him.

He whirled around – and was slammed off his feet.

His head was spinning, but he managed to get up.

Again he was hit by a sledgehammer blow. He went crashing into a stack of crates.

Dazed, he heard the howling of a wolf. He looked up to see the crate that caged the animal toppling off the top of the stack.

'No!' he screamed, throwing up his hands against the last hateful cage he would ever see.

CHAPTER
FOURTEEN

'Is Willa still in there?' asked Scully.

She gestured toward the zoo's conference room. Inside, Willa was facing the police.

'She's still there,' Mulder said. 'Did you find anything in her hideaway?'

Scully had been checking out the room where Willa had kept Sophie.

'I found this in a desk drawer,' Scully said. 'I think you'll find it interesting.'

She handed Mulder a newspaper clipping. It was yellowed with age.

'Interesting indeed,' said Mulder. In the clipping were two photos. One showed Kyle Lang and Willa Ambrose smiling together for the camera. Both were much younger. The other showed a tiny gorilla. The headline read: COUPLE SAVES BABY GORILLA FROM SMUGGLERS. Beneath it a smaller headline said: NATURALISTS WILLA AMBROSE AND KYLE LANG WILL BRING THE ANIMAL BACK TO U.S.

'So Willa and Kyle used to go together,' Mulder said.

'And I can guess what drove them apart,' said Scully. 'Kyle must have wanted to turn Sophie loose. Willa wouldn't let her go.'

'Makes sense,' said Mulder. 'A classic love triangle. Man, woman, and gorilla.'

'Except that the story didn't end there,' Scully said. She showed Mulder the note from Kyle she had found under Willa's pillow.

'It seems perhaps Sophie brought them back together again,' Mulder said. 'But only one person can tell us for sure.'

'Right,' Scully said. She opened the door to the conference room.

Willa sat in a chair. Her back was rigid and she was tight-lipped. Three sheriff's deputies stood around her. They looked tired. Willa was still stonewalling.

'I already told you, I heard the animals going crazy,' she was saying. 'I got up out of bed to check on Sophie. I saw she was gone. And then I found Kyle.'

Scully joined the circle of lawmen. Mulder chose to stand by the wall. He liked to watch Scully when she got her teeth into a case.

Now she took over the questioning. 'Do you know what Kyle was doing there?'

'No,' Willa said.

'We have a witness who saw you visiting Kyle's office last night,' Scully said. 'Is that true?'

'Yes,' Willa said.

'For what purpose?' Scully asked.

'To tell him he'd won,' Willa said. 'That the zoo was being shut down. That Sophie was being sent back to Africa.'

'Did you ask him to help you?' Scully asked.

'Help me do what?' Willa said.

'Help you keep Sophie from being taken away,' Scully said.

'No,' answered Willa. 'That would be against everything Kyle believed in.'

Scully's voice turned hard. 'But you asked him anyway.'

Willa did not flinch. 'No,' she answered firmly.

'Then what was he doing in at the zoo last night?' Scully demanded. 'And why did he leave you this note?' Scully pulled it out and read it aloud. '"Willa, let's talk. Kyle."'

Willa shrugged. 'I have no idea.'

'Did he visit the zoo often?' Scully asked.

'If he did, it was late at night – when he jumped the fence like a good WAO soldier,' Willa said. Then she added, 'Why not ask Agent Mulder what happened here? His theory is even weirder than yours. He thinks it's an alien abduction.'

All eyes turned to Mulder.

Mulder cleared his throat. 'I think the questioning has touched all bases,' he said. 'Agent Scully, can I talk to you a minute – outside?'

Scully grimaced. She had no choice but to go along with him. She could have used thumbscrews and Willa wouldn't have told her anything more.

Still, Scully felt hot under the collar. Outside, she turned to Mulder and said accusingly, 'You think she's telling the truth. You actually believe that aliens stole Sophie and killed Kyle.'

'Why do you say that?' Mulder said.

'Kyle's death and the animal's disappearance are exactly like what happened with the tiger,' Scully said.

'Yes,' Mulder said.

But Scully heard an unusual note in Mulder's voice.

A note of doubt.

'Don't tell me you're having second thoughts about aliens loose in the world,' she said.

'Not about that,' said Mulder. 'But in the case of Sophie, something doesn't add up.'

'What?' Scully asked.

'Willa's reactions,' Mulder said, still sounding puzzled.

'Reactions to what?' asked Scully.

'To losing the animal she loved so much,' Mulder said. 'No way she could mask her grief so well. No way she could stay so cool.'

'Which means?' said Scully.

'I think she knows where Sophie is,' Mulder said. 'And Kyle Lang died because he knew how far she would go to keep Sophie. He wanted to save her from risking everything. But he didn't succeed.'

'So you think she killed him,' Scully said.

'I think she'd do anything for that animal,' Mulder said.

'Even wait on top of a stack of crates for her old boyfriend to walk underneath?' Scully shook her head.

'I'm not entirely sure of what happened last night,' Mulder said. 'I think a closer examination of the body will give us a clearer picture.'

Scully nodded. 'I'll get on it,' she said.

'And I'll check out the warehouse again,' Mulder said. 'There might be something we overlooked.'

'Okay,' said Scully. 'Keep the car here. I'll hitch a ride with the cops to the station. The morgue is right across the street.'

Mulder watched her go, then headed for the warehouse. The door was open. Mulder walked among the stacks of crates. Only an occasional animal sound disturbed the silence. Most of the caged creatures must have been sleeping after the uproar of the night before.

He reached the metal box that had held the gorilla. Opening its door, he looked inside.

Nothing.

He closed the door and examined the concrete floor outside the cage.

Something.

A scattering of straw leading down the aisle to the door.

Not much. But enough to hint that the gorilla might have escaped that way – or been taken along that path by force.

Next Mulder's gaze traveled to where Kyle's corpse had been found. The crate that had killed him still lay on the ground as evidence. The wolf that had been in it was in another crate now, waiting to be shipped to California.

Mulder tried to imagine how the crate had fallen. He looked around carefully.

'Well, well,' he murmured, seeing the cattle prod hanging on the wall. 'So they found something for Ed Meecham to do to earn his pay. They had him keeping the animals in line.'

Mulder stared at the prod with distaste – until a sound outside made him move swiftly to the door.

'Speak of the devil,' he muttered as Ed Meecham let himself into the zoo garage.

By the time Meecham drove out of the garage in a zoo truck, Mulder was in his car, waiting.

He waited until the truck pulled into the street and then followed it.

It wasn't as good as tracking aliens. But it would have to do.

CHAPTER
FIFTEEN

Mulder kept Ed Meecham's truck in sight as it drove down the highway toward the setting sun.

It was dark by the time Meecham stopped beside a large building in the middle of nowhere.

From its looks, it had once been a factory. But now it was abandoned. Meecham's headlights showed broken windows and grimy brick.

Mulder had kept his headlights off. From a distance he watched Meecham turn off his headlights and get out of his truck. Then Meecham turned on a flashlight, pulled out a pistol, and disappeared into the building.

Quickly Mulder followed. His own pistol was in his hand as he went through the open doorway.

Meecham moved down a hallway ahead of him.

'Put it down, Ed,' Mulder said.

Startled, Meecham whirled around. He caught Mulder in his flashlight beam.

Mulder leveled his pistol and shook his head. 'I think there's been enough violence already. Don't you?'

'I didn't kill Kyle Lang,' Meecham said.

'Put down the gun and we'll talk about it,' Mulder told him.

Meecham stared at Mulder's weapon. Then he dropped his.

Still holding his pistol on Meecham, Mulder picked up the abandoned weapon. It was a tranquilizer gun.

'I'm only doing what she paid me to do,' Meecham said. 'I needed the money. They weren't going to give me my pension. Said they were out of funds.'

'My sympathy. I really feel for you,' Mulder said dryly. Then he demanded, 'Where's the animal?'

'Animal? What – ?' Meecham started to say. Then he saw the look in Mulder's eyes and said, 'Down the hall.'

'Okay, you're going to show me,' Mulder said. 'We're going to go there together.'

With a glance at Mulder's gun, Meecham nodded. He led the way down one hall, then another, his flashlight beam playing in front of him.

As they moved down the second hallway, Mulder heard a thumping, like the beating of a drum.

'What's that?' he asked.

'The gorilla,' Meecham said. 'She's throwing herself against the door. She's gone crazy.'

The pounding grew louder. Meecham stopped in front of a thick metal door that shook each time the gorilla slammed against it.

'She's scared,' Mulder said, grimacing. He could almost feel the impact each time she hit the door.

'Yeah, well, she's going to kill herself,' said Meecham.

Mulder shuddered as Sophie hit the door full force again. That made up his mind.

'Okay, Ed,' Mulder said. 'You're going to save her.'

He held the tranquilizer gun out to Meecham.

'But – ' Meecham began.

'I've heard you say how good you are with animals,' Mulder said. 'Now prove it.'

His jaw tightening, Meecham took the gun.

'Give me the flashlight,' Mulder said. 'I'll shine it on her.'

Slowly, cautiously, Meecham opened the door, his body rigid with fear. He moved as if he were walking barefoot on glass. Mulder was right behind him, flashlight in one hand, pistol in the other.

The flashlight showed that Sophie had retreated from the door. She was somewhere in the pitch black of the room.

'I got one shot with this thing,' Meecham said. 'You be ready with your pistol, hear?'

'Where is she?' Mulder asked.

'I think in the far corner,' Meecham said.

Mulder swung the flashlight beam in that direction.

Suddenly the flashlight flew from his hand as he was knocked onto his back.

He caught a glimpse of Sophie's angry face before she smashed into him.

Her musky odor filled his nostrils as he heard the pop of the tranquilizer gun. His hand tightened on his own weapon.

Then the gorilla was gone. She had fled back into the dark. The room was black again, except for a bar of light on the floor from the fallen flashlight.

'Ed?' Mulder said, sitting up. There was no answer.

'Ed!' Mulder shouted. 'Hey!'

He heard Meecham's muffled voice. 'I missed the shot.'

Meecham was on the other side of the door. Mulder tried to open it. It was locked.

'Open the door, Ed!' Mulder screamed.

'You've got a gun. Use it,' muttered Meecham.

'Ed, listen,' Mulder pleaded.

There was no answer. Meecham was gone.

Mulder turned back to peer into the darkness.

He longed to pick up the flashlight. But he did not want

to cross the space between him and it. It would leave him exposed to sudden attack.

He could only pray that Sophie could understand him.

He could only hope she would believe him.

'Sophie,' he said. 'I'm your friend. I want to help you. I want to help your baby.'

From the darkness came a low growling. Mulder could hear the anger and desperation in it.

Sophie had been betrayed once too often. She had stopped trusting human beings.

Mulder couldn't blame her.

Nor could he blame her for wanting to do anything that might save her baby.

His pistol felt heavy in his hand. It seemed to weigh more with every passing second.

He had never hesitated to use it on the guilty when he had to. But to use it on the innocent was a far different thing.

The situation was easy enough to see.

It was kill or be killed.

He desperately wished that making the choice was that easy.

But he had run out of time to make up his mind.

Sophie roared three times. Then she charged.

CHAPTER
SIXTEEN

Pain slashed across Mulder's forehead.

Sophie's nails had raked his skin.

The light from the flashlight on the floor turned from white to bloodred in his eyes.

In that red haze he saw Sophie standing huge above him as he crouched on all fours.

She was raising her arm for another brutal blow.

Mulder raised his pistol. His finger tensed on the trigger.

But he could not make himself pull it. The gun barrel wavered as his arm trembled. Inside him a terrible tug-of-war was taking place.

Kill or be killed?

Mulder could never be sure what he would have done if Sophie hadn't suddenly frozen.

She turned and ran back into the dark. Mulder looked around to see what had frightened her.

He blinked as glowing vapor poured into the room.

In the misty light Sophie began to melt away before him.

He saw her eyes giving him a helpless farewell. He saw her hands making three last signs.

That was all he saw as white light exploded – and he plunged again into blackness.

* * *

'Mulder . . . Mulder . . .'

From what seemed miles away came Scully's worried voice.

Mulder's eyelids felt as if they were made of stone, but he forced them open. Early-morning light filled the room. Scully was looking down at him.

'Mulder, lie still,' she told him. She turned and said to one of the two policemen behind her, 'Radio for a paramedic.'

'I'm okay,' Mulder told her as he sat up on the floor. He shook his head to clear it. He looked around the room. Sophie was gone.

'Where is she?' he asked.

'Where is who?' Scully said.

'Sophie – they took her,' Mulder said.

'Lie back, Mulder, you're still in shock,' Scully said.

Instead, Mulder got to his feet. 'Meecham –' he said.

'Ed Meecham's been arrested,' Scully said. 'He was picked up heading for the state line. He told us you were here.'

'Where's Willa?' asked Mulder.

'Outside in a squad car,' Scully said. 'I examined Kyle and found evidence that he had died a wrongful death. Seems he'd been beaten with a cattle prod. I went to confront Willa with the news just as she was getting ready to clear out. It took almost no pressure to make her fold. She confessed to hiring Ed. She said he was keeping Sophie in a building some-where on this highway.' Scully shook her head sadly. 'The threat of losing Sophie really made her flip.'

'I've got to talk with her,' Mulder said.

'Mulder. You're in no condition to –'

But he was already on his way.

He found Willa in the backseat of the squad car. She was staring dead ahead with empty eyes.

But when she saw Mulder, she came to life. 'Where's Sophie?' she demanded.

'She's gone,' Mulder said.

Pain twisted Willa's face. Then she glared at him with hatred.

'What did Ed do to her?' she said. 'I was a fool to turn to him for help. But he was the only one left.'

'It wasn't Ed,' Mulder said.

'This is a nightmare,' Willa said, her whole body shaking. 'None of this should have happened. Ed panicked when he saw Kyle. Kyle wasn't supposed to be there.' She ran a hand through her hair in despair. 'He's gone. Sophie's gone. I've lost everything.' She buried her face in her hands.

'Ms Ambrose, listen to me,' Mulder pleaded. 'I need your help. Sophie tried to tell me something.'

Willa looked up the moment she heard Sophie's name. 'What?' she asked.

'What does this mean?' Mulder asked. He imitated the signs Sophie had made before the white light had swallowed her.

'It doesn't make sense,' Willa said.

'What does it mean?' Mulder asked again.

'Man save man,' Willa said.

She and Mulder stared at each other, both trying to understand the three words.

They did not get far. A voice spoke through static on the squad car's radio. 'All vehicles in the vicinity: a large animal reported running wild. Last sighted on the interstate just west of the service road off Ninety-second Avenue.'

'It's her,' said Mulder.

'She's trying to get back to the zoo,' said Willa.

'Maybe,' said Mulder.

He caught sight of Scully and the cops coming out of the building. He shouted the news to them.

The cops jumped into the front seat. Scully got in back with Mulder and Willa. The car took off.

'Hurry, would you!' Willa almost screamed at the cop who was driving.

Half an hour later the car pulled up to a group of other squad cars parked at the side of a country road. Near them was an overturned civilian car. The scene was bathed in chill silver light under a gray morning sky.

As soon as the squad car stopped, Willa was out of it like a shot.

Mulder and Scully were right behind her.

Willa ran up to the first cop she saw. 'Where is she?' Willa demanded.

'She?' asked the cop.

'Sophie,' Willa said.

'Sophie?'

'The runaway gorilla,' Mulder explained.

'Why didn't you say so?' the cop said. 'Over there.'

He pointed toward a small clump of trees that stood lonely on the bare horizon.

Willa broke into a run. Mulder and Scully followed.

When they reached the trees they found more police.

'What happened here, officer?' Scully asked one of them.

The cop said, 'Animal ran across the road, got hit by a car. Car got totaled when it went off the road trying to avoid impact. The driver's okay, though.'

'And the animal?' Willa asked, barely able to get the words out.

'It tried to keep on going,' said the cop. 'It made it this far.'

He pointed toward some undergrowth. Two cops were standing there, looking at the ground.

Willa shoved herself between them. She knelt down by the animal that lay there in a heap.

'Oh no. No, no, no, no,' Willa moaned as she stroked the gorilla's face. She leaned forward and spoke into the animal's ear, as if trying to wake her. 'Sophie . . . Sophie . . .'

The cop nearest her shook his head. 'She's dead, ma'am,' he said.

Willa looked up and said, 'Please, tell me one thing. Which way was she running?'

The cop looked bewildered. 'Sorry, but –'

'Which way was she running – toward the zoo or away from it?' Willa asked.

The cop lifted his shoulders. 'Sorry, I don't know, ma'am,' he said.

Mulder stood beside Scully, watching helplessly as Willa collapsed in grief on top of the corpse. He couldn't give her the answer she wanted. He had questions of his own.

All he could do was stare at the animal's right hand, so very much like a human's.

The fingers were frozen in a sign that Mulder recognized. The sign he had seen Willa use so long ago.

I love you.

CHAPTER
SEVENTEEN

The next morning Mulder and Scully drove their rental car back to the airport.

They drove in silence. There didn't seem to be much to talk about.

This case was finished.

The courts would decide what would happen to Willa.

The city council would decide what would happen to the zoo.

And nobody could tell what would happen to the animals now being shipped all over the country.

'You know, it's strange what I keep remembering,' Scully said out of the blue.

'What's that?' said Mulder.

'I keep remembering that deserted shopping plaza, after the tiger cleared it,' Scully said. 'It looked so spooky. It was like a world from which all life had fled. There were only empty buildings left. Funny, huh?'

'Funny,' agreed Mulder.

Then he said, 'I might as well finish taping my observations. You'll need them for your report to the brass.'

He picked up the mike of his tape recorder.

'The crimes committed in Fairfield were the acts of desperate people who were doing more than fighting one another.

They were fighting a force none of them could have imagined, much less defeated. A force whose purpose is beyond our sure knowledge. Could aliens be trying to protect animals that we are driving toward extinction? Is it a judgment that we cannot protect them ourselves? Is it a reflection of the fact that the rate of exinction has risen a thousand times above normal in this century? Could we humans soon find ourselves alone on this planet and facing extinction ourselves? Might our survival and the survival of all other living things on earth depend on aliens who may be stocking their own zoos? Or, in the last words of a creature that could not survive, will man save man?'

Mulder put down his mike.

'I guess that sums it up, Scully,' he said.

'I'm afraid it does,' she answered, keeping her eyes on the road.

'So many questions, so few answers.' Mulder looked out the car window at a world that offered no answers at all.

Except perhaps for the billboard he read as they drove by.

On it in three-foot letters was a quotation from the Bible:

'A man has no preeminence above a beast; for all is vanity.'

SQUEEZE

To Mimi Panitch, Terri Windling, and Tania Yatskievych, intrepid traveling companions and good friends

CHAPTER
ONE

Seven thirty. As the last of a bloodred sunset streaked the Baltimore sky, throngs of working people crowded the streets, hurrying to get home before darkness fell.

All except George Usher, a middle-aged businessman. He was heading back to his office for a long evening of work. And he was less than happy about it.

As he left the elevator and stepped onto the fifteenth floor of his office building, Usher sighed. Empty cubicles. Long, silent hallways, lit here and there with Exit signs that glowed eerily in the dim, gray after-hours lights.

The office felt different at night. Creepy. *Excellent security*, Usher reminded himself. *No one can get in unless they work here.* But it still felt strange.

Usher walked into his office, turned on the light, and punched a number into his phone. An answering machine clicked on, and his wife's voice asked callers to leave a message after the beep.

'Hello, honey,' he said. 'It's about seven thirty and it looks like I'll be here awhile. The meeting didn't go so well. Call me. I love you. 'Bye.'

Usher hung up and stared into the dark hallway outside his office. Suddenly he felt an odd tremor. Fear.

Coffee, he thought. *A cup of coffee will help.* He grabbed his mug and headed for the coffee machine at the other end of the floor, making his way down a long row of empty offices.

His office, however, was not empty.

The instant he left it, a tiny noise broke the silence. High on the wall across from Usher's desk, the cover of an air vent moved, ever so slightly. The two screws holding the vent in place began to turn. First the right. Then the left. Then, very slowly, long, slender fingertips reached out from inside the vent, pushing the cover aside.

Usher started back down the hallway, his mug filled with day-old coffee. He stopped short as he reached his office door. He could have sworn he'd left the light on inside.

He stepped into the dark office, groping for the lamp on his desk. Then the door slammed shut with an unearthly force. And Usher suddenly knew that he wasn't alone.

Frantically he reached for the door. He got hold of the knob and fought to open it. But someone – or something – had hold of him.

Usher was desperate. He struggled in the stranger's grasp and slipped free. He rolled across the desk – only to feel powerful hands lock around his throat. He couldn't breathe. He couldn't make a sound as his body was lifted into the air with inhuman strength.

For a brief moment the hands left his throat. Usher's pitiful scream rang through the office as his body slammed into the door with enough force to splinter it.

And then there was only silence.

An hour later George Usher's office was blanketed in cold, white moonlight. Coffee from his overturned mug dripped onto the carpet, which was already soaked with blood. His lifeless body lay a short distance away.

Directly above the body, one of the screws in the cover of the air vent began to turn. Something inside the vent was screwing the cover back into the wall. Slowly. Victoriously.

CHAPTER
TWO

Sunlight streamed through the windows of a building in downtown Washington, DC. In the open court of an atrium, FBI Special Agent Dana Scully was having lunch with Tom Colton.

For Scully this was a relaxing break in a hectic day. The atrium restaurant was one of her favorites. And Tom was an old friend. They'd attended Quantico, the FBI Training Academy, together.

It had been a while since the two agents had seen each other. Colton looked exactly the way she remembered him: handsome, intelligent, and self-assured. He'd always liked loud ties, and the one he wore today was no exception – black with big white polka dots. And he still spoke in a low, rapid voice that made everything sound urgent. But right now Colton was just catching Scully up on gossip.

'Guess who I ran into from our class at Quantico,' he said. 'Marty Neil.'

Scully laughed. 'J. Edgar Junior?' she said. J. Edgar Hoover had been the director of the FBI for almost fifty years, until 1972. Marty Neil, their classmate, planned to have a career just like Hoover's. The problem was, Neil wasn't nearly as smart as Hoover had been. But he was every bit as paranoid.

'Neil just got bumped up,' Colton told Scully. 'He's going

to work for Foreign Counterintelligence. New York City Bureau. *Supervisory* special agent.'

'Supervisory?' Scully echoed in surprise. 'He's only been out of the academy for two years. How did he land that?'

Colton gave her a wry smile. 'He lucked into the World Trade Center bombing. A major crime that was solved. Quickly.'

'Well, good for Marty,' Scully said, shaking off a slight feeling of envy. Lately her own career didn't seem nearly as promising. Scully had an undergraduate degree in astronomy, a medical degree, and an advanced degree in physics. It was while she was getting her physics degree that she'd joined the FBI. She'd done well at Quantico, so well that she had been asked to teach there. And that was when she'd gotten her current assignment. Section Chief Bevins had paired her with Fox Mulder, an agent who specialized in investigating cases no one else would touch.

'C'mon, Dana.' Colton's voice snapped her out of her thoughts. 'Marty Neil's a loser. But look where he is now. It's where *we* should be.'

Scully studied her former classmate. She knew Colton wasn't doing as badly as he made it sound. 'Brad Wilson told me that the work you did on the Washington Crossing killer led them right to the suspect,' she said. 'The word is, you're on the Violent Crimes Section's fast track.'

Colton shrugged, as if that wasn't a big deal. But Scully knew he was pleased with his reputation. Colton had always been ambitious. Getting ahead fast meant everything to him.

'How've you been doing?' Colton asked. 'Had any close encounters of the third kind?'

Scully tried not to let the remark bother her. She knew he was kidding. Besides, she couldn't really blame him for thinking her assignment was strange. It *was*. 'Is that what everyone thinks I do?' she asked carefully. 'Have close encounters?'

'No, no, of course not,' Colton protested. 'But you do work with "Spooky" Mulder.'

Scully's partner, Fox Mulder, was known as an excellent agent. He had graduated from Harvard and Oxford with honors in psychology. He also happened to have a photographic memory. Scully had never met anyone who was sharper when it came to analyzing a case. But Mulder was even better known for his interest in unexplained phenomena. He actually believed in things like UFOs and aliens. And he'd dedicated his life to investigating them.

'Mulder's ideas may be a bit "out there,"' Scully admitted. 'But he's a great agent.'

Colton took a bite of his lunch and sighed. 'Well, I've got a case that's "out there,"' he said, his voice troubled. 'The Baltimore Police Department wants our help on a serial killer profile. Three murders. Began six weeks ago. The victims vary in age, gender, and race. No known connections to each other.'

Scully sipped her iced tea. 'I take it there's a pattern?' she asked.

'The killer's point of entry,' Colton answered. 'Actually, the lack of one.'

'What do you mean?' Scully asked.

'One victim,' Colton began, 'was a college girl. She was killed in her ten-foot-by-twelve-foot cinderblock dorm room. When she was found, the windows were locked and the door was chained *from the inside*. No one can figure how the killer got in. And then out again.'

Scully listened intently as Colton continued. 'The last incident was two days ago. High-security office building. Nothing on the security monitors out of the ordinary. It was after-hours. Everyone had gone home. The guy parked in the garage, took the elevator to the fifteenth floor. He was going back to his office for an evening of work. No one else came into the building. The guy never came out.'

'Could they be suicides?' Scully asked.

Colton shook his head. Carefully he removed a photograph from his briefcase and handed it to Scully.

Scully's eyes widened when she saw the picture taken at the crime scene.

'The victims' livers have been removed,' Colton said. 'Without tools.'

'You mean the murderer used his bare hands?' Scully asked in disbelief. Her mind searched for a rational explanation. 'There had to be a knife or scalpel –'

Colton cut her off with a shake of his head. 'I know it sounds impossible, but no. There was no cutting tool. I can't even begin to guess how he did it.'

'This sounds like an X-file,' Scully said. An 'X-file' was what the FBI called a case that involved strange happenings and unexplained phenomena. The X-files were Fox Mulder's specialty.

'Let's not get carried away,' Colton warned her. 'I'm the one who's going to solve these murders. I'm not handing them over to you and Mulder. But what I'd like you to do is go over the case histories. Come down to the crime scene. It's only a half hour from your house.'

Scully looked at him quizzically. 'If you're going to solve the case, then why do you want me in on it?'

Colton didn't meet her eyes as he answered. 'Maybe because of the cases you've been stuck with lately – you'll have a fresh angle.'

Scully took this in. Colton thought there was something crazy about working on the X-files. He was also making sure that just in case it *wasn't* crazy, he'd have her expertise. But if he really wanted someone with X-file experience, he'd need her partner as well.

'You want me to ask Mulder to help?' Scully asked.

Colton frowned. 'If Mulder wants to come and do you a favor, great,' he said. 'But make sure he knows this is *my* case.'

Scully examined the photo again. She was sure the case was an X-file.

'Dana,' Colton said. 'If I can break a case like this one . . . *I'll* be getting the bump up the ladder. And you . . .'

Scully looked at him. 'What about me?'

Colton glanced away as he answered. 'They'll stop calling you Mrs Spooky.'

Scully sat absolutely still as Colton picked up the check and left the table. That last remark had hurt. And Colton, of course, had known that it would.

CHAPTER
THREE

The next morning Scully did as Colton had asked. Instead of going straight to FBI Headquarters, she stopped at George Usher's office building and parked in the garage below the skyscraper. She glanced at the television monitors suspended from the ceiling. It was definitely a high-security building.

It was still early, just after seven. Scully stepped off the elevator onto the fifteenth floor. The office was deserted – except for one person. Fox Mulder. Scully had thought long and hard after her lunch with Colton, and she'd decided to tell Mulder about this case. It sounded too much like an X-file to leave him out.

Now Mulder stood in Usher's office. His forensic kit was spread out. He'd taken off his jacket, and his sleeves were rolled up. He wore a latex glove on one hand. He'd been at work for a while.

'Morning,' he said to Scully.

Fox Mulder looked surprisingly young for an agent with so much experience. He was a tall, slender man who wore his hair longer than was common for an FBI agent. Scully thought there was something a little deceptive about Mulder's appearance. His face seemed so innocent, almost boyish. Until you looked into his clear hazel eyes. That was when you realized that Fox Mulder had seen more than most people. And it had cost him.

Scully nodded at Mulder. She was glad Colton wasn't here yet. That gave her a chance to make her own notes on the crime scene. She surveyed the office with a practiced eye.

Usher's body had been removed, but the office was still a wreck. The top of Usher's desk looked as if it had been through a storm. Pens, pencils, and folders lay scattered. A picture of a woman, probably his wife, had been knocked over. So had the desk lamp and a coffee mug.

And blood was splattered everywhere – across the papers on Usher's desk, on his chair, on the rug, on the walls.

There was only one orderly area in the office – the corner where Mulder had spread out his forensic kit. Fingerprint powder, razors, and tweezers were all neatly arranged.

Mulder, too, scanned the bloody office. Then his eyes came back to his partner.

'So . . . why didn't they ask me?' he asked Scully.

Scully was quiet. Mulder waited patiently for an answer. He reached into his pocket for a sunflower seed.

'They're friends of mine from the Academy,' Scully said at last. She was trying to be tactful. 'I'm sure they just felt more comfortable talking to me.'

'Why would I make them so uncomfortable?' Mulder asked.

Scully faced him, hesitating. Then, as usual, she decided that the best answer was an honest one. 'It's probably because of your . . . reputation.'

'Reputation?' he echoed, sounding puzzled. '*I* have a reputation?'

Mulder was deliberately giving her a hard time, and Scully knew it. 'Look,' she said impatiently. 'Colton plays by the book, and you don't. They feel your methods, your theories are . . .'

'Spooky?' Mulder guessed. His smile was amused, but his eyes were serious as he asked, 'What about you? You think I'm . . . spooky?'

Scully paused, wondering whether Mulder deserved a straight answer. She knew he was testing her. They'd been working together only a short time. And Mulder knew that, originally, Scully had been assigned to spy on him. To give the FBI a reason to shut down the X-files. But Scully had an open mind. Although she didn't always agree with Mulder's theories, she respected his methods. She'd told her supervisors the truth: that Mulder was an excellent agent. That the cases he investigated were real. By now, she thought, Mulder ought to trust her.

Scully never answered Mulder's question. Because at that moment Tom Colton strode into the room.

'Dana, I'm sorry I'm late,' he said.

'No problem. We just got here,' Scully told him. 'This is Fox Mulder. Mulder, Tom Colton.' The two men shook hands.

'So, Mulder.' Colton spoke in a mocking tone. 'What do you think? This look like the work of Little Green Men?'

Scully shot Mulder a sympathetic glance.

'Gray,' Mulder replied seriously.

'What?' Colton asked.

'Gray,' Mulder explained. 'You said "Green Men." A Reticulian's skin tone is gray. They're known for their extraction of human livers due to a lack of iron in the Reticulian galaxy.'

Scully wished Mulder wouldn't do this. Even if Colton deserved it. She knew Colton was already prejudiced against Mulder. And now Mulder was making it worse.

Colton looked confused – as though he couldn't tell

whether Mulder was joking. 'You can't be serious,' he said.

'Do you know how much liver and onions go for on Reticulum?' Mulder asked Colton. Then, before Colton could answer, he excused himself and continued examining the office.

Colton's face flushed red with embarrassment. He scowled at Mulder, then moved off to the other side of the room. Scully sighed and followed Colton. Maybe it wasn't too late to smooth things out between the two agents.

Mulder paid no attention to Colton and Scully's conversation. He continued his investigation of Usher's office, searching the sharp corners on the desk for any fibers that might have pulled loose from the murderer's clothes.

Reaching into his pocket for more sunflower seeds, Mulder moved on to the window. Carefully he checked for points of entry. He wasn't surprised when he didn't find any. Next he made his way along the edges of the room. He was looking for anything the murderer might have dropped or touched. Any bit of evidence that might lead them to a suspect.

Mulder stopped as he saw something glittering in the carpet. Kneeling down, he gently pressed the carpet with his index finger. There *was* something – tiny metal filings.

Using tweezers, Mulder lifted a filing and held it up to the light. He thought for a second, then gazed up. High above him on the wall was the metal grille that covered the office's air vent.

Mulder stood up and went straight to his forensic kit. He grabbed the fingerprint powder, fingerprint tape, and brush. He rolled the brush handle rapidly between his hands to clean the bristles. Then he began to lightly powder the area around the vent.

This caught Colton's attention. 'What the hell is he doing?' he asked Scully in a suspicious tone.

Mulder paid him no attention. He was focused on the brush, hoping to lift a clean print.

Colton watched in disbelief. 'That's a one-foot-square vent,' he told Mulder. 'And even if a Reticulian could crawl through, the vent cover is screwed in place.'

Mulder ignored Colton and continued to stroke the fingerprint brush along the sides of the grille. Bit by bit, a print was emerging. It was long and thin. It had some of the qualities of a human fingerprint, but it was definitely *not* human.

Mulder didn't say a word. But his eyes went wide with amazement. He'd seen these prints before.

FOUR

Scully drew up a chair beside Mulder. They were in Mulder's cramped office, in the basement of FBI Head-quarters. As usual, the tiny room was overflowing with stacks of books and papers. Mulder's bulletin board was covered with photos of blurred objects. Maybe they were UFOs, maybe not. Scully wasn't sure. But Mulder's attitude toward his work was clear from the poster on his wall, which read I WANT TO BELIEVE.

Scully ignored a mountain of reports that was threatening to topple onto the floor. She focused her attention on the slides Mulder was showing her. There were six, and she wasn't sure what to make of them. Each showed an elongated fingerprint. The prints were definitely too long and thin to be human.

Mulder pointed to one of the slides. 'This is the print I took yesterday from Usher's office,' he said. 'These others are from the X-files.'

'How many murders are we talking about?' Scully asked in surprise.

'Eleven, counting Usher,' Mulder answered. 'Ten murders before him. All in the Baltimore area. No point of entry in any of them. Each victim was murdered the same way. These prints' – he lined up five slides – 'were from five of those other ten crime scenes.'

'*Ten* other murders?' Scully still couldn't believe it. 'Colton never mentioned –'

'I don't think he's even aware of them,' Mulder said. He pointed to three of the slides. 'These three prints were lifted in 1963, five years before Colton was even born. And these two were taken in 1933.'

Scully's eyes widened. 'You're saying the same murderer was at work thirty years ago *and* sixty years ago?'

'And ninety,' Muller said. 'Unfortunately, we don't have prints for that one. Fingerprinting wasn't too common in 1903. And police records weren't very complete. But there *was* at least one similar murder then.'

'Of course,' Scully said dryly. She pushed her chair away from the desk. *Leave it to Mulder*, she thought, *to come up with a completely unbelievable case history.*

Mulder ignored her tone and began adding up the evidence. 'Five murders, every thirty years. That means he's got two more to go this year.'

Scully stood up and turned away from her partner. *There has to be a more logical explanation*, she told herself. She was a scientist, a doctor. There was no way she could believe – She stopped herself. Maybe she'd misunderstood Mulder.

'You're saying these are copycat crimes?' she asked. 'Someone who knows about the old crimes and is determined to copy their pattern?'

Mulder spun his chair around to face her. 'What did we learn on our first day at the Academy, Scully?' he asked in a mock-stern voice. '*Every fingerprint is unique.* These are all a perfect match.'

Scully took this in. She knew exactly what Mulder was driving at. It was one thing for him to have weird ideas. It was another for him to expect *her* to believe them. 'Are you suggesting I go to the Violent Crimes Section and tell them these murders were done by . . . an alien?' she asked.

'Of course not,' Mulder replied, deadpan. 'I find no evidence of alien involvement.'

Scully glared at him. 'What then?' she asked. 'That this is the work of a hundred-year-old serial killer, capable of overpowering a healthy six-foot-two businessman?'

Mulder grinned at her. 'And he should really stick out in a crowd, with ten-inch fingers.'

'Mulder, if you think this is a joke – '

'The X-files investigate unsolved cases involving unexplained phenomena,' Mulder reminded her. 'This should be our case. And I'm quite serious.'

'It's Colton's case,' Scully told him.

Mulder handed her a yellowed file. 'The X-file dates back to 1903. We had it first.'

Scully sighed. She didn't want to offend Mulder. But sometimes he was so stubborn that she had no choice.

'Mulder,' she said gently. 'They don't want you involved. They don't want to hear your theories. That's why Section Chief Blevins has you hidden away down here in the basement.'

Mulder didn't seem at all hurt by this. 'You're down here too,' he pointed out cheerfully.

Scully slumped in her chair. She was tired of arguing. Couldn't he ever take no for an answer?

Mulder moved to her side. 'Why don't we agree to this,' he suggested. 'Colton and his group have their investigation. And we have ours. And never the twain shall meet. Agreed?'

Scully looked at him, unable to answer.

And unable to refuse.

*   *   *

The clock read 10:00 P.M. Scully sat alone in her apartment, her eyes fixed on her computer screen. Spread out on her desk were her notes from the case. She'd gone over the evidence they'd found in Usher's office. And she'd read through Mulder's X-files. Now she was writing a profile of the killer.

Once again she considered Mulder's theory. And then she went ahead with her own.

'After a careful review of the violent and powerful nature of these murders,' she wrote, 'I believe the killer to be a male, twenty-five to thirty-five years of age. He has above-average intelligence. His method of entry has so far been undetectable. This may be due to his superior knowledge of the inner structure of buildings and ducts.'

Scully glanced at the blueprints of Usher's office building and continued writing. 'Or he may, in fact, hide in plain sight. For example, he might pose as a deliveryman or maintenance worker. Witnesses tend to overlook such personnel. Their uniforms often render them invisible to casual observers.'

Once again Scully studied the slide of the elongated fingerprint. Then she put it down, feeling frustrated. She couldn't explain the strange print, and she wasn't about to try. Instead she dealt with another aspect of the murder.

'The removal of the liver is the most important detail of these crimes. The liver possesses restorative qualities. It cleanses the blood . . .'

The next morning Scully presented her report to the Violent Crimes Section. She knew it was important to sound professional and sure of herself. She wasn't about to mention Mulder's strange theories – or her own doubts. Both Colton and his boss, Agent Fuller, were at the conference table, listening intently.

Calmly Scully explained her theory about why the murderer took his victims' livers. 'The taking of this trophy may allow the killer to believe he's cleansing himself of his own impurities,' she said. 'I think he's acting under the classic form of obsessive-compulsive behavior.'

Several of the agents nodded at this.

'Since the victims are unrelated,' Scully went on, 'we can't predict who will be next. So we must use the fact that serial killers don't always succeed in finding a victim. When this happens, the serial killer may return in frustration to the site of the previous murder.'

'Why would he do that?' a balding agent asked.

'He'd be trying to recapture the emotional high of the last murder,' Scully explained. 'So I believe our best course of action is to target those sites where he's already killed.'

Agent Fuller stood up. 'Good job, Agent Scully,' he said. Then he turned to the agents under his command. 'If there are no objections, I'd like to begin our stakeouts of the murder sites tonight. We're looking for a male, twenty-five to thirty-five. He may be wearing a uniform: gas company, UPS, whatever.'

Fuller turned back to Scully. 'I know you're assigned to another area,' he said. 'But if you don't mind some overtime, you're welcome to join us. That is,' he added, 'if you don't mind working in an area that's a bit more down-to-earth.'

Scully forced herself to smile as the other agents laughed at Fuller's lame joke. She knew Mulder wouldn't have found it funny either.

CHAPTER
FIVE

Three days later Scully once again parked her car in the high-security garage below George Usher's office building. The Violent Crimes Section had taken her advice. Agents were conducting stakeouts at the sites of the previous murders. Scully had volunteered for this position. Now she put on a small headset and settled in to wait.

Though dusk had just fallen, the garage was deserted. Scully wondered if people were leaving work early because of Usher's murder.

'Position ten, this is a station check,' said the voice in her headset.

'Position ten, I copy,' Scully whispered back.

Her eyes scanned the area, sorting through the shadows. The garage was dimly lit. The silence was deafening. She began a second visual check. Nothing.

And then she heard it – footsteps.

She wasn't alone.

Slowly, quietly, Scully got out of the car. She drew her weapon. She aimed her flashlight in the direction of the sound.

The footsteps stopped. Scully shined her light along the grease-stained floor. Around the thick cement support columns. She saw nothing but the vast, empty garage.

And then she heard the footsteps again. Someone was

walking quickly and deliberately. Someone was coming toward her.

Keeping her back to the wall, Scully moved toward the sound. She was getting closer. Whoever was in the garage with her was on the other side of this wall.

Scully tucked the flashlight into the waistband of her pants. She rounded the corner fast, both hands bracing her gun. She aimed it straight out in front of her – and directly at Mulder's chest.

Her partner raised his hands in surrender. 'You wouldn't shoot an unarmed man, would you?' he joked.

Scully gave him a look of disgust. Then she holstered her weapon. 'Mulder,' she said in a fierce whisper, 'what are you doing here?'

'He's not coming back here,' Mulder said, ignoring her question. 'Our suspect gets his thrill from the challenge of a seemingly impossible entry. He's already beaten this place. If you'd read the X-file on the case, you would have come to the same conclusion.'

'You're jeopardizing my stakeout,' Scully said angrily. She was working for the Violent Crimes Section now. Mulder had no right to interfere. And he had no right to tell her that her theories were wrong.

Mulder held out his hand to her, palm up. 'Want some sunflower seeds?' he asked mildly.

Scully turned her back on him, steaming.

'You're wasting your time,' Mulder told her. 'I'm going home.'

He watched as Scully returned to her car. Then he walked off into the darkness.

But Mulder didn't go home. He was too intrigued by this case to let it go. Hours later he was still walking through the shadows of the garage. Night had fallen. Except for Scully, everyone seemed to have left the office building. Mulder could hear the hum of the air-circulation pump and the whine of the building's electrical system. And then he heard a dull metallic *clang*.

Quickly Mulder took cover behind one of the support pillars. He peered out, trying to see around the corner. The sounds seemed to be coming from an area enclosed by a chain-link fence.

Curious, Mulder approached the fenced area. The sounds were definitely growing louder. The fence surrounded the large motors, encased in sheet-metal, of the building's air-circulation system. Mulder stepped back, studying the system. From here the air-circulation ducts branched upward into the office building.

He moved in with his flashlight, examining the system more closely. The clanging and banging sounds were getting louder. Definitely coming from the ducts. As if something was inside them. And a metal panel that was part of the motor casing was out of place. As if it had been opened.

Again Mulder shined his light around the area. That's when he noticed that the gate in the chain-link fence was open. Not by much. Just enough for someone to slip through. What if this was the point of entry? What if the murderer had entered the building through this duct system?

Mulder stepped through the open gate and then tensed. The ventilation duct moved. It flexed from the inside. Almost as if it were breathing.

Something was scaling the duct from inside.

Mulder took off.

'Scully!' he shouted, racing toward her car. 'Call for backup and get over here!'

Scully got on the radio. 'Position ten, request backup!'

Then she got out of the car and followed Mulder to the fenced-in area.

'In there,' Mulder said, pointing toward the ducts.

Scully drew her gun. 'Federal agent!' she shouted. 'I'm armed! Don't move!'

The movement in the metal duct stopped.

'Get down . . . slowly,' Scully ordered.

There was silence for a moment. Then the duct began to creak and groan as the climber inside moved downward.

Scully and Mulder waited. The duct flexed and pulsed until whoever was inside finally stopped moving.

Scully kept her gun trained on the open panel at the base of the motors. 'All right, now get out!' she commanded. Her voice was firm, but her muscles were locked with tension. What was crawling through the skyscraper's duct system?

Scully felt her tension ease as she heard her backup arrive. Four more agents, including Colton, ran toward them. They too aimed their weapons at the open panel.

Scully watched intently. She could just make out a man, crouching in the darkness of the opening. He hesitated beyond the glare of the agents' flashlights. Then he crawled out feetfirst.

He looked to be in his early twenties. He had a boyish face with a high forehead framed by short, straight bangs. He wore a tan uniform with an emblem that read ANIMAL CONTROL. His face shined with sweat. Shaking, he raised his hands over his head. He looked scared to death. Like a rabbit caught in headlights.

'Take him,' Colton ordered.

The other agents moved in and handcuffed him.

'You are under arrest,' one of the agents told the suspect. 'You have the right to remain silent. Anything you say can and will be held against you in a court of law . . .'

Colton turned to Scully. 'Good job, Dana,' he said, making sure Mulder heard him.

Scully didn't respond. She wasn't about to celebrate – not in front of Mulder, who looked shaken.

Mulder came up to Scully. 'You were right,' he said. 'Your profile nailed him perfectly.' Then he walked off without another word.

Scully watched her partner go. She *was* right. And for once Mulder was wrong. So why, she wondered, didn't that feel good?

CHAPTER
SIX

Scully sat behind the two-way mirror. She was looking into a bleak room in the Baltimore Police Headquarters. With her were Mulder, Colton, Fuller, and two police officers. They were all watching as a woman with short blond hair prepared to give a lie-detector test to the suspect.

The suspect wore fluorescent orange prison coveralls. He was sitting in a chair, facing the two-way mirror. Scully knew that though they could see him, he couldn't see them.

One of the suspect's arms was strapped down and fastened with a blood-pressure cuff. Wires ran from the machine to sensors on his fingertips.

Scully knew that his blood pressure, heart rate, and breathing rate were all about to be measured. A change in any one of them might mean that he was lying. The suspect looked the way he had that night in the garage – young and scared. Scully was curious about what would happen during the polygraph test.

The woman adjusted the machine so that the ink flowed through the stylus and the graph paper moved.

She began the test with a simple question. 'Is your full name Eugene Victor Tooms?'

'Yes,' the suspect answered.

'Do you live in the state of Maryland?'

'Yes,' Tooms said.

'Are you employed by Baltimore Municipal Animal Control?'

'Yes,' he answered again.

The examiner watched the graph paper and marked '7/+' next to the response. So far, Scully knew, the suspect was telling the truth.

'Eugene, is it your intent to lie to me about anything here today?' the woman asked.

'No,' Tooms replied. He spoke in a monotone, and his eyes seemed glazed, as if he were in a trance.

'Were you ever enrolled in college?'

'Yes.'

'Were you ever enrolled in medical school?'

'No.'

'Have you ever removed a liver from a human being?'

'No,' Tooms replied.

'Have you ever killed a living creature?'

'Yes.' Like his voice, Tooms's face was completely neutral, empty of all emotion.

'Have you ever killed a human being?'

'No,' he answered.

'Have you ever been in George Usher's office?' the examiner asked.

'No,' Tooms answered.

'Did you kill George Usher?'

'No,' he replied again.

'Are you over one hundred years old?'

Tooms hesitated, looking surprised by the question. Then he answered, 'No.'

On the other side of the two-way mirror, Colton was also surprised by the strange query. 'That must have been a control question,' he said.

'Actually,' Mulder said, 'I told her to ask that.'

Colton gave Mulder a puzzled look, then turned his attention back to the lie-detector test.

'Have you ever been to Powhatan Mill?' the examiner asked.

'Yes,' Tooms answered.

'In 1933?'

Again the suspect hesitated before saying, 'No.' Colton scowled at Mulder. 'You again?'

Mulder nodded, his eyes locked on Eugene Tooms.

'Are you afraid you might fail this test?' the examiner asked.

Tooms looked uncertain. Now the pressure was definitely getting to him. 'Well . . . yes,' he admitted. ''Cause I didn't do anything.'

The examiner looked at the graph and nodded. 'Thank you, Mr Tooms. That will be all for now.'

A short while later, Tooms had been returned to his cell by the police officers. Scully, Mulder, and Colton all stood in the interrogation room, waiting for the results of the test.

'Eugene Tooms nailed it,' the examiner told them. 'A plus. As far as I'm concerned, the subject did not kill those people.'

Mulder didn't seem satisfied with this. He took the graph paper from the machine and sat down to examine it.

Agent Fuller entered the room with a sigh. 'Tooms checks out,' he announced. 'The maintenance people in Usher's office building confirmed calling Animal Control because of a bad smell in the building. And they found a dead cat in the ventilation ducts on the second floor.'

Colton stood up. 'Well, that ends that.'

'No, it doesn't,' Scully argued. 'It doesn't explain what Tooms was doing there in the middle of the night.'

Fuller shrugged. 'So he's one of the few civil servants we have with dedication. And we busted him for it.'

'Tooms was crawling up the air duct by himself, without alerting security,' Scully reminded him.

'Dana,' Colton said, 'Tooms passed the test. His story checks out. He's not the guy. This doesn't mean your profile is incorrect.'

'Scully's right,' Mulder said. His eyes were still on the graph paper, and he spoke with total confidence. 'Tooms *is* the guy.'

Fuller looked at Mulder as though he'd just announced that the moon was purple. 'Okay, Mulder.' He spoke in the overly patient voice of a parent dealing with a troublesome child. 'Whadd'ya got?'

Mulder pointed to the graph paper. 'Tooms lied on questions twelve and fourteen,' he explained. 'These responses nearly go off the chart.'

Fuller studied the graph paper with a skeptical expression. 'Is number twelve the question about being a hundred years old?' he asked. 'Let me tell ya, *I* had a reaction to that stupid question. And what was that Powhatan Mill thing?'

'Two murders with matching methods occurred in Powhatan Mill in 1933,' Mulder answered.

The examiner cleared her throat. 'My interpretation of those reactions –'

Fuller was out of patience. 'I don't need you or that machine to tell me if Tooms was alive in '33!' he yelled.

'He's the guy,' Mulder said calmly.

Fuller glared at him. 'Well, if he is, I'm letting him go!' With that the supervisor stomped out of the room. The door slammed behind him.

Slowly Colton stood up and moved toward the door. From

the expression on his face, Scully knew that he agreed with Fuller. And that he didn't believe Mulder at all.

'Coming?' Colton asked Scully.

Scully hesitated. She could choose to work with the Violent Crimes Section. Or she could continue to work with Mulder.

'Tom,' she began. 'I . . . I want to thank you for letting me work with your section. But I'm officially assigned to the X-files.'

Colton's eyes moved to Mulder, who was still looking over the charts. 'I'll see what I can do about that,' he said.

'Tom,' Scully said at once, 'I can look out for myself. And I don't want to –'

'You said Mulder was "out there,"' Colton broke in.

Mulder glanced up at him with a look of polite interest. Scully wished she were somewhere else. Far away.

'But Mulder's more than "out there,"' Colton went on. 'He's *insane*.'

CHAPTER
SEVEN

Scully was quiet as she and Mulder left the interrogation room and started out of the Baltimore Police Headquarters. She had just made a choice. She could have worked with Colton and the Violent Crimes Section, a position any FBI agent would respect. Instead she'd chosen to continue working with Mulder on the X-files. She hoped it was a decision she wouldn't regret.

'Mulder,' Scully said as they walked through the busy headquarters. 'Why'd you do that?'

'Do what?' Mulder asked innocently.

'After the lie-detector test,' Scully reminded him, 'you told Fuller and Colton that you thought Tooms committed the 1933 murders. You knew they'd never believe you. Why'd you push it?'

'Maybe I thought you caught the right guy,' Mulder said.

Scully shook her head. By now she'd spent enough time with Mulder to know that was only half the answer. 'And?' she prodded.

'Okay,' Mulder continued. '*And* maybe I run up against so many people who are hostile just because they can't open their minds to the . . . possibilities that – '

'What?' Scully asked.

Mulder gave her one of his rare smiles. 'That sometimes my need to mess with their heads outweighs my fear of looking like a fool.'

'I think it was more than that,' Scully said. 'It seemed like you were acting very territorial.'

'Of course I was,' he said. 'In our cases, you may not agree with what I hope to find, but at least you respect the journey. Colton only respects Colton. I guess that makes me want to keep him away from our investigation. And I don't mind him knowing that he's being kept out.'

Scully paused a moment, surprised by Mulder's confession.

'But,' Mulder went on calmly, 'if you want to keep working with them, I won't hold it against you.'

'Oh, no,' Scully said, shaking her head. 'You're not getting rid of me that easy. I know you must have something more than just the lie-detector test to back up this bizarre theory. And I want to see what it is.'

The next day Scully knew exactly what Mulder had to back up his theory. She sat with him at a borrowed computer in the Baltimore police station. Mulder had called up Eugene Tooms's arrest report.

'Here,' Mulder said, punching in a command on the keyboard, 'are Tooms's fingerprints.'

He punched some more buttons and the fingerprints enlarged, filling the screen.

Mulder entered another command. 'Now this,' he said as an elongated print appeared on the screen, 'is the fingerprint I took from Usher's office. This print matches the old ones from the X-files. Here's the print from the 1933 murder at Powhatan Mill.'

Scully didn't see the connection between Tooms's prints

and the strange ones from the X-files. She glanced at Mulder and shrugged.

'Obviously, no match,' he admitted. 'But what if ... somehow ...' He punched in another command. Now Tooms's normal-looking human prints appeared only on the left half of the screen. The elongated prints appeared on the right half.

Working quickly, Mulder used the mouse to single out Tooms's middle left finger. He hit another button, and the computer stretched Tooms's fingerprint until it was as long and narrow as the one taken from Usher's office.

Scully's mouth dropped open as she saw what he was getting at.

'Just watch,' Mulder said in a low voice. He ran the mouse across its pad, and the two images moved toward the center of the screen – until they overlapped and the computer beeped.

A small box flashed in the center of the screen. 'Match 100%,' it read. 'Match 100%.'

At first Scully's question stuck in her throat.

'How?' she asked at last. 'How could Tooms's print be the same as a print taken from a murder committed over sixty years ago?'

'The only thing I know for certain,' said Mulder, his eyes on the screen, 'is that they let him go.'

EIGHT

It was dark when Thomas Werner pulled into his driveway. He'd worked late at the office. Now he was ready for a drink and bed.

He reached for his briefcase and opened the car door. Then he stopped. Something felt different tonight. He sat for a moment, trying to pinpoint the feeling.

A cool autumn wind streamed through the open car door. Leaves rustled as they tumbled across the lawns, blew into the road, and scattered. During the day the streets of Werner's neighborhood rang with the sounds of children playing. But it was late now, and the neighborhood was quiet. It was so quiet that Werner could hear the wind in the trees and the *ping* under his car as the engine cooled. It was so quiet he could hear the sound of his own heartbeat.

Quiet wasn't a problem, Werner reminded himself. After all, he'd moved to this neighborhood because it was quiet.

He stepped out of his car. The sensor security light at the side of the house flashed on as he approached. It bathed the driveway in harsh white light. Werner glanced around, trying to shake the strange idea that something was wrong.

His three-story white house looked exactly the way it did every evening. Like his life, the house was neat, orderly, well kept. *Everything's fine*, Werner told himself. *You're imagining things.*

Werner walked up to the house, took out his keys, and let himself in through the side door.

Only pale moonlight lit the street. But the man who watched Werner leave his car and enter his house had no trouble seeing. His eyes glowed red with an inhuman fire.

Tooms crouched in the hedges on the other side of the street – waiting, watching. When Werner was inside his house, Tooms stood up. Moving swiftly, he crossed the street and went straight to Werner's house. Like an animal following a scent.

He stepped directly in front of the sensor light. It did not turn on.

Werner hadn't been imagining things. Something *was* wrong – terribly wrong. He was being hunted.

Methodically Tooms began to search for his point of entry. Keeping himself hidden in the bushes, he moved around the side of the house. Werner's home was well protected. There were no windows or doors Tooms could use without setting off alarms.

Suddenly Tooms stopped. Before him, stretching up the side of the house, was a brick chimney. He'd found his way in.

Tooms reached up, grasping the bricks with the tips of his fingers. He began to pull himself up, as easily as a lizard scales a wall. He climbed slowly, surely, silently.

Tooms moved higher, past the first-floor windows. And then past the second-floor windows. He stretched out his fingers and reached for the edge of the roof. With uncanny strength, he lifted himself up onto the roof.

He gazed around in the darkness, and his eyes lit on the

chimney stack. Now nothing could stop him. Thomas Werner didn't have a chance.

Werner stood in his kitchen. He loosened his tie and frowned as he began to read through his mail. More bills. More people asking for money. Then he stopped reading and looked up. He'd heard a noise – like a man grunting with effort. *No*, Werner told himself. *Couldn't be*. He took off his jacket and began to fix himself a drink.

On the roof Tooms peered down through the chimney opening. It was narrow, no more than six inches by twelve. This one wouldn't be easy. He concentrated, sweat beading his forehead. Then he leaned over, stuck one arm deep into the chimney, and stretched. He stretched until the tiny bones in his fingers cracked from the strain. He stretched until his hand reached down three stories – and gripped the bricks at the very bottom of the flue.

Carefully Tooms lowered his head into the chimney. The rectangular space was even narrower than he'd thought. There was barely room for his head. He tried to wriggle his shoulders in, but they were way too wide.

With a sickening dull *pop*, Tooms dislocated his left shoulder from the socket. His shoulder slipped down into the opening. There was another *pop*, and the right shoulder followed. Tooms could smell Thomas Werner's sweat. Feel the heat of the blood in his veins. With every sense focused on his victim, what he had to do next was easy. Drawing on his incredible strength, Tooms began to squeeze himself down the narrow chimney.

Werner looked up a second time as he heard a *click* coming from the living room. Curious, he walked toward the noise. As always, everything in the living room was in its place.

Except the glass fireplace doors. They were slightly ajar. Wind whistled in from outside, and tiny flecks of ash blew onto the carpet.

Werner started to close the glass doors. Then he thought better of it and decided to light a fire. A fire would make the empty house seem cozy.

He took a log from the wood basket and threw it on the hearth. Then he knelt and lit the kindling from below. Seconds later a bright yellow fire began to flicker. Werner watched the tiny flames dance.

Quite suddenly the fire died. For a second Werner wondered if something was blocking the flue. He opened the matchbox, but it was empty. He stood up, sure there were more matches in one of the kitchen drawers. He turned toward the kitchen and stopped dead in his tracks.

Something was in the house – and it was rushing straight at him. It looked like a man, but it couldn't be. Whoever – or whatever – it was had eyes that blazed red fire.

Werner never even had a chance to scream. Moving swiftly, his attacker stuffed a gag into his mouth. Terrified, Werner tried to fight back. His struggles were useless. His attacker slammed him to the floor with unbelievable force. Werner's head hit hard. The fight was over.

Thomas Werner was unconscious when Eugene Tooms took what he had come for.

CHAPTER
NINE

Thomas Werner had lived a solitary life. He'd rarely had visitors. But the next day his house was filled with people. All of them were cops, trying to reconstruct what had happened the night before. Somewhere in Werner's house there had to be a clue that would lead them to the murderer.

Baltimore Police Detective Johnson stretched out a metal tape measure. He gave the end to a uniformed officer. The officer held it at the tip of Werner's foot. Detective Johnson brought the tape to the wall behind Werner's head.

'Seventy-eight inches from the south wall,' the detective announced. He snapped the tape back into its holder. As far as he could tell, the victim had died sometime the night before. And the body hadn't been moved after the death occurred. But this murder was every bit as mysterious as the ones before it. Once again there was no point of entry. Once again the victim's liver was gone.

Johnson turned as Tom Colton hurried into the house. The young FBI agent looked stressed and frustrated.

'Let's run a check on liver transplants in the next twenty-four hours,' Colton ordered. 'Maybe this is black market. Someone who's making money selling livers to people who are desperate for a transplant.'

Johnson was not impressed by this theory. In fact, he wasn't impressed by Colton. 'Come on,' he said impatiently. 'You've got to be kidding.'

'At this point, I'll give *any* theory a shot,' Colton snapped. He ran a hand wearily through his hair. 'Any sane theory, that is.'

Colton looked even more stressed as Scully and Mulder passed the outside guard and entered the house.

Colton stepped toward them quickly. 'I'm sorry, Dana,' he said, 'but I only want qualified members of the investigating team at the scene.'

'What's the matter, Colton?' Mulder asked softly. 'Are you worried that I'm going to solve your case?'

Mulder started toward the body. Colton reached out and grabbed his arm. Mulder remained calm, but he gave Colton a glance that let him know he had no authority to touch another agent. Colton let go of Mulder almost at once. Still, he continued to block his path.

Scully stepped between the two men. 'Tom, we have authorized access to this crime scene,' she told her former classmate.

Neither Mulder nor Colton moved. It was definitely a standoff. Scully knew it was up to her to break it. Unfortunately Colton was every bit as stubborn as Mulder.

She had one weapon to use against Colton, the only thing he really cared about – his career. 'Tom,' she said in a firm voice, 'a report of your obstructing another officer's investigation might stick out in your personnel file.'

Colton's eyes flashed at her, and Scully knew their friendship was over. But he stepped aside to let Mulder examine the crime scene. Then Colton turned to Scully, his voice low and furious. 'Tell me something, Dana,' he said. 'Whose side are you on?'

'The victim's,' Scully told him.

She left Colton and went to see what the police officers had found so far.

On the other side of the room, Mulder stood watching the police taking measurements. They did their jobs efficiently, barely looking at the corpse in the center of all the activity.

Werner had died with an expression of unbearable terror on his face. Mulder made himself think of Werner as more than a body. He'd been a man, probably not all that different from the men in this room. A man who didn't deserve the death he'd gotten.

Mulder watched Johnson as he drew the tape from Werner's hand to the fireplace. Mulder's eyes widened as he saw something the detective missed – a smudge of ash above the hearth. And there was something disturbingly familiar in its long, narrow shape.

'Sixty-five inches from the fireplace,' Johnson said in a bored tone. He snapped in the tape and started to make notes on a pad.

Mulder moved to the fireplace and knelt to examine the mark more carefully. It wasn't a clear print, but the resemblance to the other prints was strong. Mulder noticed another smudge of ash leading up to the mantel.

Curious, he examined the mantel. Most people filled their mantels with photographs or knickknacks. Werner's mantel was bare, covered only with a fine layer of dust.

Mulder looked more closely. Maybe Werner's mantel hadn't been quite as bare as he'd thought. In the midst of all the dust was a perfectly clean ring. Some object had sat there, Mulder realized. An object that had been moved very recently.

Mulder turned from the hearth as Scully came up to

him. 'The victim is Thomas Werner,' she reported. 'Single, fifty-two years old –'

'It was Tooms,' Mulder cut her off. 'And he took something from the mantel.'

CHAPTER
TEN

Mulder sat in front of a microfiche machine in the basement of the Baltimore Police Station. Reels of film were stacked up next to the machine. Mulder's eyes were locked on the screen as old photographs and documents streaked past at lightning speed.

He stopped the machine with a *clack*. The screen displayed a typed form. The first line read, '1903 Census.' The census, Mulder knew, would tell him exactly who had been living in Baltimore at that time.

Mulder advanced the screen through a few more pages of census forms. He leaned forward eagerly as he found what he was looking for. This copy of the census form had been filled out by hand. The old-fashioned writing read, 'Eugene Victor Tooms.' Mulder sat back in his chair, smiling with satisfaction. Finally the pieces of the puzzle were starting to fit together.

Behind Mulder the door to the room opened. Scully walked in, holding a pad with notes on it.

'Baltimore PD checked out Tooms's apartment,' she reported. 'The address was a cover. No one's ever lived there. *And* Tooms hasn't shown up for work since he was arrested.'

'I found him,' Mulder said.

Scully gave her partner a questioning look.

'How do we learn about the present?' Mulder asked. 'We look to the past. That's where it all began – in 1903 on Exeter Street.' He pointed to the screen.

Scully began to read the census form aloud. '"Eugene Victor Tooms. Date of birth: unknown. Residence: apartment one-oh-three, Sixty-six Exeter Street, Baltimore, Maryland. Occupation: Dog-catcher."' *A profession similar to that of the current Tooms,* she thought.

'Now look at the address of that first murder in 1903,' Mulder said.

Scully picked up the X-file and opened it to the photocopy of a police report written in 1903. '"Address of victim,"' she read. '"Sixty-six Exeter Street, apartment two-oh-three."' Scully's blue eyes widened as she saw what Mulder was driving at. 'He killed the guy above him!'

'Maybe the neighbor played the Victrola too loud,' Mulder suggested.

Scully ignored his joke. 'This Eugene Tooms must be our Tooms's great-grandfather,' she said excitedly.

'What about the prints?' Mulder asked. 'Remember, every fingerprint is unique. And the other prints in the X-file are all a perfect match.'

'Genetics might explain a similar pattern,' Scully said quickly.

Mulder shrugged, neither agreeing nor disagreeing.

'Genetics might also explain the sociopathic attitudes and behaviors,' Scully went on. She was determined to find a rational, scientific explanation for these strange coincidences.

'How?' Mulder asked.

Scully thought back to the case studies she'd read when she was in medical school. 'It begins with one family member who raises kids with sociopathic behavior,' she explained.

'Little murderers,' Mulder translated.

'Or criminals,' Scully agreed. 'Most often kids who are violent. At any rate, a family whose kids are seriously disturbed. Then if that offspring raises a child who's equally dangerous . . .'

Mulder gave her a blank look, then said, 'So, what is this – the anti-Waltons?'

'Well, what do you think?' Scully asked. She was starting to feel frustrated, as she usually did when she tried to convince Mulder of something rational.

'I think what we have to do is track Eugene Tooms,' Mulder answered. 'There are four victims down and one to go this year. If we don't get him right now, the next chance we're going to get is in –'

'The year 2023,' Scully calculated.

'And you're going to be head of the bureau by then,' Mulder added without missing a beat. 'So I think you have to go through the census. I'm going to plow through this century's marriage, birth, and death certificates. And . . .' His voice trailed off as he looked at the screen and realized what a monumental task he'd set for himself.

'And what?' Scully asked.

'And do you have any Dramamine on you?' Mulder asked weakly. He nodded toward the microfiche machine with a pained look. ''Cause these things make me sick.'

Scully bit back a smile and went in search of another microfiche machine.

Mulder opened a small box and took out another roll of microfilm. Patiently he threaded it through the machine. Then he loosened his tie, rolled up his sleeves, and put on his reading glasses. It was going to be a very long morning.

Mulder and Scully scrolled through years of information on the city of Baltimore. On their screens the years flew by . . . 1904 . . . 1909 . . . 1912. And for every year, the two FBI agents scanned information on thousands of people. They were searching for something – anything – about Eugene Victor Tooms.

Hours later, Mulder sat back in his chair and took off his glasses. He rubbed the bridge of his nose. He was tired and bored and beginning to think that maybe this search wasn't such a good idea. Still, he knew he couldn't afford to feel discouraged. He forced himself to turn back to the machine and the endless records.

He felt a small tug of hope when Scully sat down next to him a short time later. 'Find anything?' Mulder asked.

Scully looked every bit as tired as he felt. 'Nope,' she replied. 'Eugene Tooms seems to have disappeared off the face of the earth. What did you find?'

'Never born. Never married. Never died,' Mulder reported.

'At least in Baltimore County,' Scully added.

Mulder sighed. Scully was right. What if Tooms had spent part of his life somewhere else? How would they ever track him?

'I did find one thing, though,' Scully said.

'What?' Mulder asked.

Scully handed him a slip of paper. 'It's the current address of the man who investigated the Powhatan Mill murders in 1933.'

C H A P T E R
ELEVEN

Scully and Mulder walked through the recreation room of Baltimore's Lynne Acres Retirement Home. A group of residents was gathered around a TV, watching a game show. Most were in wheelchairs. Nearly all of them looked to be at least eighty years old. The whole building smelled of old age.

Scully glanced at the group, then quickly looked away. Places like this made her feel sad. Would they find a clue here to the case of Eugene Tooms? she wondered.

An attendant came up to them. 'I just checked for you,' she said. 'Frank Briggs is upstairs in his apartment. Number seven ninety-three. He's expecting you.'

'Thank you,' Scully said.

Five minutes later she and Mulder stood in the seventh-floor hallway, in front of Briggs's apartment. The door was slightly ajar. Mulder knocked.

'Come on in!' called a hoarse voice from inside.

Scully led the way into a tiny studio apartment. A double bed covered with an orange spread took up most of the room. A lamp and a cheap pendulum clock sat on a tall dresser in front of a window. The clock ticked loudly. The walls gave testimony to Briggs's career as a police officer. Scully noted a photograph of a police squad and a certificate of merit.

Frank Briggs sat in a wheelchair near a window. He had
to be about eighty-five, Scully guessed. He was dressed casu-
ally in an open-necked yellow shirt that pulled tightly over
his stomach. Scully studied the retired detective's face. He
had white hair, a mustache, and the crooked, swollen nose
of a man who'd been in more than one fight. Behind gold
wire-rimmed glasses, his blue eyes were still sharp.

Briggs gestured to two armchairs at the foot of his bed.
Scully and Mulder sat down.

'I've been waiting twenty-five years for you,' Briggs said.

'Sir?' Scully asked.

'I called it quits in 1968,' Briggs explained. 'After forty-
five years as a cop.'

'Can you tell us about the 1933 killings in Powhatan
Mill?' Mulder asked.

Briggs nodded. 'I was a sheriff then . . .' he began. His
voice trailed off, as if the subject was difficult for him to talk
about.

Sixty years later, Scully thought, *and the old man still
seemed overwhelmed by the memories.*

She listened as the clock ticked and Briggs sighed. He
motioned for them to draw closer, and then he began talking
in a low voice. He spoke in short sentences, as though he
didn't have enough breath for long ones.

'Powhatan Mill was like nothing else,' he said. 'I'd seen
my share of murders before that. Bloody ones too. But I could
always go home, pitch a few baseballs to my kid, and never
give it a second thought. You gotta be able to do that when
you're a cop. You'd go crazy if you couldn't. Right?'

Scully nodded. What Briggs said was true. In police work,
you had to be able to leave your job behind when you went
home.

'But those murders in Powhatan Mill,' Briggs went on.

'When I walked into that room, my heart went cold. My hands went numb. I could feel ... *it* ...'

'Feel *what*?' Mulder asked.

Scully watched as the old man blinked back tears and struggled to explain. 'In 1945,' he said, 'just after World War Two ended, I first heard about the Nazi death camps. And I remembered that room in Powhatan Mill. And now when I see the Kurds and the Bosnians on television ... that room is there!'

'I'm not sure I see the connection,' Scully said.

The old man sighed. 'What I saw in that room – it was as if all the horrible acts that people are capable of ... somehow gave birth to some kind of human monster. And that room in Powhatan Mill held the evidence of what that monster could do. I saw the bodies he left behind.'

Briggs looked away then, as if he was embarrassed by the emotion in his voice.

Scully put a hand on his arm. 'It's all right,' she said gently. 'I think I understand how you felt.'

Briggs took a deep breath and went on. 'That's why I've been waiting for you,' he said. 'Because I knew *it* was never going to go away. And I've been waiting for it to come back.' His eyes searched Mulder's face. 'It's killed again, hasn't it?'

'Four times. So far,' Mulder told him.

Briggs pointed to a trunk in the corner beside his bed. 'There's a box in the trunk there,' he said. 'Get it out for me, will you, please?'

Mulder opened the trunk and lifted out an old cardboard box with reinforced corners. He set the box down on the bed and wheeled Briggs over to it. The retired police officer removed the lid, and Scully saw that the box was filled with thick folders.

Briggs waved his hand over the box. 'This is all the

evidence I've collected,' he told the two agents. 'Officially and unofficially. Have a look.'

'Unofficially?' Scully asked as she and Mulder began to leaf through the folders.

Briggs coughed into his hand. 'I knew the five murders in 1963 were by the same . . . person,' he said. 'The same one who'd killed in '33. But by then the sheriff's department had me pushing papers. They said I was too old. Wouldn't let me near the case. But I kept my own kind of tabs on things anyway. I knew that someday there'd be someone who could use what I found.'

Scully reached into the box and pulled out a glass jar. Inside it was a clear liquid that was probably formaldehyde. A chunk of red tissue floated in the liquid.

'A piece of a removed liver?' she guessed.

Briggs nodded. 'Left at the crime scene. You know, livers weren't the only trophies he took.'

'What do you mean?' Mulder asked.

'In each case, family members reported small personal effects missing,' Briggs replied.

Mulder's eyes met Scully's. She knew they were both thinking of the object missing from Werner's mantel.

'A hairbrush from the Walters murder,' Briggs continued. 'A coffee mug from the Taylor murder –'

'Have you ever heard the name Eugene Victor Tooms?' Mulder asked, kneeling beside Briggs's wheelchair.

The old man stopped cold. 'You know I have.' He rummaged through the contents of the box and pulled out a bulky folder.

'When they wouldn't let me in on the case in '63, I did some of my own work,' he said proudly. 'I took these surveillance pictures.'

He began to flip through a pile of black-and-white glossy

photographs. He handed a grainy one to Mulder. 'Here you go,' he said. 'That's Tooms.'

Mulder studied the photograph without comment and passed it on to Scully.

'Course that was Tooms thirty years ago,' Briggs added.

Everything in the photo – the cars, the signs in the store window – looked old. Everything except Eugene Tooms. Briggs had caught him as he was stepping out of a van. Tooms was wearing a dogcatcher's uniform. He had the same short bangs. He wore the same startled boyish expression.

A chill went through Scully as she realized that in 1963 Tooms had looked *exactly* the way he did thirty years later. He hadn't aged a day.

Mulder picked up another photo.

'Now that,' Briggs said, 'is the apartment where Tooms lived. It was located at . . . uh . . .'

'Sixty-six Exeter Street?' Mulder guessed.

'That's it,' Briggs said, looking pleased. 'Right there.'

Mulder held out the photograph to Scully and she examined it more closely. The photograph showed a tall brick building, like a warehouse, on a narrow street. A sign on it read, PIERRE PARIS & SONS.

Scully recognized the building as the sort that had been built at the turn of the century. But in 1963 it had still been in decent shape.

Mulder held his hand out to Frank Briggs. 'Thank you,' he said. 'You've been a tremendous help.' He turned to Scully and said, 'I think it's time you and I checked out Sixty-six Exeter Street.'

Scully nodded, but something tightened in the pit of her stomach. They were getting closer to Tooms; she could sense it. And she couldn't help feeling afraid of what they would find.

CHAPTER
TWELVE

Scully's hands were on the wheel. Her eyes were fixed on the traffic ahead of her. But her mind was back on the conversation they'd had at Lynne Acres Retirement Home.

'What did you think of Frank Briggs?' Scully asked Mulder. She turned onto a street that led to one of Baltimore's oldest sections. They were headed for the building in Frank's photograph – 66 Exeter Street.

'I think it's too bad Briggs is retired,' Mulder answered. 'He was a good cop.'

'I meant his theory,' Scully said. 'That Tooms is some kind of a monster. The very worst that humans are capable of, all concentrated in one man.'

Mulder shrugged. 'I don't know if Tooms is evil the way Hitler was evil,' he said. 'I'm not sure he thinks that way. Or if he thinks at all. Tooms may be more like an animal, killing to survive. But in either case, the results are the same. He's a brutal murderer who's got to be stopped.'

Scully drove faster as the traffic thinned out. There were no office buildings or stores in this part of the city. The streets were lined with warehouses and old factory buildings. Most of them looked deserted.

'Here it is,' Scully said, making a sharp turn.

Exeter Street was narrow and dark. Tall buildings on

either side blocked the daylight. Scully thought Exeter looked more like a dead-end alley than a street. She parked the car across from number 66.

'Quiet neighborhood,' Mulder observed.

'You mean abandoned,' Scully said.

Barrels of trash were piled outside the buildings. The street was covered with litter. The buildings looked as if no one had cared for them – or even used them – for years.

Number 66 was definitely the same building they'd seen in Frank Briggs's photograph. Scully recognized its red-brick face and the two shorter buildings beside it. But now the red brick was crumbling. The windows were boarded up. The sign that read PIERRE PARIS & SONS was badly faded. And graffiti covered the ground-floor wall.

Scully stared up at the building. If Mulder and Briggs were right, this was where Eugene Victor Tooms had lived in 1903. And in 1963. Was he here now?

She drew her weapon and followed Mulder to the boarded-up entry. It was time to find out.

Scully stepped inside 66 Exeter Street and switched on her flashlight. Beside her, Mulder did the same.

They were in a narrow hallway. The inside of the building was completely dark. Dust motes floated in the beams of their flashlights. The place smelled of mildew and rot.

The two agents moved silently through the old building. Ahead of them, their flashlight beams crisscrossed in the darkness.

At the base of a wooden stairway Scully and Mulder exchanged a glance. They would try the upstairs apartments if they had to. But first they'd check out the ground floor.

Scully led the way down the hallway to the apartment where Eugene Tooms had lived.

'Here's one-oh-three,' she said, stopping at a battered wooden door.

She turned the knob and pushed. The door swung open easily. Scully went in first. The floorboards creaked beneath her feet.

It was just an old apartment. The windows were boarded up. A thin trickle of light leaked through the rotting wood. Except for some garbage on the floor, the room was empty. But Scully couldn't stop a look of horror from crossing her face.

Mulder nodded, understanding. 'The old man is right,' he said. 'You can feel it.'

Nothing in Scully's scientific training had prepared her for this. This was not the sort of phenomenon she normally believed in: that you could step inside an empty room and feel something terrible. A memory trapped in the walls, lingering in the air. But Briggs *was* right. Something horrific had happened here. And the feel of it was still in this room. As real as the gun she held in her hand.

Scully played the beam of her light along the walls. She was determined to concentrate on the physical. She wanted evidence she could touch. Proof that would hold up in court.

She noted that the brick outer wall showed through the ripped plasterboard. The paint peeled from the walls. A filthy ceramic sink stood beneath a rusted medicine cabinet with missing doors. A stained mattress leaned against a wall. But there was no sign of Tooms. Clearly it had been ages since anyone had lived in the apartment.

'There's nothing here,' Scully said to Mulder. 'Let's go.'

But Mulder's interest was caught by the old mattress. He held it away from the wall and shined his flashlight behind it. He let the mattress drop to the floor. 'Check this out,' he said.

Scully saw what had drawn his attention: a rough hole about four feet high, cut straight through the plasterboard. *Big enough,* Scully thought, *for a man to fit through.* She sent the beam of her flashlight straight down – and saw a ladder dropping into the darkness.

'What's down there?' Mulder asked.

'I don't know,' Scully replied. She tucked her gun into the waistband of her pants. 'Let's find out.'

Without hesitating, Scully lowered herself onto the metal ladder. The pendant on her necklace swung out as she started to climb down.

Mulder was right behind her.

There were only about a dozen rungs before they reached the bottom. They were in a pitch-black area, even darker than the hallway above. Scully shined her light overhead. Heavy pipes crossed low ceiling joists. They were definitely in the building's basement.

It was chilly and damp. And it felt even worse than it had in the apartment. Scully fought back a shiver. She wasn't about to let Frank Briggs's theories – or her own imagination – get the best of her.

Carefully the two agents began to check out the dark basement. Finally Scully shook her head. 'Nothing,' she said, disappointed. 'It's just an old coal cellar.'

'What's that?' Mulder asked. He aimed his flashlight straight ahead. Something reflected the light to him.

Mulder walked toward the shiny object. 'Somebody having a garage sale?' he said.

On a wooden crate sat a collection of objects: a pipe, a coffee mug, a glass cigarette lighter, an enamel box, a candy dish, a snow shaker with a model of the earth inside it.

Mulder knelt down to examine the collection. He picked

up the cigarette lighter so that Scully could see its base. 'This is the shape that was on Werner's mantel,' he said.

Scully nodded, thinking of what Frank Briggs had told them about Tooms. 'Briggs said he kept trophies.'

'Does Tooms live in here?' Mulder wondered aloud.

Still kneeling, he sent the beam of his light across the coal cellar. The far wall, Scully saw, was mottled and damp.

'It looks like the wall's deteriorating,' she said.

'No,' Mulder said. 'Somebody made it that way.'

Before Scully could ask him what he meant, Mulder went over to examine the wall. Seconds later she was at his side. He was right, she saw. Someone had plastered an odd assortment of things against the wall. Greasy rags, torn strips of newspaper, and garbage were all stuck together to form a large mound. It stretched from ceiling to floor and wall to wall.

'It's a nest,' Mulder said, his voice low with amazement.

Scully saw that the nest had been stuck together with an oozing greenish yellow substance. In the very center of the mound was a hole. 'Look,' she said, 'this must be the opening. Think there's anything inside?'

As if to answer her question, Mulder gingerly reached inside the hole and touched it.

Scully was about to do the same – and then she realized what the oozing substance was.

'Oh, my God, Mulder.' She tried not to gag, but she felt sick to her stomach. 'It smells like . . . I think it's *bile*. Tooms must have taken it from his victims' livers.'

'Oh,' Mulder said. He sounded a little sick. 'Do you think there's any way I can quickly get it off my finger without betraying my cool exterior?'

Scully didn't bother to answer.

Mulder hastily wiped his hand on the floor.

Then he stood up and examined the nest again. 'I don't think this is where Tooms lives,' he decided. His mind was working quickly, putting together a pattern that would explain the X-files on this case. 'I think this is where Tooms ... hibernates.'

'Hibernates?' Scully echoed.

'Just listen,' Mulder said. 'What if some genetic mutation could allow a man to awaken every thirty years?'

'Mulder,' Scully said. This time he'd gone completely over the edge. Not even *he* could believe such an absurd theory.

But Mulder was too excited by his idea to stop. 'What if the five livers could provide sustenance for that period?' he went on. 'What if they allowed him to regenerate the cells in his body so that he never aged? What if Tooms is a twentieth-century genetic mutant?'

Scully mulled that one over for about five seconds. Then she dismissed it. The trophies and nest were eerie. Still, they didn't come close to making such a wild theory possible. But this wasn't the time to argue about it. She and Mulder had something much more serious to worry about.

'In any case,' she said, 'Tooms isn't here now. But he's going to come back.'

Mulder nodded. 'We're going to need a surveillance team.'

Scully gave him a wry smile. She knew that getting backup was not going to be easy. Colton had fought the X-files involvement from the start. He wouldn't be happy when she requested additional agents.

'That'll take some finagling,' she told Mulder.

'I'll keep watch, then,' he said. 'You go downtown and see what you can finagle.'

Scully nodded. She'd do what she could.

The two agents started out of the coal cellar. This time

Mulder was in the lead. Scully suddenly stopped, with a sharp intake of breath. 'Wait,' she called. 'I – '

Mulder spun around. 'What is it?'

'I – I think I'm snagged on something,' Scully said. She twisted a bit. Whatever had been caught was suddenly released. 'It's okay,' she called. 'I got it.'

She followed Mulder up the ladder and out of the coal cellar.

The coal cellar's ceiling was covered with pipes. If Scully had shined her flashlight directly above her, she might have seen a hand among the pipes. A hand that now held her necklace.

If she'd shined her light even higher, she would have seen the fire-red eyes of Eugene Tooms. He'd been there all along. Now his eyes followed the agents as they left the cellar. His hand tightened on Scully's necklace. A trophy for each victim. Four victims down. One to go. He'd just found number five.

THIRTEEN

Mulder sat in his car, directly across from 66 Exeter Street. Even in broad daylight the old building looked eerie. As if it held secrets. As if the darkness inside could reach out into the city and spread until daylight itself was swallowed.

Mulder reached into his pocket, drew out a handkerchief, and wiped his fingers. For the third time. He knew it was silly, but he couldn't help it. He couldn't forget what it had felt like to touch the bile that lined Tooms's nest. He knew Tooms was no ordinary man. And part of Mulder couldn't help feeling that Tooms's evil infected everything he touched.

Mulder shifted restlessly in the car. He tried not to be impatient. Waiting was a necessary part of his job. But he didn't like it.

His eyes flashed to the rearview mirror as the back door of his car opened and a middle-aged man wearing a suit got in. Seconds later another man slid into the front seat. Mulder had been expecting them. They were Agents Kennedy and Kramer, from the Violent Crimes Section.

Mulder glanced at his watch. 'It's about time,' he said.

Kramer rubbed the bald spot on his head. 'So, who we lookin' for again?' he asked.

Mulder held up the arrest report and mug shot of Tooms.

'Eugene Tooms,' he told them. 'He's unarmed, but consider him dangerous.'

The two agents nodded. Both were thick-bodied men, older than Mulder. Both looked confident. As if they'd already sewn up the case.

'Scully and I will be back to relieve you in eight hours if Tooms doesn't show,' Mulder promised. 'Right here.'

'You got it,' Kennedy said. Then he added in an undertone, 'Spooky.'

Both agents laughed. Mulder hesitated for a moment. But his face showed no reaction. They could call him whatever they wanted. Names didn't bother him. What bothered him was the certainty that Eugene Tooms would kill again.

In a small office inside the Baltimore Police Headquarters, Scully checked her watch. It was nearly six thirty in the evening. And now she had a little more than two hours before she had to rejoin Mulder on the stakeout. She might as well go home for a while. The idea of a hot bath was too good to pass up. She felt dirty somehow, as if the air in Tooms's coal cellar still clung to her skin.

She was putting the last of her things in her briefcase when the door to the office opened. Tom Colton swept in. He closed the door so hard that its frosted-glass window rattled.

Scully raised one eyebrow. Colton was definitely upset about something. He'd never been good at hiding his emotions.

Colton tossed a piece of paper onto the desk. 'We have to talk,' he said angrily.

Scully had a good idea what this was about. And the last thing she wanted to do was discuss it with Tom Colton. 'I can't talk now,' she said. 'I have to meet Mulder.'

'That's what we have to talk about,' Colton insisted. He leaned forward and pounded on the desk as he spoke. 'You're using two of my men to sit in front of a building that's been condemned for ten years,' he said.

'It's not in any way interfering with your investigation,' Scully told him calmly.

Colton's eyes hardened. 'When we first had lunch, I really looked forward to working with you,' he said. 'You were a good agent, Dana. But now, after seeing the way you've been brainwashed by Mulder . . . I couldn't have you far enough away.'

Scully stood up. She'd heard enough. Colton was acting like a spoiled three-year-old. Without looking at him, she started out of the office.

But Colton stopped her with a parting shot. 'Don't bother going down there,' he said. 'I had the stakeout called off.'

Scully whirled around to face him, her own temper finally snapping. 'You can't do that!' she told him.

Colton smiled smugly. 'You're right. I can't. But my regional supervisor can. Especially after I told him about the irresponsible waste of man-hours.'

Scully moved toward the phone, but Colton grabbed it first.

'No, let me,' he said with exaggerated politeness. 'Let me call Mulder and tell him the news.'

Scully shook with anger as Colton dialed. They were so close to catching Tooms. And Colton, with his overblown ego and ambition, was ruining it all.

'Is this what it takes to "climb the ladder"?' she asked in a low, furious voice.

'All the way to the top,' Colton assured her.

'Then I can't wait till you fall off and land on your face!' Scully told him.

Colton watched Dana storm out. He was smiling. He'd get Mulder and Scully off this case, once and for all.

He listened as Mulder's answering machine picked up. 'This is Fox Mulder,' the recorded voice said. 'I'm not here. Please leave a message.'

It will be a pleasure, Colton thought as he waited for the tone. *It will be a pleasure to tell you that your stakeout has been canceled.*

Scully was distracted as she drove home. Her mind circled the case as if it were a solid wall and somehow she could find a way through. Her thoughts went back to Briggs. She remembered his talking about how he could usually forget a case when he went home. How that was necessary if you were going to do police work and not go crazy.

Scully knew exactly what he meant. Just the sight of the beautiful old building where she lived usually put the stress of work behind her. Tonight, though, that was impossible. This case stayed with her, every second of the day.

Scully parked in front of her building and walked toward the lit entryway. What she couldn't know was that this case really *had* come home with her.

Eugene Tooms hid behind the car that was parked in front of hers, watching her every move.

FOURTEEN

Darkness cloaked the city. Rush hour was nearly over. The downtown sidewalks were empty. Mulder found himself returning to 66 Exeter Street. He'd been restless all day. He hadn't been able to eat or sleep. He hadn't been able to get any work done in his office. He wasn't due to start his next shift on the stakeout for nearly two hours, but he couldn't stay away. Not when they'd found Tooms's nest. Not when they were so close to catching him.

He turned onto Exeter and parked across from number 66. There were no streetlights here. The shadow of the building loomed tall and menacing in the moonlight. Steam rose from a vent in the sidewalk. The street seemed even more deserted than it had during the day.

The street shouldn't be deserted at all, Mulder realized. He checked his watch. Kennedy and Kramer should still be here, watching the building.

Mulder got out of his car and scanned the empty street. There was no sign of the two agents. Or even of their car.

'Where is everyone?' he asked aloud. 'Kramer, Kennedy?'

There was no answer.

'Scully,' he said, 'are you here?'

Again silence was his only answer.

Mulder had a bad feeling about this. Something was wrong. Very wrong.

He began running toward the building where Eugene Tooms lived.

Scully let herself into her apartment. She'd moved here just after she graduated from the Academy, and she'd worked hard at making it the perfect place to come home to. The airy rooms were decorated in warm, sunny colors. Everything was neat and clean and in its proper place.

Tonight, though, Scully paid no attention to what her apartment looked like. Moving with quick, angry motions, she hung up her coat and kicked off her shoes. She was still steaming about Colton's calling off the stakeout. She wondered what he'd said to Mulder, and how Mulder was taking it.

She poured herself a glass of sparkling water and picked up her cordless phone.

She punched in Mulder's number, then sighed as his answering machine played its message. Why was it that Mulder was never home when she really needed to talk to him?

'Mulder,' she began. 'I guess you went out since Colton gave us the night off. I say we file a complaint against him. I'm *furious*. Call me when you get in. 'Bye.'

She hung up the phone and went to run her bath. She loved the big old claw-footed tub and the colorful tiles on the bathroom walls. Above the tub she'd hung loofahs and little shelves filled with bath oils. A tall frosted window flooded the room with light during the day. At night the bright tiles made the room seem cozy.

Scully turned on the hot and cold taps, adjusting them until the water was the right temperature. She wished Mulder would call back. She couldn't really relax until she talked to him. Until they figured out how to get around Colton. And capture Tooms.

She was about to pin up her hair when she realized that her hairbrush was in her purse. And her purse was in her bedroom. She went into the bedroom to get the brush.

That was why she didn't see the outline of a man's body pressed against her bathroom window.

Mulder pushed through the broken door of 66 Exeter Street. He couldn't understand what had happened to the two FBI agents who were supposed to be on the stakeout. And he couldn't forget that Tooms had killed once before in this building. Mulder just hoped he hadn't killed here again.

He snapped on his flashlight and made his way down the deserted hallway to apartment 103. The door was still open.

As soon as Mulder stepped into the empty apartment, his heart began to race. He had never been so sure that Evil was a living, breathing presence. And he had just stepped into its lair. There was no doubt in his mind. Tooms had been back.

Mulder wanted nothing more than to run as far and fast as he could. But he forced himself to go forward. Even if it meant meeting Eugene Tooms.

The old mattress was exactly where he and Scully had left it. Holding his flashlight with one hand, Mulder drew his gun with the other. Slowly he stepped through the hole in the wall. Then he inched down the ladder into the coal cellar.

He shined his light around the dark space. The basement too looked untouched. It didn't make sense, Mulder told himself. Tooms must have come back; he could feel it.

His heart pounding, Mulder crossed the basement floor. He cast the beam of his flashlight onto the wooden crate.

Tooms's trophies shined back at him. Mulder recognized the snow globe and the pipe and Werner's lighter.

But this time there was a new trophy too. One that sent ice water through Mulder's veins. Dangling from the trophy crate was Scully's necklace.

CHAPTER
FIFTEEN

Scully stood in her bedroom, facing her mirror. She was pinning up her hair for her bath, but she barely saw her own reflection. Her mind was still on the case. She knew they'd gotten closer to finding Tooms today. And what they'd found made her very uneasy. *Could Mulder possibly be right?* she wondered. *Was Tooms some sort of mutant who hibernated for thirty years at a stretch? And then kept himself alive by murdering people and eating their livers? Had he really been alive since the beginning of the century? Or earlier?*

Smiling ruefully, Scully shook her head. Until she saw medical tests that proved otherwise, she'd deal with Eugene Victor Tooms as a human. A very dangerous human.

Scully glanced at her watch. If she took her bath, that would give Mulder another hour or so to call back. After her bath, whether or not she had heard from him, she'd head over to Exeter Street. Even if Mulder didn't check his phone messages, she was sure he would meet her there. And if they had to finish the stakeout on their own, they would. She wasn't about to let Colton blow this case.

She went back into the bathroom just in time to shut off the water. The tub was nearly full. She reached over to one of the shelves that held her bath oils and lotions. She chose a bottle of clear blue liquid and poured it into the steaming tub. The smell of rosemary filled the room.

Scully started to undo the bottom button on her shirt. But she stopped as she realized she'd forgotten to bring in her robe from the bedroom. The case definitely had her distracted, she told herself. Either that or her mind was going. She headed back toward the bedroom.

That was when she felt it. Something damp on her wrist. She held it up to the light and saw two drops of clear greenish yellow liquid.

It didn't make sense, she thought. The bath oil was blue. And besides, she hadn't spilled any. She thought for a second. The building was an old one. Maybe there was a leak in the ceiling from the apartment above her.

She looked up at the ceiling and felt the muscles in her chest tighten with fear. Directly above her was a heating grate. A thick greenish yellow liquid was pooling in the corner of the grate.

No, Scully thought. She fought down a surge of panic. She lifted her hand and sniffed the fluid on her wrist. Her body froze with terror as she recognized the smell.

She was suddenly horribly aware of how alone she was. And of how many hiding places there were in her apartment. Especially for someone who could squeeze himself inside a pipe. Or under a counter. Or into the air vent above her.

She touched the greenish yellow substance. She had to be sure. And she was. There was no mistaking it. It could only be bile from a human liver.

'Oh, my God,' she said softly.

Mulder sat in his car and glared at the flashing red and blue lights in the distance. He rested one elbow on the steering wheel and held his head in his hand. He couldn't believe it.

Of all the times for an accident to happen on the highway! For the past twenty minutes traffic hadn't moved.

All Mulder could think of was what he'd found in the basement of 66 Exeter Street. *Tooms has her necklace. Tooms has Scully's necklace.* That could mean only one thing: Scully was going to be the fifth victim.

Mulder reached for his cellular phone and punched in Scully's number. For the twentieth time. He'd been calling her since he'd left Exeter Street.

Once again Scully's phone rang and rang and rang. Mulder couldn't understand it. Scully had an answering machine. The machine should be picking up if she wasn't home.

'Come on, Scully,' he muttered. 'Answer!'

But all he heard was the sound of her phone ringing endlessly. Somehow this scared him even more than seeing her necklace in Tooms's lair.

Mulder sighed with relief as the flashing lights began to move. A few seconds later the cars ahead of him started to roll forward again.

Mulder tried Scully's number one last time while he waited for traffic to resume its normal speed. Then he threw down the phone and hit the gas pedal hard. He hoped he wasn't too late. He hoped there was some nice, innocent reason that Scully wasn't answering her phone.

There was, in fact, a reason that Scully wasn't answering. But it wasn't nice or innocent. She didn't answer because her phone never rang. Mulder wouldn't get through no matter how many times he tried. No one could. Because in the basement of her building, someone had cut the wires to Scully's phone.

For a second, panic froze every muscle in Scully's body. *I'm alone in the apartment with Tooms.* Her heart hammered a rhythm of terror through her veins. *Tooms is hunting me.*

She ordered herself to take a deep breath. The panic broke and instinct took over. She raced for the bedroom. Her gun. She had to get her gun.

She'd left only one light on in the room – the lamp on her bedside table. The rest of the bedroom was dark. Tooms could be anywhere. In her closet. Under the bed. Crouching in the shadows. *Please,* she thought, *don't let him be in here.*

She made it to her desk. The desk was in the darkest part of the room. Frantically she searched for the gun. Her hand closed on papers, her laptop, a box of paper clips. The gun wasn't there.

She forced herself to think calmly. Where had she left it? She knew she'd brought the gun home from work. In her bag. The gun was still in her bag. And the bag was on the bed.

She dashed across the room. She reached for her bag and yanked it open. Her heart slowed as her fingers closed on the familiar metal barrel.

Now *she* was the hunter.

She braced the gun with both hands straight in front of her. Slowly she began to move through the apartment, search-ing for Tooms.

Using her shoulder, Scully turned on the light in the bedroom. She looked under the bed, in the closet, under the desk, anywhere he might be. But she was the only one in the bedroom. Tooms was still in the apartment, she was sure of it. And he was hiding.

Carefully she made her way into the living room. Remem-bering the prints in Werner's house, she checked the fireplace. No sign of Tooms. Was he still in the air vent above the bathroom?

She edged into the hallway that led to the bathroom. She

moved slowly, soundlessly. She felt as if she were listening with her entire body – waiting for Tooms to make the slightest noise.

She glanced up at an air vent in the hall ceiling. Nothing. She whirled as she thought she heard a noise behind her. Deliberately she trained her weapon on a heating grille just above the floor. Nothing again.

She took another deep breath and turned back toward the bath.

She didn't see the cover of the heating grille opening. She only heard the ear-splitting *crack* as it flew off the wall and hit the hardwood floor.

Instantly Tooms's hand shot out of the vent and locked around her leg, pulling it out from under her.

Scully hit the floor hard. The gun flew out of her hand and skittered out of reach, across the bathroom floor and under the tub.

She managed to twist around so that she was on her back. Terror paralyzed her as she stared at Tooms. His face was framed by the rectangular air vent. He no longer looked scared and innocent. He looked like a vicious predator about to devour its prey.

For a long moment Scully and Tooms locked stares. Then a low, animal growl filled the apartment. And Tooms, using unbelievable strength, began to pull her toward him.

Scully knew that she'd never been up against anything like Tooms. That this would be the hardest fight of her life. And that if she didn't win, it would be the last.

CHAPTER
SIXTEEN

Mulder's car came to a screeching stop in front of Scully's apartment building. He got out of the car and stood for a moment. His eyes scanned the fourth-floor windows. There was a light on in Scully's apartment. She was there, all right. And he'd bet everything he owned that Tooms was there with her.

Mulder raced into the entrance of the building, then cut through the lobby to the stairway. He wasn't about to risk getting stuck in the elevator.

He took the stairs two at a time. Then he raced down the hallway that led to Scully's apartment.

'Scully!' He banged on the door.

There was no answer.

'Scully!'

Still no answer. He tried the knob. Scully had been careful, as usual. The door was tightly locked.

Mulder put his ear to the door. There were sounds coming from inside the apartment, as though some sort of struggle was going on.

At least she's still alive, Mulder told himself. But he knew that unless he got in there fast, Scully had only a few minutes left to live.

*   *   *

Scully knew she had to do two things. She had to get out of Tooms's grasp. And she had to get her gun back. Otherwise she didn't stand a chance.

Desperately she caught hold of the bathroom door frame. Using all her strength, she pulled herself toward it. At the same time she kicked furiously at the arm that held her ankle. She kicked again. This time she managed to wrestle free of Tooms's grip.

Still on her back, she slid away from the duct and into the bathroom. She paused for a second, terrified and breathless. Then she watched with disbelief as Tooms's body stretched – impossibly long and impossibly narrow – and shot out of the air duct. Scully never even had time to scream. One second he was in the air. The next he'd landed on top of her, pinning her to the ground.

Scully struggled fiercely to escape, but Tooms was too strong for her. He was on his knees, straddling her. He held her down with the strength of ten. He stank of sweat and bile.

Scully wrenched her body to the side, trying to throw him off her. Tooms didn't budge. He grabbed her chin with one hand. Then he lifted his other hand. She knew what he was planning. He was going to hit her and knock her out – so that he could take what he wanted without a fight.

Scully didn't know if she had enough strength to escape him. But she definitely had enough to make things difficult. Before he could hit her, she landed a hard uppercut on his jaw. Tooms's head snapped back, and Scully felt a flash of hope. At least he could be hurt.

Tooms drew back his arm again. This time Scully reached up with both hands. Like a cat, she went for his eyes with her nails. Scratching, gouging. If she could blind him, she'd have a chance.

With a cry of rage, Tooms grabbed her wrists. She gasped as he slammed them to the floor above her head. With one hand he pinned them there.

And with the other he reached for her right side. His eyes burned fire-red with hunger.

Scully's heart was pounding so fast she thought it would explode. Terror flashed through her like sheet lightning. This was it. She knew exactly what was going to happen. The same thing that had happened to George Usher and Thomas Werner. Tooms was going to kill her – so that he could live and kill again.

And she was helpless to stop him.

SEVENTEEN

Mulder kicked at Scully's door. His leg ached from ankle to thigh. It figured that Scully would choose an apartment with a door like iron.

He drew back his leg and sent another powerful blow into the wood. Finally it began to splinter. He kicked again – and this time the door gave way.

Mulder let himself into the darkened apartment and drew his gun. 'Scully, are you in here?' he shouted.

A muffled cry was his answer.

He threw on the living room light switch. The room was neat, perfect, empty.

'Scully?'

He heard muffled sounds again. This time he was sure they were coming from the bathroom.

Mulder reached the open bathroom door, and for a second he didn't even notice Tooms. All he saw was that Scully was still alive.

Then Mulder's brain quickly made sense of the scene. Tooms had released her. He stood with his face to the bathroom window. A shattering sound filled the room as Tooms's bare fist smashed through the frosted glass. With inhuman strength, Tooms stretched his hand up and began to lift himself toward the opening in the glass.

But Scully was up. And she wasn't about to let Tooms escape. She tackled him hard, grabbing his legs.

'Freeze!' Mulder shouted. But he couldn't shoot. Scully was in the way.

Mulder's heart sank as Tooms turned on Scully.

He grabbed her throat and pushed her backward. Mulder had a good idea how strong Tooms was. Scully was about two seconds away from having her neck snapped.

Quickly Mulder opened his handcuffs and went after Tooms. He grabbed Tooms's arm, but he wasn't fast enough to cuff him.

Tooms let go of Scully and whirled to face Mulder. Like an enraged bull, Tooms charged, knocking Mulder to the floor.

Mulder rolled, then kicked at Tooms. It didn't stop Tooms, but it bought Mulder a little time and distance. He knew that if Tooms actually got hold of him, he wouldn't have a chance.

Tooms stood over him now, roaring like a wounded animal. He raised his hand like a knife edge, about to drive it into Mulder.

Scully grabbed Tooms's other arm. She snapped Mulder's open handcuff around Tooms's wrist and fastened the other cuff to the bathtub faucet.

Instantly Mulder was up, his automatic trained on Tooms. Tooms jerked at the metal cuff. He twisted and pulled. But the old fixtures were strong. And gradually Tooms settled down. This time he couldn't escape.

With his gun on Tooms, Mulder glanced at Scully. She was leaning against the wall, still breathing hard. 'You all right?' Mulder asked her.

Scully nodded. She was trembling and she looked exhausted.

Mulder glanced back at their prisoner. 'Well, at least he's not going to get this year's quota.'

Scully smiled, for the first time all day.

CHAPTER
EIGHTEEN

Morning sunlight streamed through the windows of the Lynne Acres Retirement Home. Frank Briggs sat in his apartment, reading the daily paper. He was in his wheelchair and alone, as usual. There was no longer much he could do to change the news, he reflected. But at least he could still keep up with it.

A heavy sadness filled him as he saw the front-page headline. It read, THE CONSEQUENCES OF ETHNIC CLEANSING. Above the headline was a photograph of war casualties. *It was horrifying*, Briggs thought. *Even worse, it was endless. Why did men keep doing these things to each other?*

Shaking his head in sorrow, Briggs turned the page. His eyebrows rose in surprise as he caught sight of a much smaller headline: SUSPECT CAUGHT IN SERIAL KILLINGS. And right next to it was Eugene Victor Tooms's mug shot.

Briggs blinked back tears as he read the story. Those two FBI agents, Mulder and Scully, had done it. They'd put that monster Tooms behind bars. A case he had started on in 1933 was finally closed.

Briggs sighed, allowing himself a rare moment of contentment. Finally he'd done his part to stop a little of the horror.

*　　*　　*

In a tiny cell in the Maryland State psychiatric ward, Eugene Tooms sat on the narrow prison bed. He was holding the same newspaper Briggs held. For a moment his eyes rested on his own mug shot. Then, methodically, he began to rip the paper into long, narrow strips.

Tooms lifted one of the strips and ran his tongue across it. He crumpled the slimy paper in his hand. Then he tossed it at the wall in the corner of his cell. It slid to the floor – at the base of a growing mound of shredded papers. Tooms picked up another strip of paper and ran it along his tongue. He gazed at the corner with contentment. It looked a lot like the wall in the basement of 66 Exeter Street.

Mulder stood outside the door to Tooms's cell and stared through the small circular observation window. He knew that the door was made of steel. And that the barred cell was reinforced by a strong chain link. Tooms was safely imprisoned. So why did he still seem so scary?

Mulder watched as Tooms methodically shredded the newspaper and added the pieces to the pile on the wall. Mulder didn't look away even when he heard Scully's footsteps coming toward him from the other end of the corridor.

'Look at him,' Mulder said in a troubled voice. 'He's building another nest.'

Just the sight of Tooms made Scully's skin crawl. His building a new nest was not a good sign. Still, he was in custody. Finally.

'Everything's been filed,' she reported. 'They've got our statements. The evidence has been tagged. We can turn the investigation over to the Baltimore Bureau now.'

Mulder didn't respond.

'Colton actually tried to worm in on the case,' Scully

continued. 'But his superiors caught on. He's been bumped off the Violent Crimes Section.' She tried to keep the triumph out of her voice as she added, 'They reassigned him to the White-Collar Crime section at the Sioux Falls Bureau.'

Mulder shrugged. Colton didn't matter to him. And he never had.

'You'll be interested to know, I've ordered some genetic tests on Tooms,' Scully went on. 'The preliminary medical exam revealed quite abnormal development in the muscular and skeletal systems.'

Mulder gave her a faint smile. 'I didn't need the results of a medical exam to tell me that.'

Scully ignored his comment and continued. 'Tooms also has a continually declining metabolic rate. His body's metabolism dips way below the levels registered in deep sleep.' She hesitated. 'Did you hear what I said, Mulder?'

Inside the cell, Tooms tore another strip of paper and ran his tongue over it.

'I heard you,' Mulder said, his voice weary. 'It's just that I'm thinking about all these people putting bars on their windows. Spending good money on high-tech security systems and trying to feel safe. And I look at this guy, and I think – it's not enough. None of it is enough.'

Scully put a hand on Mulder's shoulder. 'Come on,' she said gently. 'It's time to go.'

Eugene Tooms was only barely aware of Mulder and Scully's leaving. He tore another strip of paper, wet it with his saliva, and added it to his nest. He paused as he heard footsteps on the other side of his cell door.

A narrow slot in the door opened. A guard slid a food tray into the slot.

Tooms got up and took the tray. He sat back down on his

bed. He didn't bother with the food. He'd already fed on what he needed to stay alive.

His eyes were fixed on the cell door. The guard had left the panel open so that Tooms could put the tray back when he was done eating.

Tooms listened to the guard's footsteps dying away.

His eyes glowed red as he gazed at the light pouring through the narrow slot. A smile crossed Tooms's face. It was a very narrow opening. Maybe only six inches high and nine inches wide. But that really wasn't a problem if you knew how to squeeze . . .

HUMBUG

To Mary Baginski, wherever you are

ONE

It was a night straight out of a horror movie.

Black clouds billowed around a bone-white moon.

Tropical trees cast long shadows in the moonlight.

Somewhere an owl hooted, and a dog howled.

But the two boys alone in the night were not afraid. They were only seven and five. They felt safe playing in their backyard pool. They did not see the creature silently creeping toward them.

The creature had a human head and body. But it was covered with fishlike scales from head to toe, like a nightmare sea monster. The kids splashed happily as it came closer and closer.

Smoothly it slipped under the water at the deep end. Invisible as a submarine, it headed for the boys.

Then, with a hideous roar, it exploded out of the water.

The boys had no chance to escape.

They could only scream.

Then they broke into laughter.

'Daddy, cut it out!' cried the younger one.

'I knew it was you all along, Dad,' the older one declared.

'You did, huh?' said Jerald Glazebrook. 'Well, I've got you now!'

Glazebrook grabbed his older son, Robert, and started wrestling with him in the water.

'Oh, Dad!' shrieked Robert as they roughhoused together.

His younger brother, Lionel, got into the act. He jumped on his father's scaly back.

'Two against one. No fair!' Glazebrook said. But he kept the fun going a few minutes more.

Finally he shook the boys off.

'That's enough, kids,' he said. 'Your old man has had it. I got out of shape on the road. Too many shows and not enough jogging.'

'I'm glad you're back home, Dad,' Robert said.

'I'm glad you're home too,' said Lionel.

'You see a lot of weird stuff on the road this year?' asked Robert.

'I'll have all winter to tell you about it,' Glazebrook said. 'But right now your mother wants you guys to get ready for bed.'

Smiling, he lifted each of them out of the pool. He gave each of their rumps a mock slap and watched them run back to the house.

Then he stretched. His wet scales glistened in the moonlight.

He looked at the water. Maybe he'd do a few laps. He'd start getting back into shape.

Glazebrook looked like a sea monster, but he didn't swim like one. He did a clumsy, splashing crawl. After ten laps he was gasping for air. He decided that was enough for tonight. Tomorrow he'd try for fifteen laps. Right now he'd just enjoy floating on his back in the cool water. Going on the road had its moments, but there was no place like home.

He thought of the van parked in his driveway. It was decorated with his show name, THE ALLIGATOR MAN, and a brightly colored painting of him in a water tank. Under the painting were the words IS HE AN ANIMAL? OR IS HE A MONSTER?

Glazebrook sighed happily. He'd be glad to give the van a rest for a while. To give himself a rest too.

Dimly he heard the dog howling in the distance. Drowsily he told himself he'd have to talk to the next-door neighbors. They simply had to stop chaining their pooch at night.

Then Glazebrook heard another sound. A splashing at the other end of the pool.

Had the kids come back? He'd have to make it clear it was their bedtime.

He lifted his head to spot them, but he saw nothing.

Then he saw ripples in the water.

Those kids, he thought. Trying to sneak up and surprise him. Well, he'd give them a surprise when they came to the surface.

By now he could see a pale shape underwater.

It wasn't the shape of two kids. Or of one.

It was –

He didn't know what it was.

All he could make out was a kind of blob. A blob the size of a beach ball. It was heading for him faster than he could believe.

'What the devil?' he muttered, backing toward the side of the pool.

He couldn't move fast enough.

The blob slammed into him, like a cannonball hitting his stomach.

He doubled over in pain and went under.

With a desperate effort he straightened up, spitting and gasping.

The blob hit him again. He screamed. It felt as if it were breaking him in two.

He grabbed the edge of the pool. He tried to lift himself out.

'Uhhhhhhhhh!' he groaned as he was bashed from the back. Agony knifed through him. Desperately clinging to the pool's edge, he turned his head and looked down.

He saw his own blood coloring the water.

It was the last thing that Jerald Glazebrook, the Alligator Man, ever saw.

CHAPTER
TWO

'You look like a fisherman who's hooked a big one,' Special Agent Dana Scully told Special Agent Fox Mulder.

Mulder smiled, and Scully braced herself. She knew what kinds of things made her partner smile that way. Weird things. Things that most FBI agents wouldn't touch with a ten-foot pole.

'Take a look at this,' Mulder told her.

He picked up a photo from his cluttered desk and handed it to Scully.

Scully looked at it.

Her mouth dropped open.

'Don't tell me,' she said. 'You've finally done it. You've gotten a shot of one of your aliens.'

'No,' Mulder said. 'This man is human.'

'My God, what happened to him?' asked Scully. 'How did his head get covered with those . . . those . . . scales?'

'Nothing happened to him – except being born,' Mulder said. 'Here. Take a look at the rest of him.'

Mulder showed Scully another photo.

This one showed the man's entire body. The scales covered him from head to toe.

'He had a rare disease from birth,' Mulder explained. 'It's

called ichthyosis. The outside of the skin continually hardens and sheds off. Something like the bark of a tree. Fish scales, though, is what it looks like.'

'Is it fatal?' asked Scully.

'Not at all,' Mulder said. 'It's not even painful. The suffering comes from the way other people react to it. Someone with the disease is often shunned.'

'Yeah,' said Scully. 'People can be cruel to those who look strange.'

'Beginning with the name they call them,' said Mulder. '*Freaks.*'

'Sticks and stones can break your bones – but names can hurt even more,' Scully agreed.

'Still, this man, Jerald Glazebrook, made the best of it,' said Mulder. 'He picked his own name. The Alligator Man. He used it to make a good living in circuses and carnivals, and to make a good life for himself. It wasn't sticks or stones or names that killed him.'

'What did?' asked Scully.

'I wish I knew,' Mulder said. He showed Scully another photo. 'Care to make a guess?'

Scully looked at the photo. Glazebrook lay facedown by the side of a swimming pool. Scully squinted to get a better look at the gaping wound in his lower back.

'The opening is roughly oval,' Scully said. 'About four inches across. I can't imagine what made a hole like that. Was the weapon found?'

'No,' said Mulder.

'Any other injuries?' asked Scully.

Mulder shook his head. 'The rest of him is untouched.'

'A nice little puzzle,' said Scully. 'The local police must have their hands full.'

'So do we,' Mulder said. He opened up a bulging folder

and took out a thick stack of photos. 'Flip through these.'

Scully looked at the top one. It showed a middle-aged woman with a wound in her back just like Glazebrook's. The next showed a large young man. His wound was in his mid-section.

Mulder gave her the stats. 'There have been forty-seven such attacks in the past twenty-eight years around the country. The first was in Oregon, the last five in Florida. The time between attacks can be as short as a day or as long as six years. The victims are all ages and races, male and female. We have no clues as to why they were killed.'

'Perhaps it's some weird religious ritual,' said Scully. 'There are a lot of crazy cults out there.'

'Negative,' said Mulder. 'No known cult practices this kind of slaying.'

'Maybe a serial killer?' said Scully, reaching for the last photo.

'Not likely,' Mulder said. 'A serial killer would increase the level of violence over such a long time. These crimes show no such pattern.'

Mulder put the photos back in their folder. Then he asked, 'Any more thoughts, Agent Scully, about our new case?'

Scully had picked up the head shot of the Alligator Man again.

'Mulder, imagine going through your life looking like this,' she said. 'I wonder how he did it.'

'I'm afraid it's too late to ask him,' Mulder said. 'But you'll still have a chance to find out.'

'What do you mean?' asked Scully.

'Jerald Glazebrook had many friends,' Mulder said. 'We'll see them at his funeral tomorrow. We fly to Fort Lauderdale. We rent a car there to drive to Gibsonton.'

'Florida?' Scully asked. 'I take it Gibsonton was the victim's home.'

'I think you'll find it an interesting place,' said Mulder, smiling. 'Full of surprises.'

THREE

Mulder and Scully arrived just as the funeral service was about to begin. They found the last two empty seats in the rows of folding chairs for mourners.

The minister began to read from the Bible on a stand before him. Though he was a small man, his voice was deep and powerful:

'"The Lord is my shepherd; I shall not want. He maketh me to lie down in green pastures. He leadeth me beside the still waters. He restoreth my soul: He leadeth me in the paths of righteousness for His name's sake. Though I walk through the valley of the shadow of death –"'

Scully stifled a yawn. She had gotten up before dawn for the flight down here. Sitting in the Florida sun, she had to fight to stay awake.

Then the minister turned the page – with his bare foot. Beneath his black shawl he had no arms.

Suddenly Scully felt very wide awake.

'"I shall fear no evil: for Thou art with me; Thy rod and Thy staff, they comfort me,"' the minister read.

He looked up from the Bible and went on, 'We are gathered here today to mourn the passing of Jerald Glazebrook, beloved husband, father, friend, and entertainer –'

Scully followed his eyes to where the dead man's family sat.

The two boys were dressed in dark suits. They were trying to be brave, but their lips were trembling. Their mother was dressed in black and wore a veil. The veil was not quite long enough to cover the end of her long red beard.

Scully elbowed Mulder in the ribs. 'You see what I do?' she whispered.

He nodded, and together they looked around at the rest of the mourners.

Two seats down sat a woman who weighed at least four hundred pounds. She would have taken up two full chairs – except that the man beside her was thin as a skeleton.

Next to them sat a middle-aged man. As he listened to the minister's sad words, he took a long drink from a metal flask. Then he slipped the flask back into his coat pocket. Except that the coat was not really his. Scully's eyes widened when she saw that the coat belonged to a small, headless body that was growing out of the man's stomach.

'We mourn him and recall the admiration and respect he inspired in all his fellow artists and performers,' the minister continued.

Scully heard murmurs and sighs behind her. She turned her head – and saw little children filling the row of seats. But when she focused on their faces, she realized that the small people were not children at all.

A little man saw her staring. He smiled and gave her a wave of his tiny hand. She smiled weakly back.

Scully felt Mulder nudging her. She turned and followed his gaze. She looked up and up until her gaze reached the face of the giant sitting five seats away.

Scully and Mulder looked at each other.

'Feel a little out of place?' whispered Mulder.

'Do I ever,' Scully whispered back. 'I feel like a frea –'

Mulder put a finger to his lips.

'Don't say the word,' he said. 'Don't even think it. It's a word no one uses around here.'

They turned their attention to the minister as he went on, 'Although Jerry was a world-renowned escape artist, there is one strongbox from which none of us can escape –'

At that moment the coffin began to shake.

The minister stopped in midsentence. He stared at the shaking coffin. Gasps and whispers ran through the audience.

'Tell me I'm not seeing this,' Scully said.

'I just wish I knew *what* we were seeing,' Mulder said, as the coffin shook more violently.

Someone in the back row shrieked.

A big, burly man in a sheriff's uniform marched up to the coffin. He put his massive hands on it to keep it from tipping over. Then his brow furrowed.

'Come here. Help me with this,' he barked at the four pallbearers nearby.

Together they lifted the coffin and set it down a few feet away.

Now all could see what had made the coffin shake. The spot where it had been was heaving upward.

'An earthquake in Florida?' Scully wondered aloud.

'A human earthquake,' said Mulder as the earth broke open and a man's head emerged.

First came a bush of wild, wiry blond hair. Then an even wilder face with the wildest eyes Scully had ever seen.

The head was followed by a naked upper body. And the rest, in black leather pants.

Finally the whole man stood before them, holding a railroad spike and a hammer.

'Let me introduce myself,' he said. 'Dr Blockhead is my name. Fearful physical feats are my game.'

Angry muttering greeted the intruder.

Dr Blockhead ignored it.

'I did not know the dead man personally,' he said, 'so I will not give a speech about him, though I am sure he was a real nice guy and all that stuff. But I am an admirer of his work and want to pay my respects to it. Namely by ramming this spike right into my chest!'

True to his words, the wild man pressed the point of the spike against his chest and pounded it in with the hammer.

Scully started to get out of her chair. Mulder stopped her.

'Just watch,' he said. 'This guy is good. Real good.'

Dr Blockhead stood tall in triumph. He did not even look at the red stream trickling down his chest.

'Oh dear, I think I hit my heart,' he said. 'How clumsy of me.'

He got no further. The sheriff grabbed him roughly by the arm.

'What do you think you're doing, hippie?' the sheriff snarled.

'Back off, Hamilton,' Dr Blockhead replied, giving the big man a violent shove.

Caught by surprise, the sheriff stumbled backward. He tripped over the coffin behind him and fell back on top of it. He lay stunned among the flowers.

Meanwhile the pallbearers rushed in to grab Dr Blockhead. As he struggled to free himself, the mourners left their seats for a better view.

Mulder and Scully were the only ones who stayed seated.

Scully shook her head at the weirdness.

Mulder smiled.

CHAPTER
FOUR

'I'm surprised the sheriff didn't book Dr Blockhead for disorderly conduct,' Scully said.

'I believe that you can get away with pretty strange behavior here in Gibsonton,' Mulder said.

'From what we've seen so far, I think you're right,' Scully said.

It was an hour after the melee at the cemetery. Jerald Glazebrook was safely in his grave at last. Scully and Mulder were waiting for the sheriff. They had set up a meeting in town at the Three Ring Diner.

The sheriff showed up five minutes after they arrived. He joined them in their booth.

'How do you like our local eating spot?' he asked.

'We haven't looked at the menu yet – but the atmosphere is interesting,' Mulder said.

'Yeah,' said Scully. 'Makes me want to order some cotton candy.'

The diner looked like a circus big top. Posters papered the walls. A trapeze hung from the ceiling. Life-size photos of performing animals and human performers seemed ready to spring into action.

'I see circuses are popular here in Gibsonton,' Mulder said.

'They are,' said the sheriff.

'Did Jerald Glazebrook have anything to do with the circus?' Mulder asked.

'He did,' said the sheriff.

'But my files list Jerald Glazebrook's occupation as "artist,"' said Mulder.

'Jerry was an artist – a great artist,' the sheriff said. 'He was the best escape artist since Houdini. He should have been a headliner in Las Vegas. He should have been a TV sensation. But his skin condition kept him stuck in sideshows. He traveled the country working in circuses and carnivals.'

'I didn't think there were that many sideshows left,' said Scully.

'There aren't,' the sheriff said. 'Just a few barely hanging on.'

'I got the impression at the cemetery that Glazebrook was not the only sideshow performer living here,' Mulder said.

'Well, the sideshow folk around here are pretty much retired,' said the sheriff. 'Though a lot of local people do some kind of circus or carnival work.'

'Why is that?' asked Scully.

The sheriff shrugged. 'People in Pittsburgh work in steel mills. People here work in circuses.'

'But there must be a reason for it,' Scully said.

'Sure there is – if you want to go back seventy years,' the sheriff said. 'Performers from Barnum and Bailey's big show founded this town in the 1920s. It was a place to spend their winters. That's vacation time for circus folk. But still they like to stick together.'

Scully turned to Mulder. 'I think we have a lead in our investigation. Those murders took place all over the country. Someone in a touring circus or carnival could have done them. And it makes even more sense if the killer came from a sideshow. The way he or she was treated by normal people might have made the deformed person angry. Angry enough to kill.'

Scully paused, then went on, 'Another thing. The last five murders were all in Florida – where the sideshow performer could have retired after work dried up.'

Before Mulder could say anything, the sheriff cut in. 'Hold on a second, miss. I don't know much about these murders you're talking about. But I do know these sideshow performers. Around here, we call them "very special people." That's what they are – the nicest bunch you'll ever meet. They may look different on the outside. But it's what's inside that counts.'

'That's what people say about serial killers – until they're caught,' Scully argued. 'Even their closest friends and family think they're completely normal. So if you call these sideshow performers normal, you also have to admit they may be capable of terrible crimes.'

'Let me tell you something,' the sheriff said, still hot under the collar. 'Other people have a lot harder time dealing with these people's looks than the sideshow folk do themselves.'

'I didn't mean to sound cruel, Sheriff,' Scully said. 'We're here to catch a brutal killer. It doesn't matter if he looks as odd as the Elephant Man – or as ordinary as this waitress.'

The waitress had arrived at their table. She was an attractive blonde with a good figure. She smiled. 'Hey, Sheriff,' she said. 'The usual?'

'Sounds good, Sal,' the sheriff said.

Sal turned to take Scully's order.

Scully saw her other side.

Now Scully was looking at a handsome broad-shouldered man with a neat mustache and close-cropped brown hair.

'And for the lady?' Sal asked.

Scully gulped and said, 'Coffee, please.'

'And what's your pleasure, sir?' Sal asked Mulder, giving him a good look at 'her' girlish side.

But Mulder seemed more interested in the menu.

'What is this?' he asked, pointing.

'A Barnum Burger?' asked Sal. 'It's a beef patty topped with baloney.'

'Not the sandwich,' Mulder said. 'The drawing next to it.'

Scully looked at her own menu, which was decorated with sketches of famous sideshow performers. Right next to the Barnum Burger was a drawing of the oddest creature she had ever seen. Its upper part was almost human, with a shriveled head, protruding teeth, and clawed hands. Its lower part was the tail of a fish.

'Sorry, sir,' said Sal. 'We don't serve that. It's just part of the design.'

'Too bad,' Mulder said. 'Then I'll just have some coffee, please.'

As Sal went off to get their orders, Mulder turned to the sheriff. 'The menu design is copyrighted by Hepcat Helm. Is that a local artist?'

'A bit too local,' the sheriff said. 'His workplace is right behind my station house.'

'I'd like to talk to him,' said Mulder.

Scully took another look at the drawings. It figured. Mulder and the artist could compare notes on how weird the weird could get.

Then she heard the sheriff say, 'Sure, I can take you to him. But I have to warn you – the guy's a real monster.'

CHAPTER
FIVE

The sheriff first pressed the buzzer of Hepcat Helm's basement workshop. Then he knocked on the door.

'Nobody home,' said Scully.

'Naw,' the sheriff said. 'He just can't hear us. Listen to his boom box in there.'

Scully could hear the sound of heavy-metal music from inside.

The muffled beat became a blast of raw noise when the sheriff pushed open the door.

Scully and Mulder followed him into the din.

The sheriff had been right to warn them about monsters. They saw monsters everywhere they looked.

Monsters with baboon heads and forked tongues. Monsters with eyeballs dangling out of their skulls. Monsters with screaming people writhing in their jaws. Monsters of every size and shape and fearful form, luridly lifelike, painting after painting of them.

Hepcat Helm was hard at work on his latest monstrous masterpiece when the sheriff screamed his name over the blaring music.

Hepcat put down his paintbrush and snapped off his boom box.

He smiled at his visitors, baring a mouthful of yellow

jagged teeth. He wasn't exactly a monster. He didn't look much like an artist, either. In his dirty Rat Fink T-shirt, greasy jeans, and black high-tops, he looked as if he should be working in an auto body shop. Scully could see construction tools lying among his art supplies and blueprints hanging among his paintings.

'Who are the rubes, Sheriff?' asked Hepcat.

'FBI Agents Scully and Mulder,' said the sheriff. He turned to Scully and Mulder. 'This is Hepcat Helm. He runs a carnival funhouse.'

A look of pain crossed Hepcat's face. 'Man, how many times do I have to tell you? Don't call it that. It's not some rinky-dink carny ride. When people go through it, they don't have fun, they have the bejesus scared out of them. It's not a funhouse. It's a Tabernacle of Terror.'

The sheriff shrugged. 'It's a funhouse.'

'I ain't arguing no more,' said Hepcat. He turned to Mulder and Scully. 'The sheriff here got no artistic appreciation,' he told them.

'I can see that,' Mulder said soothingly. 'Don't let it bother you. Artists are always misunderstood.'

As Hepcat's glare softened, Mulder pulled out the diner menu. 'I was admiring this sample of your work. Very effective.'

'I thought it came off pretty good,' agreed Hepcat.

'I recognized most of the famous figures here,' Mulder went on. 'But who is this?'

'The Feejee Mermaid,' Hepcat said.

'Is that what that thing is?' said the sheriff. 'I wouldn't have guessed.'

'That's because you don't do research like me,' Hepcat said. 'This is absolutely authentic. I copied it from an actual antique poster. It's the Feejee Mermaid to a T.'

'What's the Feejee Mermaid?' asked Scully.

'The Feejee Mermaid is – well, the Feejee Mermaid,' Hepcat said. He seemed surprised that Scully didn't recognize the name.

'It's famous in sideshow history,' the sheriff explained. 'A super piece of humbug that Barnum pulled off.'

'Barnum billed it as a real live mermaid,' Hepcat said. 'But when people bought tickets, all they got to see was a monkey sewn onto the tail of a fish.'

'A monkey?' said Mulder. Suddenly he looked very interested.

'A dead monkey – all dried up,' said Hepcat.

'It looked so bad that Barnum had to admit it was a fake,' the sheriff said.

'So that was the end of the Feejee Mermaid,' said Scully. 'A star one day, a has-been the next? Well, that's showbiz.'

'Not at all,' the sheriff said. 'The Feejee Mermaid kept on being a star attraction. Barnum simply changed the way he billed it. He started calling it the greatest fake in the world.'

'Barnum was a genius,' said Hepcat. 'He kept people guessing where the truth ended and the humbug began. When he said the Feejee Mermaid was a hoax, it made the crowds want to make sure it really was. In fact, maybe Barnum changed his story just to give the Mermaid a box-office shot in the arm. Maybe the Feejee Mermaid wasn't a fake. Maybe it was –'

Mulder finished the thought for him: 'Maybe the Feejee Mermaid was real.'

Scully had to smile. 'Mulder, you should have been born a hundred years ago,' she said. 'Barnum could have used you to sell tickets. No, I take that back. He would have had you buying them.'

Mulder paid no attention. He had already turned to the sheriff.

'We need to find a place to stay for the night,' he said. 'Any suggestions?'

'There's one place in town,' the sheriff said. 'The Big Top Motor Inn. It's kind of a combination motel and trailer park. A lot of traveling circus folk stay there. It's not at all fancy, though.'

'That'll be fine,' Mulder said. 'We won't be spending much time in our rooms. We have some leads to follow.'

Mulder pulled out several photos. He showed them to Scully and the sheriff.

'See these tracks?' he said. 'They've been reported at several of the past crime scenes. No one was able to identify them. But one expert said they might be simian in origin.'

'Simian?' said the sheriff. 'That means like a monkey, right?'

'It refers to any apelike creature,' Mulder said. 'But in this case, quite possibly a monkey.'

'You think the Feejee Mermaid is going around the country committing murders?' the sheriff said, shaking his head in disbelief. 'You can't really imagine –'

'You don't know my partner, Sheriff,' Scully said. 'Ever heard of the statistic that made Barnum rich?'

'What one's that?' the sheriff asked.

'The one about the kind of person born every minute,' said Scully.

CHAPTER
SIX

By now Scully was not surprised by anything she saw in Gibsonton. Not even by the manager of the Big Top Motor Inn.

She barely blinked when he stood up from the registration desk to greet them.

He was three feet tall.

At his heels was his dog. It was the size of a large rat.

'Hiram B. Nutt at your service,' he said in a deep voice. 'I take it you two want a room. Let me suggest our honeymoon suite. Lovely, really, and quite a bargain.'

'We need two rooms, near each other,' Mulder said. 'Ms Scully and I are business associates.'

'I believe I can fix you up,' Nutt said. 'We have two vacant trailers, side by side.'

'That'll be fine,' said Mulder. Then he looked at Nutt and asked, 'Tell me, have you done much circus work in your life?'

Nutt drew himself up to his full height. 'And what makes you think I've ever even gone to a circus, let alone been a slave in one?' he demanded.

'I'm sorry,' said Mulder. 'I know that many citizens here are former circus hands. So I thought –'

Nutt gave a loud sniff. 'You thought that because I am

of small stature, the only career I could have would be in the circus,' he declared. 'One quick look at me, and you thought you knew everything about me.'

'Well, I –' Mulder started to apologize.

But Nutt was not finished. 'It did not occur to you that someone of my height could have a degree in hotel management.'

Nutt pointed at a framed diploma on the wall. 'Or that I could have worked in the finest hotels in the country,' he continued. 'As a manager – not as a page boy in a childish uniform.'

'Look, I didn't –' Mulder began again.

But Nutt was not ready to stop. 'No. In your eyes, a diminutive person like me could not be a respectable businessman, but only a ... a ... clown!'

Finally Mulder managed to say, 'I didn't mean any offense.'

'Offended? Why should I be offended?' Nutt demanded. 'It's human nature to make quick judgments of people based only on their looks. Why, I have done the same thing to you.'

'Have you?' said Mulder. 'And what have you concluded?'

'I have taken in your all-American face, your unsmiling expression, your boring necktie, I have decided you work for the government,' Nutt said. 'You are – an FBI agent.'

'Am I really?' Mulder said.

'I hope you get my point,' Nutt said. 'I want to show how stupid it would be to look at you as a type, rather than as an individual.'

'But I am an FBI agent,' Mulder said, showing Nutt his badge.

There was a loud silence.

Then Nutt said, 'Sign the book, please.'

Mulder picked up a pen from the counter, signed the registration book, then handed the pen to Scully.

'You are also an FBI agent?' Nutt asked.

'Yes,' said Scully.

'But you're a woman,' Nutt said in a bewildered voice.

'Maybe you haven't noticed it, but the world is full of unusual things,' Scully said, handing Nutt his pen.

Without another word, Nutt rang the service bell.

When the bellboy appeared, Scully recognized him.

She had seen him at the funeral. Or rather, she had seen *them* at the funeral. The bellboy was the middle-aged man with the headless body coming out of his midsection.

His flask was out of sight. But from the way he was walking, he looked as if he had emptied and refilled it quite a few times.

'Lanny will take your bags and show you to your rooms,' Nutt said shortly.

'This way,' Lanny said in a slurred voice.

He picked up their bags, straightened up, and half stumbled out the door.

Mulder and Scully walked on either side of him as he wove his way toward their trailers.

'Tell me, have you done much circus work in your life?' asked Mulder.

Scully started to apologize for Mulder's crude question. The tirade from Nutt had been enough for the day.

But before she could speak, Lanny replied with pride, 'I spent most of my life on the stage. I was a headliner.'

'Didn't it bother you to have people staring at you?' asked Scully.

'Best job I ever had,' Lanny stated firmly. 'All I had to do was stand there. Every so often I'd say, "Ladies and gentlemen, I'd like you to meet my brother, Leonard. Excuse him

– he's shy."' As he spoke, Lanny gestured toward the small body that was joined to his.

'Your act went over big, then,' Mulder said.

'Big laughs, let me tell you, big laughs,' said Lanny, remembering his glory days.

'Why'd you give it up?' Mulder asked.

Lanny grimaced. 'Mr Nutt, the kindhearted manager here, convinced me to. He told me it was wrong to make my living by displaying my deformity. So I quit the circus to save my dignity. And now I carry other people's bags.'

With that, he set down the luggage and mopped his face with a handkerchief.

'Those are your trailers up ahead,' he said, handing Mulder the keys. He bent to pick up the bags again. But Mulder stopped him.

'Don't bother,' Mulder said. 'We can manage from here.'

'Why, thank you,' said Lanny, shaking hands with Mulder.

'Good night, sleep tight, don't let the bedbugs bite,' he mumbled. 'Not to say that we have bedbugs. I just meant not to, uhh, let the –'

'Feejee Mermaids bite,' Mulder suggested.

'Yeah!' said Lanny. Then his brows knit. 'Feejee Mermaids?'

He gave up. It was too much for him. He staggered away, flask in hand.

Mulder watched him go, then looked down at his hand.

'What's wrong?' asked Scully.

Mulder showed her a dollar bill. 'Lanny slipped it into my palm as a tip,' he said.

'Say, Mulder, what's all this Feejee Mermaid business?' Scully said. 'You can't be serious.'

'Every murder investigation needs a list of suspects,

Scully,' Mulder said. 'We have to keep our eyes out for any unusual person or thing. We can't cross off any possibilities.'

'I agree,' Scully said. 'But there is a problem.'

'What's that?' Mulder asked.

'In this town, your list of suspects is going to read like the telephone book.'

CHAPTER
SEVEN

That night Mulder was beset by bad dreams. He tossed
and turned on the lumpy bed in his trailer. Scully, in her
trailer, had bad dreams also.

But Hepcat Helm had a nightmare worse than both of
theirs combined.

And Hepcat was not even asleep.

Late at night was Hepcat's favorite time to work. Tonight
he was in his studio putting the finishing touches on a funhouse mirror.

He stepped back to admire his handiwork. In the mirror
his reflection looked like a long, horribly twisted snake.

'Perfect,' he said to himself. 'That'll give the customers
their money's worth.'

Then his eyes widened.

Beside his image in the glass was another twisted shape.

It too was long and pale, weirdly twisted.

'What the –' he muttered.

He wheeled around, angry that someone had barged into
his studio.

But even the hideous image in the mirror did not prepare
him for the sight that met his eyes.

'Nooooo!' he screamed, throwing up his hands to defend
himself.

His hands did no good. They could not shield him from the force that smashed into him.

Craaack!

The back of his head hit the mirror, splintering it into a thousand pieces.

Hepcat Helm's nightmare ended not with waking – but with endless sleep.

Mulder woke at dawn with his nightmare still on his mind.

He decided to go for a jog. He wanted to work up a warm sweat, not a cold one. And he wanted to clear his head.

But when he got outside, he felt as if he were back in his bad dream. Swirling mist shrouded the early morning. Nevertheless, he started running. The fog was sure to lift as the sun rose higher.

The fog was still thick when he reached a narrow bridge four miles away. Mulder paused. Should he cross or turn back?

He had run hard. He stood by the river breathing deeply. Then he saw something that made him hold his breath.

A head broke through the surface of the water. It was the head of a bald man, with a fish wriggling in his jaws.

Mulder watched the man emerge from the river onto the bank.

His dripping body was as hairless as his head. His skin was covered with blue, red, and green tattoos.

He was a man straight out of a nightmare. And the nightmare grew worse as he squatted on the bank and began to eat the live fish.

Mulder began to tiptoe over the bridge.

The man had hearing like a cat's. Still chewing, he lifted his head at the first faint sound of Mulder's approach.

Then he was off and running. He was short and squat, but he ran like a deer.

Even fresh, Mulder couldn't have caught him. Leg-weary from his jog, he gave up after a hundred feet. Puffing, he watched the man vanish in the mist.

'Coffee,' Mulder muttered to himself. 'Got to have coffee. Got to wake up.'

Scully was awakened that morning by a loud knocking on her door. Groaning, she sat up in bed. She waited a minute, hoping the knocking would go away. It only got louder.

She pulled on her robe and opened the door.

Lanny was standing there.

'Excuse me, ma'am,' Lanny said. 'But the sheriff – he wants to see you.'

'Uh-huh,' said Scully. Perhaps because of her dream, she was unable to take her eyes off Lanny's Siamese twin.

She knew she shouldn't stare, but the sight drew her eyes like a magnet.

It was her first chance to get a long, close look at the strange creature attached to Lanny's midsection. She saw that though it did not have a fully formed head, it did have a kind of hump rising from between its shoulders. On that hump were openings that could be eyes and ears. She could not see the rest of its body, though. It wore a jacket that matched Lanny's own, except that the sleeves were pinned to the sides. She supposed it had no arms.

She forced herself to stop staring at it and looked into Lanny's eyes. For a change, they were cold sober.

'There's been another murder,' Lanny said.

CHAPTER
EIGHT

An hour later Scully was kneeling beside Hepcat Helm's body. The sheriff stood nearby, watching her work. Mulder was checking out the rest of Hepcat's workshop.

Scully had a degree in medicine as well as one in science. But the wound in Hepcat's midsection puzzled her.

'It looks like the same kind of wound that killed Jerald Glazebrook,' she told the sheriff. 'Which means the same killer probably did it. Other than that, we're still at square one.'

'I disagree,' said Mulder, joining them. 'We have a trail to follow now.'

'What kind of trail?' asked Scully.

'A trail of blood.'

'I know the corpse is covered with blood,' Scully said. 'But I don't see what that tells us, except that Hepcat bled to death.'

Then she saw the blood-splattered drawing on the floor near Hepcat.

It was a drawing of the Feejee Mermaid.

'Is this what you mean, Mulder?' she asked dubiously. 'I think we should give that theory of yours a rest.'

'The drawing is interesting,' Mulder said. 'But I'm talking about something else.'

He indicated a track of dried blood that led from the corpse to a window at the back of the workshop.

'Take a look at the window,' Mulder said.

Scully saw that the inside was covered with blood.

'So the killer pushed the window open to get out,' Scully said. 'What does that give us – except more of Hepcat's blood?'

'I'm not talking about *that* window,' Mulder said. 'Examine the small one above it. I think that's the one the killer used to get in.'

Scully stood on tiptoe.

At first she saw nothing. Then she said, 'That stain, on the outside of the glass. It looks like a smear of blood.'

'I'd be surprised if it weren't,' Mulder said. 'The killer made that smear when he came in.'

'But how could there be blood before the murder? That doesn't make –' Then Scully got Mulder's point.

'I see,' she said. 'The blood on the outside of the window didn't come from Hepcat. It came from the killer.'

Mulder smiled. 'We'll have to run tests on it,' he said.

'We can find out the blood type at the local hospital lab,' Scully said. 'That'll cut down the list of suspects. But only the DNA can pinpoint the killer, and I'd have to send a blood sample up to Atlanta for that. It might not come back for weeks. The process is slow and painstaking – and they have quite a backlog.'

'We might not have that long before the killer strikes again,' Mulder said. 'It seems he's shifting into high gear. The time between deaths is getting shorter. Something is driving him into a frenzy.'

'Maybe he feels threatened because we're here,' Scully suggested.

'Maybe, maybe not,' Mulder said. 'It's hard to know, when nothing about these crimes makes sense.'

'You can say that again,' the sheriff said. He had been following their conversation. 'I mean, why didn't the killer come in through the open door? It's practically impossible for anyone to squeeze through that little window. The killer would have to be a cross between an acrobat and a contortionist.'

'Right,' said Mulder. He gave the sheriff a smile. 'You could say he belonged in a circus.'

'Or in a padded cell,' the sheriff said.

'Let's see, whom do we know who's both talented and crazy?' mused Scully.

Her eyes met Mulder's, and he gave her a nearly invisible nod.

'Could you take the blood samples to the lab, Sheriff?' she asked. 'We have to pay a call on someone.'

'There is one crazy guy,' Scully said to Mulder.

High above them, a man dangled upside down from a rope at the top of the flagpole. Bound in a straitjacket, he was wiggling like a fish on a line to free himself.

On the ground below him, water bubbled in a huge black pot over a small fire.

An automatic pulley was lowering the man slowly toward the boiling cauldron.

In another few minutes he would be cooked like a lobster.

He was a few feet from the boiling water when he pulled the straitjacket over his head and threw it to the ground.

Then he flipped himself upright and grabbed the rope with his hands. Holding the rope with one hand, he raised his feet and untied the rope around his ankles.

He leaped to the ground triumphantly and pulled a stopwatch out of his pants pocket. Only then did he notice Mulder and Scully.

'No applause?' Dr Blockhead asked. 'How many people do you know who can get out of a straitjacket in under three minutes?'

'None, fortunately,' Scully said.

'I see you have no artistic appreciation.' Dr Blockhead sounded annoyed.

'On the contrary,' said Mulder. 'We caught your act yesterday at the funeral. That was some trick with the railroad spike.'

Dr Blockhead glared at Mulder. 'Dr Blockhead does not perform so-called tricks,' he declared.

'You could have fooled me,' Mulder said. 'In fact, you did. It just goes to show, sometimes you can't believe your own eyes.'

'Well, let's see if I can make a believer of you,' Dr Blockhead said, walking to a table spread with dozens of shining metal instruments. They all looked very sharp.

'Dr Blockhead performs many feats even more astounding than the one you saw at the cemetery,' he announced. 'Feats that boggle the mind. Feats that defy the most agonizing pain.'

He picked up a pair of wicked-looking hat pins that were topped with metal human skulls.

He looked at them and shook his head. 'Not good enough,' he said. 'Not for an audience of suspicious FBI agents. I need something a bit more impressive.'

He put down the pins and picked up a hammer and an extremely long nail.

'Perfecto,' he said. 'Watch closely. And try not to blink, or turn away. I do hope you haven't eaten anything recently.'

Slowly he inserted the long nail into his right nostril. When he could push it in no farther with his hand, he pounded it in with his hammer.

Scully gritted her teeth. She did not want to give Dr Blockhead the pleasure of seeing her wince. 'You must be one of those rare people whose nerve endings do not feel pain,' she said calmly.

Dr Blockhead smiled at her with the nail sticking out of his nose.

'That's right,' he said. 'Just keep telling yourself that.'

Still smiling, he put down the hammer and picked up a pair of pliers. He gripped the nail head with the pliers and began to yank.

'Have you ever performed this tri – I mean, stunt, on anyone else?' Mulder asked.

Dr Blockhead paused with the nail halfway out of his nose.

'I tell my audiences that if they're stupid enough to try this, they'll wind up with a hole where their feeble brain was. But since you guys are obviously Feds, go ahead.'

'Thanks – but no thanks,' Scully said.

'Wise decision,' Dr Blockhead said. 'Leave this to a professional.'

He fitted the pliers onto the nail head again. But before he could give them another yank, Mulder stepped forward.

'May I?' Mulder asked.

'Be my guest,' Dr Blockhead said, slapping the pliers into Mulder's palm.

Weighing the pliers in his hand, Mulder asked, 'Exactly how does one become a professional blockhead?'

'I had my first training when I was growing up in Yemen,' Dr Blockhead said. 'After that, I traveled the world to study under the greatest masters of body control. I have been the student of yogis, fakirs, swamis, and others who know the secrets of this ancient art.'

'Then I guess it's okay for me to do this,' said Mulder, giving the nail a strong, sharp yank with the pliers.

The nail came free easily. Bright red blood glistened on its tip.

'Well done,' said Dr Blockhead, smiling. 'I could use you as my assistant if you'd ever like to change jobs. Of course, your partner here would be better. Audiences love a pretty girl – if she has a strong stomach.'

He turned to Scully. 'I'm sorry if I caused you any discomfort. But you did ask for it.'

'Not to worry,' Scully assured him, hoping her face had not turned green. 'Actually, I'm glad you put on your little show. After that, nothing is going to bother me.'

'Really?' said Dr Blockhead. 'Shall we put your statement to a little test?'

Before Scully could answer, Dr Blockhead did just that.

NINE

I'm *not seeing this*, Scully tried to tell herself.

But she had to believe her own eyes.

First Dr Blockhead went to the cauldron.

Then he gave it a sharp rap with his hammer.

A man's head broke through the surface of the bubbling water.

The head was totally bald. It was followed by a hairless body covered with tattoos as the man lifted himself out of the pot.

He stood dripping before them, wearing a loincloth and smiling broadly.

'Lady and gentleman – or I should say, FBI agent and FBI agent – meet Conundrum,' Dr Blockhead announced.

Scully saw Mulder's mouth drop open as if he were seeing a nightmare come to life.

Dr Blockhead looked pleased as Punch. He did everything but take a bow. To see shock in his audience delighted him more than applause.

'What's the matter?' he asked. 'Haven't you ever seen a man climb out of the water before?'

Mulder swallowed hard. 'As a matter of fact, I have,' he said. 'I saw him down at the river this morning. He was eating a live fish.'

Now it was Dr Blockhead's turn to be shocked. More than shocked. Angry.

Scowling, he said, 'I've told him again and again never to do that. Between-shows snacks ruin his appetite.'

'I could be mistaken,' said Mulder. 'Maybe it was a different bald-headed, jigsaw-puzzle-tattooed guy I saw.'

'Does this man, this – ?' Scully asked Dr Blockhead, then paused. 'What is his name again?'

Mulder supplied the answer before Dr Blockhead could. 'Conundrum.'

'Does Mr Conundrum practice body control too?' asked Scully.

'Not really,' Dr Blockhead said. 'I've taught him a few simple skills, like staying submerged in boiling water. But he has a different specialty. In the language of the circus, Conundrum is a geek.'

'A geek?' said Scully.

'He eats live animals,' Mulder explained.

'He eats anything,' said Dr Blockhead. 'Live animals. Dead animals. Rocks. Lightbulbs. Corkscrews. Battery cables. Cranberries.'

'What about human flesh?' asked Scully sharply. She was not talking to Dr Blockhead. She was questioning Conundrum himself.

Conundrum answered with a twisted smile. Then a crazy laugh.

'Conundrum does not answer questions,' Dr Blockhead said smugly. 'He *is* a question. He is a walking riddle, a maddening mystery. When audiences see his famous Human Piranha act, they are forced to ask themselves how he can do such inhuman things – and why?'

'A good question,' said Scully.

'Yeah,' said Mulder. 'We'll have to chew it over.'

A smile spread over Dr Blockhead's face. 'But where are my manners?' he said. 'What a bad host I am. Let me offer you a little refreshment.'

He picked up a jar, opened it, and held it out to Scully.

'Is that what I think it is?' she asked.

'The finest assortment of living crickets money can buy,' said Dr Blockhead. 'And all quite recently captured. If you don't believe me, read the expiration date on the label.'

'I believe you,' said Scully, still peering at the contents.

She reached in and picked out her cricket. Then she put it in her mouth and crunched down.

She smiled at Dr Blockhead. 'Thank you so much for the treat,' she said.

Then she gave him a dazzling smile and walked away.

'That Scully,' said Mulder, shaking his head. 'She's just full of surprises.'

He lifted his hand in farewell to Dr Blockhead and Conundrum. Then hurried after Scully.

When he reached her, he said, 'Remind me never to play a game of dare with you. I can see you'd stop at nothing to win.'

In response, Scully reached behind Mulder's ear. With a smile, she pulled out a live cricket.

'It's an old sleight-of-hand trick my uncle once taught me,' she said. 'He was an amateur magician. But he still was better than those two jokers.'

When Mulder didn't answer, she said, 'It's all trickery, right? I mean, those things that Dr Blockhead does to himself – they can't be real. And the so-called boiling water that Conundrum was under. There was some kind of machine to create the bubbling effect. And Mr Conundrum had a scuba tank.'

'Probably,' Mulder said.

'Probably?' said Scully. 'I'd say certainly.'

'I know it goes against your grain to think so – but there's nothing certain in the circus, Scully,' Mulder told her. 'It's like an onion. You peel off layer after layer of humbug to get to the truth. And you wind up with – nothing.'

'Humbug or no humbug, Hepcat Helm's bloody corpse was real enough,' Scully said.

'So was the killer's blood at the crime scene,' Mulder said. 'And so was the blood on the nail I yanked from Blockhead's nose. And so is this –'

Mulder extended his hand and plucked a long nail out of the air – a nail with dried blood on its tip.

'Everybody's uncle is an amateur magician,' he told Scully.

CHAPTER
TEN

'Maybe this nail will nail Dr Blockhead,' said Mulder. 'We'll see if the blood on it is a match for the blood on the window. I'll take it over to the lab.'

'It still won't be proof positive,' Scully reminded him. 'Just a general blood type.'

'It'll be better than what we have on him now,' Mulder said. 'Which is exactly nothing.'

He wrapped the nail carefully in a clean handkerchief and put it in his pocket.

'Coming with me?' he asked Scully.

'You go by yourself,' Scully said. 'I want to do some research on my own. This circus world is pretty strange to me. I need to find out more about it. Get my bearings.'

'How?' asked Mulder.

'I saw some kind of circus museum on Main Street,' Scully said. 'I'll start there.'

'Good idea,' said Mulder. 'We can meet tonight back at your trailer.'

Mulder took their rental car to go to the lab, and Scully headed out of the Big Top Motor Inn trailer park on foot.

As she walked along the rows of trailers, she passed an acrobatic human pyramid, one man throwing knives at another, and a crowd of tiny people who were practicing getting in and out of a very small car. Each group stopped what it was doing to watch her go by.

It was the same when she walked down Main Street. An enormous strongman carrying a mountain of groceries gawked at her. The woman behind him, carrying a shopping bag in each of her three hands, did the same. So did the man whose single leg came down from the center of his body.

So this is what it's like to look different, Scully thought. *It is not easy.*

She felt a rush of relief when she finally reached the museum. She wanted to get quickly inside and out of sight.

From the outside, the museum looked like a ramshackle country store. A big sign above the door read THE ODDI-TORIUM.

A collection box hung on the door. Scully read the notice on it: FREAKS FREE! OTHERS PLEASE LEAVE DONATION.

Do I qualify to get in free in Gibsonton? she wondered. To be on the safe side, she stuffed a couple of dollar bills into the box before entering.

A bell tinkled, and a tall old man in a threadbare black suit greeted her as she walked in.

'Welcome to my museum,' he said. 'May I answer any questions you might have?'

Scully did not ask the first question that came to her mind.

What had happened to the man's face?

Had he been born looking like that, with his features running together like melted wax? Or was it the result of a strange disease or a horrible accident?

But that's the kind of question you avoid in this town, Scully thought.

'Thank you very much,' she said. 'I may take you up on your offer. But first I'd like to look at some of your exhibits.'

'Be my guest – and I will be your guide,' the old man said.

He led her to a wall covered with large, old black-and-white photos, many of them from the turn of the century.

As Scully looked at them, the old man reeled off their names. 'This is Prince Randian, the Human Torso. Here's Frank Lentini, the Man with Three Legs. This one is the Tocci Brothers, joined together and sharing just one pair of legs. And then we come to Chang and Eng, the One and Only Original Siamese Twins.'

In front of the life-size photo of Chang and Eng was a table with a stack of pamphlets.

The old man handed one to Scully.

'Do read it when you have a chance,' he urged her. 'It is a little something that I authored.'

Scully read its title: 'The Fascinating True Life Story of the Original Siamese Twins.'

'I'm sure that their life was quite fascinating,' she said. 'But tell me, was their death fascinating as well?'

'Why do you ask?' the old man said.

'I'm down here investigating the death of a – very special person,' Scully said. 'Anything I learn about sideshow people might help.'

'Well, let me tell you that Chang and Eng's death was fascinating indeed,' the old man said. 'On a cold January morning in 1874, Eng woke to find that his brother had passed away during the night. A few hours later, Eng himself departed from this world.'

'That's interesting,' said Scully politely. But there was a puzzled note in her voice.

'I see you miss my point,' the old man said. 'Their deaths are not what is fascinating. It's the idea of Eng lying there alone.' The old man's hand closed on Scully's shoulder, and his voice turned harsh. 'You know that one half of your body is dead. And that the rest must follow. And that there is absolutely nothing you can do about it.'

The man released his grip. 'Fascinating indeed,' said Scully. 'But tell me, what was the official cause of death?'

'Chang died of a cerebral hemorrhage.'

'And Eng?' Scully asked.

'Fright,' the old man answered.

Scully felt a shudder run through her. She changed the subject.

'Do you have any information on blockhead or geek acts?' she asked.

'This is a historical collection of human curiosities,' the old man said. 'Blockheads are skilled performers.'

'Like magicians?' Scully asked.

'Like sword-swallowers.'

'And geeks?' asked Scully.

'Geeks are not skilled. They are not curiosities. They are merely – unpleasant. They do not even rate as high as gaffs.'

'Gaffs?' said Scully.

The old man pointed to another photo.

'Another pair of Siamese twins?' said Scully. The two men were joined at the waist, sharing one pair of legs.

'You have a lot to learn, young lady,' the old man said with a smile. 'Take a look at their faces. Their features are distinctly different. Siamese twins are always identical. These gentlemen are phonies. They are gaffs.'

Scully looked more closely at the photo, and nodded.

'I see it now,' she said. 'They're two guys. One has his legs wrapped around the other's waist. Their baggy pants hide it. Tell me, are such frauds common in sideshows?'

'I will only say that there are several well-known ones,' the old man said.

'Like the Feejee Mermaid?' asked Scully.

The old man's only answer was a low chuckle.

'Please, I'd appreciate anything you could tell me about the Mermaid,' Scully said. 'It might have some bearing on the murder I'm investigating.'

'If you're interested in the death of the Alligator Man, I have something you might want to read,' the old man said, handing Scully another pamphlet. Below its title, 'The Exotic Life of Jim-Jim, the Dog-Faced Boy,' was a photo of a boy whose face was completely covered with long hair.

'What connection does this have with the Glazebrook murder?' asked Scully.

Again the old man smiled. 'Perhaps something. Perhaps nothing. You will have to find out for yourself.'

'Thanks – I hope,' Scully said, tucking the pamphlet into her pocket. 'I really appreciate any help you can offer.'

The old man looked at Scully hard. He bit his lip, as if trying to decide something. Then he leaned his melted-wax face close to hers.

'If you *really* want to understand that murder,' he said quietly, 'there's something you should see.'

'What is it?' Scully asked.

'Come with me,' the old man said.

He led Scully to a door at the rear of the museum.

'I have recently come into possession of an authentic P. T. Barnum exhibit,' he told her. 'I do not show this display to all visitors. It is only for those who truly want to see it, and who have enough courage to face it. Barnum called it the Great Unknown. Tell me, do you dare to risk viewing it?'

'Will it help solve the case?' asked Scully.

'You have my word,' the old man said.

'Open the door,' Scully said.

'First I must ask you two favors,' the old man said.

'Anything. What are they?' Scully said.

'Tell no soul what you witness in there,' the old man said.

'Including my partner?' asked Scully.

The old man thought a moment. 'Well, perhaps just your partner. But no one else,' he cautioned.

'It's a promise,' Scully said. 'And the second favor?'

'An additional donation of twenty dollars – to help cover what it cost me,' the old man said.

Scully thrust the money into his hand.

The man pocketed the twenty, unbolted the door, and opened it.

Scully rushed through the doorway.

The moment she was inside, the door closed behind her.

She heard it being bolted on the other side.

She was locked in alone with the Great Unknown.

CHAPTER
ELEVEN

Scully looked around her. She was locked in a small, windowless room, lit by one weak lightbulb. The walls were concrete, spiderwebbed with cracks, sweating with moisture. The air was chill and damp.

This place is like a tomb, she thought, and shivered.

There was only one object in the room, an old wooden strongbox with air holes drilled in its sides. Massive chains fastened it to the concrete floor.

Well, at least it's not a coffin, she thought. *Those air holes mean something in it is breathing.*

Scully saw that the large lock on the lid was unfastened.

I'm in luck – I guess, she thought as she squatted down and removed the lock.

She paused. She took a deep breath. She tried to relax her tense muscles. Then, slowly, carefully, she lifted the angrily creaking lid.

She was ready for anything – anything but this.

She was staring into an empty box.

At that moment a bright red neon sign lit up on the wall.

It said EXIT.

In its light Scully saw the outlines of a door.

She grimaced.

This museum had given her a real taste of the circus world, all right.

She had been humbugged.

As Mulder approached Scully's trailer that night, he stiffened.

A scurrying noise, followed by the sound of heavy breathing, was coming out from under it. Mulder froze. He didn't like carrying a gun. But he was glad to have one at a time like this.

Weapon in hand, Mulder got down on his hands and knees. He started to crawl under the trailer.

And came face-to-face with Hiram Nutt, who was crawling out.

Both of them scrambled to their feet.

'Does Agent Scully know you were under her trailer?' Mulder demanded.

'I was merely fixing her plumbing,' Nutt replied.

'Uh-huh. Sure. And what else?' Mulder asked.

At that moment Scully opened her door.

'Mr Nutt,' she said. 'Thanks a lot. The sink works fine now.'

Nutt shot Mulder a look of triumph and strode away.

'What are you doing with your gun out, Mulder?' Scully asked.

'Just checking if it needs oiling,' he said, and stuck it back into his shoulder holster. Quickly he changed the subject. 'Find out anything at the museum?'

'You could say that,' said Scully. She held the trailer door open for him. 'So,' she said, once he was inside, 'tell me how the lab tests came out.'

'The blood from the window matched the blood on the nail,' Mulder said. 'But both were O positive, the most common blood type. I also ran a background check on Dr Blockhead. His real name is Jeffrey Swaim. He's not from Yemen, he's from Milwaukee. And he has no right to call himself a doctor of any kind.'

'Any criminal record?' asked Scully.

'Nothing but a few dozen traffic violations,' Mulder said. 'Then, with Sheriff Hamilton's help, I ran background checks on the old sideshow performers around here. Everyone was clean.'

'As a matter of fact, I ended up running a background check too,' Scully said. 'Just to keep my afternoon from being a total waste.'

'On whom?' Mulder asked.

Scully opened a folder and started reading. 'An orphan was discovered in the wild forests of Albania in 1933. He was skilled at catching his own food, but he could not speak a word, except for a few savage grunts –'

'Interesting,' Mulder interrupted. 'But what does this have to do with –'

'Keep listening. It gets even more interesting,' Scully said, and read on. 'He was brought to this country and exhibited in a locked cage. He terrified audiences with his ferocity as he devoured raw chunks of meat. He then succeeded in running away from the circus. He vanished from sight, until he reappeared in Gibsonton. Here, strange to say, he took up a career in law enforcement. He proved highly capable – and for the past four terms he has served as sheriff.'

'You're telling me this is Sheriff Hamilton?' said Mulder.

'I'm telling you that before becoming Sheriff Hamilton, he was – Jim-Jim, the Dog-Faced Boy.'

From her folder Scully pulled the pamphlet she had been given in the museum. Mulder stared at the photo of the boy on the cover.

'Hard to believe,' he muttered.

'Believe it or not,' said Scully. 'Which should be the town motto.'

Mulder sighed. 'I suppose we have to add Sheriff Hamilton to our list.'

'Just what we need – another suspect,' said Scully.

'Let's pay the sheriff an after-hours visit,' said Mulder. 'Who knows, we might dig something up.'

'I hate to think what,' said Scully.

An hour later, Scully's words came back to her.

She was crouching with Mulder in the shrubbery of Sheriff Hamilton's backyard.

The sheriff, looking menacing and massive in the moonlight, was hard at work digging a hole in the yard. At last he stopped, laid aside the shovel, and mopped his brow. Then he bent and reached into the earth.

Scully gave Mulder a questioning look.

Mulder shook his head. He couldn't tell what the sheriff had pulled out of the hole either.

But there was no mistaking what the sheriff now picked up from the grass. In the moonlight a long knife glinted.

The sheriff made a cut on whatever he had unearthed. Then he rubbed it over his hands.

Finally he bent and returned it to the hole, pushing the dirt back over it.

He stood erect, stared up at the full moon, then turned and went back into his house.

'I don't want to say what I'm thinking,' Scully whispered. 'I mean, it's not completely scientific. On the other hand, there have been reports over the centuries. And there's no denying it's a full moon.'

'True, but we have to watch ourselves,' Mulder whispered

back. 'Just because Sheriff Hamilton once had an excess of hair, it doesn't mean that he's a –'

'I agree,' Scully said. 'It wouldn't be fair to say that his affliction makes him behave abnormally. It would be like guilt based solely on skin color.'

'Right,' said Mulder.

'Right,' said Scully.

'Still –' Mulder said.

'Still –' Scully echoed.

'Well, time to find out the truth,' said Mulder. He crawled into the yard on hands and knees. Scully followed.

With his bare hands Mulder dug at the loose earth. After a minute he said, 'I've got it. I just have to pull it out and –'

He got no further.

He and Scully were blinded by a high-powered flashlight.

When their vision cleared, they saw the sheriff looming over them, brandishing an ugly-looking .45.

'May I ask what you're doing?' he growled.

Mulder held up what he had found in the earth: a piece of raw potato.

'Exhuming your potato,' was all he could say.

'May I ask why?' the sheriff asked.

It was a good question. But answering it was not exactly easy.

Scully made the first try. 'Sheriff, we know that many serial killers are fascinated by police work. Some even hold positions on their local force. So it is a normal part of our investigation to –'

'Dig up potatoes?' the sheriff asked.

Mulder tried a different approach. 'Sheriff, we found out you used to be a dog-faced boy.'

He handed the pamphlet to the sheriff and waited for the man's reaction.

Sheriff Hamilton stared at the photo.

Then he chuckled.

'Boy, look how skinny I was back then,' he said.

'Then it is you,' Scully said.

'Oh, sure,' Sheriff Hamilton said, still smiling. 'I spent the first half of my life as Jim-Jim. Then one morning I noticed a bald spot on the top of my head. I realized I was not only losing my hair, I was losing my career. Pretty soon all the hair went. My body's still pretty hairy, though. That's why I never go to the beach.'

'But that doesn't quite explain the potato,' Scully persisted.

'Well, it's a bit embarrassing,' the sheriff said. 'I – got some warts on my hand.'

'That *still* doesn't explain the potato,' said Mulder.

'Don't you know?' asked the sheriff, surprised. 'To get rid of warts, you rub a sliced potato on your hands. Then you bury it under a full moon.'

'Oh, sure,' said Mulder weakly.

'Right,' said Scully. 'I guess it just slipped my mind.'

'Anyway, how is the investigation going?' the sheriff asked.

After a moment of loud silence, he said, 'Not too well, huh?'

'Actually, we expect something to happen any time now,' Mulder said.

'Whether we want it to or not,' added Scully.

CHAPTER
TWELVE

Conundrum heard a low growling.

At first he thought it was his stomach.

His stomach was always growling. It had growled ever since he could remember. Even the yummiest treat – a nice plump live frog, say, or a canful of wiggling worms, or a squawking mother hen with crunchy feathers – could not quiet it for long.

Tonight, though, his stomach was not making the noise.

By the light of the moon, he saw Hiram Nutt's tiny dog looking at him and growling.

Conundrum looked back at the dog – and licked his lips.

For a moment, though, Conundrum tried to hold back the hunger that raged within him.

He tried to remember what Dr Blockhead had told him about eating between shows. Bad, bad, bad.

He reminded himself that Dr Blockhead had sent him out tonight on an errand. Important, important, important.

But his stomach had started growling now. Louder and louder. It drowned out every thought but the thought of fur and bones, eyeballs and blood, and a tender curling tail for dessert.

The tiny dog saw the saliva dripping from Conundrum's mouth. The dog stopped growling. Whining, he turned tail and ran.

Grunting eagerly, Conundrum ran after him. He didn't mind the chase. In fact, he liked it. It gave an extra edge to his appetite.

Conundrum was fast. But the tiny dog was a shade faster – and he didn't have far to run. He reached the Big Top Motor Inn's office door and tore through the doggie flap at the bottom.

A moment later, the office door swung open.

Hiram B. Nutt strode outside. He looked with disgust at the tattooed man slobbering on his doormat.

Safely behind Nutt, his little dog yapped defiantly.

'How many times have I told you?' Nutt said. 'Commodore is my pet – not your meal. Try that one more time and I'll kick you and Dr Blockhead out of your trailer.'

Conundrum got to his feet, his head bowed in shame. Why, oh why, did he keep doing such things? Why couldn't he listen to the greatest and wisest man in the world, Dr Blockhead?

Unfortunately, it was not in Conundrum's nature to answer such questions. Even as he groveled before Nutt, he kept sneaking ravenous glances at the dog.

'What are you doing out this time of night, anyway?' Nutt demanded. 'I would think even a blockhead would have enough sense to keep you inside.'

Conundrum brightened. At last he had a question he could answer.

He reached down to his loincloth. A piece of paper was pinned to it by a pair of Dr Blockhead's skull pins. He yanked the paper free and handed it to Nutt.

Nutt glanced at it. 'Okay,' he said. 'Now get back to your trailer – before you bite off more than you can chew.'

But Conundrum kept standing there, staring at Nutt's hands.

'I know what you want,' Nutt said. 'I'll bet Dr Blockhead promised them to you as a reward. Well, I'm not letting you have the pins – just for being so greedy. You'll have to find some other bedtime snack.'

Nutt slammed the door in Conundrum's disappointed face. Then he looked down at the check in his hand and shook his head.

'Tell me, Commodore,' he said to his dog, 'why are the weirdo tenants the only ones who pay their rent in advance?'

As if in answer, Commodore started growling, eyes fixed on the door.

Nutt sighed. 'He's still lurking around, huh? He's the one who should be turned into dogmeat.

'I warn you,' Nutt shouted through the door, 'I have a licensed gun! And I'm looking for a good reason to use it!'

Commodore was no longer growling. Instead he was barking angrily.

'What the devil?' Nutt muttered. He opened the peephole in the door. But before he could take a good look, something grabbed his ankle.

He looked down. A small hand had come through the doggie door. It started to pull his leg through it.

'Nooooo!' Nutt screamed. Bracing both hands against the door, he managed to break loose.

He landed half stunned on his back.

He lifted his head – and saw something following the hand through the doggie door.

Something that made him scream again.

And again.

And again.

Until his screams died – and there was only the sound of Commodore, whimpering in the night.

*   *   *

Scully heard the pounding on her trailer door.

She refused to open her eyes, hoping the noise would go away.

She was so tired. Sleep was so sweet.

Then she heard the voice shouting.

'Wake up! Wake up, please!'

'Okay, okay, I'm coming!' she shouted back.

Yawning, she got out of bed, snapped on the light, put on her robe, and opened the door.

Lanny stood there. His face was pale as death in the light coming out through the doorway.

'Couldn't this wait until morning?' Scully asked, rubbing her eyes.

'Sorry, miss, sorry, sorry,' Lanny babbled. Then his voice broke. 'But he's dead, he's dead.'

'Calm down, Lanny,' Scully soothed him. 'Now take your time and tell me, who's dead?'

'My best friend in all the world,' Lanny said. 'Mr Nutt! I found him. It was –' Lanny could go no further. He could only shake his head in shock.

Scully was wide awake now.

'Wait here while I get dressed,' she said. She closed the door and threw on her clothes in two minutes flat. Then she joined Lanny outside the trailer.

'Let's go,' she said. 'Show me where you found him.'

'Maybe I shouldn't,' said Lanny. 'Maybe you shouldn't have to see it. Such a horrible sight. Horrible, horrible, horri –' Lanny started to babble again.

'Don't worry about me,' Scully said. 'I'm used to bad scenes. It's part of my job.'

'You've never seen anything like this,' said Lanny. 'If you had, you'd never want to look at a dead man again.'

CHAPTER
THIRTEEN

Scully crouched down by the doggie door. She wanted a close look at the thin streaks of blood on it.

Behind her Sheriff Hamilton said, 'Lanny says the door was locked when he got here. He had to use his key to open it. All the windows are shut and locked from the inside. The only way in was through the doggie door. What could get through that, except a dog? Or maybe a cat?'

Then Mulder said, 'Scully, come here.'

Mulder was kneeling beside Nutt's body. Scully was careful not to step on the trail of blood between the corpse and the door.

'I don't know what kind of person could fit through a doggie door – but look at this.' Mulder lifted Nutt's arm to show Scully the palm of his hand.

A pin was stuck deep into it.

A pin topped with a death's-head.

'Remember where we saw this kind of pin?' Mulder asked.

'How could I forget?' said Scully. 'If he can pound spikes into himself and get out of straitjackets, who knows what else he can do? Maybe we finally have a break in the case.'

'Maybe,' agreed Mulder. 'Anyway –' A ferocious thumping sound drowned out his words.

Lanny had been standing in the corner, watching the

investigation, taking long pulls from his flask. Now he had started pounding the walls with his fists.

'He was my only friend!' he raved. 'He was like a brother to me!'

Scully took a step toward him to calm him down, but the sheriff beat her to it.

He grabbed Lanny from behind in a bear hug.

'Hey there, cool it, Lanny boy,' he said. 'You're gonna hurt yourself.'

'So what?' Lanny mumbled.

'So nothing,' said the sheriff. 'But you might hurt me in the process – so knock it off.'

'He gets like this sometimes,' the sheriff told Scully and Mulder. 'I toss him in the drunk tank till he dries out. Then he's okay – until the next time.'

'You take care of Lanny,' said Mulder. 'We'll pick up Dr Blockhead – or I should say, Jeffrey Swaim.'

'Right,' the sheriff said, hauling Lanny away. Lanny didn't fight him. His body had gone slack. Tears were rolling down his face.

Mulder saw that Scully was staring down at the corpse, shaking her head.

'What's the matter?' he asked her. 'Spot something I missed?'

'Not really,' said Scully. 'It's just that I've been having so many strange dreams lately. I almost expect the crimes to be more –' She paused, looking for the right word.

'Freakish?' Mulder suggested.

'Well – yes,' she admitted.

Mulder grinned. 'You really shouldn't gripe about this case being routine, Scully,' he said. 'Not when your main suspect is a human blockhead.'

*   ·*   *

'He's probably snug in bed, like any ordinary citizen,' Scully said.

'Complain, complain,' said Mulder, knocking on Dr Blockhead's trailer door. 'Can't you get used to the idea that these folks are just like everybody else?'

'Come in – the door's open,' Dr Blockhead shouted.

Scully and Mulder entered the trailer.

Dr Blockhead was in bed.

A bed of nails.

Scully swallowed hard. She took a deep breath, flashed her badge, and began. 'Mr Swaim. We're federal agents. We're here to question you. Please be advised you have the right to –'

'You'll have to wait a moment,' Dr Blockhead said. 'As you can see, I'm a little tied up right now.'

He held up his hands. Both of them were holding fishing lines. The lines were attached to fishhooks, and the hooks were embedded firmly in his chest.

'Gives you an idea of what a trout must feel like,' he said, giving the lines a tug.

'Mr Swaim,' Scully began again, then paused. 'Doesn't that hurt?'

'It's a variation on an American Indian Sun Dance ritual,' he answered. 'I suspend myself by these hooks, and the pain becomes so unbearable that I have to leave my body.'

'Leave your body?' asked Scully, and traded looks with Mulder. 'Where do you go?'

'You don't understand,' Dr Blockhead said. 'It's just a way to free my mind. Or, some might say, my soul.'

'I hate to interfere with your freedom, Mr Swaim,' Scully said. 'But we're taking you into custody. We want to question you about several recent murders.'

'I don't answer any questions until I talk to my lawyer,' Dr Blockhead shot back.

'Who's your lawyer?' Mulder asked.

'I represent myself,' Dr Blockhead declared.

That did it for Scully.

With one hand she pulled out a pair of handcuffs. With the other she yanked Dr Blockhead off his bed of nails.

Scully could handcuff a suspect in her sleep. She whirled Dr Blockhead around and put the cuffs on his wrists behind his back.

'What gives you the right to do this?' he snarled.

'Didn't I mention that we're federal agents?' she said, clicking the cuffs shut.

'And didn't I mention that I'm an escape artist?' Dr Blockhead replied.

'Wha –?' Scully looked down at her wrists.

How did the handcuffs get there?

She didn't get a chance to ask the grinning Dr Blockhead.

He gave her a vicious shove, and ran out the door.

She fell against Mulder, who was coming to her aid.

He stumbled backward, hitting the edge of the bed of nails.

And went tumbling right onto it.

'Mulder!' gasped Scully.

He lay motionless.

She reached down to pull him up.

But before she could touch him, he was off the bed and on his feet. He had to slide out of his jacket to do it, though. That stayed nailed down.

'Nothing like Irish tweed,' Mulder said. 'The salesman told me it would keep out the rain and the cold. Didn't mention this, though.'

'You're all right?' asked Scully, limp with relief.

'This bed is more comfortable than the one in my trailer,' Mulder said. 'Are you okay?'

Scully grimaced. She held out her cuffed wrists. Mulder had a key and unlocked them.

They went to the open trailer door and looked out into the darkness.

'Blockhead's off and running,' said Mulder.

'It was hard enough to collar him in here,' Scully said. 'Catching up with him outside will be quite a trick. If he can really leave his body, who knows what else he can do?'

At that moment a large figure walked out of the shadows and up to the trailer.

'Look what I caught,' said Sheriff Hamilton. He held up the fishing lines in his hand and gave them a tug.

'Ouch!' said Dr Blockhead.

CHAPTER
FOURTEEN

'This jail will never hold me!' Dr Blockhead angrily declared.

'We'll see about that,' Sheriff Hamilton said. 'We're used to handling all kind of prisoners in the Gibsonton jail. You're not the first escape artist to go behind bars here.'

The sheriff had Dr Blockhead firmly by the arm. Mulder and Scully, guns drawn, followed close behind as they entered the jailhouse. The place was small. The cells were just beyond the sheriff's desk.

'That isn't what I mean,' Dr Blockhead said. 'I'm mean that I'm innocent. Your case is based on coincidence. It's a bunch of humbug.'

'Humbug?' said Scully. 'Really? Well, you're the expert.'

Dr Blockhead shrugged. 'Actually,' he said, 'I'll probably thank you in the end. I'll appear on *60 Minutes* as a victim of mistaken identity. Great publicity for my act.'

'Speaking of evidence, does this belong to you?' Mulder asked.

He showed Dr Blockhead a clear plastic bag. In it was the death's-head pin found stuck into Nutt's hand.

'I may be an extraordinary individual, but I am still a US citizen,' Dr Blockhead said. 'And the Fifth Amendment to our

418

Constitution says I do not have to say anything that might incriminate myself.'

'That just means we'll have to spend your tax dollars to put you away,' Scully said.

'Another example of government waste,' said Dr Blockhead. 'Wait till I write to my congressman. Haven't you heard of the Contract with America?'

'Thinking of changing your act and becoming a talk-show host?' Scully asked.

'Dr Blockhead has many talents,' he said. 'Just watch what I do to your case in court.'

'I can hardly wait,' said Scully.

Before Dr Blockhead could respond a loud groan came from one of the cells.

'What was that?' he taunted. 'You torturing prisoners in here?'

'That's Lanny in the drunk tank,' said the sheriff. 'He was passed out when I left him. He must have woken up and seen a few snakes and pink elephants. He'll be okay once he's dried out.'

There was another groan, even louder.

Scully walked over and looked through the peephole in the steel door.

'Lanny's not going to sleep this off,' she announced. 'There's been another attack.'

Crowding around her, the others peered into the cell.

Lanny lay groaning on a bunk, his back toward them.

A thin line of blood ran from the bunk, over the floor, and up the wall to the barred window.

'How could anyone get in there?' the sheriff muttered, reaching for his keys.

'I have a strong hunch nobody got in,' said Scully. 'I think somebody got out.'

'Scully, what are you saying?' asked Mulder.

'I'm not sure myself, Mulder,' said Scully. 'The idea just hit me. But we'll know for sure when we find Leonard.'

'Leonard?' said Mulder.

'Lanny's brother,' said Scully. 'When I was in the museum, I saw an old poster describing his act.'

By now the sheriff had the cell door open. They all rushed in.

Scully was the first to reach Lanny. She turned him over in his bunk. He had been groaning in his sleep, and he was still sleeping.

There was a hole in his midsection where his Siamese twin had been.

'Oh God, somebody removed the twin,' said the sheriff. 'Tore him right out.'

'I don't think so,' said Scully. 'I think the twin removed himself.'

'Scully, that's impossible,' said Mulder. 'The twin is part of Lanny, like an arm or a leg.'

It was strange for Scully to hear Mulder saying something was impossible. It was even stranger hearing herself disagree.

'Look at the facts,' she said. 'This hole in Lanny is identical to the hole in all the murder victims. Except for one thing. Lanny is alive – and he's not bleeding.'

Before Mulder could answer, the sheriff stepped in. 'If you're saying that his twin can crawl out of his body and go gallivanting around town – you're as drunk as he is.'

'You said yourself that it's what's inside these "very special people" that counts,' Scully said. 'I think that inside Lanny there are special organs that allow his twin to leave him and then rejoin him.'

'But Scully, how could you even dream that this twin

could –' said Mulder. He could go no further. He could only shake his head.

'Mulder, tell me something,' Scully said. 'Do you think that an investigator could be led toward solving a case by a dream?'

Mulder needed only a moment to think about it. 'It's possible to pick up clues without consciously realizing it,' he said. 'Those clues are stored in the subconscious. In dreams they could surface. Dreams tell us what we don't know that we know.'

'Well, it's possible that something like that happened to me,' Scully said. 'I've been dreaming of Lanny again and again, as if something was telling me to take a closer look at him. I know it sounds weird, but –'

Mulder stopped her. 'Don't apologize, Scully. You're doing just fine. In fact, you're putting me to shame.'

'Oh, I don't know about that,' Scully said.

At that moment there was another groan from Lanny. His eyes were open and blinking dully. Scully wondered how much he had overheard.

'How . . . how could I . . . ?' Lanny mumbled.

'How could you what?' Scully asked, bending over him.

His words were weak and slurred. 'How . . . how could I turn him in? Without . . . without turning myself in?'

'Why is he attacking others?' Scully asked.

'I don't . . . don't think he knows he's harming anybody,' Lanny said with agonized effort. 'He's just looking . . . looking for another brother.'

'You in pain, Lanny?' the sheriff asked.

'It hurts . . . hurts not to be wanted,' Lanny said. 'I've taken . . . taken care of him all our lives. Maybe . . . maybe that's the reason why . . .'

Lanny reached into an inner pocket of his jacket. He pulled

out a spare flask hidden there. He started to raise it to his lips.

Scully stopped him before the sheriff could.

'You've had enough, Lanny,' she said softly.

'Had enough . . .' Lanny vaguely agreed, his eyes starting to glaze.

Before he passed out again, Scully asked, 'How long can Leonard survive outside your body?'

'Long enough to . . . long enough . . .' said Lanny, his voice fading.

Scully grasped his shoulder and shook him gently. 'Long enough to do what, Lanny?'

'Long enough to find out you can't change the way you were born,' said Lanny with sudden emotion. Then his voice slowed. 'But he always . . . always comes back. I am his . . . his only brother.'

His head fell.

Scully took his wrist. 'His pulse – it's weak,' she said.

'We need an ambulance,' Mulder said.

'I'll call one.' Sheriff Hamilton hurried out of the cell.

Meanwhile, Scully pulled a chair over to the window and stood on it to look out through the bars.

At first glance the spaces between the bars had seemed narrow. Now they looked wide open.

She touched a bar. It was wet with blood.

Mulder and Dr Blockhead had come to stand by the chair.

'I could sue you for false arrest,' Dr Blockhead said with a triumphant smile. 'But a man of my spiritual development would not stoop to an act of such crass greed.'

Then he asked in awe, 'You mean the twin can do this?' He walked his fingers up the wall. 'And that?' He stuck his fingers through the bars.

'It would appear so,' Scully said.

'My God,' said Dr Blockhead, 'I could sure use him in my act.'

'Scully, you're the medical expert,' Mulder said. 'If you say the twin is able to separate, I believe you. But how mobile can such a thing be?'

'How far can it go?' she said, peering out into the night. 'All we know for sure is – far enough to kill.'

CHAPTER
FIFTEEN

Scully and Mulder left the cell with their guns drawn.

Sheriff Hamilton looked up from the telephone as they came out.

'The ambulance will be here in a few minutes,' he said. 'I hope they're in time. Lanny doesn't look so good.'

'You wait for them here,' Mulder said. 'Scully and I will check around outside.'

Outside, Mulder and Scully circled the jailhouse until they stood under the window of Lanny's cell.

'Look,' Scully said, pointing to traces of blood on the brick. The blood led down from the window to the ground. 'The twin must have hands that work like suction cups. They'd have to be close to his body, hidden under the folded sleeves of his jacket. His legs must be short, too. You can't see them under that jacket. But we know how fast they can move.'

'You think the hands and feet bleed?' asked Mulder.

'More likely the blood comes from the internal body parts. The ones that are hooked up with Lanny,' said Scully. 'Exactly what they are, I can't even guess. It's not the kind of thing I ran into in medical school.'

'I think there's something else we can assume about our little friend,' said Mulder.

'What?' asked Scully.

'Leonard has teeth,' said Mulder. 'And they're razor sharp.'

Scully nodded. 'His mouth could be concealed in the lump of flesh where his head should be. I did notice wrinkles that might be facial features.'

'Including eyes,' said Mulder. 'Leonard seems to know where he wants to go.'

'I wish *we* knew where he wanted to go,' said Scully.

'He may be telling us,' said Mulder. 'Look.'

Mulder pointed at the sidewalk. In the glare of a street-light, blood spots gleamed.

They followed the drops around the block and down a dingy street, and then to a large, half-opened door.

'What kind of place is this?' Scully said. It was like nothing she had ever seen before, less a building than a maze of makeshift wooden corridors, spread out over a big vacant lot.

Mulder pushed the door wide open. Inside of the doorway was a switchbox.

'Maybe this will shed some light on it,' he said, and pulled the switch.

Outside, Scully's face was bathed in a bright green light.

Above the door a huge neon sign had flashed on.

THE TABERNACLE OF TERROR, it proclaimed.

Another neon light showed the faces of a screaming man, a screaming woman, and two screaming children.

'Hepcat's funhouse,' Scully said.

'The fun is about to begin,' said Mulder. He clicked off the safety catch on his gun. 'I hear noises inside. I think we've cornered Leonard. I'll go after him.'

'I'll come in from the back and cut off his escape,' Scully said. 'Be careful in there. We may not be sure how Leonard does it – but we sure know what he can do.'

Mulder nodded. He waited until Scully left. Then he

started down the long, spooky corridor that stretched before him.

When he reached its end, he saw another corridor branching off it. As he went around the corner, his trigger finger tensed – just in case Leonard was waiting for him.

Nothing came at him. His finger relaxed. Then his whole body stiffened as he saw a pale white shape moving away in the dim light.

Mulder broke into a run. But the shape was already turning another corner.

Mulder increased his speed as he went after it. He raced around the turn, but the ghostlike shape was already out of sight. Mulder didn't know what Leonard used for legs, but the thing could really run.

Mulder sprinted down the empty corridor, then tore around another corner and –

Splat!

Mulder found himself sitting on the floor, shaking his head to clear it.

He had run into a blank wall.

Hepcat must have been laughing his twisted head off, wherever he was.

Meanwhile, Scully had entered the funhouse from the other end. As she went down a corridor, she too had drawn her gun.

She turned a corner and stared into darkness. *A lightbulb must have burned out*, she thought. And there was no Hepcat Helm to replace it. What would this place do without him?

Then she heard a low growl coming from the darkness.

So little Leonard has a voice, she thought. She leveled her gun as she moved toward the menacing sound.

It grew louder.

Her finger tightened on the trigger.

Suddenly a flash of light exploded.

A gigantic head leaped up in front of her. A head with popping eyes and a hideous smile.

Scully recognized its face. It was the face of Hepcat Helm.

Scully lowered her gun as the plastic head dropped into the trapdoor in the floor. The trapdoor closed, and the sound of recorded laughter echoed in the corridor.

'Ha-ha, big joke, Hepcat,' Scully muttered as she continued down the corridor.

She reached the door at its end. Holding her gun ready, she opened the door.

She found herself staring into a shiny tubelike tunnel made of mirror-smooth metal. Before she could figure out what it was, she heard a scurrying sound from beyond its far end.

'Leonard! Gottcha!' she said under her breath, running into the tunnel.

'Hey! Whaa –' she gasped, as her feet flew out from under her.

The tube was whirling around and around, like a spinner in a washing machine. Scully was brutally bounced on her back, her sides, her front. Desperately she fought to regain her balance as she hung on to her gun for dear life.

Finally she managed to get onto her hands and knees. Inch by painful inch, she crawled to the end of the spinning tunnel and out of it.

As she got to her feet, the spinning stopped. The tube stood still, waiting for its next victim.

Scully glared at it as she waited for the spinning in her head to slow.

Then she heard the scurrying sound again, from somewhere farther inside the funhouse.

She looked down the passageway ahead of her.

It looked safe enough, so she started down it.

Her side smashed into a wall. She came off from it and hit the opposite wall. Then the floor fell away from under her feet.

She stood absolutely still.

'I should have known,' she said to herself as she took a closer look at the corridor. She saw now that that floor was on a rolling tilt. The walls were adjusted to the tilt so that at first nothing would seem strange. 'Very funny, Hepcat, very funny.'

She rubbed her shoulder. The bruises from the tube now had new bruises on top of them.

Then she heard the scurrying sound again.

Walking carefully, with one hand on a wall for guidance, she made it to the far end of the corridor.

She breathed more easily when she turned the corner and could stand on a level floor again.

Then her breath caught in her throat.

She saw what she'd been looking for. A milky shape close to the floor.

But it was coming at her faster than she had thought possible.

She had just enough time to aim her gun and fire. Once. And again. And again.

Thank God, at this range, she couldn't miss.

Except that the shape still kept coming as one bullet after another splintered one mirror after another.

Automatically Scully's brain formed the words *Funhouse . . . hall of mirrors.*

But this was no fun. No fun at all.

Pale blobs were coming at her from everywhere. She emptied her gun hopelessly as mirror after mirror shattered into showering glass – and one blob that was left kept coming for her like a living buzz saw.

She braced herself.

Then the blob stopped moving.

Maybe it was hit. Maybe it was tired. Maybe it was as confused as she was.

It didn't matter. At least Scully had a fighting chance against it now. If she couldn't use her empty gun to shoot it, she could use the barrel as a club.

She ran toward it, her gun held high. Savagely she brought the barrel down.

Another mirror smashed, and Scully recoiled in shock.

Then her mouth opened in a silent scream as hands grabbed her shoulders from behind.

CHAPTER
SIXTEEN

'Scully, you all right?' Mulder asked. 'I heard shots.'

Scully waited a moment for her heart to leave her throat.

'Mulder,' she snapped, 'didn't anyone ever tell you not to sneak up on people?'

'Sorry, Scully,' he said. 'Blame the FBI Academy. I used to have such good manners before I joined up.'

Then they heard a noise from the back entrance of the funhouse.

'It got past me,' Scully said. 'It's out there and on the loose.'

Mulder raced after the sound with Scully right behind him.

Outside, though, they had to stop.

They heard nothing but the silence of the moonlit night.

Mulder put his finger to his ear, then to his lips. He pointed to a nearby cluster of bushes.

Scully nodded. She too had heard rustling in the foliage. She slipped fresh bullets into her weapon as they tiptoed toward it.

But they weren't quiet enough.

A small shape tore out of the bushes at them.

They both raised their guns to fire.

Then both of them froze.

What was coming at them wasn't a pale blob of death.

It was a tiny black bundle of fury, barking in fierce rage.

'Nutt's dog,' said Scully as her trigger finger relaxed. 'What's he doing here?'

'Trying to tell us something, I think,' said Mulder, lowering his gun.

'But what?' said Scully.

Still barking, Commodore stopped before them. He stared up at them. When they made no move, he turned and ran away.

After a few feet, he stopped and looked at them again.

'Hey, boy, what's up?' Mulder said.

Yapping still more loudly, the dog ran back to them. He gave them another pleading look. Then he turned, ran away, stopped, and looked back at them once more.

'Okay, boy,' Mulder said. 'We get the idea. We'll follow you.'

As soon as Mulder and Scully moved toward Commodore, he started running down the street full out. Feet pounding, the agents followed. The dog slowed only when they dropped too far behind. Every time they closed the gap, he speeded up again.

'He's heading for the trailer park,' said Mulder.

'He knows who killed his master,' Scully gasped. 'Spotted him there again. Wants us to catch him. Must have a strain of pointer in him.'

'Man's best friend,' said Mulder.

'Leonard's worst enemy,' Scully said.

When they reached the trailer park, Commodore could not hold himself back.

He ran out of sight among the trailers.

They heard his angry barking from the shadows.

Then, abruptly, the barking stopped.

'I think he's found Leonard,' said Mulder.

'Or vice versa,' said Scully.

'We'll have to find out,' said Mulder, heading toward the shadows.

'I'm not sure I want to,' said Scully as she followed.

A minute later all she could say was, 'Ughh. Poor thing.'

'Leonard must be getting desperate,' said Mulder.

'We have to stop him,' Scully said, flipping off the safety catch on her gun.

'I wish those clouds would go away,' said Mulder. 'We need all the light we can get.'

Fast-moving black clouds were passing over the face of the moon, making the night dark one moment, bright the next, as if someone were playing with a dimmer switch.

Suddenly Mulder was off and running after a small shape moving between two trailers.

He came to a sharp stop when he reached it.

He took a step backward as a three-foot-tall woman looked up at him and said, 'Looking for something, big boy?'

A trailer door opened, and a three-foot-tall man said, 'Mabel, you get in here this moment.'

After she obeyed, the man said to Mulder, 'And as for you, mister –'

He raised a shotgun bigger than he was.

'Look, just a little mistake,' Mulder said. He wondered too late if *little* was the best word to use.

'I catch you with my wife again, it's the last mistake you ever make,' the man said, and slammed his door.

When Mulder rejoined Scully, she said, 'Mulder, don't you wish you had something you could handle better – like little green men from Mars?'

'Right now I feel like I'm *on* Mars,' Mulder said.

'I've felt like that ever since we came here,' said Scully.

'Gibsonton, home of humbug. Where all boxes are empty, doors turn into blank walls, and everything is as phony as the Feejee Mermaid.'

'Everything except death,' said Mulder.

They started moving through the trailer park again.

The moon dimmed and the air seemed to chill. Then the moon came out again.

Scully stopped and stared.

'Let's hope that's not what I think it is,' she said.

A man lay on his back on the ground beside a trailer.

His hands were clutched over his stomach.

And he was lying still as death.

'That's Blockhead's trailer,' Mulder said as he and Scully ran toward it.

'Yeah,' said Scully. 'Looks like the doctor ran into something sharper than a nail.'

'Something he couldn't escape,' Mulder said. 'I just hope he managed to leave his body first.'

CHAPTER SEVENTEEN

Before Mulder and Scully could reach the body, a light from the trailer came on.

The trailer door swung open.

'What's this – a night raid?' demanded Dr Blockhead from the doorway. 'You Feds better have a warrant – or I'll see you in court.'

Scully and Mulder stared at him – then turned toward the body.

Its tattoos were clear in the light from the trailer.

Then Conundrum groaned.

'He's still alive!' said Scully.

By now Dr Blockhead had joined them.

'What happened to him?' he asked.

'Brace yourself,' said Scully as she knelt by Conundrum.

The geek continued to groan as she gently removed his hands from his stomach.

'There's no wound,' she said, examining the tattooed skin closely. 'There is a bruise, though, and the stomach looks swollen.'

'Leonard must have heard us coming,' said Mulder. 'Must have run off before he did any real damage.'

'If only we knew which way he went,' said Scully.

Mulder had an idea. He squatted beside Conundrum. 'The

thing that attacked you – can you point your finger in the direction he ran in?'

But Conundrum just kept groaning and rubbing his stomach.

'Leonard must have hit him hard,' Scully said. 'That bruise is black and blue.'

'Come on, I'll put some ice on your poor tummy,' Dr Blockhead said to his partner. He helped Conundrum to his feet and led him into the trailer.

Clouds covered the moon again, and once more Scully and Mulder were left standing in the dark.

'We've lost the trail,' Scully said.

'Leonard could be anywhere,' Mulder echoed.

'We have to do *something*,' said Scully.

'I agree,' said Mulder. 'But I don't know what. Except wait here until we hear the next scream.'

What they heard next, though, was the sound of a car.

Then they saw headlights. The car stopped, and Sheriff Hamilton got out.

'I was hoping to find you here,' he said. 'Somebody in town spotted you running in this direction.'

'How's Lanny?' Scully asked.

The sheriff shook his head. 'Lanny is dead,' he said grimly.

'Killed by his own twin,' said Mulder. 'I guess Leonard tore loose one time too many.'

Again the sheriff shook his head. 'That wasn't the cause of death. The doc says that Lanny's liver gave out. Too much booze for too long a time.'

'That probably explains it,' Mulder said.

'Explains what?' the sheriff asked.

'Why the murders have become so much more frequent in the past year – and especially the past few days,' Mulder said. 'Leonard must have felt Lanny getting sicker and sicker.

He must have realized he would die too, unless he found a new person to latch on to.'

'That's it,' said Scully, remembering the story she had been told of the death of the Original Siamese Twins. 'Imagine what it must feel like when the person you're attached to dies. It has to be horrible. I mean, Leonard is human, after all. Maybe when I first got here, I wouldn't have said so. But I see things differently now.'

'Human or not, we have to catch him,' Mulder said. 'He must be desperate. He'll attack anything that moves.'

He turned to the sheriff. 'Can you help with the search? And do you have any deputies?'

'So you really think the twin is the killer?' said the sheriff. 'I mean, originally you thought it was the Feejee Mermaid.'

'This isn't humbug,' Mulder said, a touch of anger in his voice.

The sheriff shrugged. 'Okay. You're the FBI man. Tell you what. I don't have any deputies, but I do have a lot of friends in town. Special friends.'

'Wake them up,' Mulder said.

'Yeah,' said Scully. 'Maybe it takes a "very special person" to catch one.'

By dawn the search was over.

The giant, the midgets, the strongman, the fat woman, the thin man, the three-legged man, the human octopus, a squad of acrobats, and a crew of clowns had gone over every inch of the trailer park.

They had found nothing.

The sheriff broke the news to Scully and Mulder as they stood watching the sun come up. They had been searching all night themselves.

'You're sure it was the twin you saw running around

here?' the sheriff asked Scully. 'I mean, maybe it was the Feejee Mermaid and she's jumped into the river and started swimming back to Feejee.' He smirked, delighted with his own wit.

'Look, Sheriff, there *was* a twin,' Scully said, annoyed.

'Relax, Scully,' Mulder said. 'Now you know what I feel like a lot of the time.'

The sheriff turned serious. 'You better be sure it was the twin,' he said, 'if you're letting our friend there get away.'

A battered Volkswagen bug was parked next to Dr Blockhead's trailer. And the doctor was loading it up with his possessions.

Scully, Mulder, and the sheriff walked over to him.

Dr Blockhead gave them a quick look, and kept on packing. Conundrum was already in the front seat.

'Thinking of taking off?' Scully asked him.

'Wouldn't you be – with that thing still on the loose?' said Dr Blockhead as he crammed his straitjacket into the last bit of trunk space.

'Leonard is probably dead by now,' Scully told him. 'He can't have lived this long outside a living body. And his brother is dead.'

'I guess it's true what they say – you can't go home again,' said Dr Blockhead.

'I plan to do an autopsy on Lanny,' Scully said. 'I'm sure I've never seen anything like his insides.'

'And you'll never see anything like them again,' Dr Blockhead told her.

'What do you mean?' Scully asked.

Dr Blockhead's mocking face was solemn for once. 'Modern science is wiping out deviant strains of the human form,' he said. 'In the twenty-first century, genetic engineering will do more than merely eliminate Siamese twins and alligator-skinned people. It will make it hard to find a person with even a slight overbite or a large nose. I can see that future and it makes me shudder. The future looks like – *him.*'

Dr Blockhead pointed at Mulder.

'Imagine going through your whole life looking like that,' said Dr Blockhead.

Mulder shrugged. 'It's a tough job – but someone has to do it.'

'That's the reason why self-made freaks like me and Conundrum have to go out and remind people,' Dr Blockhead said.

'Remind them of what?' asked Scully.

'Remind them that Nature hates everything to be normal,' Dr Blockhead said. 'It can't go very long without creating something freakish. And do you know why?'

'No,' said Scully. 'Why?'

'I don't know either,' Dr Blockhead said. 'It's a mystery. Maybe some mysteries were never meant to be solved.'

'Yeah, like where the twin went,' said Sheriff Hamilton.

'I'll leave you with that little puzzle,' said Dr Blockhead as he got behind the steering wheel. 'Conundrum and I are off to Baltimore. We open on Tuesday.'

Mulder peered into the car.

'Anything the matter with Conundrum there?' he asked Dr Blockhead. 'He looks pretty pale.'

'I don't know what his problem is,' said Dr Blockhead. 'He kept tossing and turning all night. I couldn't get a wink of sleep. Maybe it's this Florida heat.'

'I hope it's nothing serious,' said Scully.

She went to Conundrum's side of the car. She leaned in through the open window for a closer look.

Conundrum turned his head so that they were face-to-face.

Conundrum belched.

'Must be something I ate last night,' he said.

Scully stood with Mulder and the sheriff watching the Volkswagen drive off.

When it was out of sight, she turned to the others. 'I think I'll skip breakfast this morning,' she said. 'Somehow I've lost my appetite.'